MAKALA AMOTO

Made in Malawi

Rinzi Peter Phoya

authorHOUSE®

AuthorHouse™ UK Ltd.
500 Avebury Boulevard
Central Milton Keynes, MK9 2BE
www.authorhouse.co.uk
Phone: 08001974150

First published by AuthorHouse 10/27/2010

ISBN: 978-1-4520-8293-6 (sc)

This book is printed on acid-free paper.

You can turn painful situations around through laughter. If you can find humour in anything, even poverty, you can survive it." – Bill Cosby

DEDICATION

This book is dedicated to C.F.N. Phoya, first born in my father's family of thirteen. He was a very good man, someone who had an overflowing sense of humour, always bound to leave your lungs hurting with laughter. He was a great man who encapsulated everything about the mantra; "laughter is the best medicine of all." I recall vividly the many times he made me and many who knew him laugh to tears.

May his Soul Rest In Peace.

CONTENTS

INTRODUCTION

'Made in Malawi' is a compilation of 62 short stories seen through the eyes of Makala Amoto. Sorrounded by his large clan-like family, friends and his childhood sweetheart. Makala Amoto gives snippets into current affairs/lives of Malawians at home and abroad using laughter as the vehicle.

The contents of this book first appeared on Facebook and the idea of a book came from my (Facebook) friends. They urged me that it would be phenomenal to have Makala Amoto in hard copy. It is *to* them that I owe this project... it is *for* them why I compiled these stories... and it is *with* them that I shared much with.

These are the same stories from Facebook that have been polished and tweaked up whilst trying to maintain the original core.

A few people who saw the finished manuscript before the book went into production, all gave it "three" thumbs up.

It's hilarious, ticklish, thought provoking and Malawi's first. It's not your traditional everyday book because Makala Amoto comes ridiculously hard at you in a language others have appropriately termed "Englichewa."

If you are looking for a serious book, the conventional type that you have to frown as you flip through the pages because it resonates with the norms, then probably you are reading the wrong book. But if you are looking for a book that will leave your lungs aching from laughter, then read on.

Makala Amoto "Made in Malawi" is silly, simple, outside the box and lung-buster of a book that should leave you thinking: "What possessed him to write such stuff?"

Warning: This book is not to be read at funerals or any other place where laughter is prohibited. Contents of this book may cause serious and permanent damage to your laughter glands and it may also damage your internal braking system of the bowels.

Read at Owner's risk.

Makala Amoto – Made in Malawi

AMALUME ARRIVES TODAY FROM U.K

Most of you have often heard me or some members of my family speak proudly of our uncle who we simply refer to as Amalume. Today is the day when our beloved uncle is coming back home from the UK where he has been living for the past thirty years.

Since yesterday the whole family has been very busy with preparations for this big occasion. The goat was slaughtered last night by *anyamata antchito* and *uwende* has already been cooked as I speak. My mother even insisted on cooking *mpunga*, something that is reserved for Christmas (*ndi dzikwati*) and she even surprised us by adding "*adyo*" to the meat (*koma lero zakomatu*). My favourite dish of *dzipalapatilo dza nkhuku* was being prepared by Manyuchi Darling. She knows how I like them done, a bit salty and doused in homemade *piri-piri wa kambuzi*, served while hot.

About eighty or so family members gathered at my house and the atmosphere is like some sort of a royal wedding inside the Nswati Kraal. Family members with itchy feet have been dancing *kwasa-kwasa* and laughing all night long, much to the annoyance of some of the neighbours. If this was in the UK, am sure the whole neighbourhood would have initiated litigation proceedings against us. *Poti kuno nkumudzi* all we heard were children from the house behind ours making some snotty remarks.

"*Eeiishhhh, koma ndiye kuma yadi kwalowa ghetto-tu*" one of the bigger neighbour's child said. Just because of that remark I told my nephew who was DJ-ing to increase the volume until the knob couldn't move no further.

The four massive speakers mounted on the veranda boomed so loud that everything was vibrating and shaking from the thumping bass. Even the ripe papayas kept falling off the trees as if an earthquake had hit the Amoto compound. I was positive the tremors could rival those felt in Haiti and at one point I started fearing for the foundation of the house, thinking; "can Portland Cement withstand such a pounding?"

If you are wondering why we are making all this chaotic noise and exhibiting all this happiness, it's because for all the thirty years Amalume was in Diaspora never did he once come to visit Malawi. As a matter of fact he left when I was still wearing *matewela* (the cloth ones not these disposable ones used these days).

In Amalume's absence, *ana abadwa*, have grown and even gone to secondary school. There have been *dzinkhoswe* and weddings, several unplanned pregnancies and yes, there have been one or two divorces. Unfortunately Amalume missed each and every one of these family events.

Just like any other family, ours too has been rocked with *matenda* and countless *zovuta*. But for thirty long years Amalume has never attended any of the family gatherings nor buried any of his brothers who were called by God. We have never held this against him, we understood that he had to do what he had to do – after all, a few members of the Amoto family managed to finish secondary school because of the money Amalume continuously and tirelessly sent via Western Union.

We didn't know the reason for his sudden return, that wasn't important to us, what was more important was that he was coming back *kumudzi* to be amongst us for good.

The whole clan was happy and proud that finally other people will get to see our Amalume. Someone who, as far as *apachibalefe* were concerned, was an accountant in London, *kugubuduza masamu mothinana*; Debits and Credits, *kusokerera* ma Balance-Sheet and Income-Statements.

Anthu ena ansanje were busy circulating malicious rumours that Amalume was *munthu wamba* busy *kukazinga chipisi* at Mc Donalds. Other rumours cited that Amalume *amaitanila ma* minibus *pa* rank in London, but we always doubted the validity of these stories. Our family elders kept telling us not to pay any attention to these stories because they were just misconceptions, untruths, *mabodza* that were being spread and perpetrated by bad people out to tarnish the Amoto name.

To us Amalume was more of a celebrity, especially since he was the only member of our clan to cross the border by air. Of course like most Malawian families we have a few relatives outside the country; in Mozambique, South Africa, Zimbabwe, Botswana and even Sudan, but most of these left the country by foot and most without passports (*koma izi* am just telling you *kumbali kuno* not to be repeated). Amalume was the only one who left legally, so we were told.

Azimai ena stayed behind to finalise the business of *nsima, mpunga ndi ndiwo zosiyana-siyana.* Mother, always wanting to be in-charge of the food department, stayed behind too, so as to make sure that food was ready when Amalume arrived. She cheerfully waved us goodbye as we headed for Chileka Airport.

"Make sure *kuti anawo* are not running all over the airport" Mother yelled a warning to us whilst adjusting her *chitenje* before disappearing to the back of the house where she was like a conductor for the orchestra of women-chefs who were preparing today's welcoming feast.

She sounded this warning because last time we were at the airport, one of my younger nephews, who suffers from hyperactive disorder, managed to exit the airport terminal and dashed over onto the runway. The good thing is that back then stories *zau terorisiti kapena alukayida (ntalibani)* were not in fashion yet. If back then was now – a stupid stunt like that would have guaranteed my little nephew's name ending up *pa lisiti ya anthu owakaikila* or *oletsedwa* to fly *ku Ameleka* or *Mangalande.* Just like *nyamata wachi Naijeriyani uja anamumbwandira pa* Christmas *ali ndi zophulika-phulika nthumba.*

We arrived at Chileka around 10am in style in my brother's 7-ton Bedford truck (*Penda-Penda* Transport) that he uses for his *nchenga* business. There must have been about sixty of us there jumping out of the lorry which had just come to a shuddering stop.

Penda-Penda was blowing thick dark smoke and oil was dripping from underneath it like a cow emptying its bladder all over the parking lot. Someone once commented that if a vehicle was to emit this much smoke in UK the owner would probably be arrested and sentenced to life in prison without the possibility of parole.

But *kuno nku* Malawi *Otata* – and my brother, who was oblivious to the thick smoke, commandeered his *nyamata wantchito* to go and place an empty bucket (*chigubu*) underneath the engine so that he could catch some of the oozing black oil. I thought it was a bit embarrassing since he was going to leave it running for fear it wouldn't start if he attempted to turn it off. I diplomatically whispered to my brother,

"*Achimwene* we might be here for hours, are you really going leave your truck idling and blowing this much smoke *pa* airport *pano, azungu onsewa?*"

My brother just looked at me as if I had just spoken in Greek or Hieroglyphic Egyptian writing. That's typical of my brother, I think over the years he has inhaled too much diesel smoke and fumes his brain is a bit fried, he has this annoying habit of carrying on as a zombie when someone is talking to him. He just looked past me, shouting at one of his boys to keep an eye on the bucket that was underneath catching the oozing oil from the engine.

"*Mutchezekele chigubu china nsanga-nsanga mwamvatu?*" He instructed the dark oily looking Penda-Penda assistant and simply walked past me to join the rest of the family congregating inside Chileka Airport terminal.

We all entered the terminal and made our way upstairs to the balcony lounge to wait for the plane coming from

Lilongwe. There were so many of us and people kept staring in bewilderment as if we were not supposed to be there.

Cousins, sisters, brothers *ndi akulu-akulu* of the Amoto family were all chit-chatting excitedly. We were all fantasizing what Amalume was bringing each one of us. I was hoping for a pair of Michael Jordan basketball shoes, at my age he is the only Basketball player that I associate with. A few of my cousins were fantasizing and talking about: "*ine mwina andibweretsera* lap-top", "*ine ndikuona ngati andigulira* wedding dress"....Hahahahahaha, hehedeeeeeeeeeeeeeeee...uluuuuuuuuuuu...type of laughter rang out throughout Chileka Airport.

The Amoto family had literally taken over the joint. Some of us sat inside the lounge by the bar, the young ones were holding on to bottles of Cocopina, Cherry Plum or Fanta, while the grown-ups were slowly nursing *amame* – Green, Brown and the occasional Black Stout (*dzowawa*).

The Ethiopian airlines 737 with its distinctive green, yellow and red national flag emblazoned across the fuselage touched down at exactly 12 noon, which was a bit strange for an African Airline to be on time with such specificity.

Africans – and that includes *ife achi Malawife* – tend to consider a one or two hour delay to be normal. We might start raising eyebrows after a 4 hour delay but won't get worried unless the plane is late by half a day. It's our nature, we take life easy, Africans are not *khamani-khamani* people like *azungu*.

So when that 737 touched down on time we all thought that, either the pilot *ndi wachizungu* or the plane had just taken a short-cut. But we were all happy to see the Boeing land and held our breath quietly until it taxied to a stop in front of the lollypop man wearing a bright orange vest.

The younger boys of the Amoto clan were so excited at the sight of such a big plane and couldn't care less the reason we were here for in the first place. Boys will be boys, I thought to myself as I recalled days gone by when I used to be that young, looking in awe at the now decommissioned VC-10. *Masiku amenewo.*

When the hatch door of the 737 fuselage opened, we all squinted our eyes in the glaring sun, straining them so hard wishing they were binoculars as we searched for a familiar figure. That's when we saw Amalume's recognisable shinny bald head pop out of the plane.

That big round head looked just like it did on the zillion pictures he had sent while in the UK. As soon as he stepped out into the bright Malawian 12 o'clock sun, his bald head glowed and shone like a mirror as sweat mixed with Vaseline gave it that *nyezi-nyezi* effect. It was as if Amalume's head was made out of glass from a psychic's crystal ball.

We all exploded into loud cheers, screams, *nthungululu* and a few tears as different emotions overcame us. *Malikhwelu* and shouts of Amalumeeeeeee!!! Amalumeeeeee!!! Fyoooo-fyoooooooo!!! rang out, increasing in crescendo once he started descending down the stairs purposefully just like

Obama does when coming down the stairs of Air-Force One.

Amalume waved a victory sign like the one waved by the late founder and president of Aford Party on his arrival from exile. That v-sign fuelled our screams even worse and louder than before. *Anthu ena* (*maka-maka azungu*) were just looking at us as if we were animals who did not know how to behave in a public place. But who cares *zao izo, kunotu ndi ku* Malawi and *ndife aMalawi*, Kamuzu *anatimphwanyila chitaganya…dzikoli ndi lathu.*

"*Fyoo-fyooooooo.*" More piercing *malikhwelu* were viciously launched towards the direction of the annoyed *azungu*, at an increased tempo that had an alarmingly high level of decibels likely to render one deaf.

"*Fyoooooo!!!*"

Now I know how people must have felt like when Ngwazi Dr H. Kamuzu Banda arrived from UK to the then Nyasaland back in the 60's.

My heart was racing faster than a mouse surrounded by an army of vicious and hungry cats.

"*Afikadi*" is all I could murmur to myself.

Amalume purposefully walked towards the terminal, his black shiny *nyezi-nyezi scuna* shoes glowing in the sun from the (British) Kiwi polish dragging with him a huge suitcase on wheels with one hand, a lap-top bag slung across his shoulder as he waved to us with the other. He had all the airs of someone who is confident about everything, typical *akunja*.

I wondered if he had bought me the right size of Michael Jordan Nike basketball shoes. As far as I was concerned MJ was the best basketball player of all time and

I couldn't help but make comparisons between Amalume's bald shiny head and that of the great Michael Jordan.

Amalume was really back home for good, the voice we had been hearing over the phone for so many years was finally here in person. We all rushed from the upstairs balcony back down to the "International Arrivals" gate to welcome our family hero.

I just had this feeling that with the arrival of the most important member of our family, life was about to take a new turn in the Amoto family. Even my brother looked at me with a smile and said; "things will never be the same again."

ESCOM THE MBAULA

A few weeks ago, *pa Lachiwiri t*o be precise, seventeen of my closest friends and me, together with our spouses, gathered at Simioni's house just across the street.

Simioni, as you all know by now, is both my neighbour and childhood best friend. He is one of those individuals who ranks somewhere between a friend and a sibling, more than a friend and slightly less than a relative – a frielative.

The eighteen of us had all gone to the same primary school, used to play football together, set bird-traps together and went through the whole obsession with *malegeni* (catapults) torturing the neighbourhood chickens, dogs, cats and pigeons together.

It's not a secret that my aim with a *legeni* was so bad I never had a 'bird kill' credited to my name. With such a lousy aim I only managed to smash a few house windows and once I almost blinded this distinguished Pastor. Lucky for me the righteous Pastor had some amazing reflex action for a man his age and I was thankful he managed to dodge the wheezing projectile. Out of embarrassment, fear and laziness I ended up dodging church for about nine Sundays in a row.

That is a chapter of my life I am not really proud of nor do I like to talk about.

Of the eighteen of us Simioni is the only one doing ok and by "Ok" I mean financially or economically. This is evidenced by the fact that he is the only one who owns a TV with DSTV and massive stereo system with a CD changer while the rest of us are yet to progress past the radio phase.

At least my radio has a dual-tape deck unlike a few friends who only have the basic radio. So basic and similar like the ones you see security guards carrying around with them. The ones with twenty (usually flat) batteries wrapped in cardboard held together by rubber bands.

Despite our glaring differences we all got along great, the same way we did back in primary school, even stronger. You can say our friendship is like wine, it has gotten better with age. We would often meet; drinking or chewing dzipalapatilo, laughing or watching football on telly and at times just to to talk about the good old days whenever we were in one of those nolstagic moods.

On Tuesday there was a football match on TV; Chelsea vs. Manchester United. For some reason nowadays it seems like we derive much joy watching foreign football compared to local matches.

We are constantly wowed by the likes of Kaka, Drogba, Essien and Carlos Tevez and not our own local stars. These superstar players are like some deities of football who we view as fascinating aliens from another planet earning enormous amounts of money we can only dream of.

On the other hand our local footballers are just like ordinary Joe-blokes, *anthu wamba*, claiming to be footballers on Saturday but working as butchers, bakers or sales-men from Monday to Friday. You see our local footballers standing on the bus-stop waiting for a minibus while it's pouring rain like Niagara Falls as they pathetically try to seek shelter under a PTC plastic bag.

There is no footballer in Malawi who owns an expensive exotic car; Ferrari or a Lamborghini. Compare this to the Drogbas of this world who have a car for each day of the week.

Maybe it's for that reason that we find ourselves here at Simioni's house admiring these Manchester United and Chelsea players; little gods on the football pitch and millionaires off it.

We were busy chit-chatting happily as to who was going to win while our beautiful spouses were in the kitchen preparing *dzipalapatilo dza nkhuku* and *dzabakha* to go with the drinks during the match.

I love these moments of friendship that always ended in a climax of delicious food; *nyama yootcha, ntedza okanzinga* or *mawungu* just to mention a few.

It's not a secret that Simioni's beautiful madam enjoys hosting these football-match gatherings. Of all the spouses she is the only one with a microwave in her kitchen and derives some sort of satisfaction from showing it off to our spouses.

The problem is that every night, after a visit at Simioni's house, 'microwave-talk' always ends up as the topic of choice from my frustrated Manyuchi Darling. As soon as we enter the bedroom and switch-off the lights Manyuchi would start before my head even hits the pillow.

"*Komatu a neba ndiye zikuwayendelatu, mukudziwa kuti anzanu amadya zakudya zotentha* every day?"

Whenever Manyuchi Darling goes down this road I always fake *nkonono* fully aware that she knows that I am just faking it.

The two teams came out of the dugout, Chelsea in their trademark blue kit and Manchester donned in their traditional red. The stands were packed with noisy fans in blue and red, we also felt as if we were there at Trafford in Manchester.

Manyuchi Darling handed me a plate of *dzipalapatilo* as the twenty-two players were warming up on the green pitch. Their pitches always looked so green as if someone had painted them *ndi yobiliwila* from Dulux as opposed to our brown patchy ones scorched by the equatorial heat.

I cherished these moments, our ladies sitting next to us, waiting for the match to start while chewing on these delicious crunchy chicken legs doused in *piri-piri wa kambuzi.*

"This is good living," I murmured softly while stroking Manyuchi's shoulder, knowing that come tonight, 'microwave-talk' would be the main feature of our bedroom conversation.

But until then I was just going to sit here and enjoy every minute of this football-*dzipalapatilo* bonanza. I looked into her eyes smiling and she smiled back.

Fifteen minutes into the game, John Terry crossed the ball to Drogba, who zigzagged around Rio Ferdinand, the

Manchester United defender, leaving himself one to one with Edwin Van der Sar, the Manchester goalkeeper.

Drogba, the legend from Ivory Coast, was galloping at full throttle like a mad horse with its tail on fire and was about to shoot ... we all stood up in anticipation ... I even dropped my *chipalapatilo* fully knowing what was going to happen next...

Edwin Van der Sar, went to the left as Drogba went to the right, his powerful right *Mandingo* foot arching backwards in a forty-five degree angle about to make contact with the ball....this was going to be explosive, even the ball squirmed in fear of the impact that was about to take place...

That's when the lights went OUT, total blackness, *m'dima wadzaoneni* and we all exploded like Kamenya Choir, screaming at the same time in a unified chorus.

"AAAA... ESCOM.... ESCOMUUUU!!!"

I was so angry because I didn't see whether Drogba had scored or not. I was so angry because I had just dropped my piece of *chipalapatilo* just before the lights went out. I was so angry for all the times Escom has forced us into darkness for no fault of our own making. I was so angry and mad for being a Malawian and not someone from a country that has electricity twenty-five hours a day and eight-days a week. And I was just so angry for not being angry enough.

"Escom... Escom... Escom..." I seethed in anger, anguish, despair and various other strange emotions that I didn't even know existed inside me.

I could feel warm tears of rage welling from the corners of my eyes cascading down my trembling cheeks.

Good thing the whole house was in darkness and no one could see *misonzi yanga*, but when I heard Simioni *akufwenthela* like a horse I knew I was not the only one crying in rage.

I remember there was a time, when I was growing up, when ESCOM was an acronym for "Electricity Supply Commission of Malawi".

Back in those days I used to admire Escom engineers, all dressed up in orange overalls taking care of business like professionals. They used to fix faults if you called them and they used to make these regular visits to trim down tree branches that were too close to the cables.

Escom engineers and employees used to walk with a bounce, *monjanja* and why wouldn't they? These were the people who were keeping Malawi alight with uninterrupted supply of electricity.

Looking back at that era is like looking back at a mirage, something that really didn't exist and one couldn't help wondering; 'did that really used to take place? Twenty five hours a day uninterrupted power supply? *Ayi inu mukunama.*'

I am not an engineer nor do I pretend to be one. But my father on the other hand is an esteemed electrical engineer, British qualified and as far as I am concerned the best of the best ranked up there with the likes of Jack Kilby and Maurizio Seracini.

The little glimpses I have into the world of engineering I owe to the sporadic snap shots gathered from spending too much time with my father.

He taught me how Malawi is blessed with the best form of green energy resource vis-à-vis waterfalls. Not even UK is blessed with such natural resource of fast flowing water and yet we are failing to garner electricity from these steep God-given natural water falls.

With so much water-force on tap to spin turbines at Nkula or Tedzani, there is no reason why we should be having these chronic blackouts. Somewhere, somehow, these days, Escom is selling us short.

Escom's capital assets have long aged with time and you don't need a PhD in Complex Accounting to figure out the obvious. If you are going to depreciate your assets for twenty or thirty years, they will have to be replaced at the end of that life span instead of trying to patch them up with sellotape or super glue.

I don't know the machinations or workings of Escom, but one gets an inclination or feeling that Escom's engineers are using sellotape to prolong the life of capital assets that have gone past their sell-by date. How do they expect turbines that are held together by some flimsy sellotape to power the recent explosion of homes, shops, offices and factories?

No wonder ESCOM has become synonymous with "blackouts", "*m'dima*" or "*kuthimitsa.*" It's gotten so bad that some days it comes as a surprise when we go the whole night without a blackout, prompting rude comments by fed up customers.

"Mwinatu lero othimitsa ali off.*"*

One of my friends commented, just last week, that at the rate these sporadic blackouts are occurring now is a good time to be in the candle business or *mbaula* manufacturing. Indeed what's the point of having a freezer when it ends up cooking all our meat and boiling your milk?

Cookers in Malawi are cold and Fridges are hot, Microwaves are used as cupboards for storing bread and salt… the whole notion of civilised living or normalcy has gone bananas and no one is complaing loudly.

I whispered to Manyuchi in the dark, in what was a pre-emptive strike to tonight's impending debate on 'how come we don't have a microwave.'

"That's why I don't bother investing in a microwave," I jokingly said and immediately felt her sharp elbow lash into the side of my abnomen painfully connecting with my rib cage instantly wiping the smirk off my face.

The Escom saga has gotten so sad and so very pathetic on comedic proportions it's hard to comprehend these blackouts if you don't live in Malawi.

But if you are *wakonkuno* who lives *konkuno* what else can you do? You just soldier on, after all *kwanunkwanu… palibe amasankha uko abadwile.*

Just yesterday I overheard my neighbour's wife yelling instructions at *ntsikana wawo wantchito* on top of her voice, Malawian style.

"Malita! *Iwe* Malitaaaaaa! Don't forget to Escom the *mbaula nyembazo zikabwadamukatu.*"

It took me a few seconds to realise that she was telling the worker *kuti athimitse* the fire in the *mbaula.* I thought this was funny and perhaps an isolated incident.

But again this morning, in a packed minibus, I overheard an angry man screaming his lungs out on his cell phone.

"Why having you been dodging me? I tried calling you yesterday but you had Escomed your phone!" He said in a gruff voice causing everyone in the minibus to crack out laughing.

Such is the state of electricity in Malawi that Escom now means *kuthimitsa*. I hope the *magetsi* situation will soon improve so that people can emerge out of this prehistoric era and join the rest of the civilized world that enjoys electricity twenty-five hours a day – uninterrupted that is.

At the rate we are going it wouldn't surprise me if a Stegosaurus dinosaur was seen crossing Zalewa Road because it really feels like we are back in the prehistoric age when these creatures used to roam the land. *Tikubwerela mbuyo* as a country.

There have been so many theories put forward about our electricity fiasco – the famous one being about monkeys at Nkula Falls playing monkey business.

Don't ask me to quantify and solve this dubious Monkey Theory for you because I am just as puzzled as all the people and monkeys living in Malawi.

"*Zamuanthu zeni-zeni,*" some people, especially those who lived the era when electricity was guaranteed, have proclaimed.

Although I have never quite understood what the term *zamuanthu* implies or means, I find myself agreeing with them.

"*Koma ndiye zamuanthuditu*"

Lucky for us Simioni's madam managed to light up a few candles (*za* china) and I was able to reunite myself with the prodigal piece of *chipalapatilo* that had dropped on the floor just before Didier Drogba was about to shoot the ball with his right strong *mandingo* foot.

I picked up the still warm chicken-claw, glad that Simioni's ugly cat (*Pusi*) hadn't gotten to it first. If he had I am sure he must have spat it out due to the ferocity of the *tsabola wakambuzi* that I had stolen from Agogo's *ka nkebe* before leaving home. I didn't care whether *Pusi* had licked my *chipalapatilo*, 'what the eye doesn't see won't hurt you' is the motto I operate on.

I took a big hungry-angry bite while getting ready to leave Simioni's blackout house for our own blackout house across the blackout street of the blackout neighbourhood in this blackout country. Eiishhh, *fotseki*... what a blackout life.

"*Mugone bwino-tiwonana mawa,*" we all said our goodnights while shaking hands as our shadows eerily bounced against the wall from the flickering candle light. It felt as if I was in my home village and yet I was right in the middle of what is supposed to be the metropolis of Malawi. Hahahaha what a freaking joke, 'metropolis my butt' I muttered to myself.

I walked over where Simioni was standing staring at his blank TV in rage. I whispered some good advice in his ear, which must have cranked up his rage a notch or two;

"Hey brother, don't forget to Escom the candles before going to bed."

19

INTRODUCTION TO MINIBUS-OLOGY

You don't have to be Albert Einstein to figure out that I am seasoned businessman, an entrepreneur with vast experience in general dealing and complex transactions on all things Malawian. My speciality is transport and you can tell just by looking at the two (dead) parked minibuses at the back of the house which are waiting for spare-parts from Okinawa Japan.

If you are still not convinced about my credentials as a top notch transporter then more proof can be found in the assortment of dead engines stored *mukhola la nkhuku*, gearboxes and spare axles tucked away in the children's bedroom, not to mention starter motors and brake-pads in the cupboards next to the plates, spoons and folks. Used tyres all over the garden and empty diesel drums clearly give credence to my claim as a seasoned Malawian transporter. If this still doesn't convince you then *talephelana*.

Anyone who claims to be a Malawian transporter but doesn't have his children sharing the same bedroom with a gearbox or an oily engine is not a genuine transporter. Anyone who boasts to be a transporter but his house doesn't smell of diesel and used oil is just a fake transporter, he/she is like someone who claims to be a mathematician but has never heard of the Pythagoras Theorem. In short; *nyumba ya* Malawian transporter *siikhala* ndi carpet on the floors.

Amalume came back from UK with a sizeable capital (*mpamba*) in Sterling Pounds and it has always been obvious that he was not planning on taking up employment with any of the NGO's, private firms or government agencies. He always spoke of being his own boss because he couldn't stomach someone telling him what time he needs to come in and what time he can leave.

Lately, he has been asking me a lot of questions for ideas on viable business ventures in which he can invest his Sterling Pounds. Ventures that promise returns better than the interest offered by Saving Accounts in most of these banks sprouting all over the country like minibuses.

I am always interested to know what the other person has in mind before I offer advice. So, as usual, I asked Amalume to furnish me with what he had in mind. I not-so-enthusiastically listened to his ideas as he went on to talk about all sorts of ventures from Filling Station to Restaurant and what not. He even went as far as making projections on future Cash flows, drafting Income Statements and Balance Sheets...it was all too painful for my ears I could feel the wax melting. When Amalume started talking about drafting a Business Plan that would highlight his profile and illustrate his market research and analysis of potential competition… I had to stop him in his tracks.

"Woah! Woah! Amalume! Amalume! Time out, listen *Ankolo... kuno nku Malawi eti?*" I lamented with him, telling him that if he wants a real business with future prospects of steady *makwacha* then he needs to start thinking of joining the minibus franchise.

I could tell that Amalume was somehow not impressed by my dismissal of his classroom way of doing business. *Mwina* this is how they teach and do business in UK but I was not going to sit here and listen to him talk about depreciation of assets or be lectured on the benefits of effective budgeting, *zinthu zoti* I had no clue as to what they meant or how they are supposed to make your business prosper, *zongotayitsa nthawi zimenezi.*

"Maybe in the UK things like Sales Variances or Contingency Plans work, *koma kuno zimenezo ayi.*" I told Amalume not mincing words but *kukamba mwaka-tchutchu.*

I could tell that Amalume was aghast and shocked by my staunch recommendation of a minibus business, maybe because he had already seen the number of Toyota Hiaces on the Minibus rank which superceeds the number of customers. On top of that he knew that I had two very dead minibuses at the back of the house and he must have had a feeling that the story about spare parts coming from Okinawa was nothing but *nthano.*

I remember one of my rude neighbours once told me (after we had an argument about his barking dogs) that Afghanistan stood a better chance of winning the World Cup than my minibus did of ever running again. There are a gazillion minibuses all over Malawi waiting for spare-parts from Okinawa-Japan and Amalume is well aware of this but he never interrupted me, so I carried on.

"Have you heard of Dubai?" I quizzed Amalume in an attempt to force his mind not to dwell on the downside of this lucrative business.

Most entrepreneurs will attest every business has got positives and negatives. Take BP for example; a massive conglomerate which is in the lucrative business of oil and made a profit of $14 billion (positives) in 2009 but come 2010, BP is struggling with the oil spill off the Gulf of Mexico (negatives).

Spare-part quandaries are like an oil spill dilemma of the minibus industry. You don't dwell too much on it, you clean it up as best as you can and resort to modifications if a spare-part cannot be located in Okinawa or at the local market. As part of business, you lobby the government to kick all big buses out of city routes so as to warp the odds in favour of minibus operators. I preached to Amalume who merely looked at me with a blank face.

"Do you know the capital you brought with you, it would be easier to order a minibus from Dubai and have it shipped over through TZ." I told Amalume, pausing just to make sure that we were on the same page and carried on after Amalume gave me a half-hearted nod.

"As soon your minibus gets here we have to go see Morisoni, you remember Morisoni right?" I asked Amalume referring to the first born *wa mphwawo wa Madala aku* Zomba.

"Morisoni now works for MRA, and for a small fee (*kachiphuphu*) he can get the minibus papers processed," I shared this highly sensitive info with Amalume.

Whether my words of wisdom were making an impact on Amalume or not was difficult to tell, because he kept staring at me with a blank face, nodding slightly just to show that he was listening. So I increased the tempo a little bit, showing him that here in Malawi you don't need the nonsensical nuances like depreciation of assets or variance analysis. All you need is to have contacts at the right places, relatives in the right offices and childhood friends sitting behind right desks holding the right stamps.

"As far as Road Traffic is concerned, it's not going to be a problem; you don't even need to take your minibus in for COF," I told Amalume knowing that this will surely grab his attentions.

I went on to tell him that I have friends that I went to school with who can assist in getting the minibus ready for the road. I could tell Amalume had doubts about the claims I was making but I forgave him for being a doubting Thomas. For someone who had been away from Malawi for thirty years, he couldn't really understand how things worked *kumudzi kuno*. So I continued with my lecture on minibus-ology.

"As soon as the minibus clears and is given a stamp of approval you can then employ *mwana wa-Asisi aku Chilomoni*, he has a driving licence and is currently doing nothing but *ulova*. He is such a good driver and you don't have to pay him that much since *ndi wachibale*." I saw Amalume smile for the first time since I started talking.

"*Basitu* Amalume all you have to do is sit back and count the money every evening. Am telling you minibus business is the best cash-cow in Malawi, I wonder why people even bother with some of these fancy businesses," that was my closing argument and Amalume was hooked like a chambo to a fish hook.

That was two months ago when I gave Amalume this business administration lesson. But I must confess things did not go according to plan. *Zamuanthu zeni-zeni,* am sure someone *anayilodza* minibus *ya* Amalume. Because I was confident the business technique I had divulged to Amalume was airtight.

What made me think *kuti zinali zamuanthu* started when the minibus first arrived in Malawi. MRA impounded it because of some discrepancies with the paperwork (*akuti*) and Morisoni (our MRA point man) could not help us out because he was unexpectedly transferred to Nayuchi border.

This unannounced transfer resulted after *mabwana* sniffed something fishy in Morisoni's dealings. Rumour has it that his bosses started wondering how he could afford two pairs of shoes on his current salary. Morisoni demotion-transfer meant Amalume had to pay VAT and full Duty plus penalties on the Toyota Hiace Minibus. *Anawakhapa* heavy and I had a feeling Amalume was somehow blaming me for this mishap.

As the saying goes – *ikakuona litsilo siikata* – my friend at Road Traffic got caught trying to process Amalume's COF without the minibus being present. Worse still he got fired which meant that the Toyota Hiace had to be called in for a proper COF.

Without my friend being there, the COF didn't go according to what I had promised Amalume. It failed miserably because the horn wasn't working, the brake lights would come on every time you engaged in reverse gear and the wipers wouldn't work if the radio was on.

Amalume had to spend more money fixing all these things so as to get the minibus fit for the road.

Finally when the minibus was on the road, *mwana wa-Asisi* together with the conductor started pocketing some of the money. This is typical of Malawian minibus drivers, and I had told Amalume to accept this as a business expense that can be rectified by; once in a while telling the driver that, "*mwezi uno sindikulipirani.*"

This might sound harsh but when you consider how much these drivers steal you begin to understand and sympathise with the owner of the minibus(es.) The skimming or theft is worse if the driver is a relative of the proprietor. Instead of just skimming off 20% of the daily takings he starts taking 50% or sometimes more. Every evening *mwana wa Asisi aku Chilomoni* would tell fibs to Amalume.

"*Eeeee lero sizinayende, kunathinana heavy ku* rank." He would say *m'maso muli gwaa* in his usual *kaulemu ka* fake and Amalume who was still naive and new in Malawi would just take his word as the truth.

"*Mwina ziyenda mawa.*" Amalume would usually answer. The thing is, *mawa* was always the same story simply because in the 'Owner-Driver' relationship pertaining to minibusology any notions of loyalty or morality doesn't exist.

Simply put and what Amalume didn't realise is that the minibus game operates on the Theory of dog-eat-dog.

Amalume's minibus was a 14-Seater but *mwana wa Asisi* was loading double the limit, packing them like sardines in a can, it took three strong guys to shut the door; two to push it and one to quickly fasten a string that kept it in place. One fateful hot afternoon both front tyres which had gone past their sell-by-date and looked smooth like *njoka* exploded like *chimanga cha mbuliwuli*.

The minibus swerved off the road, nearly missing a blind *wamasikini*, and smashed straight *mu sitolo ya mwenye*, beyond repair. Amalume is now being sued by the passengers who were hurt and also, the Asian store owner.

Even *wamasikini* is also claiming compensation from the trauma that was inflected on him after he came so close to dying. Some members of the public, including myself, are wondering how a blind *wamasikini* saw a minibus go past him? But then *pano mpa Malawi, nayenso akufuna aweluke*, someone must have whispered to him that;

"*Ayise* if you want to retire from *umasikini wakowu kapeze Loya.*"

It took Amalume three weeks to start talking to me again. And during those three weeks I thought to myself; how many people are abroad or have just arrived from abroad and are taking blind advice from business gurus like Makala Amoto?

To all Malawians abroad or you new-comers, think first before taking business advice from self-made business gurus or you might lose all your hard earned Pounds, Dollars or Rands like my Amalume did.

Do your homework and do the legwork before you start parting with your *mpamba*. And sometimes be prepared to spend instead of opting for short-cuts that may prove costly in the long run.

It also wouldn't hurt if you try to take the approach Amalume initially had, that of trying to do business the proper way.

Some simple Book-Keeping or even setting up a Budget would be the right way to go so that you are able to see what funds are coming in and how much is going out.

Investing in a file and a simple calculator might also be an idea, instead of counting using your fingers or toes and filing everything in your brain – *akuti* memorising as if you are dodging *anyamata* a MRA.

STARTING BUSINESS ABROAD

After giving Amalume what turned out to be erroneous business advice a week ago, I didn't think he would be talking about *nkhani ya* business anytime soon, at least not to me of all people. But strangely enough we embarked on a business tête-à-tête while driving to Lunzu to pick up a consignment of fresh *dzipalapatilo*. Upon arrival at this bustling market of all sorts, we were given some rather shocking news.

A daughter of one of Malawi's prominent Minister was getting married in two days and *Olemekezeka* himself had come at the Lunzu meat abattoir and cleaned out the whole place. My regular meat vendor, in his blood stained overalls, approached the Morris Marina before I even got out saying;

"*Iiiii pepanitu bwana Makala panabwela a Onalabo* (honourable) on his Benz followed by a Daihatsu 3-ton, *ndiye angosesa nyama yonse moti lero tiweluka kudakali m'mawa.*"

To think that I voted for these guys into power and today they come and finish all the meat at the market is a bit ironic.

"Don't these government Ministers make enough money to go and buy meat at Shoprite or Cold Storage?" I snapped at Amalume as suicidal thoughts zigzagged in my brain. I angrily slammed the gear in reverse, ignoring the vendor who was saying;

"But if you still want fresh *mbewa* meat, it's available..."

For me *dzipalapatilo* or meat from Lunzu is the best, but since there was none, thanks to *Anduna*, I guess we would have to try getting some from one of these Chinese food shops popping up all over the country.

"*Basitu tilowa* China-China," I told Amalume and this got me thinking about the influx of Chinese people into Malawi of late.

It's as if someone has just opened up a tap of Chinese people and I couldn't help wondering if we were reciprocating in equal amounts. Where Nyasalandians also flooding into China to fill up the void left by these *matchaina* coming here?

One thing for sure, these Chinese brothers are behind or responsible for much of the recent development schemes happening all over Malawi. I read recently that they are even proposing to open a school that will teach us Malawians how to speak their Mandarin language. They are also hard working people just as they are gracious, at least the ones that I have come across.

On top of their hardworking nature there is also something about these lovely, constantly smiling, Chinese immigrants. That 'something' is an undying love and fierce attachment to their food. As more and more Chinese people flood into Malawi for business ventures some of them have opened up shops that sell Chinese food to their fellow Chinese people and also to the indigenous Malawians vis-à-vis the Makalas or Simionis, in short *makadafe*.

The kinds of foods sold in these Chinese shops range from soy sauce, spices, drinks and *nyama ya mphaka* (so the rumour goes) which is flown in all the way from their mother-land China to Malawi in container loads.

It's a bit ironic that my meat vendor in Lunzu has been selling meat for over fifteen years under the same *kansakasa* made out of plywood and *nsungwi* where he spends 52% of his time chasing stubborn green flies (with a *litchowa*) that love infesting on the fresh meat. On the other hand, the Chinese (*Matchayina*) just came *dzulo-dzuloli*, yet they have managed to open up these fancy shops with deep-freezers for the assorted meat products and they have also installed check-out tills that make you feel as if you are in Shoprite.

The other thing about buying meat at a Chinese shop is that you can actually see the meat unlike at Lunzu where your sirloin steak is usually swamped by abnormally large green flies that don't even bother to scatter if you scare them, nor are they bothered by the *litchowa* being waved in their flight path.

Let's face it, *Matchayina* know how to do business, in my books they are up there together with our Asian Indians (*Amwenye*) not like us indigenous Malawians (*Makada*) still practicing business *ya masanje*, am sorry to say this. Yes, business *yaife, Makadafe,* there isn't an element or an ounce of continuity from parent to child nor is there any book-keeping involved.

The father suspiciously looks at his children as *anamponda* and the children looks at the father as *nzwanya youmila*. And we wonder why *mabiziness athu achikuda amankela limodzi kumanda* with the owner as children start selling capital assets to buy sports cars. This something you will not see with these Chinese, no way sir.

When I pointed this out to Amalume, he concurred and educated me that it was the same with the Chinese in the other parts of the world. Whether in United Kingdom, America, Australia or Congo Brazzaville, when they come into the country they establish their own little Chinas inside that country. They quickly set up shops that cater to their fellow Chinese or anyone who loves Chinese food, anyone who is not afraid of eating *nyama za maso atatu* or *miyendo* five.

Amalume went on telling me that while he was in UK he noticed that even Nigerians, Zimbabweans or Polish people have also set up shops to cater to the cuisine needs of their kind. For example there are Nigerian shops scattered all along Stockport and Gorton in Manchester, selling garri, egusi, amala, tuwoo, yam, plantain, akpu, pounded yam, banga soup, gbegiri, edikaekio, owo soup, just to mention a few.

Listening to Amalume articulate himself on foreign foods it sounded as if people from other countries have a massive array of edibles on offer compared to us. But even though we cannot match them like-for-like, I know we also have a variety of our own Malawian delicacies; *n'gaiwa, nyemba, kondowole, mbewa, ngumbi* and *Bwanoni* just to mention a few. Maybe not as many as the Nigerians but surely enough to warrant us our own shops in these faraway lands be it America or UK.

Mouth agape, I stared at Amalume and he could sense there was a question that was struggling to come out of my mouth.

"No, Makala," he answered my unasked question even before I had asked it.

"There are no Malawian Shops in the UK nor in America", he paused so that it could all sink into my unbelieving mind and just to make sure, he hammered again;

"*Sindinanvepo kuti pakuti-pakuti pali sitolo ya chi* Malawi, *mbambadi.*"

"But that's a very lucrative business niche right there. So you mean to tell me that you don't get Malawi's famous cream flour Gramil?" I asked Amalume.

"No," was his response.

"You mean to tell me there is no one selling *thobwa, Mahewu, Chibuku* or *chambo* from Lake Malawi?" I fired another one.

"No," Amalume shook his head.

"Not even Malawi Gin, *Chambiko* Milk, Gluco Power Biscuits not even *Chishango* (for the purposes of *kulela*)?" was my last futile attempt at soliciting a 'yes' from Amalume.

"*Nta ndi pan'gono pomwe,*" was Amalume's response.

I couldn't believe it, because back here we have this entrepreneurial spirit. Business runs in our blood; as can be seen by women baking *dzigumu-yoyo, mandasi, mbatata yophika, ma bin ladeni,* boiled eggs and what not. Men, on the other hand, often venture into scrap metal, chips *chanchiwaya, kaunjika,* or vending the highly potent aphrodisiac called *Gondolosi* and various other businesses.

The question that kept gnawing at my soul is 'how come, then, this spirit is not reciprocated by those *Abale ndi Alongo* abroad?' Do Malawians lose their business acumen once they leave the country? Are Malawians so afraid to go into business? Are they prohibited not to conduct any entrepreneurial ventures? I had more questions that my mouth could handle.

Why is no one importing goods or foods made in Malawi to these faraway lands? If Zimbabweans can manage to bring in Camphor body cream (so that their female Zimbabweans can have smooth skins), or Mealy Meal flour for their funny tasting *nsima* they call *Sadza* – why can't we do the same? Why do we, Malawians, have to resort to buying food from Nigerian shops instead of opening up our own?

For a brief moment I took my eyes off the road, looking at Amalume who was also looking at me, waiting for my next question.

"So you mean to tell me that you stayed in UK for all those years and never tasted *nsima* ya Gramil or fresh *chambo* not even *ngumbi*?"

Amalume had no answers to my barrage of questions, but he agreed with me that it is little things like these that make a lot of Malawians living abroad miss home. You hear them talk things like: "I wish I was in Malawi eating *ntedza ophika*" while others will be saying "*ine ndikufuna Maungu.*" There have been extreme cases where pregnant women have asked their husbands; "*inu simungawauze anzanu kumudzi kuti atitumizire dothi,* I really feel like eating *dothi la chiswe.*"

Although scientists or academicians who spend years studying soil are yet to discover the benefits of *dothi la chiswe* to pregnancy, I am sure that this is a lost business opportunity. This is a certified cash cow business that is just laying dormant, waiting to be exploited by some Malawian future tycoon... our own Bill Gates or Mark Zuckerberg. Yes indeed, this could definitely be bigger than Microsoft or Facebook combined. I could just envision the revenue generated from *dothi la chiswe* imported from Malawi to these faraway lands where *dothi lawo* looks like *utuchi*.

And to think that a lot of Malawians abroad keep calling me asking me for business ideas here in Malawi when they could easily be getting rich right there in UK or USA by just shipping container loads full of *dothi la chiswe* from Malawi. Upon arrival abroad, all they have to do is pack it into smaller 500g packets and then sell it to pregnant Malawi women, to satisfy their lucrative cravings.

Since I had this talk with Amalume I don't think I will be going ahead with my Visa application process to go abroad. I just don't think I would be happy over there if I wouldn't be able to have my daily supply of *dzipalapatilo* and Malawi's genuine Gramil first grade cream flour. Rumour has it that most Malawian abroad cook their nsima using the same flour that is used for making samosas or chapatti. Even if you put a gun to my head there is no way I will swallow *mbamu ya nsima* that tastes like samosa, heck no.

I know most of rich countries are classified as land(s) of opportunity, but if I can't get any opportunity to eat *ngumbi* or chicken heads then I am staying put right here in the Warm Heart of Africa.

We pulled up my drive-way and called *ntsikana wantchito* as soon as I got out of the Morris Marina.

"*Iwe Fane tapita ukandigulile dzigumu dza* K200 *pa nseupo* and tell *nyamata* to come and off-load *dzipalapatilo* from the boot, can you also bring a wet cloth to wipe off the chicken blood and when you are finished, go buy me today's paper from the *dzigumu* change." I spilled out a staccato of commands to *Fane* who was neither bewildered nor surprised by the endless list of what-to-do's.

Home is really best, the only place you can ask your worker to do a gazillion different tasks all at once while wondering how come Malawians abroad are not launching *dothi lachiswe* businesses or selling Malawi gin in sachets.

AUNTIE IS A WHITE BRITISH WOMAN

Today is a big day for our clan, not as big as the day when Amalume came back from UK, but still big in its own right. The only difference being; on Amalume's return a whole cow was slaughtered whereas today it is just quarter of a cow but with plenty of rice simply because *kukubwela* a very special Auntie.

Amalume returned from UK on his own so that he could organise all the paper work with the Malawian Immigration before his wife could come. I know most of you are wondering why my *Azakhali* needed legal documentation before coming to Malawi. Simple, Amalume's wife is not a Malawian but a white British lady who we have all heard about and only seen on pictures; sitting side by side with Amalume and sometimes holding hands while looking at each other like teenage lovers, *zachizungu anzathu.*

The whole atmosphere albeit festive was a bit tense, especially *ku khitchini*, because the women were not quite sure what kind of food to prepare. You could hear Mother constantly shouting and asking.

"*Kodi ndiye tiphike chiani? Nanga azunguwa amadya zathu zachikudazi ngati?*" She was so worried and petrified that our British Auntie will be appalled if not disgusted with our local cuisine of *maofozi, masamba otendela* and *ntolilo.*

Mother had actually sent Amalume to Shoprite Mall to buy a few packets of spaghetti, *mbatata za tchipisi* and some *mpunga* to supplement our Malawian delicacies. A few kids were excitingly plucking chicken feathers, constantly being yelled at.

"*Tiyeni mudzingososola nthengazi, osamalongolola chifukwa zingamelelenso.*" I almost laughed because this was the same technique that was used on my generation when we were that young just to make us de-feather the chicken(s) in record time.

Since Auntie was coming from a land of no mosquitoes, I was asked to spray some Doom (mosquito repellent) in Amalume's bedroom, the first time such tactic was used in our house. Even the unsuspecting mosquitoes must have been surprised at this new form of lethal attack.

I held my breath whilst ruthlessly spraying and waving the green canister around the room at the unsuspecting malaria carrying tiny monsters. As the lethal mist filled the room I kept thinking to myself, which was better: to die by a slap or by some poisonous chemical called Doom. It really must be hard being a mosquito, I mused while quickly dashing out of the bedroom before closing the door behind me to catch a breath of fresh Doom-less air out in the corridor.

As a family, we were doing everything possible to make sure that Amalume's British wife had the best welcome Malawian style. All children had been asked to take a bath in the morning much to their surprise, with the slightly older ones querying,

"Why are we taking a bath in the morning, I thought we already had a bath two days ago?"

As most of Amalume's *katundu* was still stuck in Durban in a 40ft container waiting for clearance, so my best friend Simioni, agreed to loan us his TV and a few VHS tapes (The Gods Must Be Crazy, Rambo, Benny Hill, The Two Ronnie's, Thriller *ndi ma* film *ena achimwenye*) so that Auntie *akafika,* she should be well entertained.

I told one of my nephews to make sure that the cassettes were re-wound all the way to the beginning. There is nothing I hate more, than sitting there and waiting for a tape to rewind to the beginning while looking at a fuzzy screen. Simioni likes to do this at his house and it always irritates me and I would always bring it up.

"I thought you told me over the phone the tape was already at the beginning?"

I figured that's why we hear in the UK, USA and even here in Malawi a few wealthy Malawians have all switched to DVD technology. This is 2010 and Simioni is still living in the VHS era (although in his defence, he said that; at least he had a video tape recorder simply called the 'deck')

Simioni offered to go and pick up my Auntie from the airport since my Morris Marina was being serviced by my trusted mechanic, Che Supanala, after I noticed it was leaking petrol from the exhaust pipe. I know some of you auto mechanics or engineers will dispute this strange phenomenon as an impossibility; well that's your opinion but I know petrol when I smell some and the fact that

Che Supanala says it is petrol pouring out of the exhaust, who are we to dispute otherwise?

The Datsun 120Y carrying Amalume and Auntie arrived from Chileka just after 6pm. The minute my British Auntie came out of the car, screams of jubilation and *nthungululu* from the army of women who had gathered rang out. If we had a gadget to measure the loudest ululations then clearly without question, Mother's *nthungulu* came first.

"*Lululululululululululu,*" she blasted away, reminding me of *mbumba za* Kamuzu back in the days of *tambala wakuda*.

Our British Auntie got out of the car smiling, shy and looking lost like a chicken *mu khola la nkhuku-ndembo*. She wasn't sure whether to cover her ears from the piercing loud *nthungululus* or jump back in the car.

She did neither and instead her shy British smile turned into laughter while holding on to Amalume as if seeking protection. I have never seen Amalume smile so wide, it almost reminded me of this crocodile I saw years back at Blantyre Zoo before it was converted into a night club, (or was it?) I get confused since so many residential homes are being converted into Disco Night Clubs – *zalowa bizimisi*. Anyway let me not side-track and let's stick to the story at hand. Where was I?

Oh yes! In respect of *miyambo ya chizungu*, Amalume had requested that *mbewa, dzipalapatilo ndi mitu ya nkhuku,* not to be included in the buffet. This did not go down well with my 102 years old Agogo, he did not put up a fight and simply mumbled something we couldn't quite understand nor did we try to. That's typical of Agogo who is always throwing tantrums like a 102 years old baby.

But when he saw the food being prepared he excitedly remarked.

"*Koma kudya kulipo lero*," he reached inside his *chijasi* since he always came to these family gatherings with his own salt and *tsabola* and today was no exception. Agogo then proceeded to pull out *ka nkebe ka* Kiwi shoe polish containing his famous home-made *piri-piri.*

The misconceptions, presuppositions or fallacies most of us had about our British Auntie turned out to be just that, misconceptions, presuppositions and fallacies.

She is such a nice woman, with good manners, something that surprised all of us. We were expecting to see someone like the famous Jordan or a WAG but we ended up with Sister Maria from Sound of Music.

She spoke so softly and deliberate but still most of us could not understand what she was saying. My primary school level of English knowledge was of no help to me against the perfect and original English coming out the mouth of a British person – *eniyake achiyankhulochi.*

I was even getting a headache from forcing my brain to comprehend what she was talking about, to the point of getting *kanfuno.*

The last academic textbook I read was Timve and Tsala and I vividly recall struggling to read the story of '*Timve's Big Shoes*' to my fellow students who couldn't stop laughing as I maliciously murdered and mispronounced the English lingo. My mouth had felt so full as if someone had attached switched my tongue for an oversized elephant tongue making me choke out the words instead of speaking them out.

That was the day I convinced myself that English and me were like water and oil, no matter how hard you try to stir us together laws of physics stipulated that we just weren't going to mix, *nta pan'gono pomwe*. From then on I foolishly ignored all the advice from my English language teacher who tirelessly tried to show me the benefits of and advantages of the Queens language.

"*Makala chizunguchi nchofunika phunzirani*," she would tell me in her typical Teacher-Parent voice that I used to find so patronising.

Why should I anyway when I always dreamt of becoming a Fireman since I was five or six years old? I had my own valid and concrete reasons.

"Who needs to learn or understand English in order to put out a fire?" I had once told her. As far as I was concerned I used to think; it's not as if you would stand outside a burning house yelling;

"Fire Fire Go Out! Fire Fire Go Off! Fire Fire Stop Now!"

With thoughts like these as a justification for my failings I used to look at my English teacher sarcastically.

"*Aaaaahhh, inu mundichedwetsapo apa.*" I would say and would grab my ball and excuse myself that I wanted to go and pee. Once outside the class I would jog down to the football pitch *kukadoda bora* with some of my friends who are now prominent *dziboli-boli*/forex vendors.

Looking back now, I wish I had listened to her. It's so sad that hindsight is a privilege we never have before we goof.

The good thing is that once in a while Amalume would translate some of the things Auntie was saying and the women would cheer with *nthungululu*, as if *ali pansonkhano wa chipani*. But that's typical Amoto of women; they never run out of things to cheer about. Last week a very ripe papaya fruit fell from the tree landing on *nyamata wa ntchito's* head while he was sweeping – we heard loud cheering and *nthungululu* as the poor guy was drenched in yellowish- orange mess with tiny black seeds all over his overalls. *Lululululululululu* went the Amoto women, anything, and pretty much everything amused the females of my clan.

But today's *nthungululu's* and cheering was loud, it got even louder when Auntie served herself *nsima* (ignoring *zakudya zina zachizungu*) and kidney beans with a bit of *thelele*. She even went as far as refusing the folk and knife given to her and instead opted to eat Malawian style – with her fingers.

Despite struggling in merging the *mbamu* of *nsima* together with the elusive *nyemba* due to the slippery *thelele* that was in the same plate with the beans – everyone was so happy and excited at seeing a white lady *akutema mbamu* with her bare fingers. The beans kept falling off the *mbamu* while in transit from the plate to her wide open mouth. This was frustrating her a little bit but we really didn't care, we were simply elated that here was a British lady getting it on just like a Malawian.

The day had started a bit tense, with a few *timanon'go-non'go* of discontent from some family members.

"*Koma Amalume mpaka kutibweretsela nzungu kusiya mbeta zonsezi zachi-Malawizi.*" I had heard some of my nosey Aunties, who have too much time on their hands to thrive on gossip, but by 9pm things were more exciting than we had all anticipated. It was now time to dance and show off various dance moves the Amoto clan possessed.

Someone suggested that a tape of Lucky Dube's songs be played, and everyone with two legs jumped up onto the dance floor. Even Agogo with his pronounced limp, hobbled on the dance floor and started shaking his hips in a funny way.

"Hehedeeeeee! *...nkoke-nkoke ...ali ndi mwana agwiritse!*" we chanted as Agogo holding *chiboda cha bakha* and his *nkebe* of *piri-piri* danced close to our bemused British Auntie.

All this time my mother was in her bedroom on her knees praying that Escom should not do what Escom does best.

"*Chonde...Chonde lero lokha musathimitse magetsi,*" she begged while looking up to the heavens, and it worked.

When Shabba Ranks' 'Mr Lover Man' song rang out from the speakers of Simioni's stereo, my Auntie who had just been dancing with Amalume came to dance with me. I didn't know whether to shake my hips, do a twist or throw my arms in the air. I did all of the above and the crowd cheered and laughed as *malikhwelu* rang out throughout the whole neighbourhood piercing the night sky as if it was New Years Eve and 6 July celebrations all wrapped up into one.

Even though *dzipalapatilo, dzinyophilo* and *mitu ya nkhuku* had been banned on this first day of the new (British) member of our family, I was having a wonderful time. Not even on Amalume's return party did I experience such happiness and a feeling of mixed emotions.

At first I had been a bit apprehensive as to how I was going to communicate with my British Auntie, but as the day wore on I realised that she was also feeling the same way if not worse. By night time all those feelings had evaporated and I found myself chit-chatting with her as if we had known each other for years.

She told me about Britain, about their foods; fish and chips, Donner Kebabs, that their evening meal is called 'Tea' but not the tea as in Chombe-Tea. She told us about baked beans, bacon and black pudding (which sounded like *uwende*) for breakfast.

I told her about our delicious rats, grasshoppers aka *Bwanoni*, the differences between *nsima ya ufa oyela* and Gramil, the technique required to cook *nsima ya kondowole* and how *chambo* is the best fish of all time. I did not forget to lecture her about our baked confectionaries vis-à-vis *dzigumu, dzikonda-moyo, ma bin-ladeni, dzitumbuwa, mandasi* just to mention a few.

Having a British Auntie was strange but such a wonderful thing, it was a true learning (and teaching) experience.

I felt as if I was sitting next to the Queen only that Auntie was more beautiful and young and her skin had this nice faint gold looking hairs, it was like the women I see in James Bond films. Before her, Manyuchi Darling was the only light complexioned person I had come close to.

Manyuchi Darling must have sensed my thoughts because she came to join me on the dance floor and I almost asked her how she knew I had just been thinking about her. Instead I just took my shirt off and waved it in the air like a helicopter, bending my knees and arching my back until I resembled an *uta* (bow).

"Hehedeeeeeee ... *ziri kuno*, Makala Amoto *wawonjeza*." The women of the Amoto clan chanted, laughed letting out their usual *nthungululus* the minute Manyuchi Darling started to dance around me in circles, shaking her hips like a Zairean woman on Kanda Bongo man's dance troupe.

"*Lulululuuuuuuuu!*" chorus resonated from my yard and beyond, this was a night to remember, it was the day the Amoto clan had added a new member to its ranks, a white British woman... my Auntie.

FILLING STATION BUSINESS

So many of you *abale ndi alongo* (abroad) have been asking me about business ventures in Malawi – and I promised that I will keep you updated if I see or hear anything in the pipeline. Well something has come up, something better than selling spoons door to door which I consider a *choncho-choncho* business especially when you consider that 99.9% of Malawians use their fingers for all their eating activities – *akuti* spoon *imachedwetsa* game.

Amalume once jokingly said in Malawi the ratio of spoons to people is 1:2000. Since my primary school arithmetic didn't cover the topic on ratios or if it did, then it must have been one of those days that I fell asleep. So I asked Amalume what 1:2000 meant, in layman terms per say.

Well, according to my learned Amalume; "It means that out of every 2000 Malawians there is only 1 spoon. This means that at the present population of fifteen million people in the country there are only 7500 spoons the whole of Malawi."

Amalume's use of ratios to illustrate the non-viability of a spoon business was a bit confusing for my brain which is allergic to numbers. But what I got from this was – don't quit your day job thinking that you are going to forge a career out of selling spoons in Malawi. We, Nyasalandians, strongly believe that God gifted us with ten natural spoons called fingers hence see no need in investing our scarce wealth by purchasing little aluminium contraptions so that we can scoop rice from a plate. The point am trying to make here is; *iwalani za gain ya masupuni* and let's discuss filling stations here.

With the recent development that Petroda might be forced to let go of some of its filling stations, business minded Malawians like myself have been getting goose-bumps *ngati nkhuku yososola*. I remember Simioni, my friend remarking perhaps what most Malawians have been thinking;

> "*Apa ndiye a Pulezident atiganilizila achi Malawife.*"

This is a ripe business venture for those Malawians with entrepreneurial drive wishing to go big time instead of wasting time with "gain" *yama* minibus; which only comprises of too many headaches with minimal returns on investment. *Kungolemeletsa ma* driver *ndi kondakitala apa.*

I still believe that the minibus venture is better (than owning Microsoft) if you are the driver or conductor, but if you are the owner then it's worse than having a having a Visa Card whose pin number is known by all the vendors in town.

Please take note that I am not trying to discourage those aspiring would-be minibus owners, I am just pointing out the obvious that; unless you are going to be driving the minibus yourself chances are your driver will be making bigger profit margins than you.

For me, I strongly believe that the Filling Station venture is the way to go if you want to be talking of six-figure gross takings (*mamiliyoni*) and Petroda might just allow you to get your foot on the ladder of this multi-billion kwacha industry.

For those *abale ndi alongo*, especially *muli kunjanu*, who have no idea what the Petroda Saga is all about, then let Makala give you a crash-course on Filling Station 101(Intro-Course.)

I am well aware that some of you left Malawi before Kamuzu even came to destroy the stupid federation (ok may be I have exaggerated a little bit – just try and stay with me here.)

You might remember a company called Oilcom, with a green looking Pentagon Shaped symbol? If you don't even know Oilcom then Makala can't help you out – *pepani*.

For those of you who do, Petroda is in the same line of business as was Oilcom. It (Petroda) came into prominence during the UDF era, back in the 90's if my history is correct. If am wrong, please forgive me, just remember this is not a history lesson and if you are one of those people obsessed with the chronological order of events then, yes, UDF came first before Petroda, not the other way round. Although in recent years Petroda's finances have peaked while those of UDF appear to have nosedived, *izi ziribe umboni weni-weni*, and this has nothing to do with what we are discussing here, which is owning a piece of Petroda.

What makes Petroda unique and different from other fuel operators is that for some unknown reasons, (which maybe political or not, Makala has no proof) this conglomerate was allowed to operate both as a Petrol Wholesaler and Retailer.

For those of you not familiar with these two terms *mutichedwetsapo apa*; a wholesaler is like Chipiku Stores and a retailer is like your average vendor vis-à-vis you cannot buy a whole bale of sugar from '*Sasamba* the Vendor.'

It is pretty obvious that this setup might (or should) have raised flags behind closed doors, but apparently if those flags were raised then they weren't waved out in the open.

Simioni's contacts in the high circles of commerce claim that for a fuel operator to wear both robes of Wholesaler and Retailer is a big No-No.

So, according to my friend Simioni and all those in the know, the government is right in quizzing and squeezing Petroda. One wonders though why just now these mumblings have started coming out in the open.

Some have rightly asked; "*koma boma lazindikila lero kuti* Petroda *ikutema nsima* using both fingers and toes?"

Anyone who has studied Filling Stationology will tell you that the retailing side of petrol is supposed to be left to small business people like Makala and some of you, business minded people, out there.

This form of business, according to Simioni who went to school further than me, is called a Franchise; something similar to McDonalds, Wendy's and Burger Kings (as those of you abroad might be aware of.)

Please note that this is just an example *tisanve muku-uza anthu kuti* Makala *akuti* Petroda *yayamba kugulitsa ma* Chicken Nuggets, Double Whopper, Angus Burgers or French Fries. *Ine ndidzakukanilani,* I will categorically deny such malicious assertions that would tarnish the Amoto name.

Anyway, back to the issue at hand... where was I? Aaaaahhh yes... now for some unknown reason(s) the government has decided to come down hard on Petroda like a hammer on a stubborn nail. The government insists that Petroda needs to let indigenous Malawians take over the running of the Petrol Filling Stations.

"*Muwasiyire anthu achi* Malawi *anyambite nawonso Dola za petulozi*," *boma latelo*, ok... ok... ok... maybe not exactly in those words, but close enough.

This is exciting news and I would advise *abale ndi alongo* abroad to start packing their suitcases, phone your respective workplaces and tell them to take you off the rota (or schedule.)

Makala strongly advises you to cancel all your shifts and tell the nurse in charge or your line-supervisor or manager that you are not going to be reporting for anymore shifts, *mwazidomoka*.

Even if you are one of the few lucky Malawians who happen to be a CEO or CFO, I strongly suggest you inform your Board of Directors or the Chairman that you are resigning with immediate effect. They don't even have to worry about giving you the remuneration package stipulated in your contract (you don't care) – because you are going back home to run your own Filling Station.

Mukukayamba "gain" *yanu-yanu*, because as I speak now, at the Headquarters of Petroda, behind *ku nkaka* in Blantyre (also known as MMM or MDI or Dairy Board – or simply *kusomilo* aka *utuchi* depending on which era you left Malawi), they are reviewing thousands of applications from would-be owners of this lucrative petrol business. And rumour has it that it's going to be on first comes first serve basis, which is strictly based on the *wayenda wapenga, wagona watsala* type of principle.

But a small word of caution from me to you *abale ndi alongo*, before you start cursing your bosses, or dumping a pile of *manyowa pa desiki ya a bwana* or spilling contents from a bedpan all over the nurses-station as a token of appreciation for all the frustration you have been through.

Yes, before you tell the Board of Directors to shove that Remuneration Package up where the sun don't shine, please take a moment to think whether you have what it takes to run a filling station.

Because this is a numbers game, a daily cash-business that will test your quantification skills to the limit vis-à-vis your 1+1 capabilities have to be up-to-date.

On top of basic arithmetic know-how, a small knowledge in measurement of liquids might come in handy too.

This means knowing that petrol is "not" measured in kilograms or inches – otherwise you are better off trying your luck in the butchery business... *kapena kayeseni kugulitsa dzitenje...* or simply stay *kunja konko* and continue doing what it is you are doing right now and let those Malawians who can tell the difference between litres from kilograms tackle this Petroda Franchise.

Most Malawians here and abroad are excited at having a piece of this business that is worth billions. Some are already envisioning themselves as the next mega rich oil barons or baronesses with so much Kwacha's to enable them buy Bata Bullets or MTL football club (*akuti Abramovich wachiMalawi.*)

Some are already dreaming of the monies they will make from running a Filling Station, money that will allow them to acquire expensive yacht and go sailing along Mudi, Nasolo or Likanga River. They already see themselves flying in their civilian helicopter from their forty-bed roomed mansion on Mulanje Mountain to their Filling Station to go and collect the day's profits. Mmmmmh… a bit of reality check here.

I have heard some prominent business gurus saying that Filling Station business requires discipline like that taught at Kamuzu Academy. The reality of this business is that the profit margins it generates are so small compared to the gross takings.

You really might want to put a stop to that order of a Bugatti Veyron or Bentley Continental because Simioni has done his research and found out that vendor *okazinga chipisi panseu* makes higher profit margins compared to a filling station.

Amalume once told me that because this business is close to what academics call Perfect Competition vis-à-vis you cannot charge higher prices than your rival filling station across the street. The gospel according to Amalume taught me that there is a theory pertaining to microeconomics which stipulates that; in such an industry like filling stations prices will be close cost. This means that you cannot make obscene profits or supernormal profits.

It's very easy to hear stories of; "*adya kapito yonse*" when it comes to *bizimisi ya petuloyi*, especially if you are one of those few who can't differentiate Revenues from Profits.

For some annoying and unexplained reason(s) it's always the case that at the end of the day Revenues look more appetising than Profits. It requires a lot of discipline to remember that most of the money vis-à-vis Revenue does not belong to you.

This is something that we Malawians have hard time grasping due to the mentality of; "*ngati ziri nthumba mwanga ndi zanga* syndrome," a crippling disease that has reduced once prominent and successful Malawian business men/women to the status of; *"awa anali anthu kale."*

Another thing is 'Business Ethics,' *nkhani yovuta kwambiri iyi. Abale ndi alongo ambiri tilibe* business ethics *ngati ya anzathu achimwenye, due* to our culture, lack of discipline and a total lack of common sense.

I am not an Asian so I cannot impart to you any of their wonderful business ethics. I think it is something that is held in secret close to their chest and only passed on from one Asian father to another Asian son, never to non-Asia people.

I am saying this because the few Asian friends that I have, can discuss very intimate and personal stuff with me but will never disclose the recipe of their business ethics that often guarantees them success. Maybe *amaganiza kuti*, if we all get rich who is going to be the security guard or the children's driver?

I might not be *m'mwenye* but I am an indigenous Malawian hence qualified enough to illustrate to you some of our indigenous-Malawian-unethical-business-pit-falls.

Take for instance Simioni's small shop called *Teki-Teki* that closed down six months ago. Every morning he would send his house girl to the shop to "take" bread, sugar and Chombe tea for that morning's breakfast. I said "*kukatenga*" not to buy but to take. After all *Teki-Teki* was his shop, why should he have to pay? Ethics... ethics *abale*, no ethics whatsoever.

The blame does not stop at Simioni alone because I also played a part in milking *Teki-Teki* shop dry. I was also a culprit in this mother-of-all-fleecing charade during my regular stops at his shop. I used to walk in and grab what I felt like grabbing and tell the shop-boy:

"*Makobidi ndiwapatsila a bwana ako madzulo.*"

The shop-boy could not protest since I was *abwana's* friend and unfortunately I wasn't the only friend doing this.

All Simioni's friends were responsible at milking his business dry, and we really milked it to the bone.

Funny enough after Simioni's shop filed for 'Chapter 11 Bankruptcy,' most of *anzinzakefe*, we became experts at pointing fingers and judging him where he had failed;

"*Ifetu tinadziwa kuti zidilizika izi chifukwa cha ana ake opanda* discipline, *amangotapa mu* till."

True, Simioni kids were the biggest culprits. Every day on their way to school they would pass by the shop for pocket money without Simioni's knowledge or consent.

They wouldn't even ask the shop attendant to give them the money, instead they would just lean over the counter, dip their fingers in the till and pocket as much as they could. *Nyamata wamu* shop would just stand there smiling at *ana a abwana*.

The shop attendant wasn't that stupid. He too would pocket his own share as soon as the kids had left, reporting to Simioni (later on) that *ana anadzatapansotu lero*.

Simioni was none the wiser and even up to this day he fails to understand how come his shop attendant managed to open his own successful shop called *Kipi-Kipi* a few months after *Teki-Teki* had gone under.

Simioni's relatives were also in on the game. Not wanting to be outdone by his friends or children, they were generously taking groceries on 'Account.' Theoretically the term "account" means you take something today which you are supposed to settle later.

But in reality (Malawian reality that is) 'Account' simply means that you take something now and there is a "slight" possibility that you might pay later. But as weeks turn into months and months into years, this "slight" possibility usually gets downgraded to "Free" vis-à-vis the Debtor status becomes a liability.

Because of the expanding and unsustainable various "Accounts" *Teki-Teki* shop had been taken to the cleaners and simply closed down, *pano amametetsalamo tsitsi*. But even this barber shop too is in danger of filing for bankruptcy because we have all been getting our hair-cuts on 'account', "*Ine mundimete* style ya Tyson ...*ndikuonani* month end."

Ethics, ethics, ethics... zero ethics in our business dealings. If only we could have a tête-à-tête with our Asian friends on ethics, *mwina bwenzi ma geni athu akuyenda bwino.* How I wish I had some Asian genes in me, just to give me an ounce of business ethics that lacks in us Malawians.

That's why it scares me to the core when I think that Simioni has also applied for this Petrol Franchise hoping to be a proud owner of a Filling Station. It's scary because 95% of Simioni's friends own minibuses and it's obvious that *adzikamwetsela mafuta a ma* Morris Marina and those minibuses at his Filling Station.

With this "*dzadinditseni* mentality" you can pretty much predict the short life span of a Malawian owned business. This can be seen in how a Malawian, in a space of ten years can launch twenty different businesses one after the other in a staccato of amazing succession; yesterday he was a transporter, today he is nightclub owner, tomorrow he is an importer of Vuvuzelas and the day after, as soon as the Vuvuzelas line has fizzled out, he wants to open a Filling Station.

No ethics, no focus, no continuity whatsoever. Imagine if Bill Gates had jumped from one venture to the next; today selling boiled eggs, then ordering used clothes, then Microsoft before switching to *yomakatenga magalimoto kunja, basi kenaka* Petroda.

Don't get me wrong here, there are already Malawian entrepreneurs who are running petrol Filling Stations successfully. But their stories always come down to "it's not a glamorous business, it's a lot of hard-work and you always have to keep a watchful eye on your petrol attendants and more important the delivery tanker."

One business guru once said that "as long as you remember that no one walks into Shoprite or McDonalds and says to *ntsikana wapa* till "*tangodindani,* I will sort you out month-end?" It's vital to emulate the Shoprite way when it comes to your business as well.

Ignore comments from your friends, "koma *ndiye zokhwimilatu, mukutchita kukaniza ndi* One *lita yomwe,*" when you refuse them *kudinditsa*. One litre here, one litre there will surely add up to a whole tanker by the end of the month. Even Agogo claims that if you are one of those people with a good and giving Samaritan heart then don't run a Filling Station try to open a Charity Shop.

Having said this, I think a lot of *abale ndi alongo* should go ahead and apply if this Franchise turns out to be true. Now is a good time because it's not like there are many of these filling stations for each and every one of you.

I am lucky because *mwana wa Achemwa a ku Bembeke* is an accountant at Petroda Head Office and I think he has managed to put my application on top of the others and will keep on placing it on top of the pile no matter how many forms come in (*wankachisi adzadya za nkachisi…* hahahaaaaa!)

I promise you all my friends in Malawi and abroad that the first week of my Filling Station opening all petrol will be half price and the diesel will be buy-one-get-one-free (litre that is, not kilogram) and Paraffin will be free for the first 2 litres. To all my friends I went to school with; feel free to open up an account – *mudzidzango dinditsa.*

But to all those of you who laughed at me when my UK Visa was declined and all those girls from primary school who used to laugh at my oversized khakhi uniform shorts, don't even bother pulling up at my Filling Station, I will instruct my attendants to fill your tank with sugar and water.

So you want to be a Petrol Filling Station owner? I hope this helps.

SOUTH BEND, SHASHA SENDS HIS LOVE

Today was the first time Shasha had visited since returning from abroad. When Shasha left Malawi years ago, he headed for America but apparently he got tangled up with the American legal system and they deported him back to Malawi.

We later on learnt that Shasha was the first Malawian to lock horns with the much feared INS, *bungwe lomwe limathamangitsa kapena kunjata anthu ophwanya malamulo a* migration *ku* America also known as Immigration Naturalisation Services. Some people say that *bungwe limeneli* is the most feared compared to the FBI or CIA for obvious reasons we won't go into. Unfortunately for Shasha, he collided with this *bungwe*.

Shasha being Shasha, instead of boarding the Ethiopian Airlines heading for Malawi, managed to outsmart the authorities by boarding an Air India 747 heading for New Delhi. How he did that remains a mystery and he has never offered us any explanation, Shasha *udolo* too much.

I must say it's nice and refreshing to have Shasha visiting my house. He really gave us an insight into an America we didn't know. Although most of the things Shasha talked about and how he talked (from his initial greeting of "wadda-up") all sounded like Chinese to my ears, it still was such an amazing experience to have him over.

He referred to things in a strange, American way that was a bit confusing for us; for example his reference to the bonnet of my Morris Marina as the "hood" and the boot as the "trunk" made us all laugh. I am sure *abale ndi alongo* who are in America could make sense of what Shasha was talking about because those of us who have never travelled were really finding it hard to keep up. *Kusayendaku abale inu*, it reminded me of Kamuzu's wise words *kuyenda nkuphunzira* or was it *kuphunzira nsi nkalasi mokha*.

Shasha started telling us about his glory days in America, how he was one of the Malawian OG an acronym for Original Gangster.

"Eeeeh *ndimayesa* gangster means *chimbalangondo*?" Simioni asked on behalf of all us *asanamayendafe*.

Of course Shasha is not in the same league with the likes of Tony Soprano, Tony Montana, Michael Corleone or John Gotti. These are real gangsters with long CVs to prove it.

Shasha's gangsterism had no credentials to back it up nor has a movie ever been made in his honour. He had never held an UZI machine gun or Nina (9mm) pistol and surely he had never participated in a 187 (drive by shooting). In short Shasha had never popped nobody not even a dog, *u gangsta was a Shasha* didn't involve *mfuti (nta mpeni)*.

Shasha was your typical Malawian gangsta wannabe like the many "Nyasa-gangsta" wannabes. The only time he got tangled with the law was via his many traffic violations. But just like many Malawian Yo's, Shasha believed or still believes he is a true OG with the same conviction Snoop Dogg believes he will one day be the president of America, a belief that is farfetched than thinking that Malawi will land a man on the moon before 2014.

Shasha was only in America for a couple of years before the traffic authorities had enough of his dangerous antics behind the wheel. Shasha's driving rap-sheet ranged from: driving while suspended, driving under the influence, driving with no insurance, driving on the wrong side of the road, driving up a one way street, driving at 50mph through a school zone in reverse, driving with his leg hanging out of the window (*kusongola* Shasha style), driving while talking on his cell phone while holding a glass of gin and juice, driving while blind-folded trying to impress a girl, overtaking a funeral procession while blowing his horn and flashing a finger and many other traffic violations that had to be added to the Highway Code because Shasha was responsible for inventing them.

One time the traffic police pulled him over but could not charge him because the offense did not even exist in the American code of traffic violations. The officer actually told him that; "Sir I don't know why I have pulled you over, but I just had to pull you over because of what you did back there on Ironwood Road." He was breathalysed and he failed the test; the Officer had no choice but to arrest him on the spot.

The presiding Judge at Mishawaka County Court had no choice but to pass a swift and somewhat harsh ruling.

"Mr. Shasha, you leave me no choice but that of deporting you back to Malawi because your traffic offences have crossed the thin line that separates misdemeanours from felonies. Your chronic disregard of the safety and well being of fellow road users through dangerous driving acrobatics now rank up there next to murder or manslaughter," the judge summed it up. Shasha case was no longer a State issue but had now become Federal issue.

A few Malawians who went to court that day claim that Shasha went out screaming civil rights cries.

"Power to the people! Abolish slavery now! Viva Malcolm X!" He was heard as far as McDonalds Restaurant across the street. To Shasha this was discriminatory simply because of his dark skin pigmentation and because he is a Bantu from Africa. Shasha threatened to appeal at the Supreme Court, but unfortunately they bundled him straight from court into a waiting tinted Federal Van with armed marshals. From court straight to Chicago's O'Hare Airport where an Ethiopian Airlines had been ordered to wait for a dangerous raving and ranting Malawian convict. *Iiiii! a Shasha munaonjenzanso nanu, kufuna kuononga mbiri ya bwino yachiMalawi.*

We asked him if he would ever go back to the US, but Shasha claims that nowadays Malawians *akuthawako* ku Bend looking for "*bata ndi ntendere*" elsewhere. If you ever want to see Malawians running away from other Malawians, then study carefully the exodus happening in South Bend.

He insists though that South Bend – still holds the title of undisputed heavy weight of "little Malawi."

South Bend has a population of *abale ndi alongo* that rivals any other Malawian population outside Nyasaland, forget Gorton, Manchester, forget Nottingham UK – South Bend is the top dog – *kumphika kwa a* Malawi – only *Jubeki* SA comes close. He spoke of this place called South Bend with a hint of nostalgia and pride, a voice of someone who was now here but his heart still longed for what he had left behind.

Shasha preached to us about a serene South Bend, a city that was all loving and encompassing when he first arrived. He claims that during his time there, South Bend was calm and peaceful. He graced us with stories of how Malawians used gather at the house of this quiet and polite Malawian on Chippewa Road. This was where a lot of barbeques used to take place, as Malawian sisters mingled with their fellow Malawian brothers. Shasha recalls those bygone days with a note of sadness in his voice, "*timanjoya masiku amenewo*."

On some weekends Malawians would travel to Niles Michigan to a place called Michiana Party Hall where Malawian DJ's would spin music to a mostly jubilant Malawian audience. African beats, Rap beats, Reggae beats and sometimes slow beats (for that *awiri-awiri* time) would resonate from powerful speakers, as the bar served free drinks resulting in uncontrollable volcanoes in the toilets.

Of course after each party Shasha would always get pulled over and breathalysed by the traffic police – how he came up with all these violations amazed and baffled the police on both sides of the Michigan/Indiana

(Michiana) border. "*Ma* driving lessons a Pemba *mwina,*" Simioni had suggested.

But Shasha says that South Bend has now changed, "*pa* Bend *padzadza ma OG achimuna ndi achikazi omwe* who don't play by the rules anymore." Shasha never stops *kuthokoza* the Judge who deported him out of America, otherwise he claims he was on a collision course with some of these Malawian OG's – "*kumene zinthu zimalowela pakadafa m'Malawi achimwene,*" Shasha lamented in a tone that betrayed a hint of anger and rage of some unfinished business he thought he had back in South Bend.

With the passing of time Shasha has come to believe that some Malawian ratted or squealed him out to the authorities. He has forgotten that it was his reckless driving that got him in the authorities' cross-hairs.

All this talk of friction and tensions amongst fellow Malawians sounded strange to us. How would someone travel all the way from Malawi to a far away land just to get tangled up with fellow countrymen? You mean to tell us there are no other nationalities that you can tangle with or have 'Beef' with? or Pork? or Lamb? or any other *nyama* that's synonymous with *mikangano*.

Shasha claims that there is something about America that changes people, he can't put it into words, you have to live there to understand it. And he was right, we didn't understand the Why's and How's of the 'beef' Shasha was proclaiming exists in the USA with much specificity to South Bend.

He claims that now Malawians have 'beef' with other Malawians just like Mike Tyson had 'beef' with Evander Holyfield (when he ate *khutu la nzake*). This is not to say that Malawians in South Bend *akudyana makutu, tangonena ngati mwa sampulo apa. Ngati akulumana makutu* we haven't been told yet – although it looks like things are heading that way. Simioni laughed out loud saying that; "*ayambila khutu lakolo iwe Makala.*"

Jealousness or *kaduka* has permeated the once tranquil Malawian atmosphere that existed during Shasha's time there. What has caused this drastic transformation is not yet known, maybe some academics studying or wanting to do a thesis on the life and culture of Malawian's in South Bend will be able to come up with the causation of such a shift in attitudes and Yo-ism that goes beyond that of Tupac or the Ruff Ryder posse.

Shasha lived in South Bend, Indiana during an era before Tupac became Makaveli, when 50 Cent was only 25 Cent and P Diddy was still Puff Daddy. The time when Public Enemy Number One was the music of choice by anyone claiming to be a Yo, the time when it was still cool to listen to Mc Hammer, the time when Michael Jordan at Bulls could fly like Mike and Shaquille O'Neal at Lakers terrorised the opposition with his Shaq Attack. This is before Beyonce became a household name, and Destiny's Child was wowing people with their "I'm a Survivor" single and also the Fugees were rocking the waves with their number one tune of "Ready or Not."

So it shouldn't come as a surprise that during this time the only beef exchanged between Malawians was at a barbeque on the House at Chippewa Road when beef meant *nyama ya n'gombe*. This was the time when all tax-returns for Malawians were being prepared by a single Malawian and all this tax-money would be spent at Michiana Party Hall...*kukazimwaza* while sipping Heineken *ndi* draft *wa* m'ma Keg.

Listening to Shasha recount the past was a bit heart wrenching, even though we had no clue whatsoever what he was talking about. He sounded like a true South-Bendian and not a Malawian. I asked him if he still craved for Obama-land, putting the question as gently as I could because we noticed that talking about it was somehow taking an emotional toll on our friend.

Shasha paused for what felt like an eternity before telling us that, for those who have never been to South Bend, it is difficult and almost impossible for them to understand or comprehend all this. There is an ancient saying that dates back to the time before dinosaur's vis-à-vis before the Ice Age that says; "You can take a Malawian out of South Bend but you can never take the South Bend out a Malawian," looking at Shasha I was starting to believe this saying.

With visible traces of tears in his eyes, Shasha's trembling voice continued, "I miss my crew and I miss my posse, especially the real OG's." With that sentence Shasha looked at his massive Bling-Bling wrist-watch and like a true South Bendian he got up and said to us,

"Yo ma bros, I gatta bounce outta here, peace out", he flashed a V sign while heading for the front door.

I had no idea what Shasha had just said and I didn't understand 91% of his whole conversation, but Shasha was the real deal. He might not have come back with a car nor built a house, but Shasha had the game. Even Amalume was in awe of this true Malawian-American, he sure was the last of his breed, the last man standing.

We all looked outside watching him run after a minibus. "Shasha... Shashaaaa for *shoh* (sure)" is all we could say.

POLITICS? CAN SOMEONE PLEASE EXPLAIN

Lately listening to Agogo talk we are beginning to think that the piri-piri (*tsabola opela*) that he keeps in his little tin (of shoe polish) has expired and become so potent that it's affecting his brains. There are those who claim that Agogo is coming down with a case of Alzheimer's or Dementia but I doubt this very much, I will bet my last One Kwacha that Agogo's recent hallucinations are due to that abnormally spicy *tsabola* that must have expired a year or so ago. Even my British Auntie made a comment that "Agogo has lost his marbles."

But today I had to agree with Agogo when he said that Malawi is a nation of very fast learners. We might not be the inventors of the Microwave but we all know that if you have a cat called Meow-meow that has gotten wet, there is no way you can put him in the microwave to dry. That is unless you are planning on having Meow-meow for lunch or as a snack.

It was a juxtaposition on a more advanced level and Agogo must have been aware of this because he took a long pause as if waiting for our brains to clearly visualise the image of a cat standing right in the middle of microwave being zapped by a zillion lethal micro radioactive waves.

After painting the Microwave-cat picture to us, Agogo then went on, talking slowly as if he was talking to 5 year olds.

"How come Malawians have quickly adapted to the complex intricacies of the microwave technology but so far have failed to grasp the simple basics of politics?"

As soon as Agogo mentioned the word "*ndale*", Mother jumped up to go and close the windows because she gets really nervous when Agogo starts politicking.

Mother is like one of those Malawians who can freely debate and criticise foreign politicians or politics, but when it comes to *ndale zakumudzi* the tone aka volume tends to be lowered to an inaudible zero. According to Mother, criticisms should be confined to one's brain or stomach never making it up the windpipe as far out as the lips, because once they come out of your mouth in form of words the probability of them being construed as mutiny or *kuwukila boma* is usually beyond 101%.

Mother is simply scared of Malawian politics, she claims its respect but we all know it is fear in its pure raw sense of *mantha*. She is so frightened of the consequences that may result from criticising *atsogoleri athu*. That's why she always starts shaking and fumbling to shut the windows whenever we start gabbing about politics.

But to understand Mother's fears or reservations pertaining to Malawian politics you need to understand that she comes from the era of *Tambala Wakuda*. Fears of that bygone period still haunt her to this very day and this is evidenced by her persistent nightmares of man-eating crocodiles.

It's not rare to hear Mother screaming hair-raising shrieks in the middle of the night as big masked men, in her dreams, always end up shoving her down a deep and dark pit full of man-eating crocodiles just because she had been overheard bad-mouthing *Chipani*. She always wakes up trembling and shaking from these terrifying nightmares, hastily checking all her limbs just to make sure that they are still there attached to her torso, pinching herself just to make sure that it was just a scary dream.

Agogo on the other hand has never been intimidated by these tales of man-eating reptiles from the sunny-side of lower Shire. He has always believed that these were just fairy tales concocted by those who wanted to instil fear in Malawians; to him these were simply *marido* or *nthano*. And because of this Agogo has always been someone who used to speak his mind 'then' and definitely speaks his mind 'now'.

Shasha was still looking at Agogo, still struggling to comprehend the connection between drying a cat in a microwave and politics. I could tell that he wanted to ask Agogo to elaborate more on this microwave-cat synopsis but wasn't quite sure on how to frame his question intelligently. Politics has never been Shasha's favourite topic, he marvelled in conversations that dealt with cars or anything on wheels, not anything that bordered on social sciences.

Suddenly Shasha's eyes lit up as he finally managed to construct an intelligent question that he could throw at Agogo.

"Has someone microwaved one of our politicians?" This was Shasha's best formulation in what was a typical Shasha classic.

I almost choked on my *chipalapatilo* as a bubble of laughter exploded from my lungs into my mouth diverting the chicken piece the wrong way down my wind pipe.

Whilst I was choking on my *Chipalapatilo* Agogo dipped his piece *muka-nkebe* of that viciously hot (*abale samalani*) *tsabola*, ignoring Shasha's question altogether. He took a bite on the chicken claw, wiping off tears induced by the ferocious *tsabola wa-kambuzi*. Auntie had once remarked that if this was UK that *piri-piri* would have been labelled 'Not Fit for Human Consumption'.

But this is Malawi and this is Agogo who just coughed and carried on talking.

"When are we going to learn that once you have had General Elections, the country is supposed to enter a period of some economic development and a fulfilment of the promises that were made during campaign." Agogo paused to sneeze as some of the spicy piri-piri powder went down the wrong way down his oesophagus.

"What are you talking about Agogo?" I couldn't help asking while looking at him struggling to swallow the spicy bits of flesh he had just gnawed from the chicken bone.

"At the rate our politics is going it's as if we are about to hold General Elections next year. Everyone seems to be in a campaign mode; people are jostling for positions, others are being jostled out of position, the media is talking about leadership crisis within the government and within the opposition, the young are getting restless and the old are getting nervous, parties are being launched while MP's are crossing the floor, people are whispering about whispers ... everything that you would expect to be happening closer to elections is happening now 48 months away. Is Malawi going to be in a campaign mode for the next 4 years?" Agogo asked that question while looking at his spicy-hot piece of *chipalapatilo* as if it was going to give him an answer.

A combination of old age and the fact that he survived the MYP era made Agogo speak as he saw it, always in black and white never grey, he never spoke *nchinin'ga*. Even back in the day, when I was still very young, I remember him entering markets or getting on public transport without his Party Card. He used to tell the Red Shirts (a *Yufi*) without mincing words.

"*Pitani mukanene kulikonseko*, am not forking out 50*tambala* to buy *khadi*."

To us we used to (and still do) view Agogo as *munthu wa makani*, but he would counter that he was one of the people present at the *indaba* that formulated the plans for Kamuzu's return to Nyasaland. And for this reason and this reason alone no one had the power to force or coerce him into buying a party card. Agogo argued that if it wasn't for him and a few other prominent Malawians, Kamuzu wouldn't have become who he became.

Agogo kept staring at his piece of *chipalapatilo* as if he was waiting to hear a response from it. My British Auntie seized this opportunity to voice her opinion "to be quite honest, I thought that Elections are next year. In the UK we tend to go through a period like this just before elections not soon after. Right now David Cameron is busy fulfilling his manifesto; tackling the immigration issue and scrapping the ID card scheme not campaigning as is the case here Malawi"

I have no idea what the 'ID card scheme' is all about but I have strong issues and reservations when people start comparing Malawi to UK. I voiced my Malawian patriotism towards Auntie, passionately telling her that, "don't forget this is Africa we are talking about. You British have had democracy since the beginning of time long before Moses saw the burning bush in the desert. Surely you don't expect Malawi to wake up one day and be like UK?"

There is saying that goes like 'blood is thicker than water', although I have never really understood the meaning behind it, I (like so many people before me) have followed its logic.

From the corner of my eye I saw Amalume clearing his throat ready to join the debate and put this '*blood is thicker than water*' phraseology to the test. I knew he was going to take my side and put Auntie in her rightful place by backing our country Malawi like I had just done. But for some unknown reason Amalume's next comment did not abide to the '*blood is thicker than water*' concept.

"Actually your Auntie is right." Amalume shocked me by siding with Auntie and I looked at him in disbelief as he continued

"Look at Mozambique or Angola these countries are doing ok because they are spending much of their energy on the economy and not on who is going to run for office in 2014." Amalume carried on realising that his response is not what I was expecting.

He spoke about facts that these two countries have just emerged out of long civil wars but so far have managed to put their political house in some sort of order. He concluded that this then could be the reason why donors are lining up to assist them with all sorts of aid.

The average Malawian doesn't really care what's going to happen four years from now. Citizen-Malawi just wants to know what's going to happen to the electricity situation today, will there be petrol or paraffin at the Filling Station today and not next week let alone 2014?

Amalume then went on to give a short sermon, rumbling about things and acronyms that didn't make sense to me.

"A couple of years ago Malawi surprised the World Bank and IMF when our economy grew by almost 8% which is more than that of UK or USA. It really felt that we had a leader who is an economist and it felt so good to read and hear such positive economic news about Malawi. What made it even sweeter is that we had done better than most countries; bar China and Botswana. These are the things we should be spending our energy on, simply because they benefit Citizen-Malawi."

I listened to Amalume's use of statistics but I had no clue what he had just said before and after the word IMF.

"But these countries you are referring to Amalume don't they have natural resources? Isn't that the reason why their economies are doing so well?" I countered Amalume's assertions but at the same time agreeing with what my 102-year old Agogo had initially said about Malawi's never ending campaign that looked as if it was going to go on for the remaining four years.

I knew I had Amalume cornered, surely he knows we are poor because of the geographical location of our country and the fact that we were never blessed with diamonds, gold, oil or an ocean like Mozambique. It is because of this grinding poverty why Malawi's sons and daughters are buying one way tickets to la-la-lands where *mipope* (taps) spew out milk and Fanta instead of water.

But Amalume was unfazed, he responded with a left uppercut-jab that caught me unawares.

"Have you ever heard of a country called Switzerland?" He asked fully knowing that I had no idea of such country. I know a few African countries and a handful Asian states; like India and China *basi*.

"Switzer-Whaaaaaaaat?" I exclaimed and Amalume looked at me, carrying aware that my geography only went as far as 'what is the capital city of Malawi? Or how many regions are there in Malawi?'

Amalume schooled me on how Switzerland's geographical attributes are somehow similar to those of Malawi. He spoke at length on how this country is covered in forests, lakes as well as mountains and has no mineral resources, drawing similarities with Malawi. Just like Malawi it, too, relies on imports, but the unique thing about Switzerland is that it reworks on its imported products to add value and then exports these goods.

It has a vibrant service industry like tourism and most importantly banking, something we can copy when you consider how many highly trained Malawian bankers, accountants and other professionals we have. Like us, Switzerland's farming is a key part of their economy too, and Amalume thinks there is no need for me to give excuses about how we don't have natural resources, after all Kamuzu repeatedly told us that *chuma chilli munthaka*. I digested what Amalume had just said

"Shaaaaaa, *koma ndiye mwalalatu Ankolo.*"

After recovering from the fiery *tsabola wakumbuzi* Agogo re-joined the conversation once more.

"Our politicians both in ruling or opposition need to get their act together and start addressing the needs of Citizen-Malawi. I wonder if these political manoeuvrings are for the good of the ordinary citizen or our politicians are just trying to gain leverage for their own financial survival. Surely you don't read in the American media that Obama is grooming someone to succeed him. Neither do you hear that the American opposition is at each other throats about who should be their leader. Do we really have enough resources to carry on campaigning for five years after just having had General Elections?"

Agogo's voice was getting louder with each sentence and Mother kept looking outside as if MYP would storm the house any minute like sharp shooters armed with live crocodiles loaded with sharp teeth cocked and ready.

Agogo picked another piece of *chipalapatilo* from the main plate, dipping it once more in his *nkebe* of that vicious *tsabola*. With his trembling hand he scooped much of the spicy-hot red powder as if he was a child stealing some delicious Cerelac, I wanted to tell him that one of these days he will Overdose on that stuff. I chose to keep quiet, digesting on the sermon he had just given simultaneously pondering on Amalume's lecture, asking myself

"Have we really let our eyes off the ball? Will any good come out of the path we are on? Or is it "everyone for him/herself...*ali ndi mwana agwiritse?*"

MALAWI YASINTHA FOR THE RETURNEES

Today is such a big day for my clan, I can already hear some of you groaning and moaning,

"Iiiiii Makala, isn't every day a big day for your family?" especially those of you who only have family gatherings once every gazillion years.

My relatives and close friends have come from all over the country in large numbers by bus, cars, pickups, bicycle and some on foot. I even heard one or two came by *ngalawa koma izi ziribe umboni* and I am currently looking into the validity of this. But whoever tells you that they have come by plane or helicopter must either be drunk or must have been smoking something that is not usually sold in a shop or grocery. Unless if it's Shasha telling you this then most likely he has done both of the above and my advice is; ignore him. No one has come by air, at least not the conventional two-winged plane unless if they are talking about the ones that use human blood for fuel (*zija zopanda mapiko zija*).

Evidence of an impending festive storm that is about to hit the Amoto Kraal can be seen simply by scrutinising the number of bags of rice and *madengu* of Gramil flour lined up against the kitchen wall. Fresh meat and *dzipalapatilo* have been ferried in from Lunzu on my brother's Bedford Truck (*Penda-Penda* Transport), the same one we took to Chileka when Amalume was coming back from UK. Yes, *yomwe ija*.

The women are busy at the back of the house; cutting *kabitchi*, sprinkling *sinjilo* in various pots of bubbling delicious *ndiwo* perched on *mafuwa* as the firewood underneath crackles like some fireworks on New Year's Eve. There is an aromatic smell of curry in the air, a smell so delicious and mouth-watering the whole neighbourhood dogs have converged along the perimeters of my yard wagging their tails excitedly as if it's mating season.

Azibambo and *anyamata* have gathered in front of the house around the barbeque grill constructed by my Welder-Mechanic, Che Supanala, from a diesel drum with wire a mesh on top, nicknamed 'Torpedo 2000'. Drinks are flowing like Shire River; *zoledzeletsa* for the big bellied relatives and Sobo, Cocopina, Cherry plums and a variety of Fanta's for the children or the religious segment (*ampingo*) of the family or simply those still conscious of retaining their six-pack until old age.

Some of my carnivorous relatives from the village have even brought succulent monkey meat, *yokonza-konza* ready to be tossed on top of the *chiwaya* aka Torpedo-2000. Some nosey neighbours even commented,

"*Eeiishhhh, izi ndiye ayitu, inu a* Makala *mpakana nyama ya nyani?*" they said even though *amakhetsela dovu*, to which my reply was;

"Hey leave my family alone, *yagwa m'bale n'ndiwo*"

A lot has been said why we are always eating so lavishly at my house, that we seem to hold parties and family gatherings at each and every opportunity. Like I hinted above, I am sure that some of you are wondering and scratching your heads why we are (again) all gathered at my house, laughing, shouting while nibbling on delicious pieces of various meats from the fired up Torpedo 2000.

I honestly don't know why we like eating or congregating so much, but as far as today's *ma hape* is concerned, it all has to do with the fact that a member of our family who most of us have never seen is coming back today. He is the first born in my father's family – *bambo akulu* – and has been released from prison or should I say been pardoned for good behaviour. He is, what others would call, the black sheep of our family – *kankhosa kolowelela* but we still love him all the same.

Apparently back in the late 1970's (when I was still young) *Bambo akulu* was a *tsotsi* known all over town for his mischievous deeds. He was involved in so many illegal activities; from selling *fodya wankulu* to stealing *chopeleka cha ntchalitchi* in broad day light. Handling stolen goods and at one time even hitting a red shirt (*wa-yufi*) who was preventing him from boarding a bus because he didn't have a party card. The story goes like '*Bambo akulu* simply head-butted the surprised Youth Leaguer, knocking him out cold and proceeded to steal over 100 party cards and K45 from the pockets of the unconscious *wa Yufi*'.

Some of you might be raising eyebrows and asking why would someone bother stealing K45? To give you an idea of how strong the Kwacha was you only have to consider that *50 tambala* (which was the cost of the *Khadi*) could get you a return bus ticket from Chikwawa to Mzuzu including luggage.

I am not condoning to what he did back then, nor have we ever tried to hide the fact that he was simply an embarrassment to our family. But am sure some of you have also got that one bad apple in your family. If you don't then your family is either blessed or fake (*nenani chilungamo*).

One day, back in 1979 or was it '78 (I get the dates mixed up,) *Bambo Akulu* decided to take his criminal career to a new level – graduating from petty criminology to the big time akuti Soprano-style. After smoking some strong Jamaican vegetable and drinking something ten-times stronger than Rider, he walked into a bank with a pocket full of quarry stones threatening to stone everyone inside if the cashier did not give him K1000. Back in the 70's, as you have gathered by now, K1000 was a phenomenal amount of money. This was a brazen armed robbery which ranked somewhere between lunacy and stupidity (although leaning more towards stupidity.)

Bambo Akulu actually managed to get hold of the Thousand *Kwacha* loot (all in crisp new K1 notes) unfortunately for him, he only managed to leg it as far as the double doors of the bank. He hadn't even planned for a getaway car as a professional bank robber would. He had simply figured that once outside the bank he would *shoot*... I mean... *stone* his way through anyone who tried to stop him.

He later on told us that his 'Plan B' was to make sure that 'Plan A' didn't fail... even though it looked as if the whole robbery had no 'Plan A' in the first place.

As soon as he was about to exit the bank he was immediately apprehended by nine Securicor guards armed with shiny *dzibonga* and his futile attempts to take out the guards with a barrage of quarry stones was pathetic at best, sad. He only managed to take out one of the guard's eye and broke a few glasses but that was all.

Two days later he was led into the dock at the Magistrates' Court, promptly tried and a verdict was instantly passed. Only one witness was called forward; the guard with a patch over his missing eye, who vehemently testified how dangerous *Bambo Akulu* was and how he had feared for his life when *Bambo* opened fire with a staccato of quarry stones like bullets from an AK-47. The Jury took one look at the crying guard with a patch over his eye and didn't even bother to deliberate, screaming;

"*Anyongedwe basi!*"

I heard that the trial was carried out so quick that some of family members were still walking and congregating into the courthouse when the Chief Justice's verdict: that *Ameneyu amangidwe* was announced.

"The Jury hereby find you guilty on all counts and I sentence you to life imprisonment, court dismissed!" A few of the Amoto women who had made it inside collapsed and had to be stretchered out and rushed to the nearby *Gulupu* Hospital.

They led our handcuffed *Bambo Akulu* to the waiting Bedford Black-Maria that was to take him to solitary confinement at Chichiri to start serving his life sentence.

Being the first person to rob a bank in Malawi the government vowed to set a good example to all would-be-bank robbers. They locked up *Bambo Akulu* and threw away the key, literally; because he went in when MCP was still *moto-moto*, he never saw the UDF era, and he will only see the second term of DPP. That's how long he has been gone but we are just thankful that he has now been pardoned and can once more live amongst us a free man. Conditions of his release stipulate that he should not come within 50-feet of any bank nor even think of walking into a bank. We honestly don't care and are just thrilled that he has come back home.

There are some *abale ndi alongo* who are abroad who left during MCP era, never lived through the yellow years of UDF and are now just coming back to a blue Malawi of DPP. That is a long time to be gone. Amalume once told us that you never realise how much your country has changed unless you go away for a long period.

The first thing *Bambo Akulu* said as soon as he walked out of Chichiri Prison was: "what happened to the red and white UTM buses?" We all looked surprised wondering what he was talking about. You mean there used to be a bus company called UTM, here in Malawi? I had even forgotten about it, until Amalume reminded me that there it was UTM, which then became Stagecoach, then Shire, then something else... or was it the other way round?

I was about to ask *Bambo Akulu* something when my cell phone rang and he almost jumped out of his skin in fear. My phone has got a unique ring-tone of Beyoncé singing "Am a Survivor" and *Bambo Akulu* was startled.

"*Imeneyo Wailesi ya makono?*" He asked looking all lost and baffled.

"No Bambo, this is a cell phone", it actually took me almost half an hour to explain to him what a cell phone is and that you can upload all sorts of ringtones on it; funny ring tones, silly ones, stupid ones and in most cases annoying ones.

As far as *Bambo Akulu* was concerned this was like Chinese mixed with Greek, it's what happens when you have been gone away for so long, *zinthu zimasintha* beyond recognition. It can be such a revelation and an experience beyond your wildest imagination when you see the world you once knew no longer exists and in its place a land that appear to have been transferred from outer space.

This is so, because when you have lived in Malawi all your life you tend to be oblivious to the changes that happen around you. I never really took a step back to see and appreciate the transformation my country has undergone; no more *makadi a chipani, Zalewa* road instead of via Zomba road, minibuses replacing buses, little shops painted with red-stars and then demolished, development and empowerment of the indigenous people, one million political parties instead of just one, electricity blackouts instead of …. [*Am sure you get the message.*]

I looked at *Bambo Akulu* who had suddenly gone quite looking outside the window as Jay-Z music blasted out of the Morris Marina speakers. For him it was like coming out of his mother's womb already a grown up person, seeing everything for the first time; Shoprite, the dual-carriage way Highway, women wearing trousers or black tights... he even asked:

"*Koma azimayi amenewa sakuopa* MYP?"

I explained to him about MYP being extinguished by the boys from Malawi Rifles during Operation

Bwezani. I also wanted to tell him that there are now a dozen banks in Malawi, but did not want to remind him anything to do with "banks" it might bring back painful memories of why he ended up *ku nzandi.*

I stopped the Morris Marina at Ginnery Corner filling station to pump K3000 worth of petrol. *Bambo Akulu* almost had a heart attack. Before he was locked up at Chichiri Penitentiary, a full tank of petrol used to cost K10. He was even amazed to know that we now have K500 notes. What happened to those K1 notes?

"*Iiiiiii, Bambo, zidanka ndi a Lidzi.*" is all I could say, referring to our first President.

In a way *Bambo Akulu* reminds me of so many Malawians who have been abroad for so long to the point of losing touch with home. When these *abale ndi alongo* decide to come back home for whatever reasons; either *kunja kwa-atopetsa, kapena zinthu sizinayendeko kumeneko, mwina akudzatsegula bizinesi* or *abwera kudzamanga banja,* you hear most of them saying, "*Shaaaaa, koma* Saigon has changed.*"

Some Malawians on their return from abroad arrive to a massive festivious family gathering where a sumptuous *phwando* has been organised especially for them; *nyama yootcha ndi zokumwa-imwa,* especially if they had been Western Unioning *makobidi* and building a house or church while abroad.

Unfortunately others arrive at the airport with no-one to greet them but a taxi driver. This is how Shasha (our primary school friend) arrived back from New Delhi, India. The taxi driver asked him "*wakuti umenewu bwana?*" Shasha didn't respond immediately, taking his time as if he had just been asked to solve a multi-complex calculus theory involving the Cauchy-Riemann equation without using a calculator.

Shasha who had never kept contact with home (for all the years he spent abroad) didn't even know what directions to give the driver. His geography of Malawi had simply disappeared from his fickle memory and he embarrassingly instructed the bemused taxi-driver.

"*Tiyeni mudzingo-yendetsa ndikaiona nyumba ya Madala ndiku uzani.*"

After driving around in circles for over two hours (and stopping at a few filling stations *kumwetsela*) the taxi finally arrived at a dilapidated house with cracks on the walls and a sagging roof. This was the same roof Shasha had left twenty years ago, making promises before leaving that;

"*Ndika-kangofika kunjako ndi kagwila ntchito ngati kapolo kuti ndika-kutumizileni makobidi* to help you *kufolela denga ndi malata a* IBR."

Unfortunately after gallivanting all over the globe all these sweet words turned out to be empty promises, *bodza lokha-lokha a Shasha.*

While some prodigal children come back matured and ready to claim their place in society, Shasha came back with a suitcase full of *mphasha* and a lot of fake Bling-Bling jewellery. Since arriving last month all he has been talking about are his Armani suits and a Bling-Bling wrist watch,

"There are only two of these watches in the whole world and the other one is owned by P-Diddy," my friend would boast

This despite the fact that none of Shasha's relatives know who P-Diddy is. All *achibale* could say was, "*chabwino tasilila nawo wotchiyi, koma denga muna promisa lija* che Shasha, program *yake ili pati?*"

Bambo akulu, just like Shasha, arrived to a Malawi that has moved on. Most returning *abale ndi alongo* are also finding this to be the case. They usually have a million and one questions, upon their arrival, on their way from the airport to the house that they built while abroad (or to a house they thought they had built.)

Usually a lot of questions tend to be based on material things, things they thought Malawi would never experience nor have. Things they thought were only confined to the likes of America, UK or only to those rich countries. But Malawi *abale ndi alongo* has changed from the Malawi of *makedzana*. It's even worse for those Malawians who left home during the era of Roy Welensky, the time when people used to go to Theba and come with assets in form of blankets.

"*Ma Benzi awa anafikanso kuno? Iiii* BMW *izi ziliponso kuno? Amalawi akukwelanso ma* Hummer? *Eeee koma anthu ndiye akumanga madenitu,*" tend to be the kinds of questions that spill out of bewildered returning prodigal children.

It's, somehow, sad to look at both *Bambo Akulu* and my friend Shasha who are trying to adjust to a new Malawi, not the Malawi of the 70's they had imagined of, but the Malawi of today.

"*Koma ndiye anthu akumanga ma* mansions, these look like American houses you would find in the suburbs of Atlanta or Texas." The inquisition and sheer mesmerisation is usually nonstop all the way from the airport to their final destination.

I could see that *Bambo Akulu* was really lost, he reminded me of a fish fresh out of water sprawled and flapping about on the sand gasping for water unable to breathe in its new alien surroundings.

I got up calling *nyamata wantchito* who was busy moving crates of soft drinks from the boot of the Morris Marina.

"Eeee *iwe Boyi, tawauza azimai ku kitchiniko kuti moto uli* ready *kuno, ayambe kubweretsa nyama.*"

Today a member of our clan was back and it was our duty to make sure that his assimilation to this new, different and changed Malawi was as smooth as it could possibly be.

Most of the times these returning prodigal sons and daughters have got a lot of stories to tell, stories of where they have been all these years, they still can't help to wonder in awe and sheer mesmerisation at what has happened to this nice little country called Malawi. I could tell by the look on *Bambo Akulu's* face that he was in such trance.

BIZINESI IS SERIOUS BUSINESS

The advantages or perks of being in Malawi are many and can range from the mundane i.e. watching your worker chase a chicken that will soon end up on the table as real fresh organic *nkhuku,* to the more serious ones i.e. knowing that you don't need a bank account to survive (although common sense will tell you otherwise).

But one of these advantages which also happens to be my favourite one is exactly what I was doing right now, sitting at the back of my house in my khaki Bermudas, no shirt with *patapatas* on my feet. I was observing my mechanic Che Supanala busy changing the engine oil of my Morris Marina. *Nyamata wantchito* was standing nearby just in case I will need another bottle of my favourite drink. This is good living, *uku ndiye kukhala abale anzanga.* Show me a Malawian who can do this in the UK or US and I will prove that you are a liar.

I can bet you my father's next pay cheque that no Malawian abroad can have *nyamata wantchito* just standing there with a bottle opener waiting, just in case *abwana* will need another bottle of *lamame.* And don't give me this nonsense that *kunjako mumamwa wandzitini* hence you don't need *wanchito.*

Che Supanala has been my mechanic for as long as I can remember, he understands my needs and he knows my car inside out more than I do. He very well knows to pour the used dirty oil *pa chulu cha chiswe* in front of the house after draining the sump, something which Amalume once commented on,

"No mechanic in the United Kingdom or United States of America can double as a "*chiswe* exterminator", he had said to me which just reaffirmed by belief that if Che Supanala was my doctor, I would have safely said that I will live beyond 100.

The Morris Marina was being serviced because it is going to be the lead car in the convoy next weekend during the wedding of *mwana wa Achimwene aku Mbayani.*

This wedding was supposed to have taken place last week, but unfortunately there was another big (Presidential) wedding taking place in Lilongwe and some of the guests invited to our wedding were also guests at the Lilongwe wedding.

Our family being as polite and as humble as we have always been, with proper Malawian mannerisms, we changed our wedding date to next weekend. *Sitimafuna za mpikisano* especially since there is also going to be a white Limo at our wedding just like was the case at the previous distinguished last week wedding.

Although there are always people in and out of my yard, I hardly get visitors early in the morning before 9am. So when *nyamata wantchito* told me that there were visitors in the living room looking for *bambo*, I was a bit surprised.

"*Mwinatu ndi a mu* committee *ya chikwati?*" Manyuchi Darling suggested while tossing me my Michael Jackson t-shirt. I reluctantly put it on, to cover my six-pack, and went inside the house to greet the morning *alendo*.

The minute I entered the sitting room I could tell that the visitors, (a young couple) had recently just come from abroad. How did I know this? The whole house smelled like *nkati mwa botolo la* perfume. *Zothila-thila anthu ochokela kunjanu*, this is how you can tell apart m'Malawi *oti wangobwela kumene* from m'Malawi *wakonkuno "nkhala-kale." Akonkunofe tili ndi kafungo ka* unique, *ka nchele-nchele* (salty) and there is even a wise proverb says '*mamuna adzinukha thukuta*' Hahahaha... *akuti chitungu...* something that always makes me laugh.

It wasn't just the perfume or cologne that told me that *awatu ndi obwela,* but also the way and manner which they greeted me, confirmed my suspicions. Malawians who have just come from abroad have got this habit of mixing English with Chichewa. They give the impression as if they have a problem articulating their conversation in Chichewa from beginning to end. Or maybe they reckon that if they keep the whole conversation in English our non-travelled brain will not comprehend what it is they are trying to tell us. Or maybe it's just a way of reminding us *kuti anali kunja... akuti* giving it to us in Kamuzu-style. This is still the case even when they have only been abroad for 4 months, *basi kumati* every sentence: "you know"... "you know," making you want to say: 'Eeeetu I know but do you know what I knew?'

"You know, sorry for invading *nyumba yanu* Mr Makala so early *m'mamawa uno*" the lady politely addressed me in the typical Englichewa of a well-travelled Malawian. The man did not say much only greeting me by mumbling "*Watsapu*" (what's up) while looking down at his shoes as if he had just seen them for the first time, *mwina anali ndi manyazi abambowa.*

From the "*Watsapu*", which literally made me look up at the ceiling of my house, I concluded that these visitors had nothing to do with next week's wedding, they were definitely here for something else and I was about to be proven right.

I have had mail, e-mails, telephone calls and even fax messages asking me for some advice on business ventures in Malawi, but this was the first time someone actually came over to my house for assistance on *nkhani ya* business. I listened carefully as the woman explained everything and I was really surprised that I had sat through the whole tête-à-tête without exploding into fits of laughter.

Apparently the couple had just come back to Malawi to start their business after a long stint abroad. One would think that being Malawians they would automatically venture into the 'minibus' franchise or 'trucking' just like everyone else is doing.

Apparently the man, who had been studying Catering at one of the many Colleges in UK (called Dubious International College) and had a Master's Degree in Chef-ology, had this clever idea of launching a Buffet business – which is pronounced as *Bafe* or *Bufe* depending on your tongue or preference.

Here was a business idea that even the great Makala Amoto has never heard of, which is why I was all ears to try and grasp each and every detail that was going to come out of the mouths of this well-travelled couple, both graduates of Dubious International College.

It seems like this 'buffet' is big business in America and UK because of the western culture of eating out. This Malawian entrepreneur wanted to emulate this business model and also make it big here in Malawi.

I had to ask the couple to start from the beginning explaining to me what buffet was all about, because I was really in disbelief and a bit perplexed. Trust me, it was really painful to try and suppress the urge to laugh and I had to pretend *kukhosomola* just to hide my amusement.

Don't get me wrong here, this nicely dressed Malawian former Alma Mater student from Dubious College looked and sounded intelligent. But just listening to him, I could tell that his business knowledge was purely theoretical classroom stuff that he had acquired from Dubious International College. He went on about how Double Entry is the fundamental concept underlying Bookkeeping and Accounting in any business and he wanted this to be emulated in his buffet venture.

I honestly don't put much faith in all this theoretical or academic mumbo-jumbo, much of which is not applicable here in Malawi anyway, so I had to interrupt him when he started talking about Cash flow projections and Capital Assets that he already had in place.

"*Achimwenewa atipweteketsa mutu apa,*" I thought to myself while sitting forward in my chair assuming the 'let-me-talk-position'

I took a sip from a mug of thobwa and cleared my throat before repeating what the man aka ex-Dubious College student had just told me,

"*Mukuti Buffet imeneyi*, people will just come, pay a fixed amount at the door and eat all they can eat until they are full?" I asked and the man nodded in agreement.

"And *bizinesi imeneyi imagwiladi nseu kunjako*?" I fired another one whilst trying to hide my sarcasm. The man nodded again and even went as far as telling me of famous restaurants like Ponderosa in the USA or Nawabs in UK, which all sounded like Greek to me.

He even wanted to show me Annual Reports with accompanying financial statements of Ponderosa Restaurant in the USA. He must have previously downloaded all this from the internet as if that would prove to me (and his wife) that just because this business *ticks* in the USA then it should *tock* here in Malawi. I wanted to tell him that it doesn't work like that, instead I kept my mouth shut and politely I accepted the financial pamphlet. It consisted of Income Statement, Balance Sheets and Cash flow Statements with abbreviations like IFRS, GAAP written all over them, things which didn't make sense and things which I thought were a waste of my time. I barely looked at this pamphlet choosing to set it down on the stool while thinking,

"Who in their right mind names a restaurant Ponderosa? *Koma kunjaku abale.*"

It seemed like this couple's buffet business idea had started off very well. It had actually taken off dramatically well so much so that in the first two days of opening their restaurant they had simply run out of food and gone bankrupt. This was proof from what I had heard some time back that Malawians eat like nobody's business and it appears they had eaten this man out of business.

The first day the buffet restaurant was packed to the brim, the array of food on display was impressive and exotic with fancy sounding names; barbequed spare ribs, sesame prawn toast, duck with plum sauce, yeung chow fried rice, chips and glazed *chambo*, fillet steak with ginger and spring onion, chicken chop suey, kidney beans boiled in honey (*nyemba za uchi*), poached crocodile eggs, raspberry ripple ice cream, marmalade ice, nsima with a hint of sugar, sweet potatoes with *sinjilo* just to mention a few.

With foods like these the result was that the flow of customers was like one-way traffic. People were coming in but no one was going out and some were actually eating whilst standing. *Munali kathithi, zakudya kumachita kusefukira* from the plates as hungry customers carefully created little mountains on their plates, drumsticks skilfully balanced on little *Kilimanjalos* of rice.

In one plate people were mixing; rice, *nsima*, chips, chicken, goat meat, bread, beans ... *nsunzi wa ng'ombe* mixed with *nsunzi wa bakha*. Everything on the buffet rack was ending up on the plate, creating a concoction that might have been exciting and delicious to the tongue but was surely ghastly to look at. Ice cream being tucked in the same plate with boiled potatoes and *mazila* as one customer remarked; "it was like a circus of food." *Zovutatu izi abale.*

People were going for second helping, third, fourth, fifth all the time filling the plate as if it was the first serving and as if it was the last day on earth aka 'the Last Supper.'

"*Tiyeni tidyeretu asanansinthe maganizo.*" People were saying as they patted each other on the back to induce burps so as to release unwanted air that was just taking up too much space in their stomach, precious space that could be filled up with more food.

And by the second day word had spread *ngati moto wantchile* throughout the whole Malawi that someone had just opened a restaurant where they were practically giving food for "Free." *Chinantindi cha a Malawi* came from all over in minibuses, cars, *njinga zakapalasa* or *wapansi* to witness this with their own stomachs. All you had to do was pay an entrance fee and you could feast as if *ndi tsiku lomaliza.*

On this second day Malawians came prepared for war, the Fourth World War, *akuti chichitike-chichitike,* no holds-barred, no prisoners taken alive. Some came with plastic bags and most men were wearing *majasi* (although the weather was boiling hot) with deep pockets while the women came armed with empty handbags (on both shoulders) ready to take home some roasted chicken, *ma banzi,* curry rice, *mpunga wangati tinjoka – akuti* spaghetti – and what not. Even table salt was being emptied into concealed plastic beakers inside women's conspicuous looking handbags, begging the questions; 'who in their right mind steals salt from a buffet restaurant *abale anzanga?*'

It truly resembled a war front, as if you were somewhere in Fallujah or Kandahar, as wives yelled commands to their husbands not to waste time and space loading their plate(s) with vegetables, *masamba* were simply treated as dangerous landmines,

"Don't go near those vegetables, go for anything that used to bleed before it became *ndiwo*", came the warning to anyone who strayed near vegetables or anything associated with photosynthesis.

"*Inu bambo a Boyi masamba mukadya kunyumba, tayikani nkhuku ina m'balemo,*" were the kind of orders coming from the female Generals.

On the flanks, young children were gorging down chips and cake simultaneously without segregation. Worried husbands kept looking at the wall clock which was getting close to closing time, it was like a worried Bomb Disposal expert staring at ticking stop-watch tied to a TNT pack of explosives, urging the wife who had been clever enough to bring empty handbags to start packing the food before time runs out.

Even those who had been here yesterday came back today with a vengeance after taking *mankhwala a m'mimba* to calm their aching stomachs from the previous day's feasting. One customer was heard commenting that this was worse than the time someone was handing out *makhwala a nchape.*

One woman who had swallowed more than her stomach could handle, fainted and was being tended to by her worried children while the husband dashed to the kitchen to try and get some water so as to splash on his madam. It worked and she got up angry that her children had wasted time tending to her instead of grabbing more food before closing time.

Of course by the third day the buffet restaurant had closed its doors for good, Malawians had literally eaten this fellow Malawian out of business. His wife who had been against this buffet idea from the start dragged him over to my house for advice. She had heard from some of her friends that I am renowned for business guruism and must have figured something could be done to resuscitate their failed experiment of a business. I wanted to tell this nice couple that I usually give advice before someone launches a business not after they have filed for Chapter Eleven-Bankruptcy.

I didn't know how to say this to them because the wife was so charged up and angry, I simply sat there looking at that useless pamphlet of IFRS Financial Statements on top of the stool. It's the only object I could look at just to try and avoid making contact with her red angry eyes. I honestly felt guilty as if it was my fault that their Malawian Ponderosa had fizzled out just after two days in operation.

I wanted to tell this couple that there are certain things that might work in these western countries but will probably look ridiculously stupid in a country like Malawi. Just because installing a smoke detector in a European kitchen makes sense, it's utter nonsense to install such a device in straw thatched kitchen at your home village (somewhere in the middle of Chipande) where the only appliance is a *mbaula* or *mafuwa*.

"*Inetu awa ndinawauza, ma business enawa nga chizungu kuno sangagwile, koma makani amuna angawa, kusamva abale. Basitu pano tilibe chilichonse* all the money we had went into the buffet idea," the young lady went on pointing at the husband, her finger almost poking his forehead.

The frustrated lady carried on angrily while the husband kept gazing at his shoes not brave enough to look at me or his wife in the eye. For the first time in my life I was at loss of words, I didn't know where to begin or what kind of advice to give. Like the husband, I too looked down at my *patapata za Bata* hoping to find an answer down there, but saw nothing apart from *dzikhadabo* ten due for chopping.

DIESEL SHORTAGE, AGAIN

There are certain stories the more you hear about them the more it feels like you are listening to a broken record. They are so repetitive it goes beyond the whole notion of déjà vu. This is exactly what I was thinking about while reading today's daily tabloids that "Diesel shortage has hit Malawi, forcing most diesel run vehicles to ground to a halt."

"Oooohhh crap, here we go again," I immediately exhaled my disgust not realising that I had said it so loud until Mother cautioned me.

"Watch your language there are kids around," she whispered while pointing to the army of my little nephews sleeping or pretending to sleep in the living room.

It's not like I wasn't aware that the country is experiencing fuel shortage. I know this because, Simioni who was just here eating with us not so long ago, had been telling us that his transporter friends have grounded their trucks because the tanks have run dry.

It's not just via Simioni's friends where we have been getting these stories about diesel woes, but from my brother too. My brother has frantically been trying to get Che Supanala (my mechanic) to modify his Bedford (Penda-Penda Transport) 7 ton truck from diesel to petrol. He has borrowed, although it looks more like taken, my

Toyota Hiace engine that was in the children's bedroom so that Che Supanala can install it in the Bedford truck.

I know here in Malawi everything is possible when it comes to modifications but I am waiting to see how they are going to pull this one off. I am eager to see how they will connect the Hiace's engine to the Bedford's large gearbox. *Nkhani yagona pa* 'bell housing' but Che Supanala thinks it's doable. I am a bit pessimistic but my brother has made up his mind and I didn't want to voice my doubts lest I provoke a sibling argument. I know right now my brother is so pissed off with the whole diesel situation it's better to stay clear out of his way. That's why when he told me yesterday that;

"*Achimwene* I need engine *yanu ya* Toyota." I simply raised my hands in a sign of surrender while gesturing towards the children's bedroom that was doubling as a warehouse.

"*Onani m'mene mungachitire a brazi*" is what I told him while thinking to myself how crazy their experiment sounded. It reminded me of my primary school days when we had dissected a frog using a Nacet Razor just to mess with its vital organs, the poor amphibious creature passed away anyway and I had a feeling that's what was going to happen to my brother's Bedford.

Agogo was just as amused as I was about my brother's futile attempts to have his truck run on a 1.8L petrol engine. But even Agogo too, didn't want to provoke an argument by telling my stubborn brother that this was the stupidest idea since human beings were created.

"Your brother is trying to attach *mapiko angumbi* to an elephant," Agogo whispered to me, an insinuation that Penda-Penda Transport was pretty much doomed.

I agreed with Agogo but I also understood my brother's frustration and anger. His whole *nchenga and njerwa* business depends on the availability of diesel. Without diesel his truck won't move, if his truck can't move he can't put food on the table. Put simply; my brother's financial survival depends on Malawi having an uninterrupted flow of diesel. This is also true for the multitude of Malawian transporters dealing in, both, local or international haulage.

Amalume agrees with me, adding that the dilemma is not only confined to transporters but to everyone else. Being a landlocked country, these trucks are Malawi's only lifeline, more like a major artery in the anatomy of our county. This artery needs to flow uninterrupted because a bigger percentage of what comes in or goes out of our country does so via these trucks. Transport is one of the most important sectors of Malawi's economy – simply put Malawi without transport is like a heart without arteries, it can beat but chances are it will eventually stop.

Agogo who doesn't mince words and has recently been aghast by some of the goings on; from electrical blackout to water shortages and now fuel crisis, simply had nothing nice to say about the current situation

"*Boma ladya ndalama zogulila mafuta*, that's why there is no diesel in the country" he said that so loud I almost thought he was trying to make sure that *Boma* hears him, as if Boma was a person lurking outside our door eavesdropping on our conversation.

"No Agogo, according to the Malawi Energy Regulatory Authority they are attributing this shortage of diesel to bad weather *ku apwitikizi*, with much specificity to the Port of Beira which is forcing tanker ships not to dock and offload the diesel *wathuyu*," I tried to correct my 102 year old outspoken Grandpa. Agogo stopped gnawing on his chicken bone, giving me a sideways look, as if I was some annoying *chitsotso*.

"You ether must be stupid or are suffering from *mutu waching'alang'ala* if you really believe that story." He said that to me with so much venom as if I was the one siphoning dry all the filling stations in Malawi.

Amalume who had been listening to our back and forth like a spectator at Wimbledon jumped to my defence.

"I think Makala is right, it says so in the papers that the weather is really bad in Mozambique," was Amalume's attempt at trying to rescue me from Agogo's wrath. Like a lion that had been concentrating on a rabbit but has just realised that there is a nice fat juicy *gwape* right behind, Agogo slowly shifted his gaze away from me and zoomed in on Amalume

"You must even be stupider than Makala then, I thought *inu munali* ku England and are supposed to be more intelligent and have a deeper perception of things and analyse them critically?" came Agogo's charge that cut through the room like a beam of light in the night aimed squarely on Amalume who shifted uncomfortably in his chair. Agogo had a way of making you feel uncomfortable in a way that was difficult to explain, his words had the propensity to inflict ticklish pain like that experienced when getting *mphini* from a rusty razor.

Amalume got up to show Agogo the newspaper article as proof of what we were talking about but Agogo waved him off before going on a stampede.

"*Aaaaa chokani nazo nyuzi zanuzi apa*, I thought all that nonsense was written by a human being. Did you see the journalist going to Beira *kukapima kuti* weather *ili bwanji*? And what about *anzathu aku* Zambia? Are they also experiencing diesel shortages? What about the shortages we had not so long ago? Was that also due to the same *nvula yamatalala* or *akanvulunvulu* in Beira?" Agogo was on a roll and I realised that no matter what we were going to tell him, he had made up his mind that this had nothing to do with Beira but all to do with the internal machinations or failures within Malawi.

As far as Agogo was concerned, believing the story that diesel shortage was due to weather was simply bollocks, it was like giving in and letting a child eat a drumstick while the Head of the family was left gnawing on *nthiti za nkhuku*.

"So you want to tell me that Mozambique, Zambia and all of our neighbours have also parked their trucks or are busy modifying their ERF or Freightliner trucks to start running on Toyota Hiace engines?" Agogo said while pointing outside where there was a clatter of spanners and hammering going on as Penda-Penda Truck was going through surgery by Doctor Che Supanala. I couldn't help wondering... mmhhh maybe Agogo had a point here. Even Amalume slowly started scratching his bald and shiny Vaseline smeared head as his mind went into overdrive asking a question to no one in particular;

"How come Malawi doesn't have contingency plans to situations like these? Shouldn't we be having diesel reserves that can last for extended periods of time?" Amalume said while slowly sitting down on the sofa.

I had no answer to those questions but I somehow agreed with Amalume line of thought. I mentioned that someone, a few weeks ago, had suggested that it's about time we had a pipeline that connects Malawi to the port in Mozambique. This would be a better alternative instead of depending on the more expensive overland mode of moving our fuel. Agogo looked at me smiling for the first time.

"Now you are talking sense Che Makala *osati nthano za* weather *mumakamba zija.*" Agogo said the sarcasm gone from his voice.

I wanted to tell Agogo that I still believe that the recent disruption is due natural havoc in form of heavy winds, but I didn't get chance to – because at that instance I heard my brother's Penda-Penda truck kick to life. It sounded like my Toyota Hiace and I jumped up to look outside.

I couldn't believe they had succeeded with what I thought was an impossibility. In the dead of night, illuminated only by a single light bulb, Che Supanala 'The Great' had managed to install a 1.8L petrol engine in a Bedford truck. This Einstein of a mechanic had miraculously managed to alleviate my brother's diesel problems. Whether Penda-Penda Transport was going to be able to haul a load full of river sand or ten thousand bricks is a story for another day *koma lero yalira. Bolani mawa tisanve kuti petulo kulibe akupezeka ndi parafini yekha. Hahahaaaa, ndiye zamu-anthuno.*

MALAWI IS AT WAR

I know *abale* from abroad have simply looked at the title and not bothered to read the whole story but rushed out to buy calling cards; Lebara, Talk Home, Malaika, Sprint, Express Call or whatever card that you use for calling Malawi so that they can start *kuimba ma foni* back home.

"*Tangonva Makala Amoto akuti nkhondo ya gundika kumudziko?*" *Akunja* will immediately start hyperventilating through the phone the minute *wachibale* answers the phone on this end.

Please, please, please calm down and at least read a paragraph or two before you start rushing calling us *kumudzi kuno* and bothering us with unnecessary stories about *nkhondo* in the Warm Heart of Africa.

Malawi's war, does not involve any guns or grenades, is being waged amongst ourselves – *pa chi* Malawi *pathu kapena titi pachiweni-weni*; neighbour against neighbour, brother against brother, sister on sister and yes even amongst friends.

For instance it's not a secret that in my neighbourhood the balance of power has always been in Simioni's favour. It's obvious that *zakhala zikumuyendera nzangayu* since primary school when we were young until our adult life. He has had so many victories over the years in our on-going cold war that has raged from as far back as I can remember. Simioni, from early on, has always been like a Super-power that had all the ballistic nuclear weaponry capable of reaching us and inflicting untold havoc.

In our adulthood his arsenal of weapons ranged from the 32inch TV that proudly stood at the far end of his sitting room. There was a big photograph of his smiling face perched right on top as a constant reminder whose TV it was we were watching. Simioni was indeed the only one with a TV in the whole neighbourhood, long before TVs became a household item.

On top of being a proud TV owner, Simioni's kitchen was the only one to have a Microwave despite the fact that it took almost 30mins to warm up a plate of *ndiwo*. Simioni's madam was a woman who walked with a bounce simply because every woman in the neighbourhood would go to their house *kukatenthetsa ndiwo*. Some of us men viewed this *ndi mangawa* although the *ndiwo* being warmed up, be it *dzipalapatilo* or *nfutso* was destined to end up in our stomachs. We enjoyed the warmed up food from Simioni's microwave while simultaneously cursing him *chapansi-pansi*

"*Iyeyo akudziona ngati ndani* flaunting his electrical gadgets and instilling envy in our women", this was said out of malice but frustration because the more Simioni's madam wound our women up, the more our women wound us up.

But ever since Amalume came back from the UK there has been tension between us. The tactics in our ongoing war have changed as I am now able to push for a counter-attack, giving Simioni a taste of his own medicine.

Now our house too has got a TV that is bigger, thinner and flashier than his. On top of that our kitchen has Microwave that works like *matsenga* warming up the same plate of *ndiwo* (that used to take half an hour at his) in under five minutes at ours.

This hasn't gone down well with the Simioni's so much that in a move of desperation, like when Saddam Hussein set his oil fields on fire as General H. Norman Schwarzkopf was closing in on Baghdad, my friend sent his Nephew to ask for a TDK Tape that I had borrowed over one year ago. I didn't know whether to laugh or be angry so I did neither. I was actually surprised and a bit disappointed that Simioni had opted for such a cheap unconventional war tactic.

"*Iyi ndiye* gimmick, because he knows that someone had accidentally taped *nkhani za n'chipatala* over his Oliver Ntukudzi songs" I told Amalume who had also been listening to the little boy's yelling.

I told my friend's little nephew to come in so that I could tell him *mwatchutchutchu* to go tell his Uncle Simioni to stop acting or behaving like a child. But like a loyal sentry in our war, the little boy refused to enter my house. To him this was like the enemy's camp, so he just stood *pakhonde* repeatedly yelling

"*Akuti mundipatsile tape ya Oliver Ntukudzi ija, koma ikhale m'mene inalili*" – a classic primary school tactic also known as the *I-want-my-pencil-back-the-way-it-was-before-you-broke-it* type of tactic

"*Akuti Chaaaani?*" I exploded but Amalume, like a seasoned General, told me to calm down and take it easy. This is typical Malawian warfare, Simioni feels threatened since *nafenso tayamba kuchita bwino.*

Amalume referred to it as "Malawianics" at work. It reminded me of the time I had just bought my Morris Marina and I used to go cruising around town blasting *nyimbo za m'maboma* on my FM radio. Some people felt threatened by this and surely viewed it as if I had declared war on them.

It wasn't long before one Bata supporter installed big home speakers in his red car. He started driving around town blasting his loud music; Lucky Dube and sometimes House music – when "Pump Up the Jam" was the tune in fashion – to the bemusement of onlookers.

It wasn't only onlookers but even teachers used to pause in the middle of their lessons as his "disco-on-wheels drove" along HHI, BSS, Blantyre Girls, Blantyre Commercial and Nyambadwe MCC route. Amused students would excitedly laugh and maybe nod their heads to the pounding loud music coming from the car of this Bata fanatic.

It was a war I terribly lost evidence by the fact that my name or my Morris were never talked about again. Everyone was talking about this guy with his tiny *mpanda-denga* who had entered and changed the face of how to wage a car stereo war. I had simply lost the mantle to this Ndirande guy, beaten fair and square.

The more I thought about this the more I am convinced that Malawi is at war, a nation infected by the 'who-has-the-biggest-thing-syndrome'.

Ever since Amalume put the Microwave in our kitchen, Manyuchi Darling has been too keen on inviting her friends over for Tea-Parties or volunteering our house for each and every *"Miyambo" ya chinkhoswe*. I can't blame her since she is just another soldier in the silent Malawi war. And after enduring years of smooching up to the Simioni's, begging to use their microwave, standing in line with the other women of the neighbourhood holding their husband's plates of sorts, I understood why Manyuchi was behaving this way.

It was our time to shine now and we felt like allied troops entering a conquered Baghdad. I knew we had Simioni cornered and I bet he was hiding fully knowing that his days as the electrical appliance king-pin were over. I could just imagine him hiding like Hitler in his bunker as the allied troops closed in on Berlin. I bet Joseph Goebbels his propagandist was in there with my friend telling him that it's all over, he had lost the war.

Simioni is sustaining heavy casualties and he knows this as he constantly peeps outside, from his living room window, looking at the flow of people (who used to go to his house) now coming to mine to watch football on our HD Flat screen.

But I suspect he is not sitting idle, and I have heard war rumours that he has made arrangements to order a 60-inch Samsung flat-screen TV from UK so that he can regain the balance of power.

"*Akuti agula yake ku Tesco Shop,*" my war spies all the way in Gorton Manchester warned me. Yes, this is war, and in war you have to have spies to tell you these things. Even Napoleon the Great had his own spies feeding him information from the enemy front.

If he orders this massive TV from UK it will surely torpedo my newly found status. I cannot let this happen; this would be worse than Iran developing the Nuke. That is why I am planning to call *mwana wa Asisi* who works for Customs to make sure that they crucify Simioni with 500% surtax duty as soon as his Samsung TV gets here.

"*Alephele kuimbola*", is what I will be whispering to my allies. *Izi si nkhaza ayi*, all is fair in war. We cannot let Simioni regain the upper hand, the status quo is ideal, am really enjoying it because it feels like the United States Army against MYP. And like any normal person, surely you would want to be the USA in this equation, unless your head is a bit twisted.

But this was not the case at last week's wedding in Lilongwe. I think I have been pouring too much energy in the battle for supremacy of electrical appliances that I completely ignored other fronts altogether. And this came to haunt me on Saturday last week.

Simioni managed to outmanoeuvre me during *perekani-perekani* time (for those non-Malawian readers, *perekani-perekani* is simply a fundraising event that is masked under the veil of tradition during our Malawian weddings and most other African weddings). Depending on your guest list or if you are well connected to the who's-who of the Malawian elite, *perekani-perekani* can net you more than most people make in a year if not 10 years. Any way let us not deviate here from our war dialogue.

When Simioni saw that during this *perekani-perekani* I was jubilantly throwing K100s in the air as if they grow on trees, he countered my show of strength and started tossing K500's in the air while looking straight at me with a winners smile on his face. This was like bringing out a 'Rocket Launcher' just because your opponent had brought out a wooden *Chibonga*. The crowd went wild, cheering and clapping hands for him, ignoring the K100s I had been tossing. Even the little boys picking up the money from the floor concentrated on Simioni's K500s as if my K100s were just Monopoly money.

I thought of dipping in my other pocket where I had a stack of K500s but Manyuchi Darling (the logistician and realist) pinched my thigh reminding me not to spend our rent money. I was so angry so hot and so chaffed up that I left the wedding before they even started serving the goat meat. I was just too angry to start chewing on food or shouting *Bevu*! *Bevu*! I stormed outside the reception, jumped into the Morris Marina, slammed the door so hard the glass-winder came off and landed on my lap, pissing me even further "*Wawina mphwanga,*" is all I could think of "*tiwona.*"

Little wars like this are being waged all over the country even amongst Malawians abroad. Women whispering to their men, "*ndava kuti anzanu agula* Benz? *Inu kodi zikuku-sangalatsani kuti tidzikwelabe Toyota eti?*"

Talks like these do not help matters, they just increase the momentum of war, often sending angry husbands or boyfriends to plot of ways how the neighbour's Benz issue can be neutralised.

Like a poverty stricken African country that invests all its meagre financial resources in procuring prohibitively expensive defensive weaponry, the angry husband gets up the next morning heading straight to the bank. There he convinces his Bank Manager to give him a massive loan, sometimes using the house as collateral, so that he can go out and buy a Hummer H2 a counter move to the Benz... *Shaaaaa! Nkhondo tu abale.*

Just last month while coming from Shoprite, I saw two brothers parked side by side at the Traffic Lights (*pama Robotsi*) by Queens Elizabeth Hospital waiting for them to turn green. Neither of them looked at the other despite being blood brothers *abele limodzi* – because today at this moment, at this instant they were simply soldiers from opposing armies. Competition had pumped their egos up to the point of no return.

It was funny and sad looking at these two as they nodded their "*watsapuzi*" while looking straight ahead as if they were disgusted with what the other was driving. One brother in his flashy 4x4 black Range Rover and the other brother in his metallic grey Ford Mustang sports car ya *mpanda denga* (convertible).

Hahaaaaaaa!! Check-mate/draw-draw...*nkhondo yachi* Malawi. When the lights turned green they both sped off like two Katyusha rockets, their V-8 engines catapulting them faster than my Morris Marina could keep up. Two soldiers engaged in their own brotherly war... *yachi* Malawi *yeni-yeni.*

Men tend to incite flames of war by making *ma* comment *a ululu ngati* that usually go like this:

"*Eee, koma tsitsi la anzanu aja ndiye ndi lalitali bwino ngati la nzungu-tu.*"

The consequences of such comments are like throwing a hand-grenade in a room packed with drums of petrol. This often causes women to march down to their

Beauty-Salon(s), issue tactical and strategic instructions to the hairdresser.

"*Ndikufuna litalike kuposa la mai a Uje* ... weekend *ikubwelayi kuli babakyu ku* Capital Hotel."

These beauty salons are like war camps were women execute their audacious strategies, as ammunition in form of 'hair weave' (also known as fake hair) is woven together with their natural hair. Others successfully pull it off, coming out of camp-salon looking spiffy and ready for battle. But, Lord behold, others usually come out with disastrous results due to either a poor choice of colour or an abnormally long hair style that stretches beyond the legal limit deemed realistic for an African woman. Rarely do you find an African woman with hair that touches her bum and those who go for this Cinderella look are often met by the question "is that your hair." A true female in a battle of the hair-do's will not be put off by such a provocative question and often proudly and forcefully answer "yes it's mine, I paid for it" ... touché, typical response of a true soldier.

Moving away from women's hair but sticking with the theme of war, there is an incident that happened about three or four weeks ago on a Sunday. A Pastor had to come out of an empty church to pull people out of their cars because everyone wanted to be the last one to enter the church.

People had simply arrived at church, parked their nice cars and never got out. In this war the first to enter loses that tactical move of showing off the latest watch, shoe, tie, suit, hat, makeup, haircut or simply that bang-bang walk down the aisle.

Someone once made a comment that all nicely dressed up people sit in front of the church, like soldiers on the front line – the back rows is for those who are not armed and prefer to stay back at base cooking and cleaning boots. Men like to pretend as if this church war is simply fought by women, but studies show that most men are full and participating combatants of church wars. Some even make sure that if they are giving K500 as tithe the whole congregation will know about it. They take it out of their wallet, studying it as if it's the first time to see a K500 note all the while giving time for other to see and comment *"che Uje apereka Chilembwe wankulu"*

But do we really benefit anything from these little cold wars we wage on our neighbours, friend or even fellow siblings? Amalume seems to think that there are advantages to all this cut-throat competition. He insists that it's this war that propels us to achieve more and do better; it gives us the incentive to acquire better things. This war has made us evolve from a nation of radio listeners to a people watching VHS and progressed to DVD (and we now hear Blue-Ray). We haven't discarded the radio altogether, but anyone will tell you that a radio looks better when it's standing next to a TV.

Of course there are sceptics who deny that there is a war out there, but that doesn't mean it's not being waged by your neighbour against you at this very moment. I looked at Simioni's nephew, who was still standing at attention like a sentry on my veranda, and told him off.

"*Ngati a Malume ako asowa chochita uwauze asanditopetse.*" I said in disgust.

I regretted saying this the minute those words came out of my mouth. But then in war every soldier regrets it the minute he squeezes the trigger and that bullet comes out of his AK47. I watched that little boy dash back to Simioni's house so eager to repeat what I have just said and maybe embellish it a little bit with his own salt and pepper.

IS MAKALA YOUR NAME?

I must admit am used to getting questions asking me about business ventures and other things related to money. Once in a while I get some strange and unique questions like the one I got a month ago asking me if I am a Pastor. Humbling as this was I had to wonder what this nice Malawian was thinking about when she asked me such a question. No, am not a Pastor and I wouldn't pretend to be one.

I figured out that my Malawian friend was just trying to have a laugh or was simply trying to inflate my already over inflated head. Whatever the motives of this dear Malawian, I thought the question was a bit unique.

Another unique question that I recently got was from someone, quizzing me about my family tree. I was just about to grab a piece of chipalapatilo when this who-wants-to-be-a-millionaire-question stopped me in my tracks,

"Makala Amoto, can you please sketch your family tree?" this person asked me politely.

"*Nkhani ya* family tree *ndi yovuta,* simply because *zimenezi ndi zachizungu,*" is all I could think of answering. Honestly speaking, trying to design a tree for my family... hahahaha... *ntengo wake ungakhale otepa kwambiri.*

The family tree business, pertaining to my clan, gets complicated because I have some *Azimalume* and some Aunties who are twenty years younger than me, I also happen to have nephews or nieces who are twenty years older than me. This would make our family tree to have its roots at the top and its leaves buried in the ground. What makes things even more complicated in my family is that *muli dzikwati dza pachiweni-weni (pachitsibweni)* for reasons that are beyond me.

Don't get me wrong here, despite our *dzikwati dza pachitsibweni* we are very careful never to cross that thin delicate line that would throw us in the realm of incest. Simply put; first cousins are out of the question but anyone outside this first cousin loop is game. It's our culture and we make no apologies for it.

But then you begin to see how this adherence to culture starts deforming our tree. That's why *tikuti, nkhani ya ma* family tree *tingoyisiya kaye apo...izi zokomela azungu ndi a Malawi ena omwe mabanja awo amatsatila zachizungu-zungu.*

Then *osalephela* I get the occasional question, the mother-of-all-questions, the crème-del-crème of questions, the 'who-wants-to-be-a-zillionaire' question; asking me, "can the real Makala Amoto please stand up?" *Iwe* Makala, who are you? *Kodi Makala ndi dzina lakodi?* What is your real name? The questions are often worded in a variety of formats but the thrust is the same.

This question always makes me sad and I find myself crying from one eye (*lakumanzele lokha*) because the right eye is strong and hasn't cried for years. The reason for shedding tears whenever I get this question is simple:

is my name that bad? Do people hate the name Makala Amoto that they wish I was called something else?

I know my name doesn't have the best ring tone to it and of course there have been those times when I wish I could change my name. I know there are those of you who are able to do this, but my culture forbids me to. I wish I was someone from abroad, *akuti kunjako umatheka kusintha dzina lako utakula.*

Unfortunately in my clan your name is like the colour of your skin – you are basically stuck with it and you have no choice but to learn how to love it and how to defend it if you meet resistance along the way.

But it seems like *kunjako* this is not the case. Apparently it is possible to adjust your skin complexion, just like Che Michael Jackson vigorously attempted and ended up overdoing it. I hear that it is also easy to change your name, and we have heard of names like Boy George, Jigga, Shabba, X-zibit, Busta, An Artist Formerly Known as Prince (although this one sounds like *nkhani)* and many other names. All these names were adopted later on in life when the owner either got tired with the original ID their parents had draped over them. Some simply figured that being called Curtis wasn't as cool as being called 50cent.

Unfortunately I am stuck with Makala Amoto just like some of you are stuck with yours. I know some fellow Malawians have got the luxury or privilege of switching to their middle name which might have a western sounding tune, a move which makes life for *azungu* a little easier as far as pronunciations are concerned. For me it's more of a double whammy because my middle name is also Malawian so I have no choice but to stick with mine.

The problem or dilemma with these names is that we don't get invited to the naming ceremony so that we can give our views or opinions. Maybe parents should wait before giving names to children at least to give them a fighting chance. *Mukuganiza bwanji?*

It would be fair if the process was set up in such a way that from the day a child is born up until they turn eighteen they should just be called "*iwe*" or "*ujeni.*" And then right on their 18th birthday, there should be a gathering (an *indaba*) of all the elders together with "*Ujeni*" so that they can draft up a bill of names.

"*Ujeni,* today you are eighteen and we have drafted up a proposal with a list of names. Would you be interested to be called Makala Amoto?" I could picture the elders asking.

I would probably have looked at the *madodas* and asked them, have you been smoking some Jamaican Vegetables? Are you out of your freaking minds? Why would you want to give me such a name? Did I do something wrong? Why can't you just call me Denzel Washington?

It is so obvious that Denzel is such a cool name when stacked against Makala, so much that if the elders were daft enough to wait until I turn eighteen and give me the option of choosing between the two... hahahaha... damn straight I will be going for the Hollywood sounding one.

Can you see what just happened here, this is exactly the rebellious outburst these elders try to avoid, hence their reason for jumping the gun which gives them a head-start while our IQ is still below 0. They are well aware of the problems this might cause, because if the naming ceremony was left to our devices, all the boys in my neighbourhood would probably be called Denzel Washington. Imagine the dilemma of trying to call your child to come home for lunch whilst he is playing with 29 of his friends identically named Denzel

"*Denzelo... iwe Denzeloooooo, tadzibwela nsima yapsya.*" A proud mother would call out to her son. Before you know it, there are twenty-nine little Denzels standing round your dining room table with their little hungry mouths and deflated looking stomachs.

Of course there would probably be a few Wesley Snipes here and there, one or two Will Smiths *osalephela ka* Billy Ocean in several houses. And of course Manyuchi, just like a thousand other females, would probably have chosen to be called Beyonce. Either that or opted for Jennifer Lopez or Queen Latifahs and other females *akadasankha kuti akhale* Cinderella. I am sure *osalephela ti ma* Lady Gaga scattered here and there. We definitely wouldn't have had females going by *Abiti Kaduku* or *Mache Ntolilo.*

Elders are intelligent enough to foresee such a dilemma. This is why they rush to give us a name and brain-wash us into answering to it before we are old and wise enough to question; "what in the freaking world just happened here?" because by the time our little milk brains start deciphering what's-what, it's already too late... game over, vis-à-vis they are calling you "*Makala*" and you are answering: "*Abeee.*"

Parents are just too clever and the odds are stacked against their children. "*Tamutcheni* Makala *asanayambe kuzindikira* what hit him," is what parents conspire while they are standing over us in the maternity ward.

So whenever I get these questions asking me is Makala your real name, I feel pain and hurt inside me, not because you are asking, but because I wish the elders had waited for me to get to the legal age before calling me Makala. They gave me that name, and so did yours, at an age when we were still addicted to milk and they were the only people who could satisfy our cravings for this drug aka milk.

I couldn't start arguing against them why they were calling me Makala because chances are, they would easily have cut off my supply of milk. So I had no choice but to go along with the idea of being called Makala. And trust me by the time I reached an age where I didn't have to depend on them for milk it was pretty much a done deal (case closed) because all my friends knew me as Makala.

Makala was officially printed on all life's documents; my driving licence, my passport, my court summons each one of them bore the name of Makala Amoto. It was simply going to be time consuming and energy sapping to start tweaking and twiddling with my name. To tell you the truth, I honestly couldn't be bothered, am very busy and life is too short to be spent calling myself, "The Artist Formerly Known as Makala" or "1 Pac or 2 Pac nor 3 Pac or whatever number comes after Pac."

But despite having said this, I will be the first one to admit that there have been nights I lay in bed looking at the ceiling, imagining... what if... what if my name was Will Denzel Washington Smith or Wesley 50cent Snipes? I would probably have over a zillion friends by now and instead of getting the same hurtful question,

"Makala who are you?" that often comes in its purity or disguised as something else, I would be getting more ego boosting questions (like),

"Will Denzel Washington Smith," can I hook up with you please?

Apparently this is not the case and as of now at this very moment, my name is what my parents said it is.

So next time before you ask me about the authenticity of my name remember this: Makala is tired of crying through one eye only, Makala was not there at the naming ceremony and Makala can never ask you,

"Wow! Is that your real name dude?" for the simple reason Makala knows that you didn't have a voice at the naming ceremony. Unless if your name is Homer Simpson, Marge Simpson or 'The artist formerly known as Prince'.

CHOICES AND LIFE BEHIND BURGLAR BARS

As human beings we have got the ability of making a million choices that impact our lives directly or indirectly. There are lucky people who can chose who they want to marry although there are some who that choice is left to their parents or village elders.

Akulu-akulu would tell a young man: "*a Che Uje inutu mukwatilana ndi namwali ujayu*"... in what others term as 'arranged marriages.'

But the majority of people are free to make this life changing decision of choosing a stranger who they will always wake up to every morning until death do them part.

Some get this choice right while others waffle it up by getting it terribly wrong. Right or wrong, it's the choice you make and you live with its benefits or pitfalls. For those whom this choice is taken by their *ntchembele or madoda*, they can only hope that the elders nail it right on the head. Otherwise it can be a lifelong *shauri-yako*.

With the exception of arranged marriages we humans make a lot of choices that affect our lives. The choices can range from the mundane to the more serious in nature. On one extreme there is the choice of not wanting to eat breakfast or choosing not to brush your teeth for a whole week. Whereas on the other extreme there is the choice of suicide for various reasons; *angongole, mavuto a m'banja,*

124

kuboweka ndi moyo, njala, mwina team *yawo yaluza* just to mention a few.

You then begin to appreciate that we have at our disposal an infinite number of choices. Yet there is one important element of our lives that affects us greatly and for some unknown strange reason, we have no choice in the matter even though the outcome impacts us for the rest of our lives.

Reality stipulates that a person cannot choose which family to be born from. *Sitimasankha banja lomwe tibadwire* – I have always wondered why not, and yet we can choose how we want to exit this lovely place we call earth through *tameki* or *chingwe*, jumping from the 2nd floor or 20th (depending on how messy you want to exit), some even put the barrel of a gun in their mouth and there are those who chose to lay down in the tub while it slowly fills with water; so many different exit choices same outcome.

And yet at no point can we choose which family we want as a vehicle of entry in this world of ours. Amalume once told me that this choice was never given to us for very good reasons. Maybe, it goes back to the whole 'arranged marriage' mentality, we cannot be trusted to make the right choice.

Most of us, if not all of us, would probably have chosen to be born in the Bill Gates family. Don't get me wrong, I love my family a lot, but if that choice was presented to me: "Makala do you want to be Makala Amoto or Makala Gates? Hahahaaaa come on – who wouldn't want to tell friends that *banja lawo* owns Microsoft. *Bwenzi ku Malawi kuno kulibe aliyense* –

*nkhalango yokha-yokha – tonsefe tikanasankha kukhala
ana a Bambo ndi Mai* Gates, *kunyauda* heavy *pa* States.

Talking of Bill Gates reminds me of what was on TV last
week. They were showing the house of this very wealthy
man, the wealthiest individual on earth (although it looks
like Warren Buffet might overtake him).

I couldn't believe how much they said his house
cost and I thought to myself *"ndalama zonsezi munthu
m'modzi?"*

I was even more flabbergasted when they
quantified that value of the assets inside Mr Gates'
mansion;

"So this man has got furnishings that are more
valuable than all the money in our Reserve Bank and his
kitchen alone is more valuable than the Reserve Bank of
Zimbabwe?" I said out loud.

But being a Malawian what struck me as odd and
out of place was that despite all these million dollar assets
in his house none of the windows had a burglar bar –
zitsulo za m'mawindo zotetezela mbava panalibe.

"Koma Bill Gates-*yu mutu wake umagwila
ntchito? Katundu yenseyu* not even *Bagla-ba imodzi?"* I
murmured.

That's when Amalume enlightened me about the
differences between these rich countries and us...*mwanja
a Malawife.* Over there *kunjako* they have a choice
whether to install burglar bars in their homes or do
without them. Most chose to do without these ghastly
looking things that end up blocking the view, something
westerners treasure a lot.

In America even in UK, *anzanthu* have got a Police that is really there to protect and serve the citizens. If thieves break into your house, you just call 911 or 999 and the police are so fast they can get to your house while the thieves are still in action.

"*Shaaaaaa…bodza inu… musatelo….you mean they actually come the very same day? Wow!*" I wondered. Amalume claims that this is why Bill Gates' house has expanse windows but not a single burglar bar, he has 101% trust that the taxes he pays ensures that the police have fast cars and will respond in no time if he needs them.

Now for someone like me who has never been outside Africa, it was hard to believe all this talk about police coming when you call them. I even asked Amalume; "Are you sure the police actually arrive the same night you call them?" Amalume nodded "Yep, in record time, it doesn't matter whether you are Tony Blair or average Joe"

I have grown up believing that the Police are only there to stop Minibuses and cars which don't have Road Tax or COF. But as far as this whole impromptu business that goes as far as them dusting for finger prints or doing the whole DNA thing, surely that's just stuff from the movies, does it really happen in reality? Amalume says that it does in these Obama-lands or United Kingdom(s) of David Cameron.

We are not claiming that America is the safest place on earth, far from it. They have their own issues there and they have even crazier lunatics that even burglar bars can't protect you from. Names like Dr. Theodore John Ted

Kaczynski aka the Unabomber or John Allen Muhammad aka the Boston Sniper comes to mind; one famous for sending letter bombs and the other for shooting people at random in America. Whereas in the UK you have taxi drivers who go on a shooting rampage killing and maiming lives.

Albeit the ominous presence of these lunatics, just knowing that their police responds promptly whenever they are called upon is surely a refreshing aspect and a feeling that your taxes are at least doing some good.

Over here if you try calling the police in the middle of the night while your house is being burgled, their first reaction will mostly likely be deflating;

"*Bwelani mudzatitenge bwana* Makala," is the response you might get from our men in uniform.

This request from our Police is a bit awkward and baffling especially if you have Ali-Baba and the Forty Thieves (with *dzikwanje*) standing between you and the Morris Marina. How do they expect you to go and pick them up? As if you would ask the thieves;

"*Bwana 'Ali-Baba* and the 40 thieves'... *ndimati ndi bwereke nawo galimoto yangayi kuti ndikatenge a polisi ndi kupezani pompano-pompano.*"

It's obvious that unlike *kunjako* where there is that choice of installing burglar bars or not, unfortunately in Malawi that is not the case. Having a house without burglar bars is like standing in the middle of the market naked. People will take one look at you and accurately conclude that you are a candidate for Zomba Mental Hospital if not worse.

The reason for this is that over here the "burglar bar" is the best, if not the only, form of defence from *akatole-tole*. If thieves broke into a home without burglar bars, they would definitely steal everything but they will also make sure that *amukalipile zedi mwini nyumba* for making fun of them by removing the only challenge to their profession.

"Do you think we are stupid, making us come all this way with heavy tools, bottle jacks, hack-saws and hammers, only to find that you don't have burglar bars, do we look that stupid to you?" They would angrily ask while slapping the owner.

It is common belief that our police will rarely come out in the middle of the night if you call them. You have to be very creative in how you put that request if you want them to jump and dash to your assistance with the same urgency and haste as their American or British counterparts.

This is exactly what happened last month when I saw twenty-five or so thieves circling my house around midnight, I rushed to the phone and called the police and worded the request in a rather clever albeit deceptive way: "Hello…Hello…my neighbour Simioni has been saying some negative and malicious things about the government, I think *akufuna ku-ukila boma*"

The minute I put the phone down, there were five or six Police Land Rovers arriving outside my street, with armed police. The thieves scattered like rats. Of course I was temporarily arrested (but bailed out the following morning) for lying to the police, but this was better than having thieves break into my house.

I later apologised to my friend Simioni for tarnishing his name. But he understood and said he could have done the same if the shoe was on the other side.

Amalume says that in America every citizen has got the choice of going to the nearest PTC, I think over there they call them Wal-Mart, to buy a gun for protection. This is stipulated in their constitution under the Second Amendment. He claims this is why an average American house has got more guns than spoons hence no need for ghastly burglar bars.

Kumudzi kuno we don't have that choice for obvious reasons.

[One] – It is illegal for Makala or any other civilian citizen to own a gun (*ayesa ukufuna kutenga boma*).

[Two] – since the thieves come in large numbers; forty, fifty or more you would have to be rich to afford that many bullets to take care of the *chinantindi cha mbavazi* outside your house.

At least we have the choice of installing burglar bars, it's cheap and it gives us a sense of security (although not always). But my British Auntie still insists that these hideous bars make her feel as if she is living in a prison.

"*Iiiiiii ndiye bwanji mungobwelela kwanu kopanda ma bagla-bazi ko.*" I almost told her.

While digesting on Amalume's talk on American police, I started thinking about our own. It's funny that every morning you see a lot of our police stopping simple people like me just because my Morris Marina doesn't have seat belts or because I am carrying 3 people in front and 7 in the back. Where do all these police officers go at night when my house or my neighbour's house is being broken into?

Just last week they impounded Simioni's minibus because it was carrying 59 people instead of the legal 15 people. Simioni made a comment to the Impounding Officer.

"*Bwanji osamakagwila akuba eni-eni.*" Simioni angrily said.

Big mistake; they arrested him on the spot. *Sanatulukebe* up to now and I can't go to bail him out because of the fake phone call I made last month, which is still being investigated, so I hear.

I fully understand why my British Auntie is very bewildered and perplexed by the relationship between our police and the citizens. But for us Malawians, since we were never given the privilege of choosing which family to be born from, this is our home and this is normal for us – *tinazolowela*.

Of course those *abale ndi alongo* who cannot take the heat and the pressures of living life behind burglar bars end up choosing to go abroad where they have the luxury of calling 911 or 999 knowing that the Police will arrive in a few minutes.

If only we had been given that ultimate choice, we would all be living in our father's (Gates) mansion looking at the amazing panoramic view not obstructed by ugly burglar bars. There would be no need to call the police and twisting stories or telling lies that your Republican neighbour has been saying bad things about Obama;

"*Zikuoneka ngati akufuna kusokoneza chipani cha* Democrat, *mwina ndi owukila Boma lachi-Mereka ameneyu.*"

ACCIDENTS AND ZOMANGA-MANGA

Someone once told me that Malawians are such fun and cheerful people – *anthu ansangala* – who can turn any situation into entertainment. We really don't need TV's, Jukeboxes or Game Arcades to amuse ourselves because we have the propensity to take any moment and turn it into a Chris Rock or an Izeki and Jakobo comedic moment. We have simply perfected the art of self-amusement, even in moments of terrible accidents.

Amalume says that in the UK when there is a car accident, life goes on as normal and people walk about their business not minding at all, that's not the case with us Malawians. For us an accident is like some sort of reality show entertainment in its true essence. We all flock to the scene of the crash so that we see with our own eyes.

"*Iiiii, tiyeni inu zakunva kupweteketsa mutu.*" We say while rushing to the sight of carnage.

I remember last month there was a bad accident along Zalewa road. People came out of their houses rushing, calling and inviting each other.

"*Amwene tiyeni kunseu akuti* minibus *yagubuduz-ika, anthu ena adakali nkati.*"

It was a horrific accident a gruesome mixture of blood, petrol and broken glass and yet people were congregating as if this was an entertaining drama. Some actually jumped out of a shower with water and soap still dripping from their hair while others came holding their plates of *nsima*, not to help or assist the injured but to observe and be entertained. Even cars and buses were stopping and people were coming out excitedly;

"*Asaa, koma pamenepa alipo watulukapo mbuya?*" They would ask no one in particular.

That's Malawian style entertainment for you, *sitisowa ma* happy. As cruel as it sounds, here in Malawi someone's broken limb is someone's amusement – if it isn't then why else do people congregate to watch and hardly assist.

It's not just car accidents that gets us Malawians excited. We even go to the extreme to amuse ourselves. I remember during Operation Bwezani when guns and bullets where flying around town as Malawi Army clashed with MYP, people were flocking from the townships heading into town to go and see what the shooting was all about.

If this shooting was in any other country; Mozambique or Angola, people would be running in the opposite direction for safety. Not in Malawi, no. We have a different style, a unique approach towards danger. Perhaps our mentality towards bullets is somehow warped in a way that defies common logic. If a gunshot rings out in the middle of Mogadishu Somalia, people dive for cover, kissing the ground because they have differing opinion towards bullets, an opinion that doesn't have an element of fun like ours does, theirs is more realistic.

This explains our reaction during Operation Bwezani, we simply viewed the whole thing as a game of *chibisalilano* not realising that people were actually getting maimed.

"*Eeee, akuti Milisha yabeba ntauni, yabwera ndi migani.*" Excited Malawians yelled and rejoiced.

It only takes a Malawian to run in the direction of where bullets are coming from. That's us; we are the true masters of entertainment thus anything including deadly whizzing bullets somehow tickles our bones.

That is why today when we saw a big house on fire down the street, everybody in the neighbourhood rushed over there. A whole upstairs house was on fire and we all stood there watching the owner, a young woman and two of her workers pathetically attempting to put the fire out with a garden hose pipe.

Every time a window would explode from the searing heat the chinantindi of Malawians would cheer;

"*Yeeeeeehhhhh ...!!!! Waiona m'mene yaphulikila?*" The gathered crowd would yell.

This woman arrived just two weeks ago from America. She had been abroad for fourteen years working somewhere called South Bend, Indiana. She had been working three jobs as a nurse, sending her hard earned money every month to her relatives to build her a house. People in America say that she never used to go out to parties or barbeques, only work and church while saving money for her mansion back home. *Namwino wanzeru uyu.*

Apparently her relatives were not as honest and were cutting corners in the construction of her upstairs house. No cement was used, which meant that this was perhaps the only upstairs house in the whole of Malawi to be built using *dothi (matope)*, *dzidina* and an occasional bag of *Kumanga* Cement.

The electrical wiring was done by some apprentice electrician who had failed his City and Guilds. The relatives only paid him K1000 and told their sister that the electrician had charged K25000. The woman nurse gladly 'Western Unioned' the funds and the relatives pocketed the change, *kupondana* Malawian style.

When this Malawian nurse arrived two weeks ago she got the shock of her life. Since not enough cement had been used during the construction of this 6 bedroom upstairs mansion – the house had more cracks than *dzikang'a dza sing'anga*.

The relatives had bribed the building inspector to sign off the house as habitable even though there was a plethora of building violations stretching from here to the moon.

The upstairs part of the house was inhabitable because the whole upper floor *chidangothifuka*, it was sagging so bad it resembled an occupied hammock.

The whole water pipe system was messed up with cold taps running hot water and vice versa. It was suicidal to stand under the shower because you weren't sure what temperature was going to come out of the jets. We often could hear agonising scream as someone got scolded or frozen whilst taking a shower.

The obvious shoddy electrical wiring meant that every time someone switched on the kitchen light, the lights of the whole house including the boys-quarters would come on too. The iron and the radio could not be on at the same time otherwise the whole electrical system would trip. It was just shambolic beyond belief.

On the very same day that this *Namwino* got back from America, there was a big fight over there with her relatives. The woman was so livid and angry that every sentence of hers was starting with "F" *chakuti-chakuti;*

"*Mwakhala mukundibela makobidi inu ma 'F' chakuti-chakuti ... mu 'F' choke panyumba panga pano.*"

We think this is how they swear and curse in America. It was really scary to listen to the swearing and I wasn't surprised to see Mother closing the windows to protect the young family members of the Amoto clan from hearing such obscenities.

"*Kwatenthatu kwa a* neighbour." I told Manyuchi Darling to lower the volume of the radio so that we could hear and amuse ourselves to these 'F-ings' coming from the neighbours. I even rang Simioni to tell him to tune in but he was already ahead of the game

"*Tichezabe achimwene, tikunvetsela nkhondo ili kwa a neba aku* America *aja.*" Simioni simply said before hanging up on me.

That was about two weeks ago when all the 'F-ings' were angrily uttered and the *Namwino* unceremoniously kicked all her relatives out soon after.

Today around 6:30pm things took a bad turn for this *Namwino*. Her house-boy had forgotten about the kitchen lights situation and accidentally flicked the light-switch on. This was a big mistake, perhaps bigger than when John Terry criticized his coach Fabio Capello.

The lights of the whole house and the boys-quarters came on at the same time. The woman screamed in horror;

"*Iwe boyi nthimitsa magetsiwo nsanga-nsa!!!*" She never finished her sentence, it was cut short by a cracking sound and something exploding from the 'electrical mains board' like *chiphaliwali*. There was this massive fireball like an atom bomb had just been dropped on

Hiroshima and Nagasaki. The whole house went up in flames culminating into this thick black smoke just like in the movies. Her fourteen-years of investment turned to ashes – *phulusa leni-leni*.

The whole neighbourhood stopped whatever it was doing and dashed over towards the fire. My Malawian instincts told me to grab my unfinished plate of *dzipalapatilo* and rush to the scene. Before sprinting off like a rabbit I excitedly yelled at Manyuchi to stop bathing;

"Darling let's go, *zagundikatu kwa a neba angobwera aja, tiyeko tingazi-phonye.*" I yelled at Manyuchi while grabbing my *patapatas* simultaneously trying to invite Amalume's British wife;

"Fire! Fire! We go see, come now." The words came out followed by vigorous hand gestures.

Amalume's wife couldn't understand what was so special and intriguing about watching someone else's house burn down, she thought the whole exercise was rather primitive bordering on lunacy.

"Iiii, darling *tiyeko atichedwetsa azunguwa asiye*", I said to Manyuchi dashing out of the house as if I was being chased by a starving lion.

The whole neighbourhood stood there looking on excitedly forgetting that this was not a game but someone's property being reduced to nothing. I couldn't help but wonder how many more Malawians are abroad working double shifts, twenty-five hours a day, eight-days a week so that they can send money to their relatives to build them little *Sanjikas*. They have no idea whatsoever that their dream home is being constructed out of *matope* and *dzidina* by these unscrupulous relatives.

Not a single person from the crowd stepped forward to help the woman extinguish the flames. Someone tried to call the Fire Brigade but was told that two of the fire engines were out of diesel. The only one with diesel had gone to drop off *abwana* at his residence *ku* Chiwembe.

I felt sorry for the woman and started thinking that it might be a good idea if all Malawians abroad would make sure to bring long hose-pipes when coming back. You just never know when you might need to extinguish an angry fire before it consumes all your life savings. For us here it will just be another day's entertainment.

ADOPTED CHILDREN ARE COMING

The country is buzzing again at the return of the two famous children of Malawi who were recently adopted by their famous celebrity singer mother from the USA. It seems these two children are known the world over by every Malawian in the country and outside it. A recent survey showed that 98% of Malawian cannot name 12 government ministers but know who these two children are.

These two children have joined the list of famous Malawians vis-à-vis Joza, Kwinyani, Amtchona, Timve and Tsala, Pewani, Taxina, Chatsalira, Sikusinja ndi Gwenembe, Akapalepale, a Nyoni, Namukhoviwa and last but not least Makala Amoto, yours truly.

If you think I have forgotten to include your name on the above list *koma mukudzithemba kuti ndinu otchuka chonde ndi lembereni email ku*: solnyam@yahoo. com.

The story of these two children has and continues to polarise my small beautiful country. Their saga has split the country into two camps, creating a chasm that is bigger than that formed by the issue of whether the national flag should be changed or not.

Malawi is usually referred by the western world as a small poor country in Africa, despite the fact, I heard on my Nzeru radio a few weeks ago, that we had posted an

8% GDP growth in the year 2009. I have no idea what all this means, (they never taught us about percentages at Primary School and am yet to be told what GDP means) but Amalume says that this was more than the GDP of America or UK.

"*Mwinatu nchifukwa chake mai otchukayu ana-sangalatsidwa* to adopt *ana aku* Malawi," I ignorantly mused to myself.

I know some of our neighbouring countries didn't like this because I overheard *abale ena aku* Zambia saying;

"*Manje Mzunguyu wakaona chiani pa Malawi, manje a Malawi amandibowa zedi.*" All I said was: "*iiii! zanunso izo mwayesa pano pa Chipata eti?*"

These two children will arrive from their American by private jet, something which will bring resentment and happiness in equal proportions, but that's Malawi for you. I know this from experience as I too encountered the same issues when I first bought my Morris Marina from David Whitehead and Sons Ltd.

My instant promotion from relying on "*Kaya-kaya*" minibus for all my transport requirements to being my own driver of a 1200cc jalopy did not go down well with some people. There was a lot of *mapokoso* caused by my new found asset but, unlike the fame of these two children, my ordeal did not involve Human Rights people, Politicians, Judges of Law or strange men claiming to be my father.

My country is one of the few places on earth where someone like me can drive a Morris Marina while someone has never owned a pair of *pata-pata* in their life. (Ok, ok, maybe *ndawonjeza*, instead of *pata-pata* let me rephrase that and say *masandozi*.)

Despite the 8% GDP that Amalume claims we achieved in 2009, the majority of Malawians still look up to minibuses if they want to move from point A to B.

Minibus still remains the weapon of choice if you are going to combat the daunting hills of Blantyre or the vast expanse stretches of Lilongwe.

By the looks of things our GDP would have to grow by 1000% if every Malawian is to afford four wheels, that are actually attached to a car, which means for now the minibus remains our only shuttle that will take us from Bangwe to there or Biwi and yonder.

If you ask any seasoned hard-core minibus rider, they will tell you that riding a minibus can be defined in so many ways; a pain, an experience, *mazunzo, nanga titani, bolani kukafika*, a torture or simply hazardous to your health and to your life.

A minibuser can throw a thousand adjectives describing what minibusing is all about, but I can bet you Fifty-Tambala that 'fun' is one word you will not find used in the same sentence with minibus.

I found this out today when I went *kunsika* to collect the battery of my jalopy from *anyamata otchaja*. I get my car battery charged once every week although Amalume advised me that I should just buy a new one.

"No!, I like this one because it's the original Exide battery made in UK *osati za* "Dubai" or "China" *zamasiku anozi*," I told him.

The minibus was so packed *mwakathithi*, once inside I realised I couldn't move or turn my head. As soon as I found a space to nudge myself in, I immediately felt someone's fingernails or teeth dig into my buttocks. The sensation at first was a bit ticklish, but after a while it got annoying, then it was painfully and ten minutes into the journey it got a bit scary.

The more passengers crammed into the minibus the deeper those fingernails or teeth dug into my butt. There was excruciating pain that shot from the assaulted butt via spinal cord into my brain I had to bite my lower lip to choke off a scream that was desperately trying to come out.

Why didn't I scream or complain? I will tell you why. While my butt was being assaulted by fingers or teeth, on the other end of my torso my head was awkwardly pressed against this woman's armpit. I thought of complaining but one look at the woman's frowning face was enough to tell me to keep my mouth shut and put up with the warm *thukuta* oozing from her armpit.

Even if I hadn't been scared of her, opening my mouth meant having a sip or two of that salty looking armpit drink. How I wish someone could adopt this sweaty woman out of this minibus right now and take her to America.

The trip only took about twenty-minutes, but with my head buried under this woman's armpit it felt like twenty-days in a maximum prison. I got off, hastily wiping my face in disgust and opened the newspaper while the auto-boys were testing my Morris Marina's battery for juice.

It was refreshing to see a non-political story on the front page and it was amusing to see that the heading was about the Mohican haircut.

The last time local newspapers talked about a famous haircut was when Mike Tyson was still Mike Tyson, *asanayambe zoluma-luma makutu a anzake.* But now I read that the whole Malawi is excited at the prospect of seeing one of the adopted children (the boy) coming back with a new haircut – which is being called "Mohican haircut."

I smiled to myself, licking my salty lips in amusement of this new haircut, not realising that my lips were salty due to that woman's sweat from the minibus. The Mohican Story was that good *ine kuiwalilatu kuti kanchele kameneka nka thukuta la madamu a mu minibus aja.*

Apparently this new form of haircut is proving to be a hit and it is being hastily added on the menu of all the barber shops in the country: Flat top K50, *Mbonga* K35, Tyson K102, Mohican K265.

"What the...? You mean to tell me that people are paying this much for a haircut?" I wondered in shock.

Exorbitant prices like these meant that only *Auje ndi Auje* will be able to afford this Mohican cut while the majority of Malawian males will still go for the K35 *Mbonga*. It really takes some courage and a little bit of stupidity to remove K265 from a monthly salary of K3000 just for a haircut. That would leave any man with a lot of explaining to do to his wife if he came home with a Mohican haircut and change of K2735 to last for thirty days (which strangely enough feels like sixty days in Malawi.)

Just last month my neighbour had done that, taking some of his hard-earned salary and investing it in a Mohican haircut. Just within minutes after I had complimented him that; "*a neba, tsitsi lili shapu,*" we overheard the wife screaming in disbelief;

"*Koma inu ndi posada eti, mutu wanu umagwila ntchito?*" She couldn't believe that her husband had invested that much money in getting a similar haircut to that of one of the adopted children.

She grabbed her *chitenje*, angrily wrapped it around her waist and stormed out of the house, not for a divorce but marching to the barber to get that K265 back. We don't exactly know what transpired when she got to the barber shop, but I can tell you that the wife came back with the K265.

Someone once said that Malawian ladies are the most polite, nice and cuddly human beings when they are in a good mood, but once they are upset and angry then it's a whole different story. (Danger*! pangozi kankhani galasi ili* type of story.)

The good thing about these two children and their Millionaire singer mother is that they don't have to go through the dilemma faced by most Malawi's young and old, surely they will never have to decide between having a Mohican haircut or paying rent. When they arrive here, in their birth country, they will have no idea what the real Malawi is all about. They will probably wonder why everyone is so interested in them, from politicians to the media.

Chances are, they have already forgotten how life used to be when they were living here in our midst. Neither do they care that the country of their biological parents might one day end up without a filling station as BP threatens to pull out and relocate. They will never experience the fear that is experienced by car owners like me and paraffin users like my grandmother at the prospect of living without Filling Stations.

The reason I am injecting the Filling Station saga into what should have been a Mohican sermon is simply because lately I have been having terrible nightmares. Bad dreams of what will happen if all Filling Stations close down and relocate. *Tikamwetsera kuti magalimoto,* where *abale* where?

These Filling Station Nightmares have been so persistent that I have been praying and hoping that these electric cars we hear about in the UK and America will be coming here *chaka cha mawa (bolani asakhale ma* Toyota *paja akuti ma* brake *a* Toyota *akumanyanyala kugula nthawi zina.)* This might alleviate these petrol fears because some of us are too old to be adopted and taken to countries which have Filling Stations that actually sell petrol, paraffin and diesel.

Amalume told us that these two are not the same children that we saw before they left with *mamina* running out of their nostrils, looking shy, scared and hungry. They have definitely changed beyond recognition, *akuti ndi azunguno.*

Having experienced and been exposed to real paparazzi, you can bet that all that Malawian shyness and propensity to stare down in fear is now gone. It is replaced by a sense of confidence and knowledge of the fact that their millionaire mother probably has got more money than the whole of Malawi put together.

They will definitely look different, most likely smell different (going abroad tends to do that to people, I noticed this with my Amalume when he came back from UK, I think it's because of the Rexona soap that they use and those things *amafefelela munkhwapa akamaliza kusamba.*)

These two children will also talk different with an accent – *kalilime kachizungu.* This too I noticed with Amalume, he says Rambo but we all pronounce it as *Lambo.* It sounds funny the way Amalume pronounces things, but I bet after a year or two he will start talking normal and pronouncing Lambo just like normal Malawians do.

Even though I still sympathise with these children but am looking forward to having them here. For those of us privileged enough to own Morris Marinas and radios that have a cassette deck we know how the rest of the country looks at us. I have also been under the scrutiny of jealousy people and am all too familiar with negative jibes like, "Mmmm *amanyada amenewo chifukwa ali ndi* toilet *ya nyumba.*"

Amalume thinks that much of the negativity directed at the adoption of these two kids has to do with the clash of the haves and have-nots. It's only human nature but I, personally think these two children are better off where they are now and I applaud Madonna for making an effort to bring them back, now and again, so that they can connect with their Malawi roots.

Compare them with most Malawians who leave the country but don't bother to bring their children born in Diaspora to come and see where their *Baba* or *Mama* came from.

Amalume, who has lived abroad, cautioned me on my assertions that I shouldn't judge those parents in Diaspora for not bringing their children home. Amalume asserts that after all these are their children, hence the parents are free to decide whether they want them to visit home or not. I could see why Amalume was articulating this and I must admit, I somehow agreed with him but I am also of an opinion that letting the children keep in touch with their roots is probably the best way to go, funds permitting that is.

What Madonna aka Material Girl is doing in bringing these two children back home for a visit should be recommended. Of course, one can argue that, this celebrity mother can afford to fly the children around the globe in her private jet without putting a dent in her bank account. But the simple notion of remembering to visit this tiny little country with her two adopted children is something which should be commended and applauded for.

FAST LANE LIKE THERE IS NO TOMORROW

Someone recently made a comment that at the Amoto household, we tend to overdo our barbeques wondering if our frequent shenanigans don't annoy our neighbours? At first, during the early days, I used think that the neighbours might take offense and perhaps file lawsuits against us because of the constant meaty smoke billowing out of the massive barbeque grill nicknamed, Torpedo 2000.

But Amalume reassured me that even in the UK where they have the 1956 Clean Air Act, it doesn't apply to *utsi* from a domestic garden, which our barbeques falls under. And since in Malawi there are no bylaws pertaining to the Clean Air Act, I can't see how my neighbours would seek legal action against our frequent usage of the Torpedo 2000 aka *chiotchelo chathu cha nyama*.

I am not a lawyer and there are no lawyers in the Amoto family, so, basically we have the benefit of ignorance in our favour. We conduct our festivities on the premise that there are no laws that prohibit us from holding loud *mahape* eight days a week if we feel like it. We are not saying that such laws don't exist – if they do then we are screwed. But as of now we are totally ignorant of their existence hence our frequent barbeques whenever we congregate as a family, something that tends to happen quiet too often because we, the Amotos, live by the credence that, 'life is too short to be wasted on being serious.'

This is why today right in the middle of the week, on a sunny Wednesday while normal Malawians are out and about being productive vis-à-vis working 7:30am-5pm jobs, you could hear screams of *mahape* coming from my yard. As usual I was the pilot in charge of the Torpedo 2000 flipping *dzipalapatilo* and beef steaks with the precision of Chef Gordon Ramsey and the skill of Chef Jamie Oliver. The crisp booming voice of *Jabulani* and *Thandeka* was wafting from the four 1000watt speakers as the Amoto women sat lazily sipping intoxicating and non-intoxicating liquids through straws, shaking their heads and hips to the tune of the African rhythm.

"Shashaaaaaa!!!!" We all exploded into laughter the minute Shasha walked through the gates because we all thought that he was wearing a motorcycle helmet.

"Che Shasha, where did you park your Kawasaki?" Agogo jokingly asked and we all laughed uncontrollably but Shasha wasn't fazed.

"Don't hate the player hate the game, this here is a Notre Dame Football helmet" Shasha simply and calmly replied in his usual American accent. I had no idea what he was talking about but I saw the letters 'ND' emblazoned on the golden helmet.

It was Amalume who enlightened us that, what Shasha was wearing was indeed a helmet worn by players of American Football.

"You mean in America they wear helmets to play football?" I couldn't help asking, but apparently they do; from helmets to shoulder pads and all the protective gear you can think of because American football is not football as we know it in soccer-sense, it's not the Chelsea or Manchester United football we watch over here on DSTV. American football is like a mixture of Rugby and Karate with a little bit of wrestling. They don't have defenders, strikers or goal keepers instead they have quarterbacks, wide receivers and running-backs.

It's a contact sport in its true form, which means that it's one of those games not for the faint hearted. It's like running in the middle of a busy highway expecting to be hit by cars while you chase or carry a funny oblong shaped ball under your arm-pit like a purse. Simply put, American Football is one of those games that will never pick-up here in Malawi for two simple reasons; [one] we don't have the resources to dress or kit a whole player, let alone a whole team, and [two] we don't have the hospitals to cope with the kind of injuries that result from the train-like-impacts sustained on the pitch or field of play (as they call it).

This was news to me; but I didn't dwell too much on it, I was rather puzzled; why would my dear friend Shasha be wearing a Notre Dame helmet in Malawi on a hot sunny Wednesday?

He had a valid reason for this new weird fashion of his, which had nothing to do with being deliriously high on weed or Jamaican vegetable.

Since he returned back from abroad, Shasha hasn't taken up a job to sustain himself while living here in Malawi. As a result he has sold everything from the Playstation game console with all its accompanying games to the rap CD's and many DVD's he had brought with him. His parents even asked me to have a word with him because he has started selling *dzifuyo dzawo* – chickens, *akalulu, abakha* and what-not.

But what we didn't know was that he had also started borrowing money from people, telling them that he has money in a Dollar Account with one of the many banks that have just sprung up in the last ten or so years. Shasha claims that he is just waiting for some paper work to be signed with his bank, National City, in South Bend-Indiana before the local bank here can release the money. Typical Shasha tales which actually don't make sense to anyone and I have a feeling they don't even make sense to Shasha himself. Just like any experienced liar, Shasha sticks to his false stories with such ferocity and conviction that people have no choice but to believe him.

But as days turned into weeks and weeks turned into months, *angongole* started smelling a rat – *panunkha khoswe apa* – they figured they will not be getting their money back, at least not in this century or the next. As a result ominous threats have been made towards Shasha, threats that have been reinforced by the tossing of a few bricks at Shasha's house, breaking one or two windows.

Shasha's cell phone is now permanently switched off. It seems he is taking these threats seriously because the last brick that was thrown through his sitting room window had a note attached to it which simply said:

"*Tikugamphula mutu wakowo ngati lambe.*"

Lucky for Shasha he hadn't sold the Notre Dame helmet and if there was ever a time to use this souvenir from South Bend-Indiana then that time was now.

Agogo blew a few puffs of smoke from his home-rolled cigarette while looking at my friend Shasha in bewilderment and pity.

"*Koma achimwene*, what were you doing all these years *kunjako* for you to come back and start hiding inside a crash helmet?" My 102 years old Agogo asked while searching for a meaty piece of chicken thigh from the Torpedo 2000.

This is one question Shasha has never answered and will probably never answer. It really was a phenomenon that Shasha had literally nothing to his name, returning from *kunja* worse than he was before he went. All those years while abroad he hadn't been going to school and all the money he made through various *timaganyu,* he never built a house back home.

He didn't even bring *mutu wa* truck like most of returning people, do but only came with piles of clothes which he ended up selling in a futile attempt to sustain himself and maintain a certain image.

"Do you really have any bank account back in the States with National City Bank, or is it all *nthano*?" I asked Shasha a few weeks ago.

"Just chill Bro," was the short reply that came from my annoyed friend. I told him that this is serious, here in Malawi there are no debt collectors sending you letters of *dzisamoni* like they do abroad.

"*Kunotu akudulani dzosadula bwana* and if you think wearing a Notre Dame helmet will save you, you better start thinking seriously."

Shasha simply ignored me, opting to remind me of a Dr Dre's Chronic CD he had left here a couple of days ago. I am sure he had run out of CD's to sell and he was looking for that one so that he can go and flog it with the vendors in town. The Samaritan in me urged to try and assist by hooking him up with a job. I told him to go meet an Asian friend of mine who owns a Hardware shop in town. There was going to be an interview but it was just for formality, he would most likely get the job because this Asian friend of mine owed me a favour. Unfortunately the feedback I got from my Asian friend was very disappointing.

That following Monday Shasha showed up dressed in big khakhi Bermudas with letters "I Don't Give a Fuck" written across his bum. He also had on a bright yellow t-shirt with a picture of an AK-47 assault rifle with the words "rat-tat-tat."

To think that I had given him my white Robin Bridge shirt and a tie so that he could look the part but had opted to dress like a gangsta-rap artist was beyond me. He later on told me that he couldn't see himself wearing a formal shirt and a tie because it made him look like "a cheap ass nerd", whatever that meant.

Since my Asian friend owed me a favour, he (albeit reluctantly) ended up hiring Shasha despite the fact that there were other candidates at the interview who were capable and suitable for the job on offer.

My Asian friend told Shasha to come and start the following Tuesday at 9:00am looking presentable. For reasons best known to himself, Shasha arrived very late saying that 9am was too early for him. My Asian friend forgave him and told him to shadow an experienced employee as part of his induction, so that he could learn what the job entails, before being let go on his own. This induction was going to take four days which meant that

Shasha was expected to start working solo come next Monday.

Shasha never made it past 2 O'clock of that very first induction day. After coming back from lunch, half an hour late, he walked into his boss' office saying that he was quitting.

"Yo big boss, am outta here, I can't do this," were his exact words much to the astonishment of his *bwana*.

"Just pay me for the time I have been here and we will call it even," with hands casually tucked into his military pockets of his big Bermudas, Shasha made a demand which had a ring of threat to it.

My Asian friend was taken by surprise by Shasha's I-don't-care-attitude. He was also a bit annoyed, he told Shasha that he had only worked for about four hours; two of which he had spent on his cell phone and an hour spent outside smoking. Why was he quitting and what money was he talking about.

Shasha calmly told him that he used to live in America where he had a nice job at University Park Mall in Mishawaka, there was full air-conditioning system and had nice fringe benefits. There is no way he was going to be selling nails and *malata* in a hot and stuffy hardware store, he just wasn't cut out for this. He wanted his day's pay and he wanted it in cash "or this shit was gonna turn nasty" were his exact words.

Mwenye posafuna zamapokoso just paid him and politely asked him to leave. That was a week ago and today he was here with us at the barbeque donning a Notre Dame helmet, scared out of his mind because half the town was hunting for him.

Simioni who couldn't control his amusement asked; "but Shasha what makes you think that *anthu angongole* will aim their *dzibonga* or *dzisenga* at your head? What about your knees or stomach? Don't you have the full American football outfit to protect your whole body?" Everyone started laughing uncontrollably at the image of Shasha looking like an American football player, a Running-back as Amalume told us.

I, honestly, didn't see the humour in all this but felt sadness for my friend. Deep down inside me I was actually grieving for him, wondering how come he was so different from Tchale our 19 year old friend who had also been abroad? Young Tchale had returned home a matured person with direction and vision, which was just the opposite of Shasha? Just yesterday he had been in Mozambique on a business scouting trip. Where had Shasha gone wrong? And was he an isolated case or were there other Shasha's out there?

All Shasha had were pictures of his heydays in South Bend, the party days as he liked to call them. I looked at him standing there like a Notre Dame football player surrounded by my little nephews as he pulled out a stack of his pictures and started showing them off and narrating.

"This was my first car in the States a Ford Mustang 5.0 V8 ... this is me arriving at Michiana Airport conquering the USA ... and that's my first chick, she is Mexican but got deported back to Juarez ... this was me at the Lakers game inside the famous Staples Centre ... this was my posse with my crew, they are still there in South Bend representing and holding it down ... this is me inside a stretch limo celebrating splashing the 'Benjamin's' (money) from Tax Returns ... this is my closet full of shoes and baseball caps, this is me sipping Hennessy at Michiana Party Hall", Shasha annoyingly went on and on talking about what used to be and how things were. Everything was in the past with Shasha, the present was too painful for him and the future held no prospects whatsoever.

My little nephews looked at him in awe they couldn't believe that they were standing next to someone who had stood next to Kobe.

"Uncle Shasha did you really saw Kobe Bryant live? Wow! You are the man uncle Shasha, you are the main man", they praised and admired him.

My friend really lived and thrived for these moments; they reminded him of the easy times, the party times before he became a shadow of his former self.

He was about to pull another stack of pictures of himself that were taken while at Lake Michigan when out of nowhere came this speeding dark blue BMW, screeching to a halt just outside my fence. These two big burly looking guys with no shirts carrying big sticks got out, before the car had even come to a complete stop, screaming.

"That's him wearing the motorcycle helmet," they yelled while pointing in our direction with their big sticks.

I have never seen any human being run as fast as Shasha did, even Usain Bolt would envy the dashing skills that Shasha possessed. He leapt over the fence in one clean jump, sprinting across the neighbours' yard, tumbling and rolling before disappearing from view as big shirtless men with *dzibonga* (followed by a few neighbourhood dogs) gave chase in the direction where Shasha had disappeared.

I wondered how all those years in America could come down to this, a true OG (original gangster) being chased through *kumayadi aku* Malawi in a Notre Dame helmet. I shook my head in sadness, grabbed the barbeque tongs and went through the process of choosing the meatiest and nicely cooked chicken leg on the Torpedo 2000 grill watching and smiling at the smoke which was billowing in the direction my neighbour's yard.

MADONNA WABWERA BOO

My eyes were fixated to the story in the local newspaper that read: "US pop star Madonna Tuesday laid the first brick at the 15 million dollar (11 million euro) girls' academy that she is building in Malawi, promising to bring quality education to young girls." I read this caption over and over, my eyes kept looking at the amount; $15million, thinking to myself; "that's a lot of dosh" which even got more when I tried to do mental arithmetic by converting it into *makwacha* at the current exchange rate.

"*Madamuwa akubwera bwino,*" is all I could think of. I must admit when I first heard about this millionaire woman coming to Malawi to adopt our kids a few years ago, I was one of the many people who stood on the podium opposing this development. I even remember running for MP elections in my area (as an independent) on the manifesto that "Our children are not for sale."

Unfortunately the elections were rigged and my race to become the first independent MP of my area died a natural death.

Now looking back I feel embarrassed telling myself; "*a Makala munaonjenzanso,*" because it's now obvious that this woman has pumped more money in my country than any other individual person that I know of. With misconceptions and presuppositions about Madonna clouding my mind I think I had hastily jumped the gun and arrived at a wrong conclusion. I am sure that feelings of jealousy and some unexplainable cultural excuses might have played a bigger part in my erroneous assertions that this woman was not fit to raise our Malawian children.

I, like so many of the anti-Madonna Malawians and non-Malawians, pathetically tried to block the adoption citing frivolous arguments like; "she goes out with a young man hence not fit to be a mother," when we knew all along that our opposition to the adoption was simply sheer jealousness to the wealth of this woman.

There are still some of my relatives, whenever we gather around for our Sunday meal under the mango tree, tend to vehemently argue that it was wrong for these children to go to America. But I know that most of these relatives of mine are tainted by *kaduka*, and baseless grudges that somewhere in this part of the world a woman can amass such wealth and power simply by melodically projecting her voice through a microphone in ear catching tunes.

At first those who held on to this line were in majority, but lately it seems like more and more of those who support the adoption are beginning to outnumber the anti-adoption movement. I will admit that I am one of those who have recently crossed the floor from the opposition to the pro-Madonna camp. It may be that people are now coming to their senses or may be more and more of us are realising that the first adoption went fine and the boy's life has been transformed beyond belief. Let's face it, this young boy looks happier than he did and there are a lot of doors that will open up for this Malawian child than would have been the case if he was still here.

The second adoption too has borne some tantalising results, the little girl who left looking like a boy has been transformed into a little beautiful princess with her own white maids catering to all her needs.

Still there are some die hard Malawians who insist that these two children shouldn't have been taken out of the country;

"They should have stayed here so that we should all suffer together in this grinding poverty."

These anti-adoption activists argue, *akuti tonse tikulukutikile limodzi basi, zatero zi njiba za pa* Malawi. The strange thing is that if you put your ear to the ground and listen carefully, you start noticing that most of the anti-adoption rhetoric comes from the mouths of those individuals who fate has denied any opportunity of ever going to live abroad for various other reasons; either they have gone past their sell-by-date so much that if they were to apply for a Visa, the embassy *would* wonder, '*inu mukufuna kukapanga chani kunjako?*'

Some of them simply don't have sufficient funds to support their Visa application, or simply that they are just one of those people *omwe kunja sikungawalole* even if *atasamba dzitsamba*. People like these are simply called BIMDIMs (Born in Malawi Die in Malawi).

Of course it's these BIMDIMs who tend to be the most vocal in trying to ensure that these two children are not adopted so that they can join the prestigious BIMDIM ranks, *asaaa, asiyeni ana akaone* snow *uku akumatafuna timadyo tofewa ta pa* Las Vegas.

It was on this basis that last Sunday during our traditional family gathering after *mapemphelo'* the debate was about

Madonna aka Material Girl. There was about forty of us; *azimalume, atsibweni, aziphwawo amadala, anyamatafe, azimayi*, all gathered for *nsima* and a buffet of *dzipalapatilo*, roasted rats, ma *ofozi, mazila a khuku-ndembo*, beans, cow hoofs and barbequed goat.

Amalume, the only member of the family to have been abroad, was the spokesperson of our side; the pro-Madonna camp. My Agogo, a typical die-hard BIMDIM, was the leader of opposition, and at his age of 102 years he was the most vocal, especially after eating *dzipalapatilo* dipped in *tsabola wakambuzi*. We have always suspected that this abnormally hot *tsabola* gives our grandfather *ukali* during these family debates. As usual, today, he was on top of his game vociferously articulating his argument;

"*Muona ana amenewa ayiwala chichewa, sadzatikumbukiranso ife, muona.*" Agogo barked so angrily, I was glad that Madonna was not here with us otherwise she would have been running for the border in fear.

Amalume stood up, countering Agogo's typical and overused BIMDIM form of argument which doesn't really hold water anymore when you consider that Chichewa is not even spoken in some parts of Malawi let alone outside the country.

"So what if they can't speak Chichewa? Surely that can't be doom and gloom for them. Madonna can't speak Chichewa neither but the whole of Malawi comes to a standstill when she coughs, and so far I haven't heard that the millions of dollars she has donated have been rejected because they are coming from the pockets of a non-Chichewa speaker." Amalume flawlessly delivered his counter argument.

We argued and debated throughout the meal and by the time we got to eating the fruits (*mango, mizimbe and matowo*), it was clear that most of us agreed that Madonna is genuinely doing something positive for Malawi. There are still those (*just like my Agogo*) BIMDIMs who oppose the notion of these Malawian children being raised outside the country. They fail to see what an asset these children will be, twenty or twenty-five years from now.

If Madonna who is not a Malawian has the potential to transform lives of so many Malawians via her orphanage, imagine what these two children will do once they become little millionaires in their own right. Even if these two children never have to donate a single *Tambala* to Malawi when they are grown-up, their lives will still turn out better than if they had been left to languish in the periphery of Malawi's poverty, where the only way out is either politics or a one way ticket to la-la-land(s).

"*Koma Otata*, if Madonnayu was to invite you to go and live in America would you refuse?" Amalume cheekily asked Agogo. My grandfather looked at Amalume, stopped chewing his *Mpinimbi* fruit, before answering,

"*Mafunso opanda nzerutu amenewo*," Agogo dismissed Amalume's cheap blow which seemed to have made an impact on the whole debate. The way I saw it, the score was; 'Pro-Adoption 1 – BIMDIMs 0'

We all cracked out laughing and a few women let out a melody of *nthungululu*. Whether we like it or not Madonna has done what neither foreigner nor Malawian has done before.

SO YOU WANT TO BE A TRANSPORTER?

Just because I have a minibus, (let me rephrase that) just because I used to have a minibus – am using past tense "used" because its resting pa *mitondo* at the back of the house and the engine is in the children's bedroom waiting for a spare-part from China so that my mechanic Che Supanala can resuscitate it back to life.

Anyway let me start all over again. Just because I used to have a minibus and I am the General Manager of my own scrap metal business and a few other businesses – which cannot be said out loud just in case MRA is listening, I have been getting a lot of mail from *abale ndi alongo* asking me for advice on lucrative business ventures that have a high probability of surviving the Malawian hostile economic environment while at the same time promising lucrative returns.

I can say with certainty that 98% of these questions, no, 99% of these questions usually come from *abale ndi alongo* who are abroad – especially ku *Mangalande* and *Obamaland*. There is something about the thinking of Malawians abroad that tends to be warped in the direction of business. Maybe it's the fact that all of a sudden they have at their disposal enough *mpamba* vis-à-vis Capital.

So far I have not received any letter asking me that; "*kodi kumudziko ma* prospects *antchito ali bwanji?*"

I don't blame them for not showing interest or not being too inquisitive about jobs. Perhaps Malawians abroad have also looked at or analysed the gleam employment statistics which speak for themselves: of the 500,000 people visiting labour office daily, only five of them will be called for an interview and of those five, only two will be offered a job. Ok... Ok maybe I have exaggerated the numbers a little bit but am sure you get the picture.

Most of these letters that I get, half of them, the owners already have in mind what kind of business they would want to pump their hard earned Dollars, Pounds, Rupees, Rands or whatever funny sounding currencies earned abroad. And this common business is none other than "Transport" aka Trucks.

These days every *Uje ndi Uje*, so it seems, wants to be a transporter and one wonders why. Is it because starting a transport venture is not as hard as starting a Legal Firm or an Accounting maybe Architectural Firm? This might be true because the common perception is that for a Transport venture all you need is a truck, a driver and mechanic who knows the difference between a hammer and a screw-driver. It's that simple, right? Wrong.

I remember when I was growing up there were only four known transporters in Malawi: Press Transport, GDC, Wheels of Africa and CARS, how times change. Now everyone is talking of;

"*Eeee mwamuona nfana anali ku* States *uja, wabwera ndi mitu itatu.*" One would think that they are referring to human heads, no. "Mitu" in trucking jargon is a reference to the "Truck-Horse" that pulls the trailer, also shortened as simply: "Horse" or *Atik* for articulated.

Yes, I will be the first person to admit that you don't need a Bachelor's Degree from Harvard or Yale in order to be successful in Truck-ology. Yes, I am well aware that most Malawian transporters are not your average-day academics but trust me, there is a certain level of science to this business than meets the eye. I am not talking about complex science involving physics or chemistry but rather a science of a different nature; that involves being familiar with the terminology and logistics of this 24-7 business.

The first term you will come across is *Mutu*. This is by no means, a reference to a human head nor that of any living species. *Mutu* is simply a trucking terminology which is a reference to a Horse or the Unit that pulls the trailer and it's categorised into two; flat face or long nose. *Mutu* is the heart of your operation because without it, you can't boast to be a transporter. Trailers can be hired or rented but as a transporter you need to own your own *mutu* or *mitu*. It's probably the first capital asset any aspiring transporter will invest in.(insert 'in') I have never heard of a transporter who started by buying spanners or hiring drivers before buying *mutu*. That is not to say that it can't happen, strange things have known to happen in this business.

The problem with these "*Mitus*" is that they have over-flooded the country as if they are being given away for free in UK or USA. But then that's the typical Malawian business mentality. We are not innovators, we like copying what everyone else is doing. Malawi is a nation of copy cats and this is also the case when it comes to the transport business. I know some of you will disagree with me here, I can even see some people coming over to my neighbourhood marching outside my house in protest carrying signs: "Down with Makala Amoto," "who does he think he is, calling us copy cats?" You can protest all you want; after all there is freedom of expression in Malawi, and now everyone thinks that they can protest over anything. Too bad we don't have MYP anymore.

Like it or not, Malawians like copying am surprised we haven't started cloning each other yet. We are not inventors we are *copy-tors* (such word doesn't exist but I bet Malawians are already copying it as we speak.)

I loathe those Malawians who visit you at your house – instead of doing the visiting activities, they get suspiciously busy analysing your house plan, design, furniture – taking pictures with that tiny camera inside their brain aka *kukopela*. Six months down the road, try visiting their house and you end up getting the shock of your life, it's like you have visited your own house, everything from the house plan to the furniture even pictures of your kids hanging on their living room wall are exactly as your home, the only difference being the smell. *Eeiishhhh!* Malawians find your own architect and interior designer instead of stealing other peoples' plans.

Coming back to business talk, I remember when I was growing up some clever entrepreneur came up with a bright business idea that if you add sugar to coloured water and pack it in tiny condom-like tubes, freeze and sell them as "*Fizesi*" on a hot summer, day people would love it. People loved it and *Fizesi* became a Malawian hit on phenomenal proportions. Unfortunately this clever guy forgot to patent his idea i.e. trademark it like Coca-Cola did so that others shouldn't copy it.

That was perhaps the stupidest business move this clever guy did, because the following week everyone, the whole country, was selling *Fizesi*. There were probably more people selling *Fizesi* than were buyers, tipping the whole concept of Demand and Supply right on its head. And every entrepreneur will tell you that there is no worse scenario for any business when supply outstrips demand, as this gives the consumer more power due to the extensive availability of choice.

You might think that *Fizesi* was an isolated incident, but a few years later, another Malawian chap discovered a business niche involving 'Public Transport. 'He observed that big buses which had been servicing the city routes were a bit sluggish and cumbersome. They tended to take long to commute between Blantyre and Limbe because they had to make scheduled stops along the way. He figured that inserting a smaller bus into the equation would cut down on time, since a fifteen-seater would be nimble and fast not having to stop on bus-stages only. The turn-around time would be faster than UTM's 100 seater mammoths.

With this blue print in his mind, this creator of the minibus idea went and bought a used minibus from Bata or was it Limbe Leaf or Admarc Tigers (I can't remember.) He was the only Malawian running a minibus the whole country, competing with Stage Coach (which used to be called UTM). Just like the blunder committed by our *Fizesi* entrepreneur, this minibus Einstein committed a similar one, that of not Patenting or Trade marking his idea so as to protect his minibus niche.

I don't need to tell you how many minibuses are currently running on the roads (and sometimes off the roads onto pavements) of Malawi today. The minibus idea was copied by everyone - on the same rate people flocked to copy Shabba Ranks's song, "Mr Lover-man" on their blank TDK cassettes, if not worse. Amalume once told me that if Malawi was a sick human being and minibuses were like a deadly virus the prognosis report would be stamped: "*za kaya-kaya*" simply because there are more minibuses in Blantyre alone than there is rice in a 90kg bag. One wonders if there are any meaningful profits being generated from this business. The same is now happening to transport because it too has been infected by the *Fizesi*-Minibus virus.

This then brings us to the inquisition by Malawians abroad about the prospects and viability of transport business. Where do I even start in responding to this? I will use as an example Simioni's cousin, who came back from UK last year with *mitu* four of ERF, Iveco and two MAN trucks. As I speak, they are still parked outside Simioni's house and they are using two of them for keeping chickens *za mikolongwe*.

Since in Malawian business is based on hearsay and never on market research, Simioni's cousin like many other aspiring transporters thought that buying a horse is a sure guarantee to start making millions of profits.

"*Ungogula mitu yama truck, udzayandama uka-bwela kuno.*"

If he had done proper market research by asking around those who are already in the field, or with a knowhow, he would have discovered that these so called *mitu* or horses need a trailer before you can start hauling goods. A trailer is now a must have asset for any transporter who hauls bulk in excess of 25 tones. Market research would have shown him that there are more horses in Malawi than are trailers. There is a prevalent scarcity of trailers making them the most treasured capital asset on a transporters yard.

The problem with these trailers is that they cost an arm and a leg. I can't remember the exact figures but when I was told, I remember getting dizzy and provoking *kanfuno*. I tend to get nose bleeds when someone mentions ridiculous amounts of money unless if it's Zim-Dollars.

After six or seven months, Simioni's cousin realised that his transport business was going nowhere. The only option was to sell the trucks. But with the internet age and the fact that every Malawian now has got someone they know living abroad, people *kumudzi kuno* are now more articulate and aware of how much these things cost abroad.

The amounts Simioni's cousin was asking for were ten times what he paid for, *kupondana masana-sana*. Maybe back in the days of Roy Welensky when people were still oblivious to prices in the UK they would have paid any amount as long as *ndicha kunja*.

But today, knowledgeable Malawians with access to websites like Autotrader.com or Trucktrader.com in the UK or Truckpaper.com in the USA or simply with a cell phone would not pay these exorbitant amounts Simioni's cousin was asking for. Even an ordinary two-tambala transporter from Chipande will tell you that he knows how much trucks cost in Michigan; "Flat-Face *iyi*

siyija amagulitsa $3500 *ku* Benton Harbor, Michigan *ija?*
Bwanji inu mukutchaja $25000?"

By the time Simioni's cousin decided to lower
his price, there were already a thousand other trucks
being sold all over Malawi ranging from Internationals,
Freightliners, Benz, ERFs, IVECOs, MAN Diesels and
others I have never heard of. Simioni's cousin had blinked,
Supply had simply outstripped Demand, like many other
Malawians trying to sell mitu, the cousin found himself
on the wrong end of this equation. The result is that a lot
of these *mitu,* owned by entrepreneurial Malawians, are
standing stagnant behind *manyumba am'mayadimu* or in
Bond Clearing Houses.

Like I said, every *mutu* needs a trailer and if you are lucky
enough to get one, (flatbed for "dry cargo" or tanker if
you are going to be hauling "wet cargo") then you are at
least half way there. Does this mean that your transport
business is a done-deal? Not really. But securing a trailer
is a big step especially when you consider that they are
going at a premium compared to horses which can be
gotten reasonably well since most sellers are just looking
to break-even.

So you have gotten yourself a horse and a trailer
which basically equates to a complete rig. What then?
This is where it starts getting interestingly complicated as
you start thinking; "what have I gotten myself into?"

The Malawian market being so small, competition
is tough, basically it's a dog-eat-dog world out there,
perhaps more brutal than the minibus arena because of
the enormous outlay of capital involved. A complete rig
will set you back several millions of Kwachas and the

sooner that thing is on the road the quicker you start generating returns on your investment.

Even if you are a novice transporter you will quickly find yourself in the deep end competing with other "seasoned" transporters who are simply referred to as the "Big Boys" and have been in the pool probably longer than you. Yes, most Big Boys have been doing this while you were still working double shifts to buy your first *mutu*. Because there is no honeymoon period in this business, you have no choice but to immediately start swimming with the sharks if you want to call yourself a Transporter, there is no induction period.

Most of these Big Boys already have more trucks than the summation of your fingers and toes and most of them can afford to buy a small Toyota for the Logistics Manager at the company that gives out transport contracts *(dziphuphu.)*

Some of these big boys are well connected in high places; either their daughter or son is married to that Minister's daughter or that Regional Governor's son. Worse still, for you, you soon realise that some of these Big Boys come from the same village with the Big People aka Politicians or *atsogoleri, eeeetu eee*, no need for me to spell it out for you. Which means that when "loads" at Admarc or Auction Floors (Tobacco) are available, the Logistics Manager will remember *komwe kumachokela nchele wake.*

Novice transporters, which most people coming from abroad are, will find out that securing a load can be quite tricky simply because there are many transporters out there chasing too few jobs, especially if your market is confined to local routes.

On top of struggling to get loads for your trucks, the other big problem is 'Payment' after you have hauled the load; tobacco or sugar or maize from point A to B. For a start-up transporter, payment is vital simply because these are the funds that you will probably need to pay for the Diesel you bought *pangongole, Mateyala angongole*, Salaries for drivers and *anyamata omanga ma lona* (tarpaulins).

As the saying goes; it takes money to have your cheque processed. *Osayina cheke adyepo zake naye,* and if a bale of tobacco or sugar was damaged while on your truck, guess who is going to pay for it? Yes, you the transporter.

Those in serious trucking will tell you that serious money is in hauling international loads. But with serious rewards comes some highly acute serious headaches that are not for the faint hearted. Trucks are very temperamental creatures and they will often breakdown without warning. Where they choose to break down can at times be a logistical nightmare that will make you think; "why didn't I just go to Medical School to become a Neurosurgeon?"

If your truck breaks down i.e. driver *wakuswela* Diff or he drank too much cerveja and decides to roll the whole rig over, somewhere in Mozambique in the middle of nowhere – the pressure and worry alone are bound to send you to a heart specialist if not an early grave. And if your Freightliner is broken down in some hostile parts outside Malawi while loaded with some highly valuable cargo with a propensity to attract thieves, definitely this is bound to cause your blood pressure shoot up to 160/100 mmHg – which again is a recipe for an early grave.

But if you are aspiring to become a transporter then these are daily headaches you would have to deal with, my only advice is to make sure you have a lifetime supply of Panado or whatever medication you chew for your migraines. If transport is the business you want to lock horns with, then prepare yourself for a roller coaster ride because the rewards can be big and the headaches bigger.

Having said all this, I think transport business is the best, if you have got the determination, strong heart, enormous drive and endurance (and of course powerful connections are a bonus.)

Common sense will show that if you are made of weak stuff, then just go to school and become an Architect or Accountant, but if your brain is not academically wired up for *Geometry and Angles* or *Debits and Credits*, then you are better off lining up at Labour Office like the 500,000 other Malawians there. It's not that bad though, they have this fun game of Bawo. Last time I checked they were split into teams playing for the *Malova* Championship. They are people who even refuse to go for interviews just because they don't want to miss their Bawo semi-finals.

I hope this helps all aspiring Malawian Transporters, Trucking is a banging business and Makala is talking to you from a point of experience. Our country is a landlocked state and we need more transporters just like the Sahara needs an abundant supply of *Fizesi*.

POLITICS, FAMILY &
CULTURAL TRADITIONS

Since Amalume's British wife came to join him in Malawi, the political divisions in my family are now more pronounced than before. Don't get me wrong, for a very big family comprising of; *a Zimalume, aziphwawo a Madala, my sisters, brothers, ma khazeni, a Zichimwene a Masiteni,* our only surviving grandfather (who is 102 years old) we all get along. We have the normal family infighting just like any other healthy Malawian family out there, but overall we are a tight bunch.

Politically my family is like a small America or a little United Kingdom because we have these political camps: there are conservatives and there are liberals and at times there are independents just like me and one or two extremists on the far right and left of the Amoto clan. Am sure you, too, have a couple of extremists in your families – *Matalibano* aka *achibale amakani mopweteketsa moyo.* I know you are all wondering why Makala is talking about *ndale?* Don't despair am coming to that, first things first.

Amalume's wife being British means that she does not abide to some of our cultural nuances vis-à-vis she does not kneel down for men, *samagwada* and she does not sit *pa mphasa* or *nkeka.*

"Why should she stretch on *mphasa* when the men sit on chairs?" Auntie has always argued and on top of that once in a while, when the sun comes out, she wears a skirt that shows her knees and a little bit of the bottom thigh. This makes Mother very uneasy and uncomfortable to swallow, especially when we get visitors from the village and Auntie dresses like Taxina.

This is when the politics in my family gets all heated up. There is the conservative camp – the Republicans – with my Agogo as its leader, who find this as a "no" "no", with a capital N. Their argument is the usual story that goes like; "women are expected to wear clothes that don't show *akatumba*, when greeting an older person (especially if that person is male) a woman needs to be on her knees, a woman is supposed to run a bath for her husband, a woman is supposed to do all the house chores, shopping for the house is a woman's task, a woman is supposed to cook for the family and most importantly a woman is supposed to address the husband as "*Bambo a Uje.*"

My British Auntie apparently does none of the above. As a matter of fact there are some things that she does not do that are not even on the list above. This is why the Conservative side of my family has more than once approached Amalume;

"*Ankolo timati tikutsineni khutu pan'gono*", they would start their *malangizo* talk but nothing ever comes out of these so-called *malangizo,* either because Amalume doesn't bother relaying them to Auntie. Or if he does then Auntie has simply made up her mind that these so-called *maulemu* only apply to Malawian members of the clan but as far as she is concerned she doesn't give a rat's ass (*thako la mbewa*).

Then there is the Liberal side of my family – the Democrats – who take a different view and are usually in minority. They recognise the importance of holding on to cultural beliefs and traditions.

"*Ife ndife Amalawi, tisamayiwale miyambo yathu koma.*" The Amoto liberals would argue pointing out to the fact that Malawi needs to move on with the times and cut the women some slack.

"It's not like we are still living in the time before the dinosaurs." Amalume likes to articulate whenever these debates come up.

Gone are the days when people used to marry from the same village with the usual arranged marriage (just because the father of the boy and the father of the girl are drinking buddies). Gone are the days when it was common to have marriages between cousins aka keeping it in the family. Nowadays it's very rare to come across a marriage set on the premise that the boy and the girl used to be childhood friends, playing *chibisalilano, fulaye* before upgrading to *masanje,* before graduating to the famous game of *abambo ndi amayi.* It sounds all romantic and ideal but this is not the case anymore.

Globalisation has warped the playing field, extended the horizons as people find themselves marrying far and beyond to what used to be the norm. The liberal members of the Amoto clan are aware of this and try to incorporate the changing environment into their reasoning, judgement and how the family ought to move forward.

Globalisations has seen embassies dish out Student-Visas, Work-Visas or Holiday-Visas igniting an exodus of *abale ndi Alongo* outside the country bigger than that experienced by the Israelites during Moses' era. This is where some *abale ndi alongo* end up meeting their future significant others who are not always Malawian nationals, just like what happened with Amalume and Auntie.

Usually when newlyweds decide to enjoy their matrimony outside Nyasaland, the political shenanigans stay dormant underneath never bubbling to the surface. A man won't mind being called by his first name by their non-Malawian wife and the Malawian ladies don't mind a Man who is always in the kitchen mixing spices and plucking the chicken. To find a man tending *mpoto wa nyemba* in UK or USA or *pa Joni pompa* is not unusual, no one will raise an eyebrow and say "eee, *koma ndiye akuvekani chitenjetu Bambo a Boyi.*"

For a woman to call her man by his first name without beginning with "A", is normal, it's a sign of affection and *chikondi*, Makala instead of *a* Makala.

I noticed this during my one week stay in South Africa, females much younger than me were calling me Makala and to tell you the truth that didn't bother me at all as they jokingly asked me,

"*Makala, kodi Mula watsala pa Saigon?*" they would giggle and smile as they called my name, *ine ku mtima myaaa*, but I know that if this was in Malawi that questioned would be rephrased;

"*A Makala Amoto, kodi Alamu sanabwere nanu?*" they would say, simply because we are within the borders of Nyasaland.

It seems that Malawians abroad tend to live a more liberal life but a conservative one once back home, a perplexing phenomenon indeed.

Of course, the game changes a little bit when a (married) couple decides to come and settle in the 'Warm Heart of Africa'. All of a sudden there is *chinantindi* of spectators made up *azichemwali a madala, azimalume* and a few nosy neighbours who can't resist the usual remarks;

"*Koma iwowa angabwere ku maliro opanda chitenje, koma zolaulatu izi.*"

"*Mabondo (maondo) anzimayi samakhala osalala chonchi*, it means she does not kneel for her elders" another nosy neighbour or that annoying Auntie would comment.

This might sound trivial but there are people out there who make it their business to be checking women's knees to ascertain whether she is a kneeler or not. *Mabize apa* Malawi, if only we could divert this energy into development we would probably be richer than America.

I have noticed that lately Amalume hasn't been very happy. He somehow looks uncomfortable whenever Auntie calls him by his first name in public. The liberal camp of my family thinks that you can't blame our British Auntie who has been married to Amalume for fifteen years and has always called him by his first name. Is it right to expect her to, all of a sudden, start calling him something different? *Koma iwowa angawaitane Amalume ngati akuyitana mwana?*

The Conservatives of the family thinks she should, they claim that as long as she is in Malawi she should do as Malawians do.

"When you are in China do what the Chinese do." Agogo screams on top of his voice.

I try to correct him that the saying goes like;

"When you are in Rome do what the Romans do."

"AAAAAA!! a Makala, *takhalani phee apa*, Rome Rome Rome *chani*? Rome *ili kuti*? *Munamvapo kuti m'Malawi wina aliyense wapita kudziko lotchedwa* Rome?" Agogo cuts me off rudely.

I have this young nephew who just turned thirteen last week and is always listening to the 'i-Pod' he got from Amalume when he arrived from UK, he jumped to my defence.

"*Koma maulemu amenewa*, what if the roles were reversed, what if it was the men who are expected to kneel down for the women or sit on the *nkeka* while the women are sitting up there on chairs? " my little nephew articulated himself like a grown up.

Agogo banged his hand on the table while reaching for his walking stick and we all feared for the little nephew's safety.

"*Kodi mwayamba kumeta liti inunso, takhalani phee*. What if, What if, What if ...*chani ...pano palibe za* What if." Agogo roared his eyes boring into the young boy who quickly and quietly sat down before Agogo could poke him with his walking stick.

We sat there eating in silence, everyone thinking about how far culture and traditions should go and how much of western traditions should be assimilated. For the first time I ate my beloved *dzipalapatilo* without sprinkling salt because the salt-shaker was right next to Agogo and after such a heated debate I didn't feel like asking him to pass me the salt. I was afraid he might throw it right at my face in anger... the political parties of this family were not known for shaking hands or hugging right after a heated debate. All you could hear were sounds of chewing and swallowing as everyone stared down in his/her plate.

IT'S TAX SEASON IN AMERICA

Today for the first time I walked into Amalume's room and found him crying. My first thought was that he had a fight with Auntie, but I was wrong. Amalume's source of grief and sorrow was something which I found strange, hard to understand and a bit disturbing. (*zodabwitsa*)

Amalume said to me that he was missing America. "But Amalume, you have been home for almost six months, *bwanji muku-ililira Amereka lero*?" I quizzed him.

What he told me not only baffled me but made me realize why a lot of *abale ndi alongo* dream of going to America more than they dream of going to UK, India, Dubai or Zimbabwe.

For someone like me who has never been to the USA, it all sounded a bit complicated to understand why a full grown man like Amalume would be sobbing for not being in America. I almost asked him *kuti*:

"*Kodi munasiyako ndani kumeneko?*"

The way he was so miserable I started to think that probably we had Auntie Number Two that we weren't aware of, *mwina ka* Black Americana, *ka kirimu kapa* States.

Surprisingly enough it had nothing to do with another unknown Auntie, Amalume was longing for South Bend because in America this is Tax season, *nyengo ya misonkho.* Unlike here where the MRA always takes and takes and takes *misonkho* from us year after year after year, in America it is a little different.

Amalume lectured me that there comes a time (at the end of their tax year) in April when their MRA, ooppss! Sorry! I meant IRS, actually gives money back to people in form of tax-refunds after you have filled the 1040 Form. This is part of the money people have been paying as tax and when it comes back as tax refunds it feels like *zaulele*.

Of course not anyone is entitled to tax-refunds – it's only those who are eligible and also *anthu ena ochenjera*. Amalume told me that this is the season *yomwe* a Malawi *amanyauda* to the extreme. These tax refunds come in thousands of dollars, *malingana ndi kuti munthu wapanga* claim *ana angati* when filing. I know...I know to all those who are not used to the American system this sounds a bit too confusing, don't worry you are not alone, Makala is confused too – especially when Amalume started talking about *kupeza ma* Social Security Numbers *kuti ukhale ngati* you have children so that you maximise *makobidi omwe boma litakupatse.* All this American jargon nearly gave me *mutu wampedze-pedze* or is it *m'mimba mwa ching'alang'ala* (did I just mix the two? It's Ok, as long as you get the picture.)

Amalume disappointed me when he said that he wasn't going to go into the minute details or intricacies and all the shenanigans that are involved in trying to squeeze the last dollar out of the American system. He says that this topic is beyond today's conversation and best left for another day, when he wasn't feeling sombre.

But even though he didn't want to dwell much on this subject, I gathered that the American tax system is not as efficient or as tight as the Feds think, vis-à-vis there are glaring loopholes that (cunning) individuals are able to exploit. It's more like tiny cracks that are prevalent in the whole concept of Efficient Market Hypothesis, *anthu ndi anthu* and will always find a way to beat the system. So it happens that *abale ndi alongo* have discovered inefficiencies in the tax system and are milking it until the peeps squeak. If you are lucky enough to be in America then *tiyeni nazo, paja amati wankachisi adzadya zankachisi* no wonder Amalume is moaning and in mourning.

Anyway – what do *achi* Malawi do with *ma sauzande ndi ma sauzande a ma dolazi*: Do they send the money home? Do they assist those people they promised they will assist before leaving Chileka or KIA? Do they at least buy *njinga ya Hamba* for Ayaya *kumudzi*? It looks like some do. But this is not the reason Amalume was crying his eyeballs out.

According to Amalume *nyengo ya ma* taxes *ndi nthawi yomwe a* Malawi live like kings and queens in America. With these tax-refunds some *abale ndi alongo* can all of a sudden afford to rent a stretch limo, even though they have nowhere to go in particular, they just tell the limo driver: "keep on driving until the fuel gauge nears empty."

This might sound laughable and baboon-like but you start to understand and sympathise with these Tax-Season Only Limo Riders (TSOLR) when you analyse the modes of transport they were riding back here in Malawi, *kaya-kaya* minibuses. But now they are in America, living lavida loca – the American dream, after all – like what Amalume tells me, that's what limos are there for. You are not going to rent a Limo to take you to your day job at McDonalds, you rent it on a weekend, when you are all dressed up, with your dressed up friends, your wallets and purses *akusefukila* with Tax-Return Dollars and you issue one instruction to the Limo driver:

"Keep driving until you reach that place where the sky and the ground meet."

According to Amalume this is the ripe time to buy that expensive piece of *mphasha* they have been looking at all year round, waiting, hoping and whispering to themselves: "*tiona ikafika* April."

Even those Malawians who haven't been going to church as often as they should, all of a sudden have the urge and desire to walk into the house of prayer. They do so not to connect with God but to use it as a cat-walk for that new Armani or Yves Saint Laurent outfit they just bought on Friday *ndi makobidi a misonkho*. These are known as the TSOCGs (Tax-Season Only Church Goers). It's possible to be a TSOLR (Tax-Season Only Limo Rider) and a TSOCG. Doctors say it's a rare occurrence but research shows there are unique Malawians who are infected by the virus of both these deadly abominations.

Sadly it is also the time of fierce competition amongst Malawians as to who has the biggest tax-refund to back up his or her ego... and According to Amalume, egos don't come any bigger than those of Malawians who never dreamt of ever having a dollar in their pocket and now all of a sudden they find themselves in a situation where the government has refunded them with thousands. People simply go bananas; they lose their marbles and think that it's all a dream. So they go on obnoxious spending sprees just in case they wake up from this dream.

Amalume even went as far as revealing to me that because of the tax-refunds, sadly, some love affairs will end and some will start, *dzikwati dzimagwedezeka*. It's not unusual to hear a man who is high on Tax-money chatting a friend's girlfriend or wife *kumati;*

"Let's do coffee when you are free after work."

Coffee *yomweyo zinthu mpakana kukathela ku* Hotel or Motel, *anvekele;*

"Room for two," even though *anthu ndinu* Mr and Mrs *Mayina osiyana.*

It's not just cheating that comes out during tax season but also bonkerism and wierd discussions between couples. Just because Bwana *nthumba lawo liri lololo ndi ma dolazi anvekele;*

"Darling, I think I can afford to send you in for a boob job." *Akuti ma* Silicone implants, *koma abale inu, akuti* bra size *ichoke pa* size 32B *ifike pa* 32ZZ.

And since these days our women have caught on to this Equal Rights bandwagon. *ndiye anvekele;*

"I was also thinking of the same thing, I think your package down there needs enlargement and an extension."

Kuwatelo Bambo, basi nkhondo yabuka pa America – they then start calling *azinkhoswe ku* Malawi *akuti nkazi wayamba mwano akuwanena kuti katundu akuchepera kaba, azinkhoswe anvekele;*

"*Malaulotu awa, bwanji mudzingobwerako kunjako ana inu.*"

This tax-disease transcends relationships all the way to employment. Most employers will report an increase in people not showing up to work in the weeks after *anthu atakatamuka*. What's the point of going for a shift at work when your wallet, purse and account *ili lo-lo-lo, kuchita kusefukila*?

Malawians can afford fancy cars for cash and even those who never used to frequent barbeque gatherings will all of a sudden start asking trivial questions.

"*Kodi lero a Malawi akukumana kuti*?"

Because, in the words of one wise Malawian celebrity, what's the point of wearing a designer outfit and driving an expensive "*mwandiona*" car if there is no one else to play spectator and pump up your ego with words that sound funny as they are shallow.

"*Mukubwera bwino Madala* or *Katundu ali nyatwa Madam.*"

I couldn't believe Amalume was actually crying over this, maybe it's because I didn't fully understand the significance of tax season to Malawian-Americans, maybe because I didn't know why it was so important to go and ride a stretch limousine while you have unpaid electricity bills at home. But as they say money – especially if you have never had it before – tends to turn people into strange creatures.

ZOKWAPULA-KWAPULA ANA
AND MATOFOTOFO

My British Auntie has got a unique way of screaming that is different from a Malawian scream. If you come from Nsimaland then you know how a Malawian scream sounds like, there is no need for me to waste ink in explaining it to you. On the other hand though, I wish I could describe the British scream to you, unfortunately it can't be explained in words, you just have to hear it. Her screams were worse during the first two weeks she arrived from the UK but they seem to be tapering off as time goes by.

My house, as most of you already know, is a typical Malawian house which means that we live side by side in harmony with *makoswe* (mice) and those big cockroaches, the ones with long antennae like some sort of aliens from another galaxy. The type of cockroaches that just look at you if you happen to turn on the kitchen light in the middle of the night. They don't even have the dignity to run away as a show of respect, *mphenvu zamatama, zojaila ...nzika za nkhitchini.*

The first two weeks the mice-cockroach tag-team terrorised Auntie so much she had to have an escort every time she ventured in the kitchen. She would scream her unique British scream every time cockroaches came out of the drawer or whenever a pregnant mouse lazily scuttled across the floor back to its hole. Am sure some of you know the kind of arrogant *makoswe* I am talking about here. The ones that have lived in your house the same number of years as you and they start thinking that they pay rent too. *Kumera mizu*, especially those that have lived in your house longer than you have.

While watching TVM, we heard Auntie scream in broad day light outside the house, the same kind of British scream that I have failed to describe to you in words. Agogo annoyingly looked at me and I knew he was about to send me out there.

"*Takawona Azakhali ako, koma iwowa sanawa-zolowelebe makoswe apa mudzi pano?*"

I, unwillingly, dashed outside to rescue Auntie only to find that her screams had nothing to do with *makoswe* or *mphenvu*. She was pointing across the street where Simioni was chasing his last born son around his house while brandishing his favourite long "*chikwapu*" crafted out of *nsungwi*.

If I was a betting man I would have put my money on the son. There was no way Simioni was going to catch him the way the young boy *amapalasila* – I thought this was funny but my Auntie found it barbaric. She looked worried.

"Is he going to use that stick on the little boy?" she asked worryingly looking at me as if I had the powers to intervene and save the boy.

"Yes Auntie if he catches him, he has to catch him first, but I don't think Simioni is in any condition to catch that boy" I responded while trying not to take my eyes off the ensuing chase.

I could see Simioni's belly bouncing with every step he took. Years of drinking and enjoying *dzipalapatilo*, ma *ofozi* and all sorts of *nyama* were taking its toll on my friend's physique. "*Tikukula anthufe eti*" is all I could think of while amusingly watching my friend huffing and puffing like a mammoth trying to catch an athletically fit and nimble rabbit.

Good thing I wasn't a betting man because, Lord behold, Simioni surprisingly closed the gap and managed to catch his son in what was a spectacular dive for a man his size and physique. Tackling the little boy by the legs in such fashion, reminded me of rugby or American football match I had recently watched on DSTV.

What followed was a series of *chikwapu* swings... ear-piercing screams... cries of agony... and Simioni's raised voice "*anakuwuza kuti ungapinse mumphika wa ndiwo usanafunse ndani!!!*" an accusation that almost made me laugh my lungs out.

In Malawi the crime committed by a child might be trivial to a Westerner's eye, but at the end of the day it's the principle that matters. Amalume once told us that in UK you won't see a father chasing his son around the block simply because that child had been caught with his fingers in a pot of *ndiwo*. But then this wasn't UK, was it?

Here in Malawi, at Simioni's house, the law had been broken the instant the child opened that pot of *dzipalapatilo*. Whether his fingers had or hadn't proceeded to the bottom of the pot and made contact with a piece of unsuspecting *chipalapatilo* is not at issue here, what's at stake is the fact that the lid of the pot had been opened without an adult's authorisation. The first amendment of any '*Malawian Household Constitution*' clearly stipulates that a minor, a child, *mwana* shall always seek a grown-up's permission before sticking his/her childish fingers in the sacred pot of *ndiwo*.

Akanafunsa kaye and since Simioni's son had callously disregarded this amendment much to his own detriment; the jury had no choice but to pass the verdict that ... *akwapulidwe basi* – so goes the Malawian "Parent-Child" Contract.

For my British Auntie this was straight out a horror movie worse than Freddy Krueger chasing the girl in 'A Nightmare on Elm Street'.

"Is someone going to call the police? He is killing that child." She pleaded, pain visibly showing all over her face.

"No, he is just teaching the child some kitchen manners, he is not going to kill his own child" I reassured my British Auntie wondering why she was hyper-ventilating on such trivialities and matters that were between a father serving parental justice to a son who had momentarily meandered on the wrong side of the strict Malawian kitchen law.

I later learnt that in UK it is illegal for a parent to spank a child. That it is against the child's human rights. I told her that in my culture a parent was always right. If you had to be spanked on the bum, it meant you had done something to deserve that walloping.

"Look at me Auntie, why do you think I turned out this way?" I proudly told Auntie.

"You mean your Daddy used to spank you? Oooh! you poor thing" she looked at me as if trying to see if I was bruised from the walloping I received when I was still a boy, during the age when I used to exhibit all the naughtiness compatible with the age of boyhood.

Of course spanking was part of growing up. If you misbehaved while your parent was still at work it was the responsibility of the neighbour to spank you on your parent's behalf. The neighbour would then tell your parent and depending on the gravity of the crime you had committed, chances were that you would get "Spanking Part 2"

I thought about my growing up. Did I turn up this way by accident or was it because once in a while I was beaten like a punch bag. I doubted if it was by accident. And it wasn't just me, even *azichimwene anganso* got the taste of *lamba wa Madala*. When you are young you know it yourself when you are being naughty, I remember once pulling on my little sister's hair for no apparent reason.

It was moments like these that served as a reminder that I had earned all my spanking sessions that followed my naughtiness. I deserved what I got and if I hadn't been nudged back to the path of righteousness by those frequent spankings, the probability of me ending up like some *chimbalangondo* was pretty high. Spanking sure kept me on the straight and narrow path just as did my siblings, especially my elder brother, *Achimwene aku Ntcheu*.

One time my brother (who we now call *Achimwene aku Ntcheu*) pinched my cheek around 2pm after I had called him a baboon. I withheld my crying until 5:30pm when I knew that *Madala* would be arriving back from work. The minute he walked through the door, I cried my lungs out, as if I had just been stabbed in the cheek at 5:29pm, ranting on my brother.

"*Chimwene wandimenya*," I sobbed holding my cheek as if it was on fire even though I felt no pain at all.

Madala took off his belt and *Chimwene* dashed for the door. They circled the house twice, but it was always like Usain Bolt chasing a one legged baby ... we heard the belt ... we heard the screams...

"*Ndidziku-uza kangati kuti mphwako si saizi yako*!!!" Madala's angry voice (with that familiar Barry White bass) could be heard throughout the whole neighbourhood just as *Chimwene's* cries could be heard throughout the neighbourhood as far out as the market.

I had my moments too, like the time I failed my standard-6 examination at primary school. All my friends were celebrating but I stood there wetting my *khakhi kabudula* uniform. Friends rushed home to show off their school reports to their respective parents while I stood there by the roadside looking at our house dreading what awaited my Fail grade. My bladder was actually oozing out its liquid contents uncontrollably. I heard my sister excitedly sell me out,

"*Makala wangoima kunseu akudzikodzela*" I heard that tiny traitor voice of hers. What followed next was a lesson on how not to fail your Standard-6 examination.

Although lessons of how to behave in my house were taught using *lamba*, I look back at those days with pride, the painful physical side to it is all but a blurry memory that hardly features at all. It's the outcome that matters. Even at my age I still treat my elders the way they should be treated, the way *lamba wa Madala* taught me how to. Maybe it's the reason why I still give my seat on the bus to an elderly people, maybe it's why I politely make way for those who are older than me... it surely has to be *lamba wa Madala*.

I looked at my British Auntie who was crying uncontrollably at the pounding that was taking place across the road.

"Easy, easy Auntie that child will be grateful for the lesson – you are probably looking at the future General Manager or president of Malawi", I reassured Auntie.

I remember when Amalume had just gotten back from abroad, he told us how unruly and misbehaved children in the UK are. You find kids congregating at bus shelters in the evening, drinking cheap beer and cider, commencing to smash up the bus shelters. Some go to extremes and start stabbing each other or innocent bystanders. These stabbings are not confined to bus-shelters or dark alleys alone; unfortunately they are also taking place at school playgrounds whereby knives tend to come out during fights which often end in fatalities.

Mother was so shocked and in a state of disbelief, she didn't really believe that such travesty could be taking place elsewhere on this planet.

"What kind of a twelve year old carries a knife to school?" Mother asked and I knowingly answered while looking at her briefly and then at Auntie deliberately.

"A kind that has never been spanked or straightened up by a nice long leather belt" the words came out directed at Auntie who cringed and recoiled as if she was about to be whiplashed with a belt.

Agogo had once suggested that just as the UK exported Big Brother to Africa we should reciprocate and export some of these lessons in "spanking" over to these western countries, this would ensure that they too reap the benefits of how *chikwapu* can shape and straighten up an individual and a nation in the long run.

"Have you seen how polite the American president is? Have you seen the pictures of the President's Kenyan father? Does he look like a man who takes nonsense? Do you think the most powerful president in the world is polite by accident?" Agogo claims and I agree with him.

Don't get me wrong, am not condoning brutality here... *ayi*. There is a line that separates punishment and *nkhanza* and that line shouldn't be crossed. If a parent had a bad day at work or his team lost and he decides to break the ribs of his child, that's *nkhanza*. But surely if a parent came home and caught his child sticking his little hand inside the wife's purse or handbag while she was taking a bath, surely that warrants a marathon around the house. And whatever happens after the father catches him...happens, or as we say in our vernacular, *chichitike-chichitike*.

This, then, brings me back to Simioni and his son. He still had his son pinned down to the ground with his knee on the poor boy's chest, like the way you straddle a chicken before slaughtering it. I yelled at Simioni in

Chichewa to make sure that my Auntie didn't understand what I was saying so as not freak her out even more

"*Dzulonso anabweretsa azinzake ameneyo ku-maonela* Blue Movie *iwe uli kuntchito*" I sprayed Doom to the already volatile situation. As soon as I said this I grabbed Auntie by the hand and quickly pulled her inside the house. I knew that the spanking that was about to be dished out by Simioni was going to X-rated for my Auntie's eyes or ears.

I grabbed the TV remote control increased the volume to drown out the screams coming from outside. Good thing they were showing Matofotofo on TVM which made me think, surely this is another thing that Africa can export abroad; Matofotofo and Spanking.

MALAWIAN CULTURE COLLIDES
WITH THE WEST

Last week Agogo was very excited after the interview given by the great Inkosi ya Makosi, blasting the government's draconian moves against Polygamy. Of course this shouldn't surprise most of you that my family is pro-*mitala* as can be seen by the multiple wives that some of my many uncles have. The fact that I come from a tribe that eats anything that bleeds (except human meat) should also tell you that my tribe and the tribe of the great Inkosi are highly correlated in some way.

According to the argument given by Inkosi, how could the government go ahead in executing such a far reaching law when that law impacts the very essence of our traditions and culture?

It was barely five minutes after the Inkosi gave his pro-*mitala* interview on TVM that Auntie's cell phone started ringing non-stop. Her friends from UK who had apparently been watching TV couldn't believe their ears. To them this is barbarism that beggars belief, a defilement of the whole female institution. They queried, how can a culture be so primitive and so backward to condone such degrading acts of marrying more than one wife?

Auntie tried to convey this to Agogo that she couldn't understand how the great Inkosi could use tradition and culture as an argument for *mitala*. Auntie claims that she has now lived in the country for some time but still found Inkosi's remarks unacceptable and her friends in the UK who have never been to these parts of the world concur with her wholeheartedly.

I sat there, quietly chewing my piece of *chipalapatilo*, digesting what Auntie was saying. She was British and there is no way she was going to allow her mind to think like that of Inkosi or anyone who is pro-*mitala*. I could see how difficult and problematic it is for someone of a different cultural upbringing to see and accept things from an alien culture.

I wanted to draw parallels by telling Auntie that while it is normal for a British youth to address his/her elders by their first name, it was unheard of and rude for a Malawian youth to call his/her elders on first name basis. But Auntie was so upset and I never got a chance to raise this point with her.

Yesterday as soon I walked in the house from the Bawo tournament, I noticed and felt some tension. The verdict on the gay couple had just been passed and Auntie was none the happier. "There is nothing wrong with homosexuality," she argued tears welling in her eyes. "It's just two consenting adults," she moaned. I remember last month she had told us that homosexuality was part of Western culture. There is even a place called "Gay Village" in Manchester UK where people go *kukanyauda* heavy.

Even powerful politicians are openly gay and she gave the examples that ranged from the recent Minister of Trade – Peter Mandelson – who was the most powerful minister in Gordon Browns government (and ironically could have been responsible for some of the British financial aid that Malawi got.) She also told us how in 2009, Iceland became the first country in the world to elect an openly gay leader called Johanna Sigurdardottir.

You could see Auntie was really trying to tell us, especially Agogo, that in Europe gay people are part of their culture and it was normal for them to co-exist side by side with everyone. But I could tell that Agogo perceived Auntie's rantings as someone desperately clutching at straws.

My small brain started digesting all this. Here was a British woman who cannot understand the culture and traditions surrounding polygamy. To Auntie, and most Western people, polygamy is simply primitive and barbaric. As far as they are concerned, culture should not be used to support such acts of marrying more than one wife.

I looked at Agogo, who sat there rolling his big *ndudu ya fodya*, happy because of the verdict. Here was a man who could not accept that homosexuality can be a norm of culture. In his eyes he couldn't understand what kind of culture allows two men to exchange intimacy? According to Agogo these two men deserved what they got from the courts, he even went as far as saying 14 years was a bit lenient, they should have gotten life or better still, the firing squad.

I looked at Amalume for help and ideas, since he has the privilege of experiencing both cultures, having lived in the West all those years. "Why is it that the West thinks that our cultural ways are unacceptable? Why do we think the same about theirs? Are our two cultures that different Amalume?" I asked without pausing between questions; "For example I have noticed that you address your brother-in-law on the phone by his first name Graham not as *Alamu?*"

Surely if we can't see a common ground on minor issues as how we address and call each other, there is no way in a million years will we ever reconcile all this homosexuality – polygamy jinx.

Amalume had no answers for me but I knew that this issue wasn't going to go away in my family. I hear that in the whole Malawian community the debate on this polygamy and especially on homosexuality is raging with much ferocity and tempo.

I noticed that some of my young nephews and nieces who are a bit exposed to the ways of the West, (via BET, CNN and Sky) are somehow liberal and exhibit some signs of compassion towards the two convicted gay couple. It is the same young ones who tend to side with Auntie on the anti-*mitala* debate.

But most of my Uncles who went up in arms when the government first announced that it will be clamping down on polygamy are the same uncles who were celebrating when the gay couple sentence was passed, and vociferously called for the two to be hanged, literally.

This debate is going on in so many Malawian homes, churches, work-places across the country and beyond. It's really hard to gauge or sense which way the winds are blowing because this is one topic where people will say one thing in public and say another in private.

Shasha, for example, who has travelled extensively tends to swing back and forth (*ngati katungwe*) depending on the audience at hand. In the presence of my uncles or elders he is the first one saying these two should be crucified and burnt to ashes. But when he is talking to his friends abroad on his blackberry, you hear him saying;

"Bro, I dun no why the gov and some peeps are dissing them two Niggaz, they ain't harm no motherfucking fly. This country is whack yo."

In my family each side, (pro or anti) has got its valid arguments and stick to them. Auntie's arguments will not convince Agogo to change his mind and neither will Agogo rantings make Auntie see things through a Malawian prism.

There is a high probability that if ex-Minister Peter Mandelson and his Brazilian male lover were to come to Malawi and flaunt their love affair in public, they would probably face the long arm of Malawi's law. And it's also likely that if Inkosi ya Makosi was to go to Britain tomorrow and start preaching polygamy in the middle of Trafalgar Square, he will also be prosecuted.

At the end of the day it's the rules of that particular country that matter most. Even when Jacob Zuma, head of State, went to UK recently, he only took one wife with him, *azungu sachedwa kunjata pa nkhani za* two or more marriage certificates... and *bambo* Zuma had to respect the laws of that land.

In a world of disappearing borders it is a bit confusing which culture has got it right and which one has goofed big time. I reached out for a second helping of my favourite *dzipalapatilo* and a few chicken heads as thoughts about culture still permeated and troubled my mind. I recalled what Amalume had once said to us that in *maiko akunja* it is against their culture to serve *dzipalapatilo* and chicken heads at the table. While here in Malawi it is against our culture for me to tell Agogo to get out of my house and go and smoke outside. *Koma abale inu, ife ndi anthu osiyanadi eti*?

THOBWA AND THE MISSING
REVERSE BUTTON

Mother says that back in the day all women knew how to brew *thobwa* but she worries that these brewing skill are on the decline. Auntie counters that most modern women are career oriented and wouldn't really be bothered on the nuances of *thobwa* brewing.

"After all most of their men don't even care about this primitive drink and are rather more interested in modern exotic drinks that come in glass bottles or cans." Auntie claims.

It would be a mistake to dismiss Auntie's claims as mumblings of a foreigner because nowadays more and more Malawian women seem to be at par with Auntie's line of thought. Hence most modern women would care less about learning the art of thobwa brewing. And as more and more Malawians fan out across the globe in search of greener pastures, for studies, for marriages or simply for the heck of it, one can predict the demise of Thobwaology with certainty.

In my family, though (despite all this globalisation), *thobwa* still tops the charts of soft drinks and that is why it's still brewed in bucketfuls. Females in my family are still lectured from a young age on the techniques and skills required to execute this tradition of turning *mapila* into a thirst quenching beverage. Even my British Auntie, who thinks little of this traditional drink, has been getting a quick-course in Thobwaology from the women professors of the Amoto family. *Jelasi* down for a white lady, Auntie has really amazed us all. If ever there was a graduation at the end of this *thobwa* course she would be graduating with a (First Class) Distinction.

According to Mother; the problem with *thobwa* brewing is that there is a very thin line that separates it from being a delicious soft drink to turning into a potent alcoholic beverage. She claims that if the fermentation process is miscalculated, *thobwa* can suddenly turn into *mowa* with intoxicating capabilities higher than those found in your daily Carlsberg or Bud and similar to your Malawi Gin or Russian Vodka.

This is exactly what happened with the *thobwa* we were drinking today, that delicate line had been crossed placing it squarely in the Vodka league. The result was that even those members of my family who usually sit quite during conversation were today flapping their mouths, laughing at everything and anything, *za mowa zenizeni*.

Simioni's madam is one of those people who hardly talks, but today that was not the case. She is a very educated lady and a boss at bank *ijayi ya ntauni ija*. Because of her position she tends to be serious and hardly talks to her juniors at work on matters not pertaining to work and she does not chit-chat *ndi anthu wamba* at home. But today's *twobwa laululu* was about to change all that because she said something which got the whole room thinking and scratching heads. Being a very educated woman I wasn't sure whether it was her intelligence or the effects *thobwa loledzeletsali* that was inducing the words that were about to spill out of her lipstick mouth.

"I wish I could go back in time and learn how to cook and brew *thobwa,*" she said it with a slight slur of someone who had been sipping on something that had over fermented. It's not a secret that Madam Simioni, albeit being the big boss at the bank, does not cook at her home. She has dedicated her time to her career and can't be bothered with the nuances of house-wifeology.

This explains why Simioni is always at my house for breakfast, lunch, supper and all the snacks in between. Simioni spends more time at my house than I do, but our friendship goes long way back and I have never thought of sending him a bill for all the food he has consumed at my house although Agogo once suggested I do. Just last week after Simioni had picked a piece of chicken which Agogo had also been eyeing and my 102 years old Gramps snapped, making a remark that made all of us pause chewing.

"*Koma ndiye mukunenepatu.*" He said it with so much sarcasm that the insinuation was not even lost on the younger members of the Amoto family. But Simioni wasn't fazed, he knew that there was no food at his house and he wasn't going to let Agogo make him give up his only source of daily nourishment. 'If only his wife could cook for him,' I thought to myself.

I digested what Madam Simioni said, and thought about the aspect of 'going back in time.' I had no idea why my mind was intrigued by that aspect, maybe it was due to the effects of the nine cups of the *thobwa* I had consumed. I found myself rumbling as if I was possessed and my mouth was going on and on as if it was detached from my brain.

"We are all given the power to shape our future from an early age and yet the future is the big unknown to all of us. No one knows with certainty what's going to happen tomorrow, let alone next week. And yet we spend a lot of resources, money and energy fighting for a better future. Our whole life is programmed in getting us ready for what lies ahead. We start with the pursuit of knowledge, the accumulation of material things, the search for life spouses and we even go as far as having children. We do this even though no one knows whether that child will become a Nelson Mandela or will turn out a Mike Tyson." I took a slight pause to have another sip, realising that everyone in the room was looking at me with the same intensity the congregation looks at its Pastor. My *thobwa* induced tongue was on a roll here so I carefully set the half empty glass on the table before continuing.

"All these pursuits are a gamble because we don't know whether they will turn out positive. For example, look at Shasha," I slurred while gesturing at my friend who sat there looking at me.

"He is been all over the world and came back home with nothing tangible apart from fifty pairs of jeans and more base-ball hats than the whole Chicago Sox players combined." I could see a few smiles in the room at this remark. Were they really smiling or was I just imagining the smiles. Damn this *thobwa*, I cursed to myself before continuing.

"Now look at Madam Simioni, a highly educated woman who makes more money than half the men in this room and yet she envies her *ntsikana wantchito's* children." I paused looking at Simioni's Madam who was smiling and nodding in agreement.

"Life took them, just as it takes everyone, on different trajectories. We all do our best to plan for the future but never know what we will end up with." I paused for another long sip.

"Everyone has got regrets, Shasha wishes he had built a house and maybe bought a car. Madam Simioni wishes she had dedicated some time learning how to cook and born some children for her husband," I paused again for another sip but the cup never made it to my lips because I started rumbling again. I tend to do this quiet a lot.

"Why did God set things out in such a way? Letting us deal with the unknown future?" I took a short pause as if expecting God to answer me, but after realising that there wasn't going to be an answer forthcoming I pressed on.

"Everyone knows their past but nobody knows their future. Poor people have no idea if they will ever get rich before being buried six-feet under and on the same token rich people do not know if their riches will see them to the end." I paused to let this rather awkward illustration sink in.

"Even Mike Tyson at the peak of his career had no idea that one day he will be poor. Such is the mystery of the future – the inability to predict it. If only God had given us a '*Reverse*' button on life." my *thobwa* brain made me say and I paused, struggling to hear what had just come out of my own mouth. If I couldn't make sense of my own words, did anyone in the room make sense of what I was mumbling about? Who cares? So I carried on, high on the disorienting effects of thobwa that were increasing in intensity.

"Couldn't it have been better if we had the power to work on our past, instead of messing with the unknown future? Imagine if it was possible for Madam Simioni to go back in time and learn how to cook for Simioni. Imagine if Shasha could go back in time and do something worthwhile with all the money he earned while working abroad instead of spending it on designer clothes? Imagine if the Mike Tyson's of this world and all of us had a 'Reverse' button on life."

I looked at the blurry faces that were staring back at me with blank looks, I couldn't quite make out who was who because the room had started to spin, not too fast, but spinning is spinning. I thought to myself, wow! This thobwa sure packs a punch, and carried on with my seminar.

"Life would have had zero regrets because we all would have shaped it the way we want it to be. I, for one, would have pressed my 'Reverse' button to fix a few things," people were nodding in agreement to this, were they really nodding or was it the thobwa that was making me think they were nodding?

"In primary school I constantly ridiculed, embarrassed and made fun of this one boy who now happens to be the big man at the passport office. Because I don't have a 'Reverse' button that is why my dozen attempts of applying for a passport have all ended in *Declined.*" This revelation caused the whole room to burst out laughing, they already knew that my attempts to leave the country for greener pastures have always been frustrated by the failure to get a passport in my name, but every time I brought it up, they always cracked up so I waited for them to stop laughing before continuing.

"Take for instance *Achemwali aku Bangula,* I am sure if she had a 'Reverse' button she would have used it so that she could marry the boy she rejected while in Form-2." I didn't have to tell the room that this boy turned out to be a prominent Pastor and respected member of the community. Everybody knew this and often chided *Achemwali aku Bangula* for missing on this jackpot, especially that she ended up marrying a man who uses her as a punching bag every night he comes home drunk. The words came out of my mouth like sharp needles as my red watery eyes zoomed in where *Achemwali aku Bangula* was sitting.

"The future is tricky, it throws all these tests at us and if you make the wrong decision the consequences can be catastrophic. Ask Shasha who has been reduced to selling off his nice sneaker shoes just to raise transport money," the whole room turned its gaze in Shasha's direction.

I know I was talking like this due to the effects of the *thobwa* but I wasn't the only one thinking this way.

Tchale's fifty-five year old British partner said she would definitely have used her 'Reverse' button so that she shouldn't have given birth to a child when she was only fifteen years old. Her first born child is now forty which makes it a bit awkward because Tchale (her lover) is only eighteen; I started seeing why she too would have welcomed the privilege of having a "Reverse" button.

Of course there are other *abale ndi alongo* whose lives are perfect, they dreamt of becoming astronauts and they now work for NASA, they married the perfect person, live in a perfect house, their kids go to perfect schools and get the perfect grades, in short everything is just so perfect for them. But for most of us we wish there was that 'Reverse' button that would at least give us the power of going back in time to change and make a few minor adjustments.

Everyone knows where in their past they went wrong and what needs rectifying. Yes there are those who claim that they wouldn't change a thing because the mistakes they made in their past turned them into a better person. What a bunch of crap this is. Why would you want to do something wrong first before doing something right? Why not nail it right in the first go? I remember I started respecting dogs after one had almost eaten my thigh. But if I had a choice I would chosen to earn a dog's respect without having to go through the whole scary rabies painful experience. To say that being bitten was a good learning experience is a load of crap in its purest form.

Imagine how life would have turned out for most people it they had just listened to the Arithmetic teacher more, instead of thinking what time was break. Imagine how life would have turned out if you had hooked up with that quite boring girl or boy instead of chasing after the one everyone was talking about. Maybe start thinking of being your own person instead of floating on Daddy's wealth.

But I am sure there is a strong and good reason why were never given the "Reverse" button on life. But I also know that if we had *ka rivesi batani*, we would all have been a happier and content people.

Thobwa lili boo ili and if you are sitting there contemplating on life's 'Reverse' button or giving this whole talk a serious thought, then you must have been drinking Makala Amoto's intoxicating *thobwa* too.

WOMEN TRYING TO MOVE A MOUNTAIN

According to Amalume the recent Cabinet of the Conservative government in UK is made up of only (white) men and four women *basi* which, Amalume claims, represents only 17% of the total cabinet. Auntie has always cried foul at how women are severely underrepresented especially if one equates the cabinet's male-female composition to the male-female ratio of the whole UK society. She had a valid point there, although she forgot to mention that there isn't a single black person in the whole cabinet, but I felt like saying this would be diverting away from the point she was trying to make, which was the plight of women.

It was quite a revelation for me to learn that even in UK women are still fighting for their rights. I thought of my Malawian sisters and wondered if things pertaining to equality have really changed for them? I tried to stretch my memory as far back as I could to see if there has been any convergence of the male-female positions. Has it just been cosmetics or have women really moved closer to the rights enjoyed by their male counterparts?

Agogo seems to think so; he often backs his chauvinistic stance with a rather shallow argument whenever the gender issue comes up.

"*Ndimayesa masiku ano azimayi akuvalano ma* trousers." He had a point there, but I didn't want to clarify it to him that women's rights went beyond just wearing trousers or miniskirts. I know there are those who will claim that the dawn of a trouser-wearing female in Malawi was a Rosa Park moment.

You really can't argue with the fact that burning their *dzitenje* and sticking their legs into trousers was a liberating step for a lot of Malawian sisters.

But in the grand scheme of things the issue about trousers is a mere side show when one looks at the bigger obstacles that loom in front of women vis-à-vis corporate glass ceiling(s) which women find themselves bumping into. I don't know for sure how many female General Managers sit on the helm of Malawi's businesses nor am I aware of the composition of the male/female ratio of our Cabinet. To figure this out (so that I can present an intelligent argument to you) would take up a lot of time and honestly speaking my tiny tired brain is not inclined to go down this path. There is a high probability that some learned and highly qualified Malawians will dismiss my arguments as shallow and lacking in substance. So for the sake of simplicity (and the fear of clashing with these Malawian Einsteins) I will latch on to this trouser issue and use it to illustrate how women are still struggling in catching up with their male counter-parts.

The question then we should ask is; "Are women in Malawi 'really' free to wear trousers of their choice?" I ask this question because of an incident that happened last week when I went in town with Amalume to go *kukasunzumila* on his minibus by the rank.

Those *abale ndi alongo* not familiar with minibus business, "*kukasunzumila*" is another word for spying on your driver to make sure that he is doing his job, and that he has paid *anyamata oyitanila ma* customers (commonly called *Ojiya* Minibus *kapena Majiyamen*). These drivers have got the habit of just parking idle on the rank (so that they can pocket the petrol money), blasting *kwasa-kwasa* music while sitting in your minibus with their friends whistling and jeering at passing girls. And they have the nerve of reporting to you at the end of their shift in the evening that "*lero kunathinana*" so as to justify the meagre takings generated on that day.

For those of you who have recently walked from the Blantyre bus stands – through the stalls of vendors (that were recently set on fire by *boma*) all the way to Mudi Bridge (near Blantyre market) you know how intimidating this short strip of land can be.

Someone once referred to this area as Afghanistan *ya pa Mudi*. This is the only place the whole of Blantyre where there are more vendors than customers, more thieves than victims and more merchandise from China you start thinking you are in Beijing. *Akamati* "Malawi *yalowa* China" this is where you can see it with your own eyes, this is the only China without Chinese people. It's the only China you won't hear any Mandarin being spoken and the chances of you meeting any person by the name of Wang Cheng Lee are zero, although you might hear rap tunes by the Wu-Tang Clan coming from the vendors' music boom boxes. Even though I like to think of this area a Chineseless-China, the merchandise on sale is enough to make you think you have just been dropped in the middle of Beijing.

It is the place where women walk while clutching their handbags close to their chest as if they are holding a baby. Even the men are not immune to the theft that is so ever prevalent here. This is the reason why my wallet is always securely tucked in between my trousers and my boxers when I visit this area. If someone is going to steal my hard earned cash they would have to undress me first. That's how intimidating this little Afghanistan in Blantyre is.

For those of you who left Malawi a long time ago (before Zinjanthropus was even born) and you still picture this area as the tranquil place simply known as *kuma Standi,* famous for romantic rendezvous during Kamuzu's crop inspection tours, forget that picture. If Mogadishu and Darfur were to have a baby that child would look like Afghanistan *wapa* Mudi River. It's not a place you go for romantic walks with your loved one anymore unless you are planning on breaking-up your affair in style (*Kuchithetsa mwa stailo*).

Having given you this rather bleak prologue you can imagine my surprise and shock when I saw this girl dressed in a pink jogging suit with the words "Yo Baby's Mama" emblazoned on her chest. She also had on matching pink tight jogging shorts with the words "Bootylicious" written across her Jenifer Lopez behind.

This might have been ok if she had been walking somewhere in Namiwawa or Area 43, but this was neither of the two. I really had a bad feeling about her being in this environment dressed like a Hoochie Mama while shaking her behind so obvious it was like looking at two balloons filled with some of that BP oil spilling out of the Gulf of Mexico.

Amalume was busy negotiating with a vendor to come down on price of this Ziggy Marley CD when I tapped him on the shoulder while pointing to Bootylicious. Amalume, who had managed to squeeze a 50% discount and was hoping for more, shook my hand off his shoulder dismissively telling me that *maiko akunja* a woman wearing tight jogging shorts with the words "Bootylicious" on her behind is a normal thing and no one would take notice or sweat over it. I told Amalume that *kuno nku Malawitu* women are still not that free to dress in clothes of their choice, there are still certain lines that shouldn't be crossed.

I remember Simioni, who did some correspondence studies on International Political Economy, once told me that the era from 1976 all the way up to 1985 was classified as the international Decade for Women but there are telltale signs that this era somehow bypassed Malawi altogether. Simply put, the concept of feminism missed this country completely evidenced by the fact that any man is free to wear jeans with the words; "Your *Mandingo* Lover" printed on his butt and no one would be bothered or feel apprehensive about it. Unfortunately this curtsey is not extended to my Malawian sisters, which is why the minute this girl entered Afghanistan *wapa Mudi* River, the whole place exploded as if an innocent cute cuddly rabbit had just been dropped in a cage full of starving lions.

Pandemonium commenced with *malikhwelu* from an army of drug dazed vendors and I immediately knew that this was going to get nasty. The rude chants started gathering momentum as vendors slowly converged around the poor girl, a cacophony of swear words and crude references spewing out of their over-stretched mouths. It was like watching an allied forces soldier (who had run out of bullets) in the middle of a market in Kandahar-Afghanistan surrounded by angry Taliban fighters armed with AK-47 assault rifles and explosive vests.

I told Amalume, who is respected by most of the vendors, "we need to do something." My Samaritan instincts came over me and we rushed towards the crowd, pushing ourselves through the circle of vendors who had completely surrounded the athletically-dressed girl.

You could see the loathing in their eyes and the profuse sweating due to excitement of seeing a girl dressed in such a way. It was difficult to tell whether their twisted rage was directed at how the girl was dressed or whether it was due to the fact that a girl like this was way out of their league.

Machipisi, a big-mean looking vendor who fries and sells the most unhealthy but delicious chips the whole of Blantyre appeared to be their leader. He is simply referred to as 'Chips Technician' and he annoyingly but respectfully looked at Amalume as if we had just spoiled their party

"Bwana, kodi Madamuwa ali ndi inu?" Machipisi who was standing right next to the scared girl growled at us.

Amalume had to lie through his teeth forgetting that very sacred commandment Thou Shalt not Lie, but maybe telling a lie if you know that such lie is going to save a life is not such a bad gig afterall

"*Tamusiyeni uyu ndi mwana wanga wangobwela kumene kuchokela kunja*" Amalume said as the petrified girl looked at my Uncle as if he was *Mose* and immediately started crying tears of relief.

Like a military General, Machipisi barked on top of his voice to his battalion of vendors.

"Guys, *asiyeni madamuwa adutse, ndi mwana wa a* Biggie *uyu.*" The vendors who respect and fear Machipisi as if he is Idi Amin Dada made way for the trembling and shaken-up girl. We watched her walk away *mwandawala* until the "Bootylicious" letters on her J-Lo behind disappeared from our view.

As she disappeared from view in the direction of Mandala I couldn't help but wonder about women's freedom to dress and how it conflicts with the expectations of our culture. There are some women who will tell you that the threat of vendors is their biggest worry just like Bootylicious girl had found out.

When we got home later on that evening and explained what had just transpired at Afghanistan *wapa* Mudi, Agogo simply dismissed us alleging that she had deserved every insult that was dished at her.

"*Zofuna zake ameneyo*" he said in a 'you-get-what-you-ask-for' tone of voice. Of course views like these are to be expected from someone of my Agogo's age and anyone who is still fiercely cultural and cling on to the ways of the past.

Simioni, who is a strong advocate for women's issues once said that "females have got a long way to go especially when you consider that two-thirds of a billion illiterate people are women", a fact which coming from my learned friend Simioni must have had some validity to it. And the more you listen to Simioni talk about the plight of women, the more you start feeling that the male dominated society as a whole is against women; and judging by what happened by Mudi River I was beginning to think he had a point.

But strange enough not all women would side with Bootylicious. There are some women in my family who are church elders, *amayi amvano, amayi* a Dorica etc and claim that there is a certain way a woman should dress. According to them a Malawian woman should always dress "appropriately", although that word is open to debate.

Simioni claims that the whole game is balanced in favour of men and disadvantages the females. He argues that "How come we see all these fashionable young men walking around with trousers that hang so low you can see the rest of their underwear? But you don't see them being harassed"

Simioni had a point there, never in my whole life have I ever seen a mob of *mavenda achizimayi* chasing a young boy because he is dressed in a way that gets them so worked up. I could just visualise how intimidating it would be if a man was to be surrounded by *azimayi ogulitsa dzigumuyoyo* and *dzikondamoyo* chanting and yelling obscenities, to the point of wanting to molest and rape him.

The more I thought about the "Bootylicious" girl incident the more I realised that like the new Conservative government in UK which is dominated by men, here in

Malawi and elsewhere *azimayi ndi asungwana* still have a long way to go. Simioni articulated it better when he threw a question:

"Name 5 presidents in the whole world who are female?" he said while observing the whole room for any takers. But there was simply this loud silence, until Agogo raised his hand like a Standard 4 Primary student:

"Winnie Mandela" Agogo said with a cheeky smile on his 102 year old face. The whole house exploded into laughter, *nthungululu* and chants:

"*Lulululululululululu* ... Agogoooooooooooo!!" and I had to laugh too, but Simioni was the only one who was not laughing and we all stopped laughing and looked at his serious face. In a quite but tense voice, Simioni told us that we wouldn't be laughing if we knew the realities facing the female species.

"In a space of 100 years they have only been twenty-four females elected as head of state and that only one percent of land in the world is possessed by women", my friend lectured us in a sombre voice. If it was anyone else saying this, I would have thought they were just yanking my chain, but coming from my academically adept friend I knew these must be factual details he was spewing at us. I really felt sorry for all my Malawian sisters just as I had felt sorry for Bootylicious.

Later on that night I thought of my Malawian sisters abroad who are planning on visiting Malawi for holidays or to change their passport details or simply to get married. If you are a fashionista and have got clothes that you know will arouse unnecessary attention, just be careful where you plan to walk. The world is dominated by too many males with the mentality of guys like Chips Technician the Vendor. This means that women will continuously have a mountain to climb here in Malawi and so too elsewhere. Those who disagree only have to look at the female-starved UK Conservative cabinet or go talk to jogging Bootylicious girl who we rescued at Afghanistan *ya pa* Mudi.

AKUNJA AND AKUMUDZI

Amalume was just telling us how *ku maiko akunjawa,* the issue tax tends to dominate their current affairs. In America most people believe that they will be paying higher taxes due to the recent Health Care Bill and in UK wealthy people threaten of transferring their investments to countries that have a more lenient tax regime than that of UK.

For the sake of not wanting Malawi to be left of this tax issue, Simioni jumped in saying that word on the street is that here in Nyasaland, women entrepreneurs who specialise in selling sex will also have to start paying *misonkho* (tax.) I had a feeling this was going to turn into a healthy debate until Shasha barged in through the door interrupting and changing the whole tax mood.

"*Kodi iwe,* how many times should I tell you *kuti udzigogoda?*" I confronted him because I was actually interested to hear more about what Simioni had to say about these so called hookers paying tax.

"Ma bad...ma bad bro," is all what Shasha could utter, whatever 'ma-bad' meant.

Lately Shasha has been looking miserable and sad. Rumour has it that he has sold most of his clothes, shoes, DVDs and pretty much everything that he brought with him from abroad. Because of his dwindling wardrobe he has even stopped going to these weekly weddings *pajatu kuno dzikwati ndi lololo.* Unfortunately Shasha's lack of *mphasha* means that he is no longer the centre of attraction at any gathering – *chikwati, chinkhoswe* or even at our weekly *Bawo* tournaments.

As a matter of fact he has become a source of ridicule for most people, especially those *abale ndi alongo* who look down upon Malawians from abroad. The more you open your ears wide, the more you start hearing whispers of war – a cold war that is raging between *akumudzi ndi akunja* and Shasha's plight has brought this to the fore.

Two weeks ago someone approached Shasha ku *chikwati cha mwana wa Asisi aku Dowa* during *perekani-perekani,*

"*Inu munangotayako nthawi kunjako, palibe tiwona ife apa,*" this guy sarcastically chided our friend. Shasha who is short tempered almost jumped on this guy and we had to hold him back.

Shasha is our friend and we love him to bits, but this guy, albeit mouthing off something that was unwarranted, somehow he had a point. Shasha is just like one of the many returning prodigal sons and daughters who arrive here and cause a stir in the first few weeks or months at parties but then start asking for handouts once their forex runs out, *zawathela.*

Shasha, so it seems, got the wrong data while he was still abroad by jumping at someone's advice,

"*Amwene bwelani kumudzi, zinthu zikuyenda masiku ano,*" and sure enough Shasha packed his suitcases with clothes, i-pod, Playstation 2 and 3, a Blackberry and DVD's then bought a ticket for Malawi without any game plan.

My advice to those in Diaspora is always return home when you think you have accomplished your mission abroad, not when someone who is in Malawi tells you; "*bwelani* Malawi *yatukuka*," because most of them *akufuna mukatuwile limodzi.*

And neither should you listen to someone who is also abroad together with you encouraging you that; "*pitani Bambo*, my brother who is Malawi says *kuti zinthu zikuyenda kumenek.*" Ask yourself this, *iyeyo ngati achimwene ake* says *kuti* things are running back home, how come he is not buying a one way ticket? How come he has picked up double shifts for the whole year including half of next year *m'malo momanyamuka poti zinthu zikuthamanga kumudzi?* The answer is that *akufuna muchepeko kunjako, kuti aphange ma shifiti onse iyeyo.* Shasha, stupid enough, ended up listening to *manon'gon'go ngati amenewa* and came back with no game plan, no strategy whatsoever.

This seems to be the problem of many prodigal sons and daughters returning to Saigon (Malawi), they blindly fly in *ndi timasutikesi tawo* without having laid out their long-term strategies or short-term tactical plans on how they are going to sustain themselves while trying to maintain the standard of living they got used to while abroad. Some would classify that as: *kubwerela mwaumbulimbuli.*

It's 100% true, *zinthu zikuyenda*, but it's also 100% true life is tough in Malawi, perhaps tougher than it was years ago. Now, there are so many educated Malawians chasing very few jobs, never in Malawi's history has the job market been as competitive as it is now. I remember during my father's time, for those coming back from abroad chances of getting a job were somewhere in the regions of 99%. Nowadays you have to have something uniquely special to compete with fellow job seekers or applicants who are either home grown graduates, foreign trained graduates or simply *ana a Uje* whose father or mother are on first name basis with the President. It's tough and it's ugly and anyone who tells you that life in Malawi is like Las Vegas, either hates you dearly or has been smoking those cigarettes that happen to be illegal on both sides of the border.

Shasha is now talking of heading back abroad because he doesn't see any potential here, an observation which is not 100% true, because there are people who will tell you that life is good in here in Malawi. *Ena zikuwayendera mwaliwilo...ma* program *awo agwira nseu.*

You just have to look at this boy who *mwana wa Asisi* was marrying. He manages his family's business; we know that his family own a fleet of about forty or so tankers, they own properties in the most exclusive areas of Lilongwe and Mzuzu – and there is an unsubstantiated rumour that they want to buy Delamere House in Blantyre.

"*Koma anthu amazitenga kuti ndalama?*" one Malawian was overheard asking. This is one of the most common questions in Malawi, but no one has yet come up with a convincing answer. Simply because if all knew where *omwe zikuwayendela* get their money from, we would all be singing *lokoma ambuye*. A balanced society must comprise of the haves and the have-nots... *asilizi ndi asilizidwe... Eeeetu eeeee.*

Just looking at the cars outside the wedding reception hall, one would think it was an American/ British/Germany dealership with all the shiny-gleaming 4x4s, Hummers, Chrysler 300's, latest BMW's with lazy dropping eyes, dolphin shaped Mercedes' and executive Jaguars (and my Morris Marina of course.)

One wedding goer even commented; "*koma Malawi abale inu?*" He didn't have to say much, you could extrapolate whatever you wanted from that short sentence and you would still arrive at the same juncture. There is that Malawi that people read like a fairy tale novel and then there is the Malawi that Shasha was going through right now, the impoverished one. *Umphawi wadzaoneni* whereby Shasha was a *nsilizidwe* or *namasilila* someone English speaking people would classify as: 'The Admirer'.

Shasha told us how life is so rewarding abroad, if you put in the time you get rewarded. He talked of how at one time he had three cars, one for work, one for *mapemphelo* and one for going out to parties or barbeques.

"*Musatelo Che Shasha,*" Mother had to remark, she was surprised that Shasha was actually going to church while he had been abroad, but what surprised her even more was that Shasha used to have a keychain which had a car key on it. Apparently in Obamaland he really had more than one vehicle, this is a fact that has been substantiated by some Malawians who used to be his friends and still residing in South Bend.

But since he came back, Shasha has been a frequent minibus addict. They know him at the rank and he has even started getting on minibuses and paying his fare by giving the drivers DVD's in what can only be classified as barter type of trading – goods in exchange for a service. An action or kung-fu DVD allows him a full week minibus access but a romantic DVD only buys him 2 days of free minibus ride.

We could see why Shasha was starting to despise and hate Malawi. He even started thinking that everyone hates him because he just got back from abroad.

Shasha is convinced that one cannot make it in life here, without resorting to shortcuts and *katangale*. This is not entirely true because you find people like Simioni's wife, a very successful manager at one of the many banks here, whose life of a lucrative and illustrious career disapproves the theory that all is doom and gloom in Malawi.

There are many like her who are not complaining; for example *Achemwa* aku Road Traffic or *Alamu apa* Mwanza border. At the end of the day Malawi is like a coin with two sides; heads and tails, a country of 'Admirers' and the 'Admired' with no in-betweens.

The "heads" aka 'The Admired,' go about their business, eating bread dipped in honey and caviar imported from abroad, while the "Tails" aka 'The Admirers' are constantly screaming: "blue murder! This is a cursed poverty stricken country the how come we don't have enough money to see us up to the second day of the month."

How the "Heads" are able to stay afloat in this country is not the issue at hand here, the point being made is that Malawi, like it has already been stipulated above, comprises of the Haves and Have-nots.

Amalume calmly told Shasha that life is not about where you are, but what you make of it. He talked of his own experiences while abroad. While *maiko akunja* might appear glossy and might reward hard work, he had some friends who *zinthu sizimawayendela*. On both sides of the border you will find those who eat sausages and those who don't. Amalume spoke with conviction.

"I cannot stand here and tell you that everyone who is outside Malawi *akumwa nkaka* that would be a blatant lie." Amalume said to us and this was new to me because I thought it always rains milk in these countries abroad.

"Even those who drink milk eight days a week will tell you that milk does not come easy because they have to work hard and sometimes they work long anti-social hours in the night," Amalume shocked us.

"And not all Malawians abroad are accountants just like here at home not all Malawians are Managers too." He said not clearly elaborating, but leaving the rest to our imagination.

He carried on his lecture on life, looking at Shasha as he spoke, as if he was trying to save a single lost soul amongst many.

"Right now there are a lot of Malawians who are dreaming of getting a Visa and disappearing *kuma* greener pastures. And yet there are Malawians abroad who have had enough and cannot wait to come back home." He paused to let us digest this.

"But in the middle of these two extremes you get those die-hard Malawians who claim that there is no way they can ever leave Malawi *kupita kunja.*

Then there are those die-hards who vow they can never (leave *kunja* and) come back to Malawi, not even at gun-point. Some Malawians *amalumbila kuti ine ndiye a* Immigration *adzachita kundikhwekhweleza* by my toe nails."

I listened to Amalume and concluded that it is a confusing picture that no one really knows what's what.

The cold war seems to be hot between this "middle-group" of die hards – those in Malawi who can't be forced to go abroad and those abroad who can't be forced to go back home.

You hear *akumudzi* constantly saying aMalawi *akunja "amagwila ntchito zonvetsa chisoni."* This often rubs those Malawians *akunja* the wrong way and they always hit back claiming that yes but, "we make more money than you."

Akunja claim that they make more in a month than *Akumudzi* would make the whole year... *shaaaaa musatelo inu.*

And *akumudzi's* response: "yes, but here in Malawi we only work 7:30am to 5:00pm, Monday to Friday and we go to the lake on weekends, *kukanyauda kudzikwati,"* Hahahaha *ntchito za nyofu-nyofu, zovala tie kapena gogoda asati majombo ndi ma golovesi.*

To which those *akunja* counter while laughing sarcastically; "hahahaha but I can go and watch L.A Lakers or Manchester United play while you only watch it on TV hoping that Escom doesn't interrupt you." *Iiiii!Abale anzanga, mwabweretsanso za* Escom.

A lot of bullets and missiles are often exchanged and will go on being exchanged. *Akumudzi* will always claim; "*mudzingobwelako kumeneko*," but *akunja* will stick to their guns; "*mukufuna mudzandidyele zanga, betele kuno* I can eat spaghetti for breakfast," one *wakunja* claimed... to which *wakumudzi* cracked up laughing; "*kaninso anthu mumadya spaghetti for breakfast, chimidzi inu.*"

Agogo coughed to clear his throat swallowing the phlegm before continuing.

"I don't know why *ife achiMalawife* like chiding one another? We need each other and we reciprocate one another." He said whilst gazing around the room.

"Just look at Malawi's three presidents, so far two of them did their stint abroad and only one was home grown." Agogo said, bringing the whole room to a dead silence that was silent than silence itself. He never stops to amaze us how he comes up with these things.

"So for now we can conclude that: *Akunja 2 – Akumudzi 1.*" With that Agogo paused having used the presidency as a proxy, leaving all of us scratching our heads.

"*Nkhani yatha basi*, full stop... continue with *zija mukuti azimayi antchito zamu m'dima ayamba kudula nsokho...*"

NYU-NYU CARS, BUT SERVICE ABALE

Amalume once said that in UK a dog is a man's best friend and in America a car is man's best buddy but as far as Malawi is concerned *Galimoto sabwerekana ngati silipasi ya patapata*. I have been pondering on this to try and make sense out of it but I am still coming up short. I have even tried to translate it into my own vernacular, still I have no clue what Amalume is trying to say here. That's Amalume for you who sometimes say things that only make sense in his head.

Some sayings are best understood when backed by incidents, Amalume's saying got a bit clearer last week when I stupidly let Shasha use my car. He wanted it for a shindig that was taking place at Grin Bamboo, a local spot that is becoming popular for a lot of Blantyre's young who's-who.

Anyone who owns a car knows that there is a cardinal rule; "if there are five pot holes on the road, prudence and common sense stipulates that if you are sober, do your best to dodge at least four of them, if you are tipsy from *dzakumwa dzowawa* then try to dodge at least two." Apparently Shasha who was sober like a Priest, disregarded this cardinal rule and ploughed right through the pot-holes as if he had issues with them. One of my friends who had been driving behind him later told me.

"*Anangoipemelela* Morris *yako* straight through pot-holes *osadoja nta imodzi yomwe,*" were my friend's exact words.

This is why today I was sitting outside with Che Supanala my mechanic, trying to rectify the extensive damage Shasha had inflicted on my Morris Marina. So far we had established that the whole suspension system (two shocks in front and leaf springs in the rear) was damaged. He had hit the pot-holes so hard that the indicators wouldn't go off, the fuel gauge was showing 'full tank' even though there was only three litres of petrol and on top of that one mirror, on the passenger's side was missing.

All Che Supanala said to me was; "*zazin'gono izi bwana, tikonza.*" This is why on the list of important people and Che Supanala ranks second from Manyuchi Darling. He is the only person outside my family I would go and visit if he was admitted in hospital – my Morris Marina is still on the road all thanks to Che Supanala's ingenuity. He is a mechanic, an auto-electrician, a welder and also tyre fitter, Che Supanala is what *aluya* would classify as 4-in-1, but here we just call gifted people like him, *a misili*.

With Malawi's booming economy and the positive effects of globalisation, there are now more cars on the road than any other time in history. I remember when Amalume first arrived from abroad and he couldn't believe his eyes at the mind boggling traffic jams on Malawi's highways. Nowadays traffic jams are a Malawian way of life and now people use it as an excuse whenever they are two hours late at the office, telling the boss; "*lero* traffic jam *inamangana mwa kathithi.*"

For some reason, facts show that people don't seem to mind these morning traffic jams but hate and loath the evening ones when they are going home – especially *lachisanu* when people *ali pakala-pakala* rushing to Iponga's, Kamba's Bar or Chez Ntemba.

Someone once said that if the number of cars on Malawi's roads were a barometer for the health of our economy then, for sure, we are about to catch up with the GDP of America. We are not talking about Anglias or Tatas, but about cars that cost more than the average four bedroom house(s). These are your top of the range Mercedes', Toyotas that look like BMWs and Jaguars that look like something from a science fiction movie.

And it's not just men behind the wheels of these sci-fi autos, but women have also gotten into the act of riding posh. Shasha who is a car-addict calls this, "ridin' dirty,"and he never stops gawking at each and every nice car that passes by, always commenting; "Yo check out that ride dawg, that shit is tight yo, daaaamn it's pimped like a muthafucker, even my nigga Exhibit would be impressed, for sheezy." We are now getting used to Shasha's ghetto-talk, Simioni always laughs;

"Che Shasha *tangoyakhulani bwino-bwino kuti galimotoyo ili mushe* for sheezy... for sheezy *ndiye kuti chani apa?*" Simioni always chides him.

Whatever opinion is about Shasha; from his rap-style of dressing or his mouth that spews out obscenities of an X-rated nature, you cannot deny it that the boy has an eye for detail when it comes to cars. Shasha knows his cylinders from his valves, a turbo from an intercooler, and this is why I found myself agreeing with him when he said that, as far as cars are concerned, Malawi is punching its weight with the best of them.

To say that I don't notice these flashy cars would be like saying that I don't notice the sun during the day, while taking a walk across the Sahara. Yes, like any man who has petrol running through his veins, I find myself drooling at these cars, but deep down I am still a staunch Morris Marina guy. As long as Che Supanala is still alive, I know that my Marina has got twenty-five more years and I wouldn't trade it for all the flashy BMWs in the world. Not only do I love its unique shape but I admire the simplistic engineering. Che Supanala claims that most of these new cars don't even have an engine; the bonnet (hood) is filled with computers.

"*Bwana muli makopyuta okha-okha* you can't even use a shifting spanner to fix them, when they start coughing *basitu kupachika.*" He seriously told me or rather he warned me just in case I was contemplating on buying one of these cars that are all shaped the same – like a bottle of Malawi Gin.

My mechanic is right because if you go to some of these houses *zaku-mayadi*, you will find these latest fancy cars resting on *mitondo* waiting for computerised spare parts from abroad. Most of these cars only last for six or seven months tops before disappearing from the roads of Malawi – *azipachika-pachika.* Compare this to my Morris Marina, even though it has gaskets made out of Chibuku packets, it's never been off the road due to a lack of *ma-speya* parts. If in need, I simply call my guy at the market for a part, who then gives it to *ntsikana wantchito* when she goes to buy *matimati.*

Tell me of a place in the UK where you can buy brake-pads simultaneously with tomatoes, tell me of a place in the USA where you can buy ball-joints together with *dzipalapatilo*. If the market vendors are out of stock I simply text my boys at PVHO *kuti adumphitse mpanda* and sort them out *madzulo* or month end. The same cannot be said of your fancy *nyu-nyu* cars, *akuti ma* hybrid running on both fuel and electricity or batteries... *za feki basi*.

Take for instance, Shasha's friend who went to Dar-es-Salaam (TZ) two weeks ago to collect his latest BMW 750 V12. Malawi being a tiny happy country, people make it their business to know what everyone is driving and it's no surprise that the whole town heard that *kukubwela* machine from Germany. Unfortunately for Shasha's friend the much publicised car never made it to Malawi.

Its sophisticated computer system had simply inhaled too much dust while cruising on our African roads which are a far cry from the tarmac autobahns of Düsseldorf Germany. Computer *yamu* BMW *inakumana ndi dothi la katondo laku Bantu land* and had simply been overwhelmed and died just before crossing the Malawi-Tanzania border. The computer system simply shut everything down, the lights died, all four tyres deflated and the doors locked permanently. In order to get out, Shasha's friend had to break the glass which was a struggle because it was a reinforced double glazing glass.

Shasha's BMW friend tried, unsuccessfully, to convince Che Supanala to go back with him to Tanzania and resuscitate his car. Che Supanala told him that he was better off getting a BMW auto electrician from Automotive.

After three days Shasha's friend went back with the auto-electrician and got the shock of his life upon arrival at the side of the road where he had left his prized BMW.

In the middle of the night scrap metal boys had descended on his expensive piece of Germany engineering like scavengers stripping it off with meticulous precision. They peeled off anything that could be sold for scrap metal; it was easier to quantify what they didn't take than to try and list what they took. They left the BMW's computer but pretty much took everything that didn't have chips or circuits.

I joked with Shasha to go and tell his friend that he might be able to buy bits and pieces of his BMW if goes to the market. Shasha didn't like my twisted sense of humour and told me so.

"Bro why are you hating, just because your car is a lemon, doesn't give you the right to diss other people's rides."

In a way, he had a point and I mumbled a half hearted apology, but went on to tell him that it really takes a lot to maintain a car. If you are going to buy a car that is 100% computerised then don't expect Che Supanala to start cutting packets of *Chibuku* to modify a gasket for you, if your car has broken down because its computer system has shut down.

Simioni whose madam drives a Sports car concurs with me that it's a very expensive affair maintaining a car especially if it's a modern one.

Since we don't manufacture anything here, it means that all our spares come from abroad. Being a landlocked country means that we get them at premium because to start with; the middle men add exorbitant mark-up rates, and on the other end of the equation, MRA will quantify VAT using formulas that don't make sense. This often means that your heart will start doing summersaults as you reach for the wallet or purse.

And if your spare-parts are for a Benz or Lexus, the MRA bill is bound to give you diarrhoea and a cardiac arrest simultaneously. As you lay there clutching your heart which is, by now, beating after every other ten minutes, the MRA boys will casually tell you; "*bwana imeneyo* is a luxury car that's why there are so many zeroes on the Invoice Bill."

Simioni once told me that here in Malawi it's normal for the price of Mercedes-Benz headlamp to be more than the price of a Toyota Corolla's gearbox once MRA has done some fiddling with their nonsensical formulas.

I will admit that my Morris Marina does not turn heads the same way these *abale ndi alongo* are turning heads with their exquisite jalopies. Just last week, a whole minibus veered off the road and smashed into a lamp post because the driver was busy admiring two girls driving along-side in a BMW 330i Convertible.

Shasha who had been in the same minibus at the time managed to escape with minor bruises and a sprained right arm. You would think he would be talking about his lucky escape, but all Shasha talked about were the girls and the BMW.

"Yo dude them two Honeys in that ride were tight and that Beemer 330 was moving like the f-ing Apollo space shuttle," my friend surprised us, unconcerned about the plaster of Paris (*chikhakha*) that was held by a sling around his neck.

"Hahahaha Ashasha *inu mukanafatu.*" Simioni said while laughing out loud.

TIME FOR THE YOUNG GENERATION

Today there is more meat at my house than you would find at Lunzu abattoir. There are carcasses of a cow, goat, lamb and an assortment of *dzipalapatilo* of chicken and duck. Some of my relatives from the village brought with them their already prepared monkey meat – this was perhaps the biggest gathering of the Amoto family.

I know you are sitting there thinking; come-on Makala wasn't the last gathering bigger than the previous one? I know-I know and I am positive that there will be bigger festivities at my house, bigger than this in the coming weeks or months. But for now, at this point in time, today's bash was the mother-lode, it's what others call grande-la-grande aka *phwando ladzaoneni*. It was so massive I even met some of my relatives that I haven't seen for a very long time.

Our 102 year old Agogo was doing something that has never been done in the history of my family. He was stepping down as the leader of the Amoto family, his reason being; "the family needs a young head now, someone with energy and fresh ideas." And unlike in the past when the mantle had automatically passed to the eldest child this time round he wanted us to vote for it.

Agogo wasn't going to impose a leader on us – but wanted us to vote. Amalume was so excited, talking about the dawn of a new era in our family politics.

"*Zoonadi* we need someone young and fresh. I mean just look at the most powerful countries in the world, America's president, Barack Obama, is only 48 years old. Russia's President Dmitry Medvedev is only 45 years old and United Kingdom has just elected David Cameron as their leader aged only 44." Listening to Amalume was always a lesson in current affairs.

"It is only right and plausible that Agogo is recognising the young talent that can take the Amoto family forward." My friend Simioni remarked with a hint of admiration for my clan, noticeable in his tone of voice.

But it was obvious that some of the old guards in my family were not at all pleased with Agogo's surprise move. The likes of *Madala Akulu* in his 70's and other *azimalume* thought the time was not right for the likes of me and my age mates to carry the Amoto mantle. They didn't even touch the meat offered to them... *akuti kunyanyala.*

I wish that we had been given an opportunity to at least hold one or two debates so that other members, especially the older generation, of the family get to see us, young-ones, articulate our policies on what path we wanted to take the Amoto family.

Amalume once said that the freedom of aspiring leaders to articulate themselves and be judged by *m'mene akusinjira nfundo* is one of the significant aspects that distinguish *mabanja achi* democratic from *mabanja omwe nkhani za dibeti siziloledwa*. Unfortunately the Amoto family was still not a fully-fledged democratic family and we still had a long way to go before debates could take hold. But at least we were allowed to cast a vote and chose who was going to lead us.

Although Simioni and Shasha came to this *msonkhano/phwando*, they couldn't cast a vote because they were not part of the family, we don't recognise dual nationality in the Amoto family, but that didn't stop them campaigning on my behalf – Shasha was the most vocal, canvassing on my behalf, telling the women on how I was planning to build *Chigayo* in my backyard where the Amoto ladies could come *kudzakonoletsa* for free.

But of course some of my cousins were also canvassing for votes with the same intensity as mine. Voting was going to be held after lunch when everyone's stomach was bloated up with food and the men had loosened their belts, the women loosened their *dzitenjes*.

Every time I went to the back of the house to check on the food, I just had to smile at the rainbow of colours from the women's *dzitenje* which was befitting the occasion taking place. It reminded me of how politically diverse my family is.

Women were wearing MCP's party cloth with the famous *tambala wakuda* and that familiar face of the late Life President. There was the bright Yellow *dzitenje dza* UDF with the face of a *Tcheya*. There was the Blue of DPP with the face of the current President. The late Aford's President and Founder had a strong following in my family as well as could be seen from the Aford's party cloth worn by some of the women, especially by those relatives of mine from the northern part of the country.

"*Koma ndiye United Nations tu.*" I remarked to Manyuchi Darling who funny enough has political affiliations that are different from mine. Manyuchi had explicitly made it clear long time ago that she would be more than willing to switch churches and join my religion or adapt to my strange foods but political affiliation is something she will not be following me.

I guess you could say me and Manyuchi Darling are like the Republican Governor Arnold Schwarzenegger and *mai a kwawo*, Maria Shriver who is a Democrat.

Not many Malawian families can boast such show of freedom of political affiliation – where the husband is DPP and the wife is Aford or husband is UDF and the wife is MCP. Such was Manyuchi's fierce independence that I wasn't sure which direction she was going to vote in today's family leadership contest, for me or for big *Khazeni*?

What makes my clan diverse is the fact that unlike other families that only marry within the borders of their village; we tend to cast our nets far and wide and that is why we ended up with this rainbow coalition of Yellow, Blue, *Tambala wakuda* and the rest. If UK Labour Party had its own *chitenje* with the face of Gordon Brown, am sure Auntie would have been representing it. But for now it was only Malawian Parties on show, although there were no *dzitenje* for the newly formed party called United Democratic Party (UDP). This rainbow of colours borne out of Malawi's political parties spiced up our own little family election convention.

It was obvious that our family leadership contest was going to mirror the politics of Malawi, a kind of African politics that is devoid of any ideology or beliefs. Amalume once told us that; "in the West their politics is a bit simpler and structured because they adhere to set ideologies – you either are "Left" (i.e. Labour or Democrat) or you are "Right" (i.e. Conservative or Republican) or somewhere in the "Centre." If you happen to be a "Leftist" you will have certain ideologies which might be pro-immigration or anti big business and if you are 'Right leaning' then the opposite is true, and you might view all immigrants as stealing jobs from the indigenous citizenry."

Amalume reckons that Malawians; we vote because a candidate comes from our village or because he/she speaks the same language like us."

Simioni agrees saying that; "this is sad because it means that those who come from a village of only twenty people will never have a chance in hell of ever having their candidate grab the keys to Sanjika Palace or the State House."

If Americans were to vote like Malawians, then Obama would not have become the 44th president because all white people (who are in majority) would have voted for John McCain, giving him a landslide victory.

Staying on this prejudicial path, I knew that today's leadership race was between me and big *Khazeni waku* Zomba, simply because we come from two of the biggest families within the Amoto family. They were those who were going to vote for me not because my manifesto on how to run the Amoto family was better than that of *Khazeni*. They would vote for me for the same reason Simioni votes UDF, or Agogo votes MCP or Shasha votes DPP and Tchale Aford. My other *Khazeni* who comes from a smaller family was not even a threat to me. I knew after today's election, he was going to be swallowed up by either me or big *Khazeni* from Zomba (in alliance talks). Even our family politics was mirroring that of my country, how sad.

Amalume once said that; "90% of the people who voted for Tony Blair or Bill Clinton had no idea which part of the country these two gents came from. They voted for them because of what they stood for, because they had an ideology similar to theirs." It was obvious Amalume was trying to convince the family to take this route, but you could tell that most family members had already made up their minds on who they wanted as leader of the Amoto family.

The *nkhalambas* of my family were not thrilled about this whole leadership contest, and we overheard some of them saying that Agogo should rescind the move he had just made.

"*Ife timayesa Agogowa ndi ntsogoleri wathu wa-muyaya?*" The elderly vehemently voiced the concerns.

We understood why the 'old school class of *makedzana*' feared our generation of the internet age. Because under Agogo's leadership most of these elders benefited a lot; the ability for them to take home left-over nyama, the privilege of being served first during meals or sitting under the cool shed at funerals. With Agogo's exit from family politics all this was going to change – but I had a feeling they were not going to go down without a fight. These were the dangerous people to watch for, not Agogo but those around him, *anamadya nawo*.

Just like in real life politics where no one wants to let go off *mpando onona* and Benz *ya nyofu-nyofu*, it was the same with these grumpy old men of the Amoto clan – but today was another day, the dawn of the new era in the Amoto family, *nthawi ya madala* team was coming to an end, *tiyendetse zinthu achinyamatafe*. With this thought in mind I walked over to the back of the house, "*azimayi-azimayi* listen up ... Yes We Can!" I yelled on top of my voice like an Obama wannabe.

Thungululu rang out from women and most of them shouted jubilantly: "Amakala *omwewa atitsogolela basi.*" They chanted while dancing around me.

It was obvious I wasn't the only one whipping up morale because I heard the cheers coming from the front yard as big *Khazeni* from Zomba was also rallying his base. As for my other *Khaze* from a smaller family, I knew that, just like in the politics of my country, this was not his time yet.

FAMILY DIVERSIFICATION
AND THE FLAG ISSUE

If there is one thing I am proud about my family is its size. My dear friend Simioni has always commented how he envies and wishes he had so many relatives like I do. Whenever he starts talking like this I always tease him that his grandparents weren't as productive as mine, a friendly joke which has a 99% element of truth in it.

Since Agogo had fathered so many children, the result is a family abnormally large that we basically can claim the title of the biggest family in the whole of Malawi. If family size was like boxing, then the Amoto family would definitely be Muhammad Ali - undisputed heavyweight champ of all time, our family would simply be king of the ring.

But if there is anyone out there *akudzithemba kuti* their family deserves this mantle then please stand up; let's have a duel – your family against my family, going head to head in twelve gruelling rounds inside the ring, I bet your family won't make it past Round One… Hahahaaaa (*zochezatu izi.*)

The multiplication and quadruplicating of our clan has come about as a result of blessed fertile seeds of the Amoto men, coupled with the active producing wombs of the Amoto women, the consequences of *mitala*, helped by the absence of any contraceptives (injected, pills or worn) and boosted by the fact that we as a family have never confined our marriages to just our village or district alone opting to spread the Amoto seed far and wide.

Agogo once warned us that sticking to the borders of your district weakens the genes of the clan as it can become prone to all sorts of ailments or hereditary health risks.

"Diversification is the way to go," Agogo always reminded us, stressing on the word *diversification* as if he was lecturing about Finance and artistic cherry picking of Stocks or Bonds.

Amalume who is married to a lovely British lady (and also happens to be more knowledgeable than most of us) concured with Agogo.

"Just as diversifying your financial portfolio reduces financial risk and this technique also works in reducing diseases in my family." Amalume claims.

I am so very proud to have in-laws, cousins, nephews and nieces, uncles and unties from all the regions of the country. This then should explain the variety of languages that can be heard whenever we have family gatherings at my house.

This variety of dialects also extends to the array of foods that can found on our family gatherings; from dishes of *Mulamba* fish, to the salty tasting monkey meat or dark looking crocodile soup, not forgetting the in-house favourite *dzipalapatilo* relish. Even our *nsima* comes in a wide variety of *n'gaiwa, ufa oyela* or *ya Kondowole*. You will also find chips, rice or bacalhau (*bakayawo*) to cater for those relatives from across the border (yes I do have relatives who are not Malawian by birth.)

Globalisation means that some members of the Amoto family have married outside the borders of Malawi maximising the already diverse clan something which should explain the broken English, Swahili and Portuguese you hear at our family gatherings vis-à-vis muito obrigado meu amigo *kapena* Tafadhali nataka bia mama, shauri yako.

You then begin to understand why and where Simioni's envy comes from, especially since his family comprises only of people from his own region – *akuti* keeping it pure. As a result, they have a tendency of viewing anyone who isn't from their region as being against them. *Zao izo, akuti amafuna onse adziyankhula chiyakhulo chimodzi* because their language is superior, how sad, narrow and shallow...*hehedeeeeee...* in this day and age? *Zachi kale-kale zimenezo,* something that I once told my friend Simioni; *dzikwatilanani nokha-nokha* and he wonders why *m'banja mwawo mulibe tidziphadzuwa tachikaladi.* Look at my Manyuchi Darling and some of my cousins *ali myaaa* skin complexion *ngati kirimu bwana.*

For some unexplained reason my house has always been the venue for *dzinkhoswe, miyambo* 6 July Independence Day celebrations or any family gathering you can think of. Having relatives who are scattered all over the country created a unique problem. It was simply impossible for *achibale* coming from *kumudzi* and other far away areas to locate and find my house which is in the middle of so many houses (you know *m'mene zimakhalila ntauni muno.*)

The problem was further acerbated with the missing road signs that plague the country. It was simply a logistical nightmare giving directions to relatives who were coming from far and wide. Most of them used to get lost and would simply go back in frustration whilst others would struggle to find my house only to arrive when the ceremony they were coming for was drawing to a close.

This used to result in some unsavoury and tense moments especially when there was no meat left by the time my carnivorous relatives from *kumudzi* finally arrived. They would find only pots of vegetables and meatless bones...*dziboda dzotsopatsopa...* discarded and strewn all over the floor now being gnawed on by an army of excited neighbourhood dogs.

It was a recurring problem until one day the Amoto elders came up with a very ingenious plan. A plan that has so far worked and eliminated all the logistical problems we used to have. A plan so simple but powerful, I have often wondered why I never thought of it in the first place, perhaps this reinforces the phenomenon why elders are wiser than the young.

These old school wise men simply suggested we cut down the tallest blue gum tree, attach one of Mother's David Whitehead *chitenje* on one end and stick the other end of the long tree into the ground. In one swift eureka moment our elders had created a flag, a flag that has come to symbolise the Amoto clan and also acts as a beacon, guiding those trying to locate my house, *nzelu za akulu-akulu akwathu zimenezi*.

Due to this rather engineering feat, nowadays it's very common to hear; "*Mukufuna nyumba ya bwana*

Makala? Simungasocheleyi, mwayiona mbendela ikuuluka apoyo? Basitu pamenepo ndiye pa Amakala Amoto." Some even add; "*mukanva kununkhila nyama yootcha ndiye kuti mwayandikira.*"

With the passing years, I must admit, I am more proud of our flag than I am of my house. Now most of my relatives look at this flag as part of them, because it unites and binds us together as one unit. It's like the glue that binds a book, without it you have nothing but separate pieces of paper fluttering all over the place.

I was surprised and pleased to note that some of my cousins from Mzuzu, Chikwawa, Thyolo, Lilongwe, Mangochi and Rumphi have also planted identical flags outside their houses. It really makes life easy for us to find each other's houses when we are visiting. Just as a flag compliments the name of a country, this flag compliments the Amoto name so much that whenever people see it they think of our clan.

The two reciprocate each other in such a powerful way, giving us a unique identity... think of the flag, and the Amoto name comes to mind, think of our name and the flag comes to mind, on the same lines as Malawi and the Black-Red-Green symbiosis.

For those of you who follow the goings on of my family, you will remember that we just had elections after Agogo had announced he wanted the young generation to lead the Amoto family. This was an exciting period for us when you consider that Agogo has been the leader of our clan for thirty years.

There are those in my family who would have loved Agogo to lead us for life. Actually I never thought a day would come when Agogo wasn't our Head of State... ermmh excuse me... I mean Head of the family, our family.

During Agogo's reign there were those who claim that he was a bit autocratic and that the Amoto women didn't have as much freedom as they do now. But then some family members will tell you that there used to be order and a sense of normalcy in the family when Agogo was the Head. Which story you believe about Agogo's rule depends on what you went through during his reign as the Life Head of the Amoto clan.

But now times have changed and so has the leadership of my clan. There is, now in my family, a fully fledged democracy and a sense of freedom that didn't exist before. Freedom which at times tends to be flaunted excessively as can be seen by the open dissent that is now prevalent but was absent when Agogo was Head.

As much as I had looked forward to the time when my generation would be calling the shots and initiating policies in the running of the family, I never expected that this would also give rise to a seeds of disorder and an element of chaos. I guess, like they say, democracy comes with its own pitfalls. Albeit all this as a family we have so far stuck together as one, after all that's what families do.

The recent suggestion that we need to change the colour of the flag outside my house (and outside all the Amoto houses) looks to expose the underlying divisions of my clan. Those who are proponents for a new flag articulate their reasons that the clan has now moved on, we have changed and achieved a lot as a clan, thus we need a flag that will portray that change. *Akuti banja la* Amoto *lapanga* develop and this warrants a new and different looking flag. The fact that there has been commendable economic and development in my family is evident compared to the yesteryears, *kumayamika Chauta zikutiyendera*, no wonder all this talk about fiddling with the colours of the flag.

On the other end of the spectrum, advocates of the status quo have dug in, arguing that this flag is who we are and tinkering with it robs us of our identity. And they go on to argue that there are other pressing issues we can divert the family resources towards. They vehemently point to the fact that a few nephews and nieces need assistance with school fees and books. Splashing money on changing the Amoto flag is simply a misplacement of priorities. *Akutelo abale otsutsana ndi zosintha ma* colours *ambendera yathuyi.*

It's really a tough debate but the ones who are opting for a new flag have got the upper hand, since they are the ones currently wielding all the power in the Amoto clan. They are the ones with deep pockets, they are the ones who tend to finance most of the development projects or celebrations that take place in the family and they are the ones with the keys or the access to *matapu a madzi amoyo.*

We are hoping that today's gathering and ensuing deliberations will resolve this matter once and for all. You can sense the tension even though we are trying to chat as if everything is normal. Deep down I know that the seismic tremors will soon erupt damaging the already shifting tectonic plates of the Amoto clan. Sometimes I get the feeling that Agogo's heavy hand during his reign as leader had successfully managed to put a lid on the Amoto diverse volcano that contains the dangerous lava and magma within its belly. You now get the feeling that this lid is somehow wobbly and threatens to erupt into a volcano that would probably be bigger than that seen at Mount St. Helens in 1980.

I looked up at the flag that was lazily fluttering in the calm June wind. This flag was older than some members of my family, and I wondered if they had any strong sentimental attachment to it or whether they too wanted a new one. I didn't realise that I was crying until Manyuchi Darling using her soft tiny hand gently wiped a warm tear that had cascaded down my cheek.

"You are really attached to this flag aren't you?" She gently asked in her calm soothing voice sensing the dilemma and conflict inside me.

How could I tell her that it wasn't really the flag that was causing the tears, it was the fact that my diverse clan that has always stuck together was now divided over a piece of cloth and what colours we should print on it.

I thought of other families that have feuded because of bigger issues, issues relating to wealth and distribution of resources. Like the family of my friend Shasha which we always referred to as Congo, as they viciously feuded over *dzifuyo* just like Congo tears itself apart over diamonds. We have never had an abundance of *dzifuyo* in our family, but rather concentrated on farming, and yet here we were, letting something as simple as a flag expose our prejudices and perhaps be a catalyst for something big and ugly.

"Should I go and get you a plate of *dzipalapatilo* and rice?" Manyuchi offered while getting up; "you need to eat before the flag deliberations take place dear." She could sense the turmoil inside me and knew that I needed food to try and get my head thinking straight before the debate and deliberations start.

I said yes to the *dzipalapatilo* and no to the rice, "I think I will have nsima ya *kondowole* that my sister-in-law from Nkhata has prepared." I lovingly told Manyuchi Darling while looking at the chinantindi of relatives eating and laughing. I know that each one of them was also apprehensive as to which flag was going to be flying come tomorrow.

Our current flag cut a lonely figure out there in the yard, the wind had died down and it drooped low, the cloth hanging limply against the pole as if it wasn't too sure of its own continued existence. I wondered if flags have feelings. Did it have any idea or suspicions that its days were numbered? Surely it must have known that it was an endangered species, the way it looked down at us, as we were about to begin deliberations pertaining to its future, I swear that flag was shedding tears up there.

FOREX TRADE AT DZIBOLIBOLI

Shasha claims that there are more Forex transactions conducted *Padziboliboli* compared to those transacted by banks. This statement is open to debate, but I will probably not be part of that debate because I am sticking with my friend Shasha on this one. The word *"Padziboliboli"* (a market-place of wooden curvatures) comes from the noun *"chiboliboli"* which means a carved wooden curio. The place *Padziboliboli* is synonymous with a currency exchange (black) market.

A bit of caution here, before people get carried away, especially those of you who trade in complex financial instruments like Derivatives. If you are into Options, Futures, Forwards or Swaps then *Padziboliboli* is definitely not a market for you. But if you are in the market for currencies vis-à-vis going Long or going Short on Forex then *Padziboliboli* is the place you want to be. Amalume once said that *"Padziboliboli* is on par with the London Stock Exchange (LSE) or the New York stock exchange (NYSE) two of the biggest money markets in the world." Of course Amalume was not comparing trade-for-trade but rather the mind boggling speed and ingenuity exhibited by the currency dealers of *padziboliboli.*

Unlike the highly educated (university) dealers who work on the LSE or NYSE using powerful computers, the local dealers of *Padziboliboli* mostly got their education from Dharap F.P School or the other primary schools around Blantyre. They don't use powerful computers, instead they are only armed with calculators on their cell phones. Yet these money savvy forex dealers control one of the most lucrative money markets in Malawi.

Don't be fooled by the funny wooden elephant or zebra curios on display, behind this façade there is serious money exchanging hands – from Pounds, Dollars, Rands, Rupees, Euros and more. Shasha, who has contacts there, claims that on a good day K12.5 million (£50,000) changes hands there. This statement coming from Shasha, of course has to be taken with caution and a pinch of salt, but gut feeling tells me he might be right. K12.5 million in a single day (at a venue that does not have a computer or landline telephone) is not bad business at all.

To fully comprehend how serious this under-ground lucrative trade is, you only have to see the re-sources the government is pouring in policing the forex trade. When you quantify the man hours dedicated only for *Padziboliboli* and convert them into wages, you start seeing what a pain in the butt these dealers are to the government.

One dealer once claimed that there are more plain clothes police personnel dedicated around *Padziboliboli* than those assigned to the presidential motorcade. They claim that these Policemen, who patrol in an unmarked Land Rover 110's, are amateurs. There is some truth to this claim when you consider that some of the older dealers (*nkhala-kale*) have been trading since I was in primary school and so far they haven't been caught... and they are still there, shouting *"wawa Angoni"* whenever I drive past in my Morris Marina.

Then there are those who became dealers when they were still teenagers and are now in their 60's nearing retirement, they even boast that they have been in operations throughout the tenures of all Malawi Police Inspector Generals.

What makes *Padziboliboli* unique is its strategic location at a prime site in the heart of Blantyre, ironically flanked by Banks on all sides. Shasha told us that his dealer friend claims that more customers transact with them because; there are no limits to the amount you can exchange, there are no questions asked, no ID required and their exchange rate tends to be better than the banks.

The dealers admit that the government has changed tactics which has forced them to adapt with their own counter-measures. They now have look-outs posted on strategic places along Victoria Avenue, TNM, Apollo and near Mount Soche Hotel armed with cell phones. The job of these look-outs is to raise alarm if suspicious Land Rovers with anyamata a Fiscal are spotted.

They claim that it's not difficult to spot these Fiscal undercover agents; their obvious haircuts, the warm jackets even though the weather temperature is one million degrees Celsius, their darting eyes like those of a prey stalking its kill are all give away signs. The look-outs will just text *"five-o"* and the dealers just disappear into the crowds.

Most transactions are now conducted via texting where arrangements on monetary amounts and exchange rates are agreed. The actual face-to-face transactions where monies change hands are done away from public view – usually inside expensive cars or taxis on parking lots of Hotels or business premises around the city.

Contrary to common belief the people exchanging currencies are not drug dealers – instead they are your everyday tourists or entrepreneurs who have been declined by the bank. Most of these are in the auto-trade, buying cars from abroad for re-sale in Malawi like Shasha's friend who goes to Europe and brings trucks.

Four months ago he managed to bring in three Iveco trucks and sold them for K15 million each, grossing himself a cool K45 million, ka mpamba equivalent to £180,000 Sterling. But when he wanted to exchange half of this into Pounds (so that he could go back for more trucks) the bank told him that £1,500 is the best they could help him with. He ended up *Padziboliboli* to exchange (kusungunula) part of his K45 million.

Although he had to make repetitive transactions spanning a period of 2 weeks, it sounds as if he has exchanged enough to venture back into UK. But surely hard-working entrepreneurs shouldn't be going through this.

Simioni's female relative who is a transporter has been complaining of problems with forex. She can't get any at her local bank for her drivers who haul containers to and from Durban for AMI-SDV. These drivers need dollars as allowance and for toll fees along the highways of South Africa. But the banks have been saying that they are out of forex, and this transporter lady has turned to *Padziboliboli* for forex.

Tchale, who just came last month from UK, says that he exchanged all his Pounds *Padziboliboli* because their rate was good compared to the banks.' According to him, not only was the rate good but so was the speed of the service. With Banks you have to call them first and when you go there you sit there waiting as if you are at Queen Elizabeth Central Hospital waiting for a kidney or a lung that is coming in from the North Pole from an Eskimo who hasn't even donated it yet.

The booming trade of the currency black market confirms my suspicions that this industry is here to stay. Every time I drive past *Padziboliboli*, my primary school friends who are now big time dealers always wave and politely greet me; "wawa aBiggie." Occasionally I will stop for a chit-chat and pick their brains about business.

I once asked; "I hear *kuti anyamata a boma avuta?*" And the defiant response was; "*Hahahahaha pan'gono* aBiggie, they cannot close us down, we are here 24-7...365. Even during Operation Bwezani when the Army was shooting it out with the MYP, we were still open for business." Wal-Mart, Tesco, Asda or Meijer (US and UK biggest retailers) cannot make such a claim.

Amalume also concurs that the government may be fighting a losing battle. As long as the banks maintain these ridiculously low limits as to how much forex people can apply for, individuals will just resort to the black market.

Closing forex bureaus run by Asians might temporarily appear to be addressing the problem, but this just channels business in the direction of *Padziboliboli* (and not the banks.) Some dealers claim that they have some influential clients who can't be seen loitering around *Padziboliboli*. Instead they send couriers to go and conduct the transaction(s) for them.

Clamping down on money bureaus just channels forex not towards the high street bank but into the hands of dealers at *Padziboliboli*, and as disturbing as this sounds, this is exactly what is happening.

The more forex ends up *Padziboliboli*, the more the government loses out. This has serious consequences as seen by the recent fuel shortages because *boma* doesn't have forex to pay for fuel. The fact that *maiko akunja*, like Canada, are not buying our tobacco just compounds the government's forex reserves woes.

Dispatching an army of Fiscal Police for an all-out war with *Padziboliboli* dealers just drives the trade further underground. This then affects the exchange rates because the dealers have to factor in the increased risk associated in dealing with forex.

Sarcastically the dealers claim Fiscal Police is not their main problem; their worry is the current Ash cloud that is grounding planes in Europe and the impending British Airways staff strikes. Apparently this is slowing down the flow of tourists who are the major source of forex for the dealers.

If you listen to most of these dealers, you would think that you are talking to a Harvard PhD graduate in Finance or Business. They are so up-to-date with the current economic affairs. They are able to quote exchange rates of any currency including the Zim-Dollar (a currency that is highly volatile and fluctuates by the second.)

Stories by Agogo that *Padziboliboli* amagulitsa *chamba* and stolen items are both unfounded and untrue. These dealers have got an unwritten code of ethics that includes zero drug tolerance. You might come across a latest phone or blackberry for sale but this doesn't mean that they are stolen merchandise – items like these are from tourists who want *maKwacha* but don't have the Dollars or Pounds to trade. *Padziboliboli* will often accommodate this by resorting to barter form of trading.

This is perhaps why *Padziboliboli* will be the likely place to buy an apple i-Pad even before it has hit any major shops in Africa; chances are it will be available at this market of sorts. There is no way a tourist can walk in a bank to exchange a cell phone for *maKwacha, zosatheka abwana*. But the flexibility with *Padziboliboli* is such that anything can be currency and that includes the fancy expensive leather jackets you see these dealers wearing ... *mphasha yapa* States. Where do you think I bought that Louis Vuitton hand bag you see Manyuchi Darling carrying?

DZIPANI, DZISANKHO & DZIPALAPATILO

Today Mother must have been in a very good mood whilst cooking because she really surprised us with a buffet of assorted *dzipalapatilo*. Chickens, Ducks and even *nkhunda* feet were all mixed together in the *dzipalapatilo* basin. One can't help to wonder though that if this was an election then the fight was between chicken-feet and duck-feet. *Dzipalapatilo dza nkhunda* were clearly a third party that stood no chance, everyone was going for *nkhuku* or *abakha's* feet. It reminded me of the just recent UK elections Conservative (chicken), Labour (ducks) and Liberal Party (*timiyendo ta nkhunda*).

While chewing what appeared like *chipalapatilo cha bakha*, at least from where I was sitting. Amalume started his lecture on how America is the richest country and has the biggest economy than any other country. My uncle has got the tendency of backing his facts with figures so it came as no surprise to us when he started spicing his talk with facts.

"America's nominal GDP last year alone was $14.2 trillion," Amalume went on sounding like an Oxford University Professor lecturing to students from standard 5 at Chilomoni Full Primary School.

I have no idea how big a trillion is, my arithmetic skills don't go that far, (*timathela pa 100,000 ikakhala khani ya za manambala*) but I knew that a trillion must be big because when I tried to type it on my cell phone it flashed a message of "*mutipweteketsa nazo mutu izi a* Makala."

The reason why Amalume was talking about the USA economy was because of what he had just read in the local tabloid about the creation of another Malawian political party, which I am sure most of you are well aware of.

According to Amalume, in America (*kuchimake kwa* democracy) there are only two prominent political parties, the Democrat Party and the Republican Party. In UK it's the same story with only two parties dominating their politics vis-à-vis Conservatives and Labour.

Like an excited and elated standard 5 student who just realised that the teacher has written 1 + 1 = 3, I jumped up.

"But Amalume, I thought there are Liberal Party and Green Party in UK and USA respectively?"

Amalume looked at me smiling, that smile a teacher gives to a student who thinks he knows it all but knows doddle squat.

"Exactly my point Makala, the parties you are referring to will never end up in the White House or at No. 10 Downing Street." Amalume started honing his eyes right on my forehead as if he wanted the words to stay imprinted like some sort of a number plate.

"These parties are too minuscule to cause any waves that could turn into a tsunami, propelling their leaders into government. The only reason why these so called third parties have managed to survive this long is because they have very wealthy and powerful American, like the Billionaire Ross Perot willing to finance these parties from their deep pockets." Amalume paused to swallow a stubborn *chipalapatilo* that had to be washed down with a glass-full of *thobwa* before he continued.

"Unfortunately the same cannot be said of Malawi. We don't have wealthy individuals who are willing to pump money at a third party and neither is our GDP of national wealth comparable to that of America. It's actually pathetic to start comparing ourselves with them as that will be like comparing a grasshopper to an elephant to see which of the two makes the loudest *n'didi* when walking."

It took me a while to realise that Amalume had used GDP to illustrate the level of our economic plight. It's suicidal to be in Opposition in a poor country like Malawi and it is a massacre to be a third party. The life span of a small party in Malawi can be unforgivingly short.

I then queried Amalume that, "how come when it comes to the number of political parties we seem to have more than our rich Atlantic neighbours?"

What Amalume said next almost made us choke with laughter, even Agogo who hardly laughs unless it's something to do with food or drink just had to laugh the minute Amalume started talking.

"It surely feels like some people after eating breakfast have a conversation that goes like ... '*akazi anga*, thank you for that delicious breakfast, I have come up with an idea to finish the house, I think I will launch my own political party today, *kuti tikonze za malata*." Amalume said it while mimicking his voice to that of a politician.

"Hahahaaaa, *Amalume mwaonjeza!*" We all cracked up in delight.

But Amalume was on a roll, it's as if our laughter was giving him fuel to increase the tempo.

"You really wonder what these old school politicians are thinking when they launch a party to *chinantindi* of 25 or 30 of their village people." Amalume had a point there, we all agreed.

Amalume was not implying that Malawians should not launch their own parties. To the contrary, he thinks that this is healthy for multiparty to thrive in this country. Amalume claims that it is the right of every Malawian to launch his/her own party if one feels that there are enough people willing to propel him/her into Sanjika Palace. But it's obvious for all to see that most of these tiny small briefcase parties lack that Wow factor, their leaders lack charisma or certain airs about them. According to Agogo he says they lack that, "*I came to break the stupid federation*" factor.

It is not a secret that no other politician has had an explosive entrance any where near to that of the late Ngwazi Dr. Hastings Kamuzu Banda. Indeed some might disagree with this reality but such a person will simply be exhibiting characteristics of someone who is in denial, a person who argues that the Lion is not the king of the jungle but the antelope is.

Indeed some have tried to copy Dr. Hastings K. Banda but none comes close. HKB was a man of average built with a strong command of the Queens language, (that is yet to be surpassed) highly educated and well-travelled (although some will again chose to refute this, *iiii kaya zanu izo.*) Behind his dark sunglasses HKB viewed the white man as his equal in an era when this was not the norm. Compare this to today's presidential wannabe with their briefcase parties, view *azungu* as beings that should be placed on a pedestal. You see these so called leaders smiling and agreeing to whatever is asked of them to do (especially if that *mzungu* happens to work for the IMF or World Bank.

That is why when you compare HKB's entrance to some of these so called *atsogoleri* of today, (most who have never walked past a secondary school let alone ventured inside a classroom) you can't help to laugh, wondering: "*komadi atilamulila amenewa?*"

Hahahaha, some of these wannabe presidents *abale anzanga*, can they really go to the UN and articulate issues about economics, greenhouse gas effects, balancing budgets on behalf of Malawi? Ok forget about economics, can they even be able to say; "good morning?" Can they honestly say *mwadzuka bwanji yekha* in English while addressing the head of IMF or World Bank (at least to increase the chances of *bwana* IMF signing us a cheque) or will they just stand there smiling like *bubu* saying: Yes! Yes! Yes! …to everything?

And after saying a gazillion '*Yes Bwana* IMF' and not a single '*No Bwana* IMF' they still come back *m'manja mbeee.*

Ifenso achiMalawife ndi umbuli wathuwu we don't even ask these so called leaders why they even bothered using tax-payer's money by going there in the first place. Couldn't they have just scribbled these gazillion: '*inde… inde bwana*' on an A4 paper and sent it via mail or fax instead of going to New York just to mumble *yes bwana*

IMF and then do window shopping before coming back *kumatinamiza apa kuti mumaphinjako nfundo*... Aaaaaaaa *Fotseki*.

Hate him or loath him one cannot deny Kamuzu had a certain mystique, an aura about him that will probably never be replicated by this generation or the next, especially when we have these tiny little parties popping up like mushrooms in season.

Why Amalume finds the whole 'start-up' party phenomenon a bit unappetising is that it seems to be the same people who started a party last year (*kenaka ziiiii*). The year before that they had also launched another party (*kenakanso ziiiiii*) so forth and so on.

It's normal, albeit ridiculous, that after General Elections to hear that *a Pulezidenti akachipani kajaka ajoinano boma*, they have been offered a seat in Cabinet. Which makes, the sober voting electorate, wonder and question; was he really serious? Is his head firing on all cylinders?

Yesterday he wanted to be the President of Malawi but today he is accepting to be nominated as Minister of Portholes and Vendors. Talk about being power hungry.

And you can tell such characters, even the way they sit in their ministerial car, that they have no clue what their job or portfolio entails. They sit in the back looking so scared and in bewilderment you would think the one driving the Benz is the minister. Yes, in most cases it's the driver looking so composed at his job and not *Anduna* in the backseat. Oh my God and to think that he wanted to be my President.

Sometimes it's also us the electorate who are to blame, just because someone comes from the same village like ours, we then start giving them false hopes and pumping their egos. Blindly supporting a homeboy with the notion that once he makes it *atinyambititsa ka* ministerial job. *Fotseki.*

"*Tiyeni nazoni bwana, chaka chino ndi chanu.*" We stupidly encourage their unattainable ambitions with what will definitely never be. Hahaaaa, *abale ndi alongo* how do we expect him to win when the only people voting for him comprise of the population that makes up his village which only totals 260 including children and *dzifuyo?*

Some of these small start-up parties, even if vote rigging was to be legalised, they still wouldn't garner enough votes to make it halfway to Sanjika, not even as far as Dharap F.P. School (ooh it's now called Namiwawa.)

I queried Amalume how come they have smaller parties in America, surely we can only emulate what the Americans are doing, can't we? Amalume looked at me the same way a tiger looks at a fragile *gwape.*

"When was the last time you heard that someone has just launched a party in the USA?" He asked knowing that I was not going to come up with an answer to that.

Indeed I had no answer for him, but surely you don't expect our young multiparty culture to be similar to that of America, I quizzed him while keeping my eye on the plate of *dzipalapatilo* noticing that everyone kept avoiding the *nkhunda* feet.

I wasn't happy the way the *dzipalapatilo* elections were going, *nkhunda*-feet was losing poorly according to the exit polls.

Surely we have to start somewhere and you can't expect a new party to be as big as the big Four.

Amalume looked at me knowing that I had just wandered into a trap without realising it.

"Exactly my point Makala, for a country the size of ours, for an economy as poor as ours, going beyond four parties becomes a joke," my uncle said to me while reaching for the glass of thobwa that was perched preciously on the edge of the stool next to the basin containing *dzipalapatilo.* He paused taking a sip from his mug of *thobwa.*

"But you are right that launching new parties in a way keeps multiparty phenomenon burning. But what would you think of a person who launches a party every month?" He paused to give us a moment to think of names that have recently done just that. And a few names came to mind.

"This month he is launching UNKP, last month he launched URJOP, the month before that it was UZSDP … will you really take this person seriously?" Amalume said and we all started laughing.

Amalume had a valid point; I even stopped chewing briefly to digest although my right hand dashed to grab the last piece of *chipalapatilo cha nkhuku* before Shasha made his move. Amalume ignored our little *chipalapatilo* war being waged and continued.

"And don't you really think if ever we are going to be launching parties it should be the young generation doing that?" Came another intelligent remark from Amalume.

He was right in suggestin that these old school guards should either retire or stay on as advisors to the young bright Malawians and Shasha was clearly hooked by Amalume's reasoning.

"Ankolo *mwalasatu ap*a, even me I get nervous when am in a minibus that is being driven by someone Agogo's age." Shasha cheekily remarked while looking in the direction of my 102 year old Agogo who had just passed out so suddenly as if someone had flicked a sleeping-switch in his brain.

There was a rumbling snore coming out of Agogo's partly opened mouth as he lay slouched on the sofa while flies kept landing on his mouth because of *nsunzi* smears around his lips from the *dzipalapatilo*.

The thought of Agogo zooming down Zalewa road at 99mph behind the wheel of a fully packed minibus got my head spinning. Is this what has become of our politics? In a crazy way Shasha made me realise that some of these politicians have been in politics since I was a baby and they are still here launching and re-launching parties so that they can continue telling me, my children and probably my grand children the same lies.

"*Koma abale ma* driver *onsewa achi youth wa bwaa?*" I couldn't help wondering whilst thinking of what I had just read in the papers two days ago that the son of an ex-president might be throwing his hat in.

Amalume looked at me like a tiger that was laying on top of an injured *gwape*.

"Imagine if Obama had launched his own party in 2008 called UPAO (United Party for Africans *Obwela*) do you honestly think he would have become President?" Amalume quizzed knowing that he had landed that punch exactly where he wanted.

"We have enough parties in Malawi, join these parties – whether through front door or back door – but once you are in there, try to change things from within." These were the wise words from the master himself, Amalume was really a genius, I thought to myself while looking at my snoring Agogo.

"We can't seriously be launching *tidzipani* whose life span is only 6 months at the most," with those words Amalume dipped in his pocket taking out a K500 note;

"Is anyone willing to bet with me that some of these newly formed parties will not be here next year?"

I looked at the K500 laying there on the table, the last bet I made with Amalume, he won but I was sure this is one bet I could not lose if I tweaked it a little bit

"Ankolo, decrease the period from six months to at least two months then I am in on the bet." I said with a cheeky smile on my face, all the while thinking about the full plate of *dzipalapatilo dza nkhunda* which no one had bothered to touch and how that resembled these briefcase parties. I dipped into my wallet fishing out a crisp K500 slamming it on the table.

"*Nanenso nda betcha Amalume.*"

IMMIGRANTS & GROOMING LEADERS

Someone once asked me why I always smile whenever people talk about something that I have no knowledge about. The answer is simple; I just don't want to look foolish by making the wrong comment just like what happened about a month ago. It wasn't some sort of a life threatening gaffe; it wasn't like an operation or surgery whereby a doctor forgets a pair of scissors inside someone's abdomen. It was your simple everyday gaffe, still Shasha made it sound as if I had committed a crime of the highest order punishable by a firing battalion of T42 Tanks.

Shasha, as you know by now, is someone who is very knowledgeable and articulate when it comes to anything that involves cars. He, pretty much, knows the engine size of each and every American car; from your Chryslers to your Lincolns. This is why he laughed and made fun of me when I once commented that a Ford Mustang has got a 1.2litre engine. In Shasha's auto-world where he was the ruler, I had committed a crime.

He didn't stop talking and making fun of my blunder for two weeks straight, telling everyone about it, even my garden boy who has no idea what a Ford Mustang is.

"*Iwe Boyi, abwana ako ndi opepela eti, akuti Mustang ili ndi 1.2lita injini...Hahahahaha!*" Shasha roasted me.

Since *Boyi* knows where his salary comes from, he just carried on sweeping the leaves, ignoring the jibe, although I heard him later on laughing hysterically with the *khukhi*.

That was about a month ago and today, after watching some British News on TV, we were engaged in UK current affairs. It turns out that James Cameron's Conservative government just announced that all immigrants going to Britain will have to take an English language test, *mayeso a chizungu*.

I didn't see anything wrong with this, it's their language and it's their country so they could do as they pleased. Even Simioni agreed with me, adding that our government here should do the same.

"All immigrants coming to Malawi should take a Chichewa Test." Simioni said, because Malawians are tired of jumping in a minibus and having to listen to two Nigerians talking and laughing in their own language be it Igbo, Yoruba, Ibibio, Kanuri or any of their gazillion languages. To us it all sounds the same, they might be talking about a funeral back in Nigeria but since we can't understand a word they are saying, it just sounds as if they are ridiculing us.

"Look at all these stupid Malawians... kikikikiki!"

If Nigerians or Somalis or Ethiopians want to come to Malawi for greener pastures, they should at least be able to communicate in our language, that way they can integrate easily within our society.

It is only right that this then should also apply to those seeking greener pastures in United Kingdom, *phunzirani chizungu* otherwise *mukakwera* underground train *yopita ku Ndirande* when you wanted to go to St Pancras or Kings Cross.

Amalume, who had been sitting quietly listening to us, joined our conversation pointing out an important aspect we had just missed.

"I see what you mean," he started in his usual authoritative voice while setting his mug of thobwa carefully on the stool.

"Do you know that this new British ruling does not apply to Polish people or any of the white people coming from the European Union countries?" Amalume paused looking at us as we looked at him.

"They can still go to UK without taking this English Test," Amalume said pausing to take a sip from his mug of thobwa, waiting for his words to sink into our perplexed minds. It took me about four minutes before his words reached the inner most crevices of my brain and it took me the same length of time before I could churn out a response.

"Whaaaaaaaat?" I exclaimed sitting upright from the sofa almost knocking my drink over.

"So basically they are targeting Malawians and other Africans, *sichoncho*?" I directed this question at my British Auntie who was looking at me with a cheeky smile.

"Yes, it's because most Africans don't want to integrate with the British people. They like to keep to themselves and their own kind. You hear them laughing or arguing in Chichewa and it really annoys us British people." Auntie said while looking me straight in the eye.

This made me realise that the British people are also annoyed with African gibberish and obnoxious sounding *malilime* just as we Malawians take offense whenever these Nigerians start rapping in Igbo or Yoruba dialects while sitting in our luxurious minibuses or walking along the high streets of Mzuzu or downtown Zomba?

Before I could formulate an intelligent response to Auntie's assertions, my friend Simioni's beat me to it.

"Auntie, it's nearly impossible and a bit harsh to expect a Malawian to be arguing in English. When tempers hit boiling point it is better to resort to your mother language."

Simioni had a point here, because any futile attempts to curse (*kutukwana*) in a second language, just makes it sound ridiculous and funny. Instead of inflicting fear in your opponent you just make them laugh, which makes you get even angrier than before. There is nothing worse than someone laughing at your anger because it is has been conveyed in broken English.

Even Amalume had to agree, wiping some thobwa dregs from his upper lip, he told us that while he was in UK most of his arguments were conducted in his beloved Chichewa regardless of whether he was arguing with a fellow Malawian or a British.

"Anger comes out better in your own language." Amalume said while carefully setting his mug of Thobwa, claiming that his opening used to be in English but the core of the argument was best served in Chichewa.

"There are certain strong words that tend to lose their meaning if you try to translate them into *Chingelezi*." Amalume said while reaching for the mug of Thobwa.

Agogo agreed that an argument is not about the words, syntax or grammar but it's all about how loud your voice is, how much saliva is coming out of your mouth as you speak. This according to Agogo is a proven strategy that will force your opponent to take two or three steps back making him/her look as if he/she is retreating in fear.

"More importantly an argument is how twisted or viciously contorted your face is, the more wrinkled your face is, the more nerves protruding from your neck, the more convincing you will be in an argument, that's the art of a perfect argument." Agogo said while looking around the room as if he was about to argue with someone just to prove his statement.

I had to agree with Agogo because what he had just said reminded me of my growing up days, the days of going to Customs or Iponga's to watch Kung-fu movies. In most of these oriental martial arts movies they would often argue in a language I couldn't understand but I could easily surmise who was the angriest just by looking at their facial features.

Go and watch the film called "Enter the Dragon" by Bruce Lee, look at the bulging nerves on his neck and contorted facial features and you will understand what Agogo is implying here.

Now all along this debate, my dear friend Shasha had been sitting quietly unable to contribute. If this were a debate about cars he could have been the main speaker. Issues that had a social or political connotation to them were not Shasha's cup of tea. He always sat like *bubu* resembling a spare wheel locked up in the boot. But today Shasha decided enough is enough; he was going to make a contribution too, *basi nawonso che* Shasha *akuti akufuna kutsila nawo ndemanga pa nkhani za* current affairs.

His contribution took the whole topic on a totally different trajectory. We all paused in silence; mouths wide open, looking at him the same way you would look at a person who has three eyes and no neck. Shasha's contribution reminded me of the Ford Mustang gaffe I had made two weeks ago, it reaffirmed my strong belief that if you don't understand a topic it's better not to comment.

Shasha gulped down a mouthful of thobwa and out of blue said something that startled all of us.

"Western politics is really crazy." He paused and we all looked in his direction surprised that he wanted to contribute to the conversation. He did by dropping a bombshell on us.

"I hear Obama is grooming someone to take over from him when his term expires." Shasha said with a tone of conviction as if he was a worker in the White House and had heard this from Obama himself. Even one of my younger nephews who had been busy playing with my cell phone looked up in disbelief.

"*Izi nde zitinso uncle Shasha?*" My nephew asked, probably a question that everyone in the room would have loved to ask Shasha.

To start with, the topic we had been discussing had nothing to do with politics and nothing to do with America. Where and why Shasha came up with the notion that Obama is grooming his successor is really beyond belief. I am not very conversant with the politics of USA but I had doubts if Obama could really be wasting his time trying to handpick his successor. And even if he did, would the American people really swallow it.

Amalume, who is more knowledgeable than my friend, joined in the condemnation of what Shasha had just said.

"It's undemocratic as it is appalling to suggest that one man can make a decision for the whole country, there is a system in place and aspiring leaders are chosen via that system" Amalume rubbished Shasha's claims and even Auntie seem to think so.

"You can groom a dog to behave accordingly and you can groom your child to take over your business, but surely you don't expect a president to groom his successor?" She more like continued where her husband, Amalume, had left of. We all levelled our disagreements to Shasha's assertions.

But then Shasha is Shasha and in his mind years of living in South Bend made him more qualified than the rest of us as far as USA is concerned. Because my friend had lived through the Monica Lewinsky scandal and survived the whole hanging chard fiasco that denied Al Gore the Presidency, he was convinced that he was the professor of Americanology. He wasn't going to shut up because of rebukes from people who had never been outside the borders of Malawi (with the exception of Amalume and Auntie.)

Instead of sticking to the topic he had just started, he unexpectedly changed course again just like a drunken pilot, catching all of us off-guard. His next comment was even hard hitting than the first, which he delivered in a calm way.

"I wonder if they will investigate Obama too after his term comes to an end like they always do to ex-presidents?"

I thought this was too much now; Shasha was simply off the rails. I had no clue what my friend had been smoking or injecting himself, because I don't recall hearing Obama's predecessors ever being investigated with the exception of President Richard Nixon with the whole Watergate scandal.

"*Shasha, koma mutu wako ukugwila nchito bwino-bwino, wasuta chani lero?*" I lamented at my friend who didn't look bothered the least.

"Why would they investigate their president?" Simioni asked also failing to see Shasha's reasoning.

Auntie, who had been sitting quietly since the immigration issue, sat up excitedly like someone who had just figured the last piece of a complex million-piece jig-saw puzzle; "Oh! Shasha you mean like how you do it over here in Malawi?" she asked.

The minute Auntie said that, it downed on me, and everyone in the room, that we have actually dragged our ex-presidents through the courts and I found myself agreeing with Auntie.

"Yes we have, haven't we?" It was a question directed at my inner self than at the audience.

I never really thought of this and I found myself scratching my head. But surely Obama didn't accumulate any assets while in office did he? Last I heard is that once his term is over he will be moving back to the house he used to live (in Chicago) while he was still a Senator.

Which was rather peculiar that these presidents from rich nations don't usually go about building massive mansions while they are in office or did he ever build his own mansion while in office? I don't think so.

Did Obama start his own transport business, or build office complexes, maybe have shares in Filling Stations while in office? Not that we have heard of.

Why is it not the case? Can it be that the most powerful man on earth is afraid and in respect of the laws of his country that much? It looks like it.

All along I thought I had been thinking and asking these questions inside my mind not realising that I had actually been saying them out loud. I was surprised to see that everyone in the room was looking at me with their mouths wide open.

Mother who had been listening quietly started getting nervous with how our talk on UK immigration had suddenly turned into prosecuting ex-presidents.

She uncomfortably stood up to go and shut the windows, just as Agogo started complimenting the questions I had just posed. He reminded us about the whole saga of Press Corporation that took place years ago. Agogo also hinted on the ongoing case with some Office buildings rented to MRA, both cases involving ex-leaders.

"Is this a Malawian trend that our political leaders retirement will always be spent commuting between the court house and the lawyers office because of assets?" Simioni asked while looking at Agogo.

Agogo took a moment before responding, which was strange that he bothered to give Simioni's question a serious thought considering the way he hates Simioni's guts.

"We can't really say for sure, because so far we have only had two ex-presidents who have tangled with the law after their term. To draw conclusions from such a small sample would be erroneous." Agogo responded to a surprised Simioni. Maybe Agogo was right, or was he? Should we really wait until we have had forty-four presidents like America? And only if all forty-four end up in court because of dubious ways of asset accumulation while in office, then we can start drawing conclusions.

"I guess time will tell, but so far we can say that 67% of our Presidency has tangled with the laws of the land over assets." Amalume said interjecting his love of statistics in this case with percentages. I didn't know how he had arrived at the 67%, lucky for me Simioni was there to show me how.

Mother who had just finished shutting the windows and closing the curtains waded into the debate, speaking louder than usual.

"So this English Test that immigrants have to take in UK, are they allowed to use a calculator?" Mother jumped in the conversation in an attempt to derail this whole conversation about Presidents into safe neutral waters.

Hahahahaha, Masteni mpakana calculator pa Chingelezi eti?" Shasha laughed out loud and a few on my cousins had mischievous smiles on their faces.

We knew this was simply Mother's tact of trying to change the subject back to shallow waters, I don't think

Mother had made a gaffe like the one I made that a Ford Mustang has got a 1.2 litre engine.

The thought of trying to take an English Exam with the help of a calculator sure did lighten up the mood and caused us to move away from the talk of wealth accumulation by *atsogoleri athu.*

MIGRATING TO MOZAMBIQUE?

I pulled up at the filling station parking the Moris Marina next to the petrol pump as the cheerful petrol attendant in a yellow top and blue trousers approached, asking me how much should he pump.

"*Thilani mpaka idzadze mbuya.*" I replied as I got out of the Morris Marina and entered the Filling Station Shop to buy some Mahewu for myself, Sprite for Amalume, Cherry Plum for Shasha.

We were going to Mwanza to pick up our friend Tchale who was coming in from Mozambique. He had already sent us a text that he was just approaching Zobue and should be arriving at Mwanza border in an hour's time.

At nineteen-years old, Tchale might be young, but there is something matured about the way he talks and conducts himself. Maybe that is why he ended up with a fifty-something year old madam. But I must admit she looks young, *poti anzathu achizungu kuzolowela kudya zofewa*. Tchale had gone over to Mozambique scouting for business prospects after hearing that the economy there was doing so well.

There was a newspaper article about this company, Maputo Port Development Company, which was planning to invest close to a billion US dollars in the port of Maputo and was looking for sub-contractors.

Upon hearing this, Tchale sniffed an opportunity and went to Mozambique without second thought.

For one so young, Tchale is an amazing go-getter, someone who believes that opportunity doesn't come knocking. In his usual high pitch voice, Tchale likes saying that in life you make your own luck. To him Mozambique was the new frontier, the new gold rush.

I thought this was a bit strange and the day Tchale left for Mozambique I brought this up with Amalume.

"Wasn't Mozambique at war some time back?" I asked as memories of refugees seeking safe haven in our peaceful and tranquil Malawi came flooding back to mind. *Masiku amenewo* Renamo and Frelimo *itabeba*, this was when landmines were robbing people of their legs and lives.

I remember back in the day whenever we drove along the M1 near Ntcheu overlooking Mozambique, all you could see were dilapidated and bombed out houses spread across a vast expanse of open land. *Ku apwitikizi* land as we used to call it, a place where no normal person would want to go unless that person has fallen out of love with his/her legs. Even Malawians living near the border knew what the ominous sign written: "Peligro Minas!" meant... (Danger landmines!)

When we picked up Tchale at Mwanza border post, we could tell he was elated, he immediately started telling us of a Mozambique we didn't know existed. Initially I thought he was simply making it all up, surely Mozambique with all the fighting that took place over there cannot be better than Malawi which has never seen war?

Yet, no matter from what angle one looks at it or whether one compares the two countries Macro and Micro economic indicators. Malawi, as a country, is pathetically lagging behind.

We were getting facts straight from the horse's mouth because Tchale had penetrated deep into the bowels of Mozambique. He had gone beyond Tete as far down as Maputo the capital city, to go and meet with the big kahuna's of this conglomerate aka Maputo Port Development Company.

"*Koma iwe,* weren't you scared of Peligro Minas?" I asked him while checking him out via the rear-view mirror to ascertain that he still had all his limbs intact.

But he surprised me that the days of landmines and AK47's are long gone. *Akuti kuli bata ladzaoneni, moti anakanyauda* at Costa De Sol, which is like Mangochi *ya apwitikizi.*

Tchale spoke of the amazing food in Mozambique; *nsomba ya bakayawo* (bacalhau) even *dzipalapatilo* (pés da galinha) claiming that it is better than what we eat over here. He thinks that this is why Mozambican women have got skin *yosalala ngati kakhanda.* I told him not to repeat this in the presence of my sisters and Aunties otherwise they will chew him alive.

Amalume seems to agree with Tchale, not about the women's skin but that Mozambique's economy has overtaken ours the same way Usain Bolt would overtake Zabweka in a race. I smiled at the thought of Zabweka in jogging shorts; sprinting huffing and panting, his belly bouncing like a balloon full of *phalala* trying to catch up with *Bwana* Bolt.

My funny visualisation of Zabweka the athlete was abruptly interrupted when Tchale started telling us about Mozambique's infrastructure; their massive modern roads with funny sounding *apwitikizi* names like Eduardo Mondlane, 24 de Julho and even a Chinese sounding one Mau Tse Tung.

I mused over this, wondering how come we don't have a Chinese road in Malawi, surely it would be nice to ride my Morris Marina in a road called Bruce Lee, Jack Chan or Chuck Norris, Amalume later corrected me that Chuck Norris is not Chinese. I didn't want to argue with him because I have seen the way Chuck Norris fights and no American can fight like that.

Tchale told us that many foreign businesses are investing in Mozambique. He was even amazed at the number of BP filling stations being opened in that country.

"I thought BP is closing all its filling stations in Africa?" I asked while checking the petrol gauge of my Marina (half tank.)

"No, I think it's just here in Malawi that they are pulling out." Amalume chipped in. I couldn't understand why they would want to close down here and open up just across the border (*mwina atopa nawo ma Kwacha athu akufuna* Meticais.)

But I thought Shasha had once told me that BP is closing up shop and going back to UK because the *chitsime* where they used to get their oil from in the USA was destroyed and it's been leaking oil non-stop.

Since I have always looked at Shasha as 5% Malawian and 95% American, I had wholeheartedly believed his story without a doubt. But now it seems that my friend's explanation was nothing but a pile of *ndowe*.

The massive oil spill in the gulf has no bearing on BP's move to shut down operations in Malawi. As a matter of fact according to Tchale, BP is very much in business and pumping serious money into neighbouring Mozambique.

The only thing that Shasha told me, which Amalume agrees with, is that a lot of Mozambicans abroad are now exodusing back to their homeland because of job opportunities in their country.

It's not just BP setting up businesses in Mozambique, but a lot of foreign companies are flocking to our neighbour, companies like AME, Mineral Economics and Riversdale just to mention a few, *nchifukwa chake anzathuwa akumabwerera kwao.*

Even white farmers chased out of Zimbabwe by Zanu PF, are also setting up farms in Mozambique resulting in massive food production. *Pajatu anzathu achizunguwa samalima ndi makasu*, they use farm machinery and instead of depending on rain, they set up massive irrigation infrastructures – pipes and sprinklers. *Zipangizo zothilila madzi* instead of waiting for clouds of rain especially in this day and age when the weather patterns have gone bonkers.

How can such good economic developments be happening just across the border in Mozambique, a country where not so long ago had more AK47's than *makasu* and where its people were busy planting land mines in the ground instead of maize.

I looked at Tchale in disbelief as if surprised that he made it back alive with all his limbs still attached to his torso.

"You really saw all this in Mozambique but you didn't even see a single land mine?" I asked a bit perplexed because the impression I had of my neighbouring country is that, it was infested with land mines to the point that no one ventures outdoors anymore. But now Tchale was giving me a totally contradicting picture to the Mozambique that I knew, as a result this was really troubling me down to the core of my unknowing Malawian soul. I looked at Amalume for some clarification; surely this didn't sound right.

"Amalume, how come Malawi boasts real peace backed by the fact that we have never experienced war and yet a country like Mozambique that was ravaged by sixteen years of civil war seems to be doing better than us?" I asked briefly taking my eyes off the road.

"Mozambique is now the envy of all these *Azungu* and they are pumping in money into their economy more than they are into ours." Tchale added not really answering my question but compounding it even further.

"Is there some favouritism going on here? Or is our neighbour doing something right and better than us?" I posed this to Amalume.

What Amalume said next didn't address my queries, if anything it just made things a bit more complicated for me. I could feel my brain lumbering and straining to decipher all what Amalume was saying, it was like asking *bubu* to break the Davinci Code. He spoke while looking outside the window as we passed the famous Thambani Turn off.

"Right now Zimbabwean economy is one of the worst in the world, but there is something that tells me that once they sort out their political quagmire, they will also overtake us just as Mozambique has. We will be flocking to Zimbabwe for greener pastures." He said with a hint of realism.

I almost slammed on the brakes because of Amalume's claim. First Mozambique overtakes us and now the thought of Malawians queuing up at the Zimbabwean Embassy for work permits to go work in Harare or Bulawayo, was something I just couldn't contemplate.

Amalume reminded me that not so long ago Zimbabwe was the jewel of Africa and their comeback from the brink is surely just around the corner. Especially now that they have just discovered large deposits of diamonds which, it is being claimed, would propel Zimbabwe as the contributor of about 25% of the world's diamonds.

"Have you forgotten that delicious drink called *Mazoe* we used to drink when you were still young?" Amalume tapped into the part of my past that had faded with the passing of time.

Memories came flooding back; I had forgotten that *Mazoe* had been an import from Zimbabwe as was Cerelac, Camphor and more. Amalume had a point there, just like Mozambique has overtaken us, am sure it's only a matter of time before Zim does the same. I started to think, of all the cruel and bad tasting jokes I have said about the Zim-Dollar and wondered if they will ever let me into their country if things got tough here, which is probably just a matter of 'when' not 'if' due to the obvious tell-tale signs of our economy which is, probably, rapidly sliding into oblivion.

How I wish I was like my young friend Tchale, to have that ability of dropping everything and relocating to a different geographical region all together. I looked at him via the rear view mirror.

"So you are seriously thinking of relocating to Mozambique? How are you going to communicate *ndi apwitikizi*? Do you know any *Bondia-Bondia*?" I bombarded him with a staccato of questions that had a hint of sarcasm.

"Eu falar Portuguese bem." Tchale surprised us with his command of *chipwitikizi*. I couldn't help but laugh.

"*Hahahahaha, aTchale inu musatitukwane apa*, you have only been there for two weeks and already *mwayamba ku phoza*. Do you even know what you have just said?" I asked while keeping my eye on a stupid-brainless goat along the road that appeared as if it wanted to cross, typical Malawian *mbuzi*. I almost didn't hear Tchale's translation of what he had just said I had to ask him to repeat as the Malawian goat darted back into the bushes.

"It means I can speak Portuguese well." Tchale repeated, but I didn't believe him because *ziribe umboni*.

Tchale ignored my sarcasm telling us that he will most likely be settling in Mozambique.

I tried to convince him to stay in Malawi because things will also pick up here as can be seen by the recent development by this American company called Millennium Challenge Corporation (MCC.) A company that has embarked on a project to modernise our energy sector and facilitate the possibility of setting up a private electricity company here in Malawi because, let's face it, Escom *zikuwavuta.*

I am sure once we sort out all these electricity blackouts companies will start investing in Malawi, creating job opportunities so that all Malawians who are abroad can come back and do something for their country, *kudzathandiza chitukuko kumudzi kuno abale.*

I have never heard Tchale laugh so loud I had to take my eyes of the road again watching him on the rear view mirror thinking that someone was tickling him to induce such laughter, *kuseka mwachikhakha.*

"Hahahahaaa, *m'mene ndikuwadziwila aMalawi a kunjawo,* I have my doubts about that." He said sarcastically.

I wondered why Malawians wouldn't come if foreign companies started investing here. Let us not forget there is also that massive initiative the President has been proposing down in *Nsanje* District of developing a port, which would cut the cost of transporting goods by road and create jobs; although transporters, especially heavy goods hauling both dry and wet cargo, will have issues with this.

Tchale gave me a look of someone who knows something you don't, a look of a knowledgeable person, clearing his throat like a pastor about deliver a sermon.

"Yes these are important steps, but I have lived with Malawians abroad and most of them cite certain aspects that prohibit them forever returning to Nyasa. Things like education for their children, medical facilities, fair job opportunities, and security among other things."

He said with the emphasis of someone who knows what he is talking about.

"*Iiiii, koma nanga enafe tikukhala bwaa?*" I queried.

MAULEMU WERE DRAFTED BY MEN

Today I had a very strong feeling that Simioni was going to be asked to leave my house by Agogo before even lunch was served. It's one of those feeling you can't exactly explain, the feeling that just originates from the pit of your stomach, the one that feels like a bubble of air that needs to come out – yes that kind of feeling.

It's the way my dear friend started the whole subject about the origins of our Malawian *miyambo* or *maulemu*. I even told Manyuchi to tell *ntsikana wantchito* not to bother setting the table with Simioni's plate on it because Agogo was going to throw him out in a few minutes. The minute my friend opened his mouth I knew that he was surely on collision course with Agogo.

"Guys, I really want you to have an open mind, think outside the box." Simioni started and I immediately sensed trouble brewing like Hurricane Katrina from the direction of where Agogo was sitting. Simioni must have sensed it too because he was trying his best to dodge Agogo's eyes with the same difficulty New Orleans had hoped to dodge Katrina.

At 102 years, everything about Agogo is very old except his eyes. If Agogo was a packet of biscuits then he would have been past his sell-by-date, but it's his eyes that betray his age. Agogo has the fiery eyes of an angry teenager capable of staring at you with the same intensity a fifteen yr old concentrates at a shoot-em up Playstation Game.

If looks could kill, then Simioni would have died a thousand deaths by now because Agogo's lethal stare was honing in at Simioni in what a sniper or a rifle marksman would categorise as 'dead in his cross-hairs.'

Agogo had the capacity to disarm a whole army with his look alone, a look so defeating and at times so frightening you had no choice but to look the other way. It always appeared as if he was trying to read your soul and see beyond the realm of your imagination.

My friend Simioni tends to stand up for women's issues and that always wins him some bonus points in my house from the feminine sector of the Amoto clan. I have even noticed that he gets served more rice and bigger pieces of *dzipalapatilo* even though he is not a relation of ours. This prospect of an outsider coming in and enjoying best pieces of *nyama yobaya* is like adding petrol to fire, it intensifies Agogo's dislike of my friend. I remember Manyuchi Darling once commented.

"*Adzaphana awa.*" Manyuchi said it with a serious tone that made me fear for the safety of my friend because I know Agogo is one of those characters who brings a bazooka to a fist fight. While you are busy rolling up your sleeves and clenching your fists he is slowly loading a bazooka shell and taking aim.

"Have you ever wondered who came up with all these cultural nuances that we blindly follow?" Simioni started while signalling at one of my young niece who was holding a basin of water for washing hands not to kneel down for him.

Simioni always confused the Amoto females with his liberalism and I could tell that my little niece was struggling whether to kneel or not. She looked at Agogo in fear and looked at Simioni pleadingly, but my friend reassured her.

"It's ok for you to give me the water while standing up." Simioni said whilst stealing a glance in Agogo direction and gesturing for the young girl to stand up.

The minute Simioni gave that unauthorised authorisation that a girl of the Makala clan could go ahead *kuperekela madzi* while standing up... *mayo ine...* from the corner of my eye I saw Agogo breathing fire like a two-headed dragon.

Everyone in the room knew that Agogo had the authority to authorise the cancellation of Simioni's unauthorised authorisation. We all held our breath as Agogo started making some hand gestures that Generals make at the start of a major war. I could also see Agogo's hand slowly reaching for his walking stick, which was more of a weapon than walking aid.

"What do you mean by cultural nuances?" I jumped in before Agogo could blow a gasket in his 102 year old brain.

"You know I have always wondered if the constititution for our *maulemu* was arrived at in the same way America's founding fathers came up with their constitution." Simioni went on ignoring Agogo fiery gaze.

Shasha, who tends to get excited at the mention of anything American, looked up from the plate of groundnuts that had been keeping him busy since he got here. I looked at him wondering how anyone can eat groundnuts just before *nsima* was served. I figured maybe that's how they do it in South Bend USA especially after Auntie, once, told me that groundnuts are like "starters"... *akuti* appetiser or *kandzutsa lilime*.

Ignoring Shasha I quickly switched back to Simioni trying to discern the point he was articulating. Even the women who had been making trips to and from the kitchen started to gather around lending him their ears. I saw Mother with two of her sisters come in from outside where they had been tending to *m'phale*.

The congregating females seem to energise Simioni who shifted his conversation into 2nd gear. He knew that with the women captivated by what he was saying, it would be hard for Agogo to throw him out. Agogo is stubborn but he is also wise enough not to upset the women before food is served, *pachizungu akuti* he knows which side of his bread is buttered (don't ask me what this means, ask my British Auntie.)

"Did our ancestral elders gather around a village fire to create all these traditions? We just didn't pluck them out of the air, did we?" Simioni said while making plucking gestures with his hands.

"Surely there must have been an *indaba* of wise people drafting up these things that became almost traditional laws." Simioni paused to let the packed living room digest his words before continuing.

"I have always wondered, were there any women representatives at this *indaba* of wise people?" He quizzed while looking at the section where most of the females were sitting or standing, all looking at him in a trance like state.

"For the benefit of doubt, let's presuppose that indeed there were women at this *Indaba for the Formulation of Malawi's Cultural Norms.*" Simioni paused briefly just to abbreviate this into I.F.M.C.N as if it was some sort of an International Organisation that arose from the Bretton Woods Conference of 1944.

"Did these female representatives really cast their vote that a woman shall always kneel down for her man, that a woman shall always carry the baby on her back, while balancing a bucket of water on her head and carrying plastic bags of *matowo* and *m'bedu* on both hands, obediently following her husband who has his hands in his pockets while smoking a Tom-Tom and yelling; *inu a mache boyi tamayendani zansanga-nsanga mukandiphikile nsima apa tisanagone.*"

With that Simioni took a long pause, the women in the room looked at him the same way a congregation looks at a pastor and I noticed that some of them had tears welling in their eyes as his funny but true narration struck a chord in them.

Agogo couldn't take this treason sermon anymore; he sat upright from his chair, so ubrupt I thought he was going to fall but he regained his balance with by planting his walking stick in front of him.

"Have you got nothing better to talk about?" He started while walking toward Simioni, I sensed trouble.

"Don't start coming in here spreading your bad manners and rebellious seeds among our well cultured women." Agogo shot at Simioni while gesturing to the packed living room of women.

My British Auntie who, all along, had a wide smile cutting from ear to ear urged Simioni on, ignoring Agogo as if he hadn't spoken something which caused Amalume to shift uncomfortably in his chair forcing himself to stare at the ceiling trying to avoid Agogo's stare.

Ever since Auntie came to join us in Malawi there are so many things she has said or done that go against the norms. But the mere fact that she is British gives her a free pass that is not enjoyed by some of the Makala females. But there are times I feel that perhaps Auntie has overused that free pass and perhaps her privileges are about to come to an end. Lately she has been rubbing Agogo the wrong way and lately Agogo has been giving her that 'don't push your luck' look.

Simioni who had been sitting down all this time whilst delivering his sermon got up to his feet. This looked like a tactic to avoid Agogo who was menacingly approaching where he had been sitting. Simioni started pacing the room reminding me of the charismatic Evangelist Reinhard Bonnke preaching on the area where they later on built Shoprite.

"I think that this Indaba must have comprised of only men." Simioni said while locking eyes with Agogo for the first time. But Simioni couldn't stand the fire originating from those 102 year old twin retinas thus he broke eye contact opting to carry on with his sermon while walking to the other side of the room.

"Imagine if it was the other way round that the IFMCN was comprised of only our wise ancestral women without a single male in attendance." He said with some emphasis on the word 'female' while looking at the women.

"The outcome would surely have been drastically different. It probably would have been the men kneeling down for their women and most likely it would have been the man carrying buckets of water on their heads while the woman walked in front with hands tucked into her chitenje." Simioni stopped pacing after noticing that Agogo has stopped following him round the room.

"You are just talking *ndowe zaziwisi.*" Agogo gave out a weak response showing signs of defeat.

Simioni knew that he had Agogo by the ropes. It was like a 'Mike Tyson vs Sikusinja fight' – and Sikusinja was surprisingly pounding Tyson's head *ngati thimati.* The crowd couldn't believe it, most of the women got to their feet as if Sikusinja aka Simioni had just landed a sharp uppercut to Tyson's chin.

Simioni used the momentum gained and shifted into 3rd gear. He now had the courage to look at those teenage eyes embedded in Agogo's 102 year old skull.

"I know Agogo thinks am being rebellious, but shouldn't we really question some of these norms?" Simioni asked and I saw smiles from most of the women in the room

Simioni had shifted gears so fast most of us our brains were still in 2nd whereas he was engaging 3rd.

"What were they thinking when they accorded *alendo* such vast importance?" Was the surprise change of direction that came from my friend leaving all of us perplexed but to Agogo it was deflating so much that he slumped in the nearest chair in what looked like a sign of surrender or defeat.

"What do you mean by that?" I asked on behalf of the whole sitting room which was now packed. Even the garden boy's wife was in attendance including the wife of *akhukhi* and some women who must have been her friends.

Simioni turned his gaze to me the same way Evangelist Reinhard Bonnke would look at the local pastor knowing that this may be your country but the congregation is here to see me.

"Most of us are doing ok right, which means that we don't have to wait until Christmas to eat rice. Then how come when we visit the village, we are regarded as important visitors (*akutauni*) and we are worshiped to the point that they slaughter a whole chicken for us? And yet these are the same people who have been eating *ntolilo, nkhwani* or some greens that taste like quinine medicine day in day out." Simioni paused, taking a sip from his glass of thobwa before continuing.

"Why did our ancestral elders come up with this tradition that we should worship *alendo* with such blind madness?" Simioni articulated this with some air of authority knowing that he had the room under his spell and at this moment in time Agogo was absolute.

Shasha who had now finished *kutafuna* the roasted groundnuts, *mosusukila*, thought it was wise to contribute.

"Yo bro that shit is deep, but 'em village dudes are just showing their love, innit?" Simioni looked at Shasha the same way Evangelist Bonnke looks at someone who desperately needs to have evil demons cast out of his soul.

"Exactly my point, why should a whole village full of malnourished young children lacking in protein slaughter a whole chicken just for one over-weight visitor who looks like he eats margarine and drinks kazinga oil daily." Simioni paused looking at Agogo who was pretending to sleep.

My friend Simioni had just shifted into 4th gear and everyone was captivated including Agogo behind his fictitious sleep, as could be seen by his twitching lips.

"That is why I think that the elders who came up with these cultural norms were a bunch of crazy men." Simioni said it stressing on the word *Crazy*.

"I can't see women concocting such norms that deny skinny malnourished village kids chicken meat but blindly slaughter the biggest *tambala* for the *chinamadya bwino* with a figure like Zabweka from town." The minute Simioni said this you could see the Zabweka-look-alikes of my family shifting uneasily as if they were sitting on hot nails.

"Wouldn't Zabweka-man benefit from the *nkhwani* and *ntolilo* growing behind the toilet?" Simioni said with the airs of someone who was enjoying himself.

My friend had shifted into 5th gear with some skill and finesse, walking with a spring in his step he sat back down to let his words sink in our heads.

Simioni's sermon like speech was slowly trying to force its way into my hardened brain when behold out of the kitchen appeared a big plate of rice with tender *dzipalapatilo* just for him. I heard Shasha whisper to Amalume who had a look of bewilderment.

"Damn this boy is good, damn he is so good." Shasha cursed while licking his dry lips either from hunger or the salty groundnuts he had been munching on.

We all sat there licking our dry mouths too while watching Simioni enjoy his hard earned food. He scooped a forkful of rice and we all followed that fork as it took off from the plate orbiting towards his open smiling mouth. We swallowed our own saliva as we watched Simioni methodically and deliberately chew the delicious looking rice. He swallowed and then set both knife and fork down the same way a soldier sets down his weapons when he is getting ready for hand-to-hand combat. He then purposefully reached down to pick a delicious and sumptuous looking piece of *chipalapatilo*, winking at me as he did so.

I couldn't take this torture in my own house anymore. I looked at the girl who had just set the plate for my friend.

"What's taking so long with our food?" but she just shrugged her shoulders and dashed back into the kitchen.

After a few minutes which felt like eternity, a damning report came from the kitchen via the same smiling girl.

"*Akuti chakudya cha enanu madzi sanaphwele mubadikilabe.*"

TAKING OVER OUR LAKE

I want to categorically deny all these malicious rumours being spread about me being seen driving near Chipata, Zambia. And those who are claiming to have seen me at St Pancras underground train station in London need to stop saying these things. The same goes to those Malawians who claim that I was pulled over by the traffic police for speeding along Lincoln way West in South Bend. And a big massive "no," because the person you saw on the 192 bus along Stockport road Manchester was not me. I know *ndinati ziii,* but that does not give people the right to start claiming that they have seen me in places where I have never been before. And to the one who says that I have been locked up at Mwanza Prison .... *Iiiiii abale, imeneyo ndiye nkhanzano. Ndalakwa chani kuti mpakana anditsekele ku ndende?*

To all those Malawians (and a few non-Malawians) who came over to my house and didn't find me, *ndati ndikupepeseni, ngakhale zikuoneka ngati munasangalala* in my absence. I don't mind you people coming into my house for *ma hape* – eating and drinking as if there is no tomorrow.

What I don't like is, when you start taking my empty bottles with you when leaving. And what I despise most is, when you start barbequing my *dzipalapatilo* when you can read the notice on the freezer that clearly stipulates that; "*dzipalapatilo dzili* strictly off limits to *alendo.*" If I ban you to come into my house most of you will start complaining;

"Makala w*ayamba kunyada.*"

Some of you know that I was at the lake and yes, I was surprised to see you there just as you were surprised to see me there. But just like you (not all of you though) I am a very busy person too who needs a break once in a while. Seeing that I have never been to the lake for leisure or relaxing, I thought to myself.

"Flipping 'eck, why not!"

It's not like I have never been *kunyanja* before. The thing is the only time I went to Mangochi was years ago when I was still working for David Whitehead (*idakali mʹmanja mwa azungu.*) I had to go to the company cottage with some documents for the *bwana nkubwa* – General Manager – to sign. That time the lake was mostly for *anzathu achizunguwa.*

So you can imagine my apprehension when Simioni suggested that we go to Mangochi and relax, lay on the sand, *mwina kubantila mʹmadzi.* I told him that *zobantilazo ndiye ayiwale*, no way will I be taking my shirt off in public.

The first impression I got upon arrival at the lake was typical of anyone who has hasn't been at the Lake for ages.

"Malawi *yasinthadi abale.*" Was the first remark that came out of my mouth, because back in the day the only Malawians at the lake were *opalasa ngalawa* and maybe a few cottage houseboys, *khukhi's* and maybe, one or two, Honourable *Ujenis*. That's not the case anymore because *ma Nyasa* have taken over *nyanja yawo*.

I know some of you go to the lake every weekend and are probably wondering what Makala is on about. If you are, then you must be one of those people who never experienced the lake when it was the domain for *azungu* only. This has nothing to do with a black and white thing nor should anyone ascribe racist connotations to it. The fact of the matter is that back in the day *ife achiMalawife* did not know the relaxation that could be had simply by laying half naked on a sandy beach.

The lake transforms your senses; laying on a beach with your legs spread wide open in a 45 degree angle (90 if you are adventurous) is considered chillaxing. But if you try to pull a similar stunt in the middle of Blantyre, right by Clock Tower, people will look at you disgustedly. Most Malawian back in the day used to have this mentality, no wonder they never frequented the lake thinking; "zopusa ine ayi, zomagona pa nchenga."

On the other hand, let's face it, not a lot of Malawians had disposable cash that one needs in order to spend a day or two at the lake.

But things have changed, *zinthu zasintha*, I was so impressed and so gripped by the whole lake fever that I started regretting not bringing *kabudula wanga* so that *nanenso ndi bantile nawo* in this lake of ours. *Ine kusilira.*

I just had to smile though, thinking *a*Malawi *talandadi* our lake and in the process *zinthu zalowa chikuda osati masewela*. Back *nthawi ya azungu* the men wore 'bathing shorts' – *akuti* swimming trunks – and the women were usually in bikini's or swimming costumes. Funny enough or sad enough this is not the case with us Malawians today.

The reason I am bringing this up is because, while minding my own business and looking at the distant mountains across the crystal blue waters, I saw this one man (*wachi-Malawi*) strolling along the golden sandy beach not wearing swimming trunks but clad in a full office suit and a tie sticking out of his pocket. I know that *aMalawife mphasha* is our way of life, but *abale anzanga* who wears a formal suit to the lake? Or was Makala missing something here? Does this Malawian want to tell me that taking off his tie and sticking it into his pocket constitutes to beach wear? *Zovutatu izi.*

And what made this even more perplexing was that whenever the waves crashed on the beach and a few drops of water splattered on his *skuna* – shoes – the gentleman would flip out his handkerchief to wipe the droplets off.

"Why go to the lake if you don't want to get wet?" I wondered to myself, at least the girl he was with (am assuming it was his teenage daughter) was dressed more appropriately for the lake in a matching yellow bikini that made her look like a Brazilian Samba dancer.

I could see that Simioni and Shasha were not new to this lake charade, they appeared to be enjoying so much; laughing and splashing about that I felt like screaming a fake threat.

"Hippoooo!!!" But I did not, figuring that this would turn me into a spoilsport and worse it would end up giving Simioni a coronary heart attack.

Shasha claims that while he was in America he was a regular swimmer at St Joseph, Lake Michigan, although *izi ziribe umboni,* something which is a problem *ndi a Malawi obwera* from *kunjaku* – they come with all sorts of stories knowing that we cannot verify, qualify or quantify them. We don't even know if there is a lake called Michigan. Whatever the case though they were really having more fun than me.

They had, both, jumped in water and Simioni was pretending to swim although I could tell that he was just walking, pretending *kumapalasa* with his hands. There is no way that Simioni could float above water, not with that physique of his coupled with his fear of depths and or heights. He forgets that he has told me how he can never take a bath in a tub not even at gun point claiming that they would have to shoot him first.

Shasha on the other hand was elated and couldn't stop screaming ecstatically and I had to admit that for someone who suffers from aqua-phobia it was a bit impressive to see him venture out as far deep as his knees.

"Did you know that this is the 3rd deepest fresh water lake in the whole world?" Shasha shouted elatedly even though he didn't venture in too deep to put that factual claim to test. As matter of fact I don't know why he jumped in because the water level was just above his *akatumba* it would have been safer just to walk in than dive.

"Is this how *mumachitila ku Lake Michiganiko?*" I sacarstically asked him although I wasn't expecting to get an answer from him.

While my two friends were having fun pretending to swim and float, a dugout canoe aka *bwato* had just docked by the beach and most of the women flocked to buy the fresh *chambo, milamba ndi nsomba zina zosiyanasiyana* that the tired but constantly smiling fishermen had just caught. Some of the fish was still alive flopping and flapping in the shallow water at the bottom of the *bwato*.

I am not a fish guy – some of us it's *dzipalapatilo* for life – so I opted to not to congregate on the fish auction sale that was taking place.

I kept on strolling along the beach, I saw *azungu awiri* who were smiling – that fake smile *azungu* like to give when they are in minority – I fake-smiled back.

I wish Amalume's wife, my British Auntie, was here, you never know maybe they might know each other. Even if they didn't, am sure it could have been a good experience for Auntie to come in contact with her own people.

I remember Amalume once told me that in UK it's nice if you get on a bus or train full of strangers and all of a sudden you hear someone talking in Chichewa. It takes you back home, *akuti*.

There is something about the lake though, everyone looks happy and people are friendly to each other, even if you don't know them. Even Shasha, who had just come out of his fake-swimming, commented.

"You don't see this much friendliness among a *Malawife kunjako, maka-maka ku* Bend, *aaaaaa! Nta ndi pan'gono pomwe.*" He said while drying his chest, arms and neck with a fluffy looking beach towel that had a picture of Sponge Bob Squarepants. I resisted the urge to query him about having a towel with children's favourite cartoon character.

I thought Shasha was exaggerating a little bit here, but he insisted and stuck to his story.

"You see how those women are happily chit-chatting there while buying *chambo* and *matemba?*" He said while pointing to the happy looking women who couldn't believe the good deal they were getting on the fresh fish when compared to extortion prices in Blantyre.

"What about them?" I asked while looking at the women who had now completely surrounded the dugout canoe much to the excitement of the smiling *asodzi.*

"If that was South Bend, the police would already have been called in, *chifukwa a Malawi adakaphana because of nsomba ya iwisi.*" Shasha said while shaking water off his breaded hair the same way a dog does when it's wet.

I don't know what it is about our lake – *mwina mpweya wake ndi wa* special but I found it relaxing and felt like spending a night here. I honestly wished I could stay for the whole week maybe a whole month, but I knew that this would simply not happen. Especially when I have been getting a lot of texts that *abale ndi alongo* have congregated at my house for *macheza.*

I know it's nice and relaxing at the lake, but there is a side of me that thinks am better off at home than being here watching a man walking in a suit along the lake or staring at a few women who were pretending to swim while wearing *dzitenje*.

"Who jumps in the lake wearing *nsalu ya chipani? komadi aMalawi tatengadi nyanja yathu.*" I said it loud without realising, and my friends both looked at me quizzically.

POOR MILLIONAIRES SYNDROME

After last night's ma happy at Grin Bamboo I was in no mood for any activity this morning. I was just going to sit here and listen to Boyz 2 Men music wafting out of the Sony surround-speakers with the volume appropriately low for a Sunday morning. Sipping a nice cold glass of *thobwa* while reading the Sunday Times was, perhaps, the best peace and quite a man could ask for.

Unfortunately this peace and quiet didn't last long. Shasha barged in like some sort of hurricane wind without the decency of knocking on the door.

"Hey *madala*, this is not South Bend you know, *kuno timagogoda* before entering someone's home"

But Shasha being Shasha he either pretended to ignore me or didn't think I was serious enough and continued to smile tossing a Forbes Magazine at me. "Here read this" he gestured to an article about the 'World's Richest People'

I didn't think knowing who the world's richest *dzikhwaya* would help me in any way whatsoever. I know it wouldn't help me pay my bills nor will it have any effect on my dwindling bank account, but just to keep Shasha quite, especially since my head was still spinning from last night shindig at Grin Bamboo I grabbed the Forbes Magazine and flipped through the pages.

There was *che* Bill Gates, *abiti* Oprah, *ada* Lakshmi Mittal and some names I have never heard of. It was bwana Bill Gate's wealth that caught my eye... shaaaaa... I couldn't help wondering.

"How could one person have so much money?" I wondered while reading where it said that his net worth was at $54 billion. I couldn't believe my eyes I had to confirm this with Amalume who seem to agree with what was written in Forbes and even proceded to tell me that this was eleven-times bigger than the nominal GDP of the whole of Malawi which is slightly under $5 billion, *zovutatu izi*.

What struck me as odd wasn't the mountain of wealth these individuals had – what I couldn't understand was their pictures, *zithunzi-thunzi*. As you know being a typical Malawian I get carried away with pictures or photographs of myself, which should explain the thirty-two photo albums in the bedroom and sitting room.

On top of these albums there is also a gazillion pictures of me on Facebook, most of which I am posing on expensive cars, which is a common Malawian fallacy called "Snap and Run" vis-à-vis identify a flashy car stand next to it and take a picture real quick and run before the owner of the car catches you.

As long as you are not caught, 'Snap and Run' is a cheap way of showing off to your Facebook friends all the expensive cars you own. There is a Malawian in UK who works at McDonalds but on his Facebook pictures he is standing next to a Ferrari, Lamborghini and Porsche with a narration at the bottom of each my weekend car, work car and girlfriend's car respectively.

But there was something odd and peculiar about the photographs of Bill Gates and his billionaire colleagues. My Malawian eyes and mentality told me that there was something strangely missing from their Kodak moments. That's when it hit me, like a ton of bricks, right on the head.

None of these very wealthy individuals was posing next to a fancy car like our fellow Malawian friend employed by McDonalds. None of these gentlemen was wearing a flashy bling-bling wrist watch, something which I found a bit perplexing seeing that they had all the money in the world and didn't have to resort to Snap and Run. As a matter of fact they could afford to pose next to their own 80 foot yacht or Gulf Stream Jet and yet and they weren't. For example; Lakshmi Mittal who has £23 billion (yes billion with a B) in the bank was wearing a shirt that looked as if it was bought at *Zalewa-Kaunjika Ltd.* And yet this is the man who is four times richer than the guy who owns Chelsea football club, what's his name?... Oh yes, Roman Abramovich. But here he was, looking simple and ordinary, *zikutheka bwanji?*

Now contrast this with a typical average 2 tambala Malawian like our McDonald's friend or even like me. Like I have said previously, it's not a secret that ever since I discovered Facebook, a thousand pictures of my Morris Marina, my shoes, my flip phone and what not have been posted without regard or remorse for my Facebook friends time.

I have never even paused to wonder, who really want's to see my Morris Marina or my flip phone especially when you consider that people are now using

Blackberry's and next generation smart phone capable of sending e-mail, browsing and even making you toast.

With only twenty-four precious hours in a day, do people have that much time to be looking at what car Makala Amoto drives (a common car for that matter?)

And who wants to see my expensive but fake jewellery or designer shoes? Is it because I am desperate to tell the whole world that; "Haaallooo, look at me, I can afford an expensive wrist watch or hand bag, even though I am still in arrears with my electricity bill from two years ago."

Should I be surprised then why God took one look at my Malawian mentality and materialistic perception towards life, shook His head thinking.

"*Awatu ndi matama awowa tisawadalitse ndi* $53 billion otherwise *atipweteketsa mutu.*"

Isn't it funny that most of us who flaunt fake wrist watches and appalling clothes don't even know our own personal net worth? Of course we wouldn't know it because we don't have it.

Isn't it amazingly sad that if our friend from McDonalds or Makala Amoto was to stand next to Bill Gates people would think that I have more money than *bwana aku* Microsoft-*wa*.

That is why Amalume claims that Malawians are affected by the deadly virus of "Poor Millionaires Syndrome" – *amphawi olemela?*

Reading the Forbes Magazine it said that *bwana* Bill Gates buys his shirts at Wal-Mart. And according to Amalume that's like buying *mphasha* at PTC – and yet Shasha once vowed that he can never wear anything from Primark or Value City shops, especially not from Goodwill (*akuti akaunjika akunja amenewa*) – *akuti zotchipa* – because he has an image to protect. This sounds ironic coming from someone who seems not to have minibus-fare on a regular basis; which, according to Amalume, is a classic example of Poor Millionaires Syndrome.

Just yesterday I stopped to fill up 2-litres at Petroda on my way to Grin Bamboo when this young Malawian boy in his twenties or thereabouts dressed in flashy clothes that looked as if the flag of Mozambique had collided with a flag of Congo jumped out of a flashy Range Rover V-8. He looked at the petrol attendant who had come running.

"*Tathilani wa 2 hanzi.*" He said in what was a whisper aka *manon'go-non'go* much to the bewilderment of the Petroda employee. I just had to smile; those flashy can-you-see-me-clothes, that flashy car which must cost more than my house and yet this boy wanted to pump petrol *wa K200*?

As if he was reading my mind, the shocked petrol attendant looked at the young boy's expensive flashy attire and repeated the question on top of his voice just to make sure that he heard what he heard.

"*Mukuti tithile wa K200 bwana?*" Came the question a pitch higher than was comfortable for flashy boy. You could see him squirm in his baggy clothes which made me laugh, wondering who drives such an expensive gas-guzzling 4x4 Range Rover Vogue and only pumps K200 worth of petrol (that's less than £1) *abale azanga,* poor Millionaires Syndrome *iyi.*

Ignoring the fact that I had come just for 3-litres myself, I yelled at the petrol attendant who was not even ready to serve me yet because he was waiting for the K200 from Range boy.

"*Ife mutipopele wa* K6000." I said it with all the airs of *matama*, a show-off tactic which I later on regretted.

Since I am a regular at this Filling Station, the petrol attendant looked at me in disbelief. He was fully aware that I don't pump this much petrol in my Morris Marina and must have suspected that I was trying to outdo this young Malawian.

This was a big mistake that was going to have some dire domestic repercussions once I got home. I knew I had some explaining to do to Manyuchi why I had spent both electricity and water bills money on petrol. Was I also suffering from the Poor Millionaires Syndrome? You bet.

Why do we try so hard to tell the whole world that we have two-Tambala in our pockets, why can't we just be like these billionaires who appear as if they have no money at all and yet they have more wealth than the whole Africa?

This reminded me of way back in primary school when Shasha used to walk around town carrying video cassettes although we all knew that they didn't have a video at their house. They didn't even have a radio cassette if I remember correctly. The girls used to love Shasha for that but this might have been the early symptoms of the Poor Millionaires Syndrome.

When Amalume arrived with his flat screen TV for once I felt like 'somebody' (*munthu ochita bwino*) and I was eager to have visitors at my house; friends and relatives. I even went to the extent of telling *nyamata wantchito* to go stand by the road side and ask *anthu odutsa* if they want to come and watch football at my house. Was Poor Millionaires Syndrome peaking in me as well? Most likely it was.

It's like the time Manyuchi Darling refused to go to church because she didn't have a new outfit to wear? According to her she had a valid excuse.

"*Anthu adziwa kuti ndikubwerenza zovala.*" Manyuchi had said to me and I failed to comprehend this reasoning looking at her in amazement.

"Do you really think God cares whether you are repeating what you wore? God doesn't care whether you are wearing jeans or beremudas, show-maso t-shirt or uniform *ya Sefu-gadi.*" I said to her as if we were having a father-daughter conversation.

But Manyuchi, who has a mouth sharper than a butcher's knife countered back at my rebuke.

"If God doesn't care why do you always ask *boyi* to polish *mateyala a* Morris Marina with Kiwi shoe polish on Sundays and always park it next to the Church door?" She said giving me the check-mate look.

Oh my God, Manyuchi had a point, a valid one for that matter – I too had the Poor Millionaires Syndrome, touché.

Even my friend Simioni has got the Poor Millionaires Syndrome running through his blood like the deadly Ebola virus. About two months ago he asked me to accompany him to Shoprite to buy some kitchen salt. While inside we saw this girl who Simioni had proposed to a gazillion and one times during our school days but he always got the same repetitive negative answer, like a gazillion and one times.

"*Ayi ine sindikufuna za uchitsilu wanva.*" This girl would always tell Simioni day-in-day-out.

So when Simioni saw her again, Lord behold, the agenda of buying salt suddenly morphed into something Machiavellian aka Devious. He dropped the basket as if it had just burnt his fingers and reached for the trolley.

"Surely you are not planning on carrying one packet of kitchen salt in a trolley are you?" I asked but my friend had already sped toward the isle where the girl had disappeared.

I managed to catch up with him and found that he had started loading it with items he doesn't usually buy for his house: sausages, yoghurts, corn-flakes, apples, air-freshener and a bit of everything even meat (he gets his meat supplies from Lunzu.)

There were these students from Polytechnic who were there to buy condoms commented.

"*Shaaaa,* trolley *kuchita kudzadza ngati chi* truck *cha Glens Removals.*" One of the Poly students jokingly teased.

I know why my friend was doing this – and I tried to caution him, I tried to wake him up and bring him back to reality, back to planet earth and maybe to resort back to our initial plan of simply picking up a packet of kitchen salt, paying and going back home to our waiting women.

"*Bwanawe*, madam *sakanyanyuka* with all this unplanned expenditure?" I could tell my question fell on deaf ears, the Poor Millionaires Syndrome had taken over all Simioni's judgement and mental reasoning – he had to impress the girl no matter what, by any means necessary.

I will not go into details of what happened when Simioni arrived home with a mountain of shopping. He had tried to give it to me, but I had sternly refused; I wasn't going to have a fight with Manyuchi because of shopping that Simioni had done in order to impress a girl who bombarded him with a gazillion 'No's' back in our school days.

Let's just say that we are thankful that Simioni lived through that day, although his worker later on told us that "*kunatentha* bad."

I looked at the billionaires in Forbes Magazine with their not-so-expensive clothes. They were talking of investing their money so that they can make more money. I have heard of such thing and I have been meaning to do but never gotten round to it.

There was this Billionaire by the name of Warren Buffet who says he started investing when he was only six years old by selling chewing gum but now ranks up there with the Bill Gates, as a matter of fact there are rumours that he might become the richest man in the world overtaking the Microsoft Mogul.

Whilst the Buffets of this world talk about Efficient Market Hypothesis and the Time Value of Money, me on the other hand the only investment(s) I make is when I visit Penda-Penda bottle store on a Friday evening screaming on top of my voice to the barman so that everyone should hear.

"Anyone wearing a shirt and trousers and anyone who is a female, the drinks are on me."

Abwana Makala *amenewo, akuti* buying rounds for everybody even though they don't help me with school fees for my nephews and some don't even know my last name. Yes, isn't it sad and heart breaking that I, Makala Amoto, takes pleasure in buying *dzakumwa* for total strangers even though I have unpaid bills at home.

The clientele at Penda-Penda bottle store usually applaud and cheer – but are they really cheering me up or are they laughing at me? Perhaps even talking behind my back.

"*A Makala ngopusa, tiyeni tiadyele.*"

I looked at the rich billionaires and wondered do che Bill Gates and co. buy rounds of *dzakumwa* at a bottle store? I don't think so because I know for a fact that they don't suffer from our Poor Millionaires Syndrome.

Maybe this is why most of Malawians live on mentality of 'if-I-was-like' aka '*ndikadakhala-ngati*' which is exactly how we were talking like.

"If I had money like Bill Gates Malawians *akananva n'bebe.*" I told Shasha who reciprocated

"If I had money like Bill Gates …Aaaaaa… Facebook *ikananvetsa*, everyone could have been saying '*Shasha ukubwela dunyu, game ili boo.*" Shasha said while standing up getting ready to leave.

I could tell he was about to leave because he started padding his pockets as if to tell me that he had just forgotten his wallet and will be needing some minibus funds. A typical Shasha stunt which he had overused it had ceased to be genuine and was now flat-out pathetic and embarrassingly ridiculous.

"Yo my bro, can you loan me 2 *hanzi ya* minibus, I gat to bounce, keep the Forbes though." Shasha said struggling to surpress a smile.

"Hahaaaaaaa, Poor Millionaires Syndrome *yachi Malawi yeni-yeni.*" I thought to myself.

NGONGOLE

Amalume, who has done some courses on Finance, once told me that *ngongole* is simply a financial claim that has to be repaid on a specified future date. But sometimes when you hear of the amounts of some *ngongole* it makes you want to have diarrhoea.

It was on this premise that my eyes almost fell out of their sockets when I saw on the news how much money the EU countries were willing to loan to Greece. Over £100billion ... shaaaaa ... and we are not talking about Zim Dollars here. £100billion (Sterling Pounds) is a lot of money. I am not a mathematician but I think that a '*hundred bil*' is equivalent to a mind boggling K25trillion (if based on the current exchange rate according to Amalume). That's when I realised that *azunguwa amakondana* but most importantly they trust each other.

Take two steps back (three steps if you are short) and think for a minute. Greece is not a struggling country according to Amalume. Actually the last time Greece had an electricity blackout was ninenteen years ago. Even during their worst fire disaster a few years ago, the country was still able to churn out electricity to its citizens. Bottom line, Greece is not what you would consider to be the average poor country aka LDC (Least Developed Country).

You then wonder why one *nzungu* would lend another *nzungu's* country such *makobidi* when that particular recipient country is not even in need of new electricity equipment at their Nkula Falls nor does its Airline need to buy new planes with new engines like ours does? Are Greek hospitals in need of medication and equipment like ours? The list of questions is endless and the answers obvious – we are in need of much more than Greece does unfortunately we cannot be trusted with £100 billion.

I am not an economist but I am sure £100billlion would extinguish most of our economic woes; maybe enable us to buy new equipment for out ailing hydro-electric power stations or fill all our hospitals with Panado and aspirin. Do these *azungu* think instead of buying Panado we will buy Mercedes Benzes? Toyota Prado's for our MP's or Regional Governors?

We can't blame them for thinking like this can't we? Imagine if you saw a street beggar aka *thandizeni bwana* – parking a Mercedes Benz 500SEL and then rolling out his begging mat and a plate, would you be willing to throw in some change (coins) in that plate? If you would then surely there must be something wrong with you. I know I wouldn't but I know I would squeeze this beggar by the throat, punch him in the stomach and take the keys of that Benz away from him.

It all comes down to trust and respect. *Ulemu anzathuwa* when it comes at *kubwerekana makobidi* and most importantly, *kubwenzera kwa makobidiwo* is paramount. I will stick to this reasoning although there are other well informed Malawians out there who will articulate academic arguments.

"Makala your thinking is narrow and shallow; don't you know that there is politics and the whole aspect of EU allegiance at work here?" I can just hear the academicians coming after me with sharp knives of knowledge.

Shaaaaa, musatelo anthu ophunziranu, but since I have no idea what EU is nor what allegiance means, I will stick to the simplicity of what I know, which is "they are all azungu, that's why *amakongonzana okha-okha.*

Agogo once told me that there was this great white magician called Houdini, *akulu-akulu azamatsenga – a njiba a za ufiti-fiti wachizungu. Bambo* Houdini was good at this disappearing act which amazed a lot of people throughout his life. But now it seems like Malawians have perfected this disappearing act to the point where even Houdini would be impressed. Malawians are good at borrowing money but tend to become Houdini's when the pay date comes around. In short they start playing *matsenga achibisalirano.*

Last month Simioni loaned some money to one of his brother-in-laws (*Mlamu*) who was a bit tight on rent ya Malawi Housing. We are not talking money's like the K25trillion – but at the end of the day *makobidi* is still *makobidi.*

Someone once said that *ukangongola makobidi* 30 days feels like 3 days. And sure enough after 30 days Simioni's *Mlamu* started playing Houdini games, *chibisalilano cheni-cheni.* He was nowhere to be seen or found, like a Houdini Ninja he had simply vanished into a puff of smoke.

It was proving harder to find him at his house, harder than trying to milk a chicken. And for those of you who have attempted *kukama nkaka wa nkhuku* you know what am talking about here. I am not suggesting that you should go out there chasing your neighbour's female chickens, *no-no akakugwirani muzidzati* Makala told us so.

On twelve occasions I escorted my friend Simioni to his *Mlamu's* house and on twelve occasions the wife (Simioni's own sister) told us nada.

"*Mwango-phonyana nawotu amenewo, anali pompano* two minutes ago," She would say nervously. I could tell my friend was angry because he started talking *mwachibwibwi*.

"D... d... d... did he take his cell phone with him?" He would stutter angrily, asking a question which was basically stupid as it was daft because everybody knows that anyone owing anyone money, their first act of the day is usually switching off the phone and slotting in a spare sim card. It is a known fact that those people who have *ngongole* all over town tend to have *ka* plastic *jumbo* full of sim cards for dodging *ofunsa angongole*.

We have a friend called Nyenga, who is like that – he walks around with a gazillion sim cards of TNM, Zain and even some foreign Sim cards of Vodafone, T-Mobile and Lebara. You have to wonder who in Malawi walks around with a Vodafone Sim card *abale? Zovutatu izi.*

For some obvious cultural reasons or beliefs, *ife achi Malawife* have got great respect for Zovuta (Maliro), it brings us together *mwaunyinji wathu*. And last week we were doing just that, paying our last respects to one of our elders who had just passed away. The women were doing their thing vis-à-vis crying sorrowfully and the men, sitting around the fire, looking down between their knees in grief, *kumafwenthela mwachidala-dala*, while waiting for the *nsima* to be distributed and *dzipalapatilo* to be shared.

It was your typical Malawian funeral different from the American type where men are all dressed in black suits and dark sunglasses accompanied by sombre looking women in massive black hats and abnormally large designer shades, everyone sipping red wines and Tia Marias or Amarulas chewing on meatballs. This here was a Malawian funeral; bare-footed men in overalls and majasi accompanied by screaming women in dzitenje, the smell of nsima and smoke wafting from somewhere behind the pit-latrine, sounds of a bleating goat running for its dear life because it's about to become funeral relish.

From the other side of the funeral fire Simioni saw his *Mlamu* who had also seen Simioni. And at that brief moment our cultural beliefs were temporarily suspended – put to one side. *Njonda zaonana* and Simioni was the first to break the silence.

"*Mlamu!!! Makobidi anga aja alikuti?*" he shouted the question, got up and started taking off his *chijasi* revealing his big arms that resembled the size of a young boy's legs. Arms which, in the body building world, are simply referred to as '12 gauge shot gun' because their massive size and potentiality to inflict untold damage.

Mlamu had obviously heard of Simioni's boxing/karate/kung-fu/judo/weight-lifting history and he was not going to wait and find out the validity of that history. Well aware that this *zovuta* would turn into a double-funeral if Simioni manages to wrap those two massive arms around his throat in a choke-hold, *Mlamu* hastily got up and dashed towards the forest *yaku manda*. Simioni gave chase right behind him, *kuthamangitsana pa zovuta... eeeisshhhh... zovutatu izi.*

This reminded of what Amalume once said that the topic of ngongole is too sensitive no matter from what angle you look at it, as long as you are dealing with a Malawian.

"It's always a 'lose-lose' situation" he had told me, if you say no, *ndilibe ndalama*, you are labelled a bad person – *kuumila ngati makobidiwo munakhwimila.* But then if you say, 'yes, here is the money' you still become a bad person when month-end comes around and you go to ask for your money.

"*Eeeeehhh koma ndiye nyela-nkuleketu*, I thought I just told you *dzulo-dzuloli kuti panopo ndilibe*," is the reception that you are bound to get as if you are the one who is the culprit.

And it's even worse if you try and express an observation that pertains to your money.

"How come you say you don't have money but I just saw you buying eggs?"

This is the sort of question that the borrower doesn't like to hear and it's most likely to make him/her more angrier resulting as they turn the tables on you, making you feel guilty because of your own money.

"*Kodi mwayamba kundi londa-londa chifukwa cha timakobidi tanuto?*" is the snorty remark made while the borrower walks away from you leaving you mouth open, amazed and still without your money.

Agogo's explanation is even simpler; he reckons that *achi Malawife never* invented money how do you expect us to understand the ethics of *ngongole* – that *ukabwereka* you are supposed to pay back.

With our Malawian mentality that cannot differentiate a loan from a gift, it's no wonder Azungu cannot come to our assistance with £100billion or K25trillion. Maybe they just don't have the time to start chasing us through graveyards or cemeteries, maybe *nchifukwa chake amangotikon'goza timachenje basi.*

Lucky enough so many women were mourning on top of their voices, their cries and wailing camouflaging the cries and screams that were coming from the direction of the forest were Simioni and his *Mlamu* had just disappeared. I couldn't help wondering why we Malawians are problematic when it comes to the issue of *ngongole.*

I remember before Shasha went to the States I had loaned him K5, yes you heard me "Five Kwacha" when it was still money back then. You would think that now that he is back he would repay that loan, including inflation which should now be something in the regions of K5000.

We could hear the screams coming from somewhere inside the forest where the two had disappeared three or four minutes ago. It sounded as if Simioni had apprehended his *Mlamu* which must have given Shasha a wake-up call, a reminder of some sort, because all of a sudden he whispered to me.

"Hey bro, I haven't forgotten about that Fiver (K5) I borrowed from you back in the day, I swear I will sort you out next week." Shasha said sounding a bit nervous as if he thought I was going to ask Simioni to come collect on my behalf.

I felt like choking him by the throat right there and then but I whispered back to him without even looking in his direction.

"*Ingosungani achimwene.*" I said with a hint of sarcasm because I know from experience that when someone who owes you money starts his sentence by 'I swear' it means that *wakupondetsa.*

If Greece had said to the EU "I swear to pay you back this £100 billion", the EU would have definitely sniffed a rat from a mile away. Like Amalume always say 'never put the words *swear* and *debt* in the same sentence' because doing so is equivalent to saying 'screw you, I ain't gonna pay you back fool.'

It was towards the end of the funeral when Simioni finally reappeared from the forest. His shirt was missing a few buttons, his trousers were dirty by the knees and he was holding a few K500 notes in his clenched fist but there was no sign of his *Mlamu.*

He sat next to me, cracking his knuckles like someone who had just administered some painful physical punishment, and whispered.

"*Wandibwenzela zanga, amati atani.*" He said whilst sitting down and I could see specks of blood on his knuckles and I didn't have to ask whose blood that was. I was happy for him and wanted to know what had happened to his *Mlamu* but I was too afraid to know the answer.

All I could think was '*kunatenthatu kunkhalangoko*' and I was silently hoping *kuti sanaphaneko kumeneko* because I honestly didn't want this funeral service to turn into a 2-in-1 ordeal.

It's sad that for most of us this is the only way we know how to repay back *ngongole* and we wonder why rich countries don't loan us such big amounts like the £100billion Greece will be getting from *anzawo achizungu*, instead *amangotinyambititsa ndi timachenje* which we still have issues paying back.

FOREIGN SPOUSES & VILLAGE LIFE

I have a feeling that if we looked in the Guinness World Book of Records we would find, right on page 1, a fact that the road going to my home village is the roughest, bumpiest and worst road in Malawi and indeed the whole world. Even cow-propelled carts – *ngolo* – have to engage their 4-wheel drive in order to tackle this road, which doesn't even deserve to be called *nseu* in the first place.

It shouldn't come as a surprise then that on the way to my home village I broke two coil springs on my Morris Marina. Now I understand why most of these well-to-do Malawians invest in 4x4's; Pajeros or Land Cruisers.

Most *dzidya-makanda* or small time business entrepreneurs claim that owning a 4x4 is a necessity. I know Simioni's young step-brother Ntimasuvalasanza who sells sour milk (from Zimbabwe) just bought this massive V8 Land Cruiser VX. *Anthu akuti wadya kapitolo ya bizinesi,* but who cares, it's his business. Makala thinks if the boy can afford a 4x4 from selling Chambiko milk, who are we to judge him otherwise? *Musiyeni mwana ayende m'malele, masiku omaliza ano.*

On Thursday we took a trip to my home village for the sake of my British Auntie who hasn't seen the birth place of the Amoto name and where we bury each other when the time comes.

331

Those of you who visited my home village last year during *zovuta zinationekela zija*, I remember you complained of the condition of the road. You should feel lucky that you came that time because it has gotten a hundred times worse. Of course carrying passengers beyond the legal limit of four wasn't good for the health of my suspension.

I won't disclose how many people were in the Morris because I know some of you have got relatives who work for the Road Traffic, *muti mutilanditse ma* driving licence *apa*.

I wasn't surprised when the springs broke simultaneously, making a terrifying sound as if someone was frying gigantic popcorn the size of footballs. The car sagged and I could hear the tires scrapping against the wheel-arch fender.

This meant Che Supanala will have to do his magical modifications once I got back to town. *Pajatu ku* Malawi we are good at *ma modi* – even *ma* mechanics *akunja* can't compete with our home-grown mechanics. For example last year Simioni's Land Rover 110 was modified to be powered by a Datsun engine. That's *talent* for you right there, and if anyone disputes this, let them stand up.

There is something about going to your home village that puts everything in perspective. The feeling of connecting with your roots and the realisation of how we take everything for granted especially when we spend years living in the city. For example my little nephews have got this reflex action that as soon as they enter a room, their hand automatically reaches for a light switch. (*Ana okulila ntauni.*)

I know some of you are lucky and blessed to the point of having electricity *kumudzi kwanu*, but I am sure that the majority of Malawians are like Makala Amoto. *Nyali* is the way to go and the smell of burning paraffin reminded me of my childhood. The memories of me and my friends running into the bush like little hunters – *tialenje* – stalking *mbewa* and *dzitete*, all came flooding back to me, I was actually feeling nostalgic.

I remember how we used to light fires *m'mauna a mbewa* (rat-holes) to flush them out. Occasionally a dizzy *mbewa* (high on smoke) would dash out, only to be met by an army of fifteen or twenty little hunters armed with rocks, sticks and what-not. The thrill was in the chase, yelling and diving hoping to catch that little long tailed rodent and take it to the young girls who were waiting for us by the fire with salt and yesterday's *nsima* aka *nkute*. Aaaaahhh! The good old days.

My British Auntie looked a bit lost and frightened because of my village relatives who still cling to the old ways of carrying with them big *panga* knives with the same affection you carry your wallet or handbag around.

I come from a tribe of hunters and fierce meat lovers who thrive on the motto: 'if it's not human meat then it's definitely ndiwo.' This is the reason why my village is one of a few in Malawi where monkeys have become extinct; you are more likely to meet a dinosaur than a monkey in the forests surrounding my village.

Atha kudya anyani onse, oti pano ayamba kulowelela in the jungles of the neighbouring village to the point that *nkhaniyi idakali kwa* T.A *a m'mudzi mwathu ndi mwa enawo.* They are trying to sort out the litigious issue pertaining to *azibale anga* depleting *anyani* in the forests of the neighbouring village, *akuti* we are encroaching and poaching. My relatives are vehemently denying these allegations saying it's the monkey's fault because they keep crossing the village border into our territory. Once they step over the border-line then all bets are off, they become our property, our relish. Anyway we are awaiting the outcome.

The way my village folks were greeting Auntie was really scaring the living daylights out of her. My relatives' habit of shaking your hand and never letting go, to the point where you start thinking that they are contemplating of keeping it for good, is a bit scary because while they shake with their right hand the left has that panga knife, which compounds the element of fear surrounding the whole handshaking proceedings. This is what Auntie was going through right now.

I could see Auntie's hand was changing colour due to the squeezing and vigorous pumping, she was freaking out. I whispered to Amalume who was busy going through a plate of *bwemba* fruit that had just been given to him by a smiling young lady who was kneeling and giggling shyly.

"Amalume, I think you need to rescue Auntie because *akuwafinya kwambiri ndi ma moni achingoniwa.*" I said to him with some urgency which he chose to ignore, his mind distracted by the *bwemba* on offer. Lucky for Auntie the announcement that food was served under *m'bawa* tree ensured her freedom. She retracted her hand so fast before anyone else could grab it again (for another torturous handshake) and she kept looking at it as if in disbelief that her whole arm was still attached to her torso.

The meal was a typical Malawian delicacy. There was a big plate of *nsima ya n'gayiwa* and two big plates of *ngumbi* and *bwanoni* accompanied by that smell of *zokazinga-kazinga*. All of a sudden I felt the familiar sensation and the excitement of being back at my village. I looked at the shiny roasted *ngumbi* and wondered why some Malawians crave for Chinese food when we have such sumptuous foods of our own fit for a royal buffet. I was surprised that I had forgotten how to eat dry *nsima* vis-à-vis without relish that has soup. (*nsunzi.*)

I saw the look of worry on Auntie's face at the sight of the village buffet in front of her.

"What's thaaaaaat?" She asked worryingly whilst pointing to the plates of *ngumbi* and *bwanoni*.

"Auntie this is called *ngumbi*, it's a delicious Malawian relish that tastes like half chocolate and half roasted chicken." Shasha who had asked to accompany me on this trip answered before I could.

"This is good food Auntie, I guarantee you it will leave your British taste buds confused and your tongue excited." He went on flaunting his expertise and knowledge of Malawian cuisine to my Auntie. He was on a roll and I didn't feel like interrupting him. After all, anything or anyone who could convince Auntie to experiment with this strange cuisine was welcome to do so.

I could still tell that she wasn't sold on the idea of eating a relish that looked like murdered insects. But being married to a Malawian man she had no choice but to adhere to that universal law; 'when you are in Rome do what the Romans do.'

So she agonisingly shut her eyes, picked up a nice sumptuous *bwanoni* by its tiny legs as if she was scared to hurt the already dead grasshopper. We all paused, watching her hand move in slow motion towards her partly opened mouth. As soon as the *bwanoni* disappeared between her lips the whole crowd exploded into a cheer ... *nthungululu* rang out and even my serious Agogo muttered with a smile,

"*Ameneyu ndiwathu-wathudi basi.*" He said while looking at Amalume as if to tell him that *munapatatu pamenepa*.

I don't know how long it took Auntie to chew that one *bwanoni* but I could tell she was having difficulties swallowing because she kept drinking buckets of water trying to wash it down as if it was some sort of a nasty suicide pill. This really didn't bother us one iota, the fact that she was here breaking bread with us was joy in itself.

Shasha must have read my mind because he started talking despite having a mouthful of *ngumbi* and *bwanoni*,

"Boss-man, you know I don't understand those Malawians who claim that they can't eat *bwanoni*," he said while pointing to the plate of the grasshopper-like relish.

"That's like a lion boasting that it can never eat rabbit meat, innit?" We all laughed at how Shasha said it but I had to agree with him though. There is something unique about this true Malawian dish that boggles the mind.

Agogo, who all along had been looking at Auntie chewing as if in disbelief that a white person was munching on Malawian delicacy, finally looked in our direction, cleared his throat before saying,

"*Ngumbi* and *bwanoni* relish is God sent. On top of that there is no religion or belief that bans this traditional relish, if there is such a religion then *changoyamba dzulo-dzuloli*." Agogo said and he went on further to tell us that *bwanoni* is neither meat nor vegetable which is good news for both vegetarians and meat-arians.

I corrected Agogo that no such word aka meat-arians exists, but he told me that it will stay.

"*Ndiwo izi zili chapakati-kati*... it's neither meat nor *masamba*." Agogo said with finality.

This relish is also versatile it can adapt to a *nsima* environment, rice or chips, although common sense and strict cultural norms encourages to go with the *nsima* option.

"*Ngumbi* and *bwanoni* can be consumed as a snack, at work, at school, or even in bed if you are feeling peckish." Amalume said while looking at Auntie who gave him a look of disapproval, as if to say, no way is she allowing insects in her bed at night, alive or dead as a snack or otherwise.

I was really cherishing being *kumudzi* it was really fun and such a change of green scenery, soothing sounds of *dzifuyo* and aromatic village smells that tickled my nostrils. I was enjoying myself despite the fact that you couldn't get any cell phone network, which made me wonder why Shasha kept poking at his Blackberry as if he was texting someone else, but that's Shasha for you, *chi Mereka nfanayu chidzamupha.*

We were all laughing and talking loudly NOT about politics, bills, work stress, school problems nor marital issues. Instead we were deeply engrossed in simple talk about the deliciousness of *ngumbi*, *bwanoni* and the impending litigious issue involving murdered monkeys that have ended up in my relatives' pots.

I looked at the *ngumbi* in the plate, laying there so still and shiny from its own oil. This was good living at its maximum, a family having a special moment, communicating and laughing without all the additives that you find in city environment(s). There was no flat screen TV, no microwave nor stereos, in short... there were no gadgets or gizmos. This place was so pure, it was not infected by technology. Even my Morris Marina looked out of place parked under the mango tree, no wonder the skinny village dogs kept peeing on my Michelin tyres as if they were trying to wash it off its *chitauni.*

TIYAMBE KUYANKHULA CHINESE

I almost choked on the piece of *chinyophilo* because of the headline in the local Daily Times. I had to fold the paper just to check the front page to make sure that I was not reading the China Daily or hallucinating.

No hallucinations here, I was really reading our one and only Malawian Daily Times. Could this really be true that 'Confucius Institute will open its doors soon to offer Chinese language to Malawians especially business people and students?' I wondered.

I grabbed the cup of *thobwa* to try and wash down that piece of *chinyophilo* which had gone down the wrong side of my oesophagus. Simioni who was busy reading last month's Newsweek Magazine looked at me worryingly,

"*zabwino-bwino mkulu?*" he asked while setting his magazine down on the stool next to his sofa.

"Can you believe this; they want us to start learning Chinese?" I said to Simioni who looked at me questioningly as if he wanted to know who this 'they' was. I informed him that I was referring to the government and couldn't understand *why* boma had this daft idea that I would want to start learning another language at my age when even my English is still work-in-progress.

It's not a secret that I have been battling with English since primary school like some sort of terminal hereditary disease, why would I want to compound my linguistic nightmares by compiling another foreign language on top of the Queens language?

My standard 7 English teacher had struggled with me, constantly pleading and insisting that I study and read more so that I can better my English before she finally gave up altogether in obvious frustration.

"*Makala uli ndi lilime lokanika, chizunguchi muyiwale.*" She had angrily told me one afternoon after I had failed to spell the word '*No*'.

"And yet the govt expects me to learn Chinese at my advanced age? Aaaa come-on, *tisa-namizanepo apa, tisiyeni tibalimbana ndi chingelezichi*", I told Simioni who had picked up his Newsweek magazine and was about to start reading it again.

My friend who is always on top of world affairs folded his magazine while clearing his throat the way pastors do before they start preaching the good word. I knew there was going to be some long sermon coming from him, so I called *nyamata wantchito* to bring *ntedza okazinga* and some more *thobwa*.

Simioni claims that the whole world is now making an economic exodus towards China, a country regarded to be one of the emerging economies, a powerhouse in its own right.

"Do you know that while *ife tikudumpha-dumpha ndi ma* Visa to go to Australia, America or UK, the American's, Australians and the British are flocking towards China?" Simioni imparted his words of wisdom to me.

How my friend comes up with these facts about the world beyond our borders is beyond me, maybe it's all this extensive reading that he does. According to him if anyone wants to do business – big time, business *osati tima-geni ta 2 tambala* – then China is the place to be and knowing their language was like the much needed lubricant, easing the rigidity that exists during business transactions.

In a way Simioni had a point because all the spare parts for my Morris Marina were now 'Made in China'. It wasn't just spares but also edible products like *mkaka wa ufa* were also made in China, prompting someone to comment that '*zonse zalowa China*'.

Maybe my friend was right, he was always right anyway, except that one time he told me that rubbing piri-piri in your eyes cures your migraine headache. Despite Simioni's words of wisdom I still had lingering doubts if Malawians could learn this language and speak it with fluency?

Most of us English is still '*choncho-choncho*' because we think in Chichewa and the message is sent to our tongue to be translated into *chizungu*. Depending on the distance between your brain and your tongue or what kind of obstacles are in-between your medulla and your vocal chords, the outcome is usually catastrophic. These obstacles vary in size depending on the level of education. Someone of meagre English education like me will have massive obstacles compared to someone who has a Masters in English.

A person who English is not his/her first language will have an accent which can be classified into three categories: Light, Medium and Heavy.

Light accent; means that any British person will be able to understand the Malawian English without needing a translator.

Medium accent; means that the Malawian English coming out can be understood, but the British or American person will be saying a lot of 'pardon me... what was that again?... can you please repeat', which means that a conversation that would normally have taken 5 minutes will go over ten or more minutes.

Heavy accent; means that the British person will need the services of a translator or a dictionary just to have a conversation with you and depending on their level of tolerance or politeness, they might just even give up all together saying: 'Sod this, I can't be bothered', and walk out on you.

This accent is prevalent in us Malawians even though English has been with us long before Nyasaland became Malawi. And now try to imagine how bad it would be for us to start articulating our thoughts and/or arguments in Chinese.

This will most likely cause many of us *kudziluma milomo* with devastating consequences. I can just picture the queue of tongue injuries ending up at ERs of our Hospitals with paramedics screaming out to nurses,

"Here is another one who was attempting to speak mandarin; he has a lacerated tongue and massive deformation due to his own bite." The nurse(s) would say while trying to shove some gauze inside your mouth to stem the bleeding.

Let's be realistic here and call a spade a spade for us Malawians, Chinese is not really our cup of tea.

The only time I came across Chinese language was when I used to watch Kung-Fu films at Iponga's or Customs as a young boy. I never really cared what Bruce

Lee was saying as long as he kicked the other guy hard, that's what mattered.

We would all scream and cheer throughout the fight scenes, "Iwe eee! Iwe eee! Iwe eeeee!" We honestly didn't care what was being said unless if it sounded like "Huwaaa!.. Hiyaaa!"

During these kung-fu glory days there was this handicapped Malawian on clutches, Nodie as we used to call him, who used translate these mandarin kung-fu movies for all of us.

"*Pamenepo* Bruce Lee *akumufunsa mfanayo kuti – iwe* Cheng-Wu *dzulo lija umati chani*?" Nodie would talk us through the movie from beginning to end and at no time did I question whether Nodie actually understood the Chinese being spoken in the movie. If he did, (which is highly unlikely) he probably was the only Malawian who understood the language.

But Simioni says that these days there are Malawians who speak Chinese fluently – Mandarin as they call it – but, as far as I am concerned, I haven't personally come across one with the exception of Nodie our translator at the Custom's Movie House.

"Makala my friend, Globalisation is here. Whether we like it or not,China is taking over the economy of the world. Do you know that China has the fastest growing economy in the whole world? Do you...." I had to stop him right there and then.

"Hey Simioni, don't start with your big words of Globalisation, *mutipweteketsa mutu apa*." I said while reaching for the roasted groundnuts while giving him the time-out sign.

Simioni likes talking these big terms and giving advice about doing things *ngati azungu.*

"Time out *achimwene tiyeni tidzingotafuna mtedza okazingawu.*"

Simioni argued that China will be another destination for Malawians. We started with *Jubeki masiku amakedzana* when *Theba* was in fashion. Then one clever Malawian thought, "Hey! I can do better than *Jubeki*, why not *Mangalande*? Before you knew it, people were talking of America.

Malawians *ayika maziko* in so many countries all over the world – but these tend to be English speaking countries. Simioni is positive that this is about to change, China watch out here we come, he claims.

If this is the case then all I can say is *"mumvetsa ma Jupa* - teach us your language and I am pretty sure we will invade China like Napoleon invaded the whole world. *Ndife ma Nyasa*, we don't mess around – boat or plane we are coming", maybe learning this Mandarin language can't be a bad thing after all I thought to myself.

And the more I think about it, the more I come to the conclusion that China is better than America or UK. I have heard some mumblings that *maiko a chizunguwa* are very unhappy that Malawi hasn't passed a law banning smoking in public. They are so pissed off with us that countries like Canada have stopped buying *fodya wathu. Akuti kutikhaulitsa...* Eeeisshhhh! *akagwele uko*, I know that *ma Jupa apa* China *atigula fodya wathu.*

I also heard in the grapevine that in China smokers can puff away like *ma chumuni* and no one minds. Compare this to what Amalume told us that nowadays life in the UK is tough for smokers.

"You can get arrested for thinking about smoking in public." Amalume once said.

So, maybe, before we start frowning and ridiculing the new initiative of teaching Chinese here in Malawi, we might want to take a step back and put everything in perspective.

I am not a big fan of smoking in public, especially after someone almost set my hair on fire once in a packed minibus, years back when I used to use curl-kit in my hair. This stupid man had to light up *ndudu ya Tom-Tom, akuti dzibaba.* I told myself that if I was to run as an MP in my area, my manifesto will include 'to ban smoking', although I know that Agogo's vote will not be coming into my ballot box. And I am not the only one in Malawi who harbours anti-smoking sentiments.

I shudder with fear what will happen to my Agogo if Malawi suddenly introduces a law that bans smoking in public. At 102 years old Agogo has been smoking for 90 years – maybe it would be a good idea to convince him to take Chinese lessons just in case there is a clamp down by *boma* on smoking.

The Government have already started making gestures that they are about to clamp down on our polygamy vis-à-vis *mitala*, surely it's just a matter of time when they will introduce a blanket over lighting up anything that has nicotine in it.

Am sure Agogo wouldn't mind getting a "Student Visa" to China just like a lot of *abale ndi alongo* who smoke would jump at the prospect of going to this prosperous country where you can smoke freely until your lungs fall off with no threat of ending up in Prison.

Of course there is also an economic angle to learning Chinese that we as a country might benefit from. As an entrepreneur, I have always wanted to know what is written on most of these Chinese products, especially their food products that I sell through my network of vendors.

You never know *tinyama tokoma tamdzi-tiniti from china ndi ti a mphaka.* Wouldn't you want to know? I know I would love to, so that I can make some informed decisions or recommendations to my customers. I am tired of telling my customers that what they are buying is beef, when deep down I have no idea whether that tin actually contains beef especially when it smells like a mixture of fish and *mphaka* once it's cooked.

No wonder Agogo vows that he will never put anything in his mouth that comes out of a tin unless it's his *tsabola wa kambuzi* from *ka-nkebe* of kiwi shoe polish.

I think I am sold on this Mandarin development and I am 110% behind our government. I can confidently stand here and say that bringing school *za Kwacha* specialising in Chinese curriculum is the best thing to happen to Malawi, better than when King Jetu knocked out the Chilomoni Baby in less than 2 boxing minutes.

Grab you pens and pencils *abale ndi alongo*, dig out those note books you threw away years ago because we are about to learn "*a- e- i- o- u*" in Chinese.

IMMIGRANT vs EXPATRIATE

I cannot exactly remember when I first encountered the English language, just like I cannot remember the first time I ventured into the toilet by myself without needing assistance of a grown up. I have had a rather rocky on-and-off relationship with the English language, I just couldn't quiet commit myself to staying faithful to this rather slippery language. The reasons stem from the problems that have existed between my tongue and some of the strange English words.

It's not only the pronunciations that have tortured my Malawian tongue but also their meanings, words like prolepsis or sombre stand out the most. The first one I have never used in a sentence because I have no idea where to place it and the second one,(sombre), I just couldn't pronounce it properly until I was in my late 20's or thereabouts.

I remember when I first tried to pronounce sombre I literally pronounced it as it is written, as if I was reading a Chichewa word. My father, who had been nearby reading the Daily Times, corrected me that it's pronounced as '*so-mba*.' My young sister who had been sitting on the floor with me, playing with her one-legged doll, cracked out laughing as if someone was tickling her armpits. She never stopped laughing until it was bed time and she woke up the next morning still laughing calling me *so-mbre* all day long. I slapped her on the cheek hoping to make her stop, which turned out to be a grave mistake, because Father found out and gave me a serious belt walloping, which left me in a sombre mood all day long.

Another word, apart from prolepsis or sombre, that I grappled with throughout my childhood was the word *Expatriate.*

My father's illustrious career spanned through a period when most of the bosses were white. As a result I grew up thinking that the word Expatriate meant *azungu.* I remember one day telling my father,

"Today *ku PTC kunali ma* Expatriate *ambiri,*" I said it with a boyish grin, what I meant to tell him was that there were a lot of white people at PTC that day. Good thing my little sister wasn't around when I goofed again in my ongoing wrestling-war with English words.

It was later on in life that I learnt that expatriate simply meant any foreigner who came to Malawi to work in companies like David Whitehead, Sucoma, Portland Cement just to mention a few. Most of these Expats were usually *azungu* from Europe or America. What made them standout in the Malawian working community was that they really had such a good life because of the benefits that were accorded to them. These fringe benefits ranged from a company car, a company house, company *khukhi* and garden boy, private schools for the children just to mention a few.

It was based on this new found meaning of the word expatriate and what it entails to be one, I quizzed Amalume who had just returned from UK a couple weeks ago.

"Amalume," I started, looking at Amalume who was busy on the computer while trying to eat nsima at the same time.

"Why did you leave UK for Malawi? I mean, why did you leave behind the luxury life of an expatriate?" I asked him as best as I could, struggling to pronounce the word expatriate.

Amalume almost choked on his *nsima*, gasping for breath like a chambo fish out of water.

"The life of whaaaat?" he choked out the words, putting much emphasis on the word 'what.'

"No, I mean when these Europeans come here we call them expatriates, right?" I stuttered a bit and he nodded in agreement while gulping down a mouthful of water to clear his oesophagus of the piece of nsima that had meandered the wrong way.

"So that means when you were over there in UK you were also an expatriate, with all the benefits of an expatriate, right?"

Amalume struggled to swallow his *nsima*, washing it down with a mouth full of homemade thick *thobwa*, ignoring the now empty glass of water. Amalume was the only member of the house who always had two or three different types of drinks in front of him during a meal; water, thobwa and Sprite if not the Cherry Plum. I am glad I wasn't his bladder because that's one organ in his body that was always working overtime.

I was jolted back to the subject at hand when he set the mug of thobwa next to the empty glass of water saying,

"My dear Makala," he started with much emphasis on the dear as if he was referring to Auntie.

"When I was in UK, I was an immigrant and all Africans in UK, even in the USA are immigrants. We are not referred to as expatriates over there." Amalume said with a hint of sadness.

This was breaking-news and a bit confusing for me and I looked at my Amalume not sure how to word my follow-up question.

"How come we don't call westerners immigrants when they come over here? And why are Africans not called Expatriates when they are in Europe or the USA?" came a staccato of questions fired at my bemused uncle.

"Because Africa is Africa and Europe is Europe mphwanga." Amalume simply responded in a quite despondent voice.

"But Amalume, did you have a company house, company car and anyamata antchito?" I carried on a bit perplexed by his response. I figured that maybe expatriate is the same as immigrant which meant that the same benefits accorded to these white expatriates over here would also apply to my immigrant brothers and sisters over in the UK, USA or any of those *maiko akunja*.

I have never heard Amalume laugh so loud. I thought that a rat had jumped inside his trousers and was doing a marathon like Usain Bolt around his private parts. I noticed that not only was Amalume laughing his lungs out but he was also crying at my innocence and ignorance of life on the other side... but something told me that he was actually crying at the double standards of the way we treat them over here to the way they treat us over there.

After what felt like an eternity, he looked at me, wiping his tears, and said in a whisper;

"My dear Makala ... Europe and America are very rich and wealthy nations but everyone is a slave, a slave to time and a slave to money. Africa is poor in comparison but we live like royalty, don't you ever forget that Makala my son."

With those words Amalume got up wiping his tears and went to bed without even saying goodnight nor washing his *nsima* tainted fingers. I looked at the plate of unfinished *nsima* and the smaller plate which still had a small army of red beans floating around in the soup, I knew Amalume was not coming back to finish his meal.

While pondering on what he had just told me about Malawian immigrants abroad, I dug my fingers into the warm *nsima* and with it I attacked the plate of beans, all the while wondering; "why immigrants and not expatriates?"

All this was so very confusing and a bit perplexing for me; as confusing as to why the word sombre is pronounced *so-mba* and as perplexing as the word prolepsis.

AZUNGU ARE JUST LIKE US

Ever since Amalume's British wife came, I have been taking more interest in UK and the affairs of this far away Kingdom. I just found out recently that they don't have a President in UK; instead they have a Queen and also Prime Minister. It looks like the Prime Minister calls all the shots but it's the Queen who has all the wealth. The Prime can only serve for a specified term but the Queen is there for life. These British people have got a strange way of ruling themselves and they sure know how to complicate politics.

And yet *Azungu* have always looked (and at times ridiculed us) for all the faults and failings we exhibit when it comes to politics and most importantly corruption. And I have always asked myself why can't *ife achi Malawife* (and most African Countries) emulate the good example set by these *azungu*? *Kodi ifeyo ndi umbuli umatipangitsa corruption* and *tribalism? Mwinatu.*

Why do we have all these shenanigans when we don't have to juggle with Monarchy or Prime Ministerial chairs? Is it because Azungu possess an IQ that is miles ahead of ours? Is it because of their complexion or colour of their eyes? Is it perhaps the long strandy hair compared to our curled afros that makes their politics excel over ours? Let's see.

Last Thursday, UK held its general elections and my British Auntie proudly told us just before the voting began; "I want you all Malawians to see democracy at work." Sure enough we were glued to the flat screen TV – the two basins of *dzipalapatilo* making its rounds, in one basin, piri-piri flavoured for the adults and in another, salt only for the kids – as DSTV broadcasted the voting process.

"*Tiphunzire nawo m'mene anzathu amavotela,*" I heard one of the women exclaim and I knew what she was alluding to. She was trying to say: 'voting without rigging and an instantaneous announcement of results followed by an immediate change of power without *mapokoso,' anzathu ma Britso ndi m'mene asewerela ndale zawo*.

Then we all got a shock. At a few polling stations, people were turned away before they could vote, this happened in Hackney South and the same was the case in Withington Manchester. In Sheffield Hallam, over 500 people were turned away and told that they could not vote.

One would be forgiven to think that Sheffield Hallam is in Zimbabwe and the 500 voters belong to Morgan Tsvangirai's party who have just come to a polling station that is Pro Mugabe. But we are talking about UK here, the Kingdom of the Queen, *kuchimake kwa* democracy.

As if things couldn't get worse, in another polling station in Liverpool they run out of ballot papers which meant that some people could not cast their vote. Sounds like Sudan, one would think that the Janjaweed militia had ridden through Liverpool on their horses and camels stealing all the ballot papers the night before.

I thought this was interesting and a bit intriguing for a country that claims to be the First World, *kodzuka*, aren't they supposed to be better than us these *atsamundas*?

By Friday morning after all the ballot papers were counted, UK still didn't have a President – I think he is called Prime Minister over there – which was a bit amazing. Even my British Auntie who is always one of the people to get up early in the morning was still locked up in the bedroom.

When she later came out around 11am, in what appeared as a pathetic attempt to exonerate her country's goofyism, Auntie said something that brought up more question marks.

"The British were not voting against Labour Party, they were voting against Gordon Brown because he is not British ... he is Scottish." She said.

My 102 year old Agogo almost chocked on his piece of *chipalapatilo* as he latched on to Auntie's admission.

"So you mean to tell me that you *azungu* are also tribalistic?" Agogo quizzed looking at Auntie and Amalume nodded much to the disapproval of my Auntie who just realised that she had set a trap for herself.

It was looking like we are the same after all. Shambolic voting, a healthy tribalistic presence – it was so amusing to learn that UK has got its own Tutsi-Hutu thing going and I wondered what next?

I soon found out the next item on the list that confirms our identicalness with our light in complexion relatives from the Kingdom a yonder.

Simioni who never misses an opportunity to contribute to a conversation brought up a good point.

"*Even nkhani ya* corruption, weren't the British MPs involved in some shady dealings – *amaonjeza ma* zero *ku ma* IOU, and were claiming extra rent allowance."

I thought Simioni was just making this up. How can a British MP *wachizungu-zungu* be involved in corruption, *zabodzatu izi*. But Amalume acknowledged that: yes, a lot of MP's *amathyolela makopala m'matumba awo*. But in UK they don't call it corruption instead they call it 'Expenses Scandal.' I think corruption is a word reserved for African politicians. That's why you will never see or hear the western media saying that Malawi is embroiled in an expenses scandal, that expression is only reserved to be used for British politicians, *achikudafe lathu ndi* corruption. Make sure you keep them separate or else *atumiza anyamata awo a nkhondo* claiming *kuti tonse ndife ma Talibano.*

Agogo who had now managed to clear the piri-piri stuck on his throat jumped back in the conversation;

"So, *azunguwa nchimodzi-modzi ndi ife eti*? They are tribalistic, their voting system is not as straight forward too and they also have corrupt people like we do over here?"

The women in the room broke into *nthungululu*, cheering as if Malawi had just won the World Cup.

"*Mwalasa* Agogo *mwalasa*!"

All of a sudden I didn't feel embarrassed being m'Malawi or African. Even Shasha who had remained quite throughout remarked.

"*Kaya nkhedu, kaya nkada* we all bleed red blood, *tonse nchimodzi-modzi.* Why do you think they are giving Obama a tough time in the States, tribalism *imeneyo.*"

Shasha, despite his lack of academic achievements but vast knowledge gained from traveling the globe, went on to say that;

"*Ku Amerekanso kuli mizwanya ya* corruption *kuposa kumudzi kuno. Bwana* Rod Blagojevich and there is also *Ambuya* Ted Stevens *omwe anali* Senator of Alaska, *onse ma tchale azoponda-ponda.*"

I was surprised by Shasha's knowledge and grasp of America current affairs. But I told him that at least American voting system was better than Africa. I have never heard Shasha laugh so loud.

"Hahahaaaa, better *kutiko*? If it was any better then Al Gore could have been President instead of George Bush. *Anaba upulezidenti a Bush – kodi simunanve* scandal *ya ma* hanging chards in the State of Florida?" I didn't hear of this but Shasha was kind enough to keep us up to date on the shambolic proceedings that went on in American back in 2000, with the Presidency being decided by the Supreme Court in December of that year. Hahahahaha, *musatelo inu...* even *ma* Yankees (Americans) *apa Yusa* (USA) *ndi akambele-mbelenso?*

Ndikutitu tonse ndife ofanana – kuponda, zau tribalism, *kaya vuto la mavoti...* they just call it different names in these Western countries. Even one of my teenage nephews got up talking on top of his voice.

"Expenses scandal – expenses scandal my butt, just call it corruption."

But Mother cautioned him to be careful, these British and American have got unmanned drones flying all over trying to listen to voices of dissent, *timau toukila* and if they hear that we are calling them corrupt, they might accidentally drop a Bunker Busting Bomb also known as earth-penetrating weapon (EPW) on our gathering; claiming they thought *unali nsonkhano wachitalibani.* So for the sake of our safety we will classify their politicians as Expenses Scandal Specialists (ESS) not corruption technicians (CT's.)

I quickly grabbed the basin of *dzipalapatilo* at the same time Agogo did, there was only one piece left in there. Yes he was older than me but this was my house. The only way to see who was going to eat that last piece of *chipalapatilo* was to cast a vote.

After 30 minutes of the whole house casting their secret ballot, it was dead heat – as we say it in Malawi it was draw-draw – there was no clear winner as to who was going to eat that last piece of *chipalapatilo.*

All of a sudden I began to feel what Gordon Brown and David Cameron were going through. Too bad my house was not America else we would have taken this *Chipalapatilo* deadlock to the highest court of the land, the Supreme Court to see who gets to eat it.

MEN CHAKA CHINO MUNVETSA

Agogo claims that *azibambo achi* Malawi are an endangered species. The way he stressed the word "endangered" one would think he is talking about the Bengali Tiger – the endangered feline found in the jungles of India. But Agogo was simply referring to the Malawian Homo-sapiens descendant of Zinjanthropus, the *Mandingo* brother aka *Bambo a Boyi*.

"Gone are the days when the Malawian male was king," Agogo laments while his gaze roamed around the living room.

"There was a time when being born male meant you had the same rights like those of Simba the Lion."

What Agogo was alluding to, were the rights of being able to marry as many wives as ones' libido would allow or wallet would permit.

For someone who enjoys buying or spoiling *mai akwao* with chocolates, diamonds, *zibangili*, shoes, handbags, *makabudula ankati* or even cars, they know that servicing a relationship from an economical (not emotional) point of view can be a costly endeavour. That's why I have always wondered how some men are able to do this for two, three or more wives.

"Only *amuna-muna* are able to do this." My Uncle once told me.

Polygamy is a status symbol and it is not a secret that some of my uncles can compete with the likes of Zuma, Nswati or the big man himself, late King Sobuza, when it comes to wife-ology. I have an uncle who buys two goats every Friday so that his army of wives (and hordes of children) can split the meat amongst themselves. By Sunday the whole *nyama ya mbuzi* vanishes like *matsenga*.

It's common Malawian knowledge now that the government will soon be coming down hard on polygamous arrangements. It seems like the days *a zokwatila azimai angapo* are about to come to an end. And like I said a couple of weeks ago, most male members of my family are alarmed by this development. *Mphwawo wa Amalume* put it better when he said; *"chaka chino azibambofe tinvetsa."*

Amalume *an'gono* had a point especially when you consider what just happened to Tchale, Simioni's young brother, although his case had nothing to do with *Mitala*.

Tchale, who is nineteen old, arrived from UK with his *mai akwao*. She isn't a girlfriend and she isn't a wife neither – in UK *amati* Partner, someone who is more than a girlfriend and less than a wife... *mwina kuno tingati kati-kati*.

Tchale's partner is a lovely lady but a bit older than him. As a matter of fact she is fifty-five years old, which according to my Sanyo-FX calculator makes her thirty-seven years older than him – but as they say *maiko akunja*, "love knows no age" and Tchale *ndi* his madam look to be in love like two characters in a Mills and Boon novel.

Upon their arrival, they came through customs and immigration holding hands while bumping hips, a sure sign of *chikondi abale azanga*. Not like us, *achi Nyasafe*, whereby Bambo walks in front and Madam following at a safe cultural distance of not less than 20-feet, according to Section 4 chapter 9 of Malawi Cultural Code of Ethics and Conduct (in Public Places.)

To Tchale's surprise, the serious looking officials with permanent *tsinya* groves engaved on their foreheads, pulled him *pambali* and gave him a caution – *chenjezo* – because here in Malawi there might be a law coming into play, banning and arresting young men who go out with older women, something which is being vigorously pursued by our Minister of Gender and Something-something. Madam Tchale is deemed simply to be too old for him. It was ok for now because the Bill hasn't hit parliament yet, hence the caution. Like Agogo said earlier on, *chaka chino amuna tinva n'bebe*.

One wonders why Boma is not contemplating on passing a law banning older men gallivanting with little girls. It seems that Shuga Daddyism is still practiced by a lot of well-to-do men. The government will arrest young boys philandering with older women but will not clamp down hard on Shuga Daddyism.

Is it because most of these laws are concocted by njonda who are themselves Shuga D's and don't want *kudzisokonezela* game? Or may be boma doesn't have enough resources to combat ma *Shuga Dadi*, especially when most of these skilful Shuga Deez are deploying their sophisticated weaponry also known as 'tinted windows' on their cars.

Everyone knows that tinted windows on a Benz, BMW or Lexus are a powerful deterrent because what the government can't see, the government can't catch. That's why some heavy type of tinted windows is against the law in the UK or USA for obvious reasons.

This sophisticated deterrent weapon also gives the Shuga D's protection just in case their young girlfriend happens to be the granddaughter of one of their friends. It's like killing three birds with one stone; the wife can't see inside the car, neither can the father of the teenage girl nor the government.

This is one weapon of choice that Shuga Mommy's will have to adopt and adopt quickly if they are to be on par with their male counterparts.

Ndikutsineni khutu pan'gono ... those wanting to launch a business specialising in tinting glasses, Makala thinks you can't go wrong with this one because there is a niche market out there waiting to be tapped into.

What made Agogo even more agitated and mad are the rumours that smoking in public places is going to be banned as well. This is another cheap blow aimed at the male genitalia, because it's a known fact that a bigger percentage of smokers in Malawi are men.

Others will argue that this also will inconvenience Malawian sisters – *mbumba zathu* – but research has shown that there is a higher chance of coming across a small box full of K500 notes in the middle of Ndirande market than finding a female smoker.

Amalume claims, while in the UK or USA a lot of Malawian females enjoy the privileges of lighting up *ndudu* just like their male counter-parts, here in Malawi there are not that many, it's only *azibambofe* who seem to be lighting up *mwaunyinji wathu*. And it looks like *azibambo osutanu simunati, Boma likunjatani pompano.*

Because of all this, Agogo thinks the world, for the Malawian male, is coming to an end. As far as I am concerned, the ban on smoking is one law I might end up supporting, considering the way Agogo has been burning my sofas whenever he falls asleep while holding *ndudu* ya Tom-Tom.

But according to him he thinks that the government is concocting a 'conspiracy' against the Malawian male. Listening to Agogo I had to agree that *amuna mukhaula chaka chino, muona tapedze-pedze.*

Shasha cleverly puts this conspiracy theory into perspective. *Indedi* the government has got an axe to grind with the male citizenry? He sends out a warning to those Malawians abroad thinking of coming back home.

"If you are one of those dudes who fancy this game *yogiligishana-giligishana* with fellow dudes, also known as gay or homo, then chances are you will find yourself at Dzeleka Hotel or Zomba Lodge or perhaps that motel near Shoprite commonly known as Chichiri Penitentiary – handcuffed to your gentleman lover whilst paraded on TVM." Shasha finished talking, surprising everyone because what he had just said was factual.

Both Shasha and Amalume concur that in these western countries, gays and non-gays co-exist side by side in harmony. This is unbelievable to most Malawians *kumudzi kuno*, because over here fashion *imeneyi siinagwile nseu*. As much as achi Malawife are so good at copying everything from the West: Rap, Bling-Bling, Spinners on Wheels, Mohican haircuts, John-T shoes, low-hanging trousers, black female tights and what not – it seems like Gay-ology is having problems being copied, *ikukanika kugwila nseu kuno*. If it's being copied then it's being copied in secret, by *ya usiku okha-okha*. The truth is that if you are a man and try to come out to practice gay-ology in broad daylight – well you heard what happened to those two dudes; *Anti Tiwo ndi Bambo akwawo* who we are still waiting to hear *kuti zawathela bwanji a Jaji akagamula mulandu pa 18 May*. Like Agogo says, *amunafe chaka chino sichathu*.

I don't want men who are abroad to feel or think that it's all doom and gloom over here in the warm heart of Africa. It's not as bad as it sounds and shouldn't make someone who had plans of coming back to this beautiful country change their mind, *kumudzi ndi kumudzi basi, bwelani*.

The government is just trying to protect its citizenry from harm (so we are being told). And after all, why be alarmed when most of these things haven't been passed into law yet – apart from gay-ology.

Like I have said already, if you come to Malawi and start dancing to the gay tune, chances are you will be wearing those silver *dzibangili* on both wrists while we all watch you on TVM.

A claim by Agogo that 2010 is going to be a tough year for all Malawian males, is both true and false depending on individual perspective, *enafe tikukhala bwanji?*

Like I told you some weeks back, the *mitala* ban has got loopholes. Simioni's uncle came from South Africa six weeks ago and had a unique wedding ceremony. He married four women at the same time – *akuti kupha mbalame zinayi ndi mwala umodzi* – beating the system.

He has since gone back to Jubeki satisfied that even if the government passes the anti-polygamy law, he is covered. He already has another South African wife *ku Jubeki ko* and these four women *adzingo-dikilira* until he returns back for good.

As for the pending anti-smoking ban, Agogo has consulted our lawyers – *Tidyenawo and Tidyenawo* Associates – to see if the ban will include *fodya wamphuno* or *otafuna.* We are still waiting to hear from them and I will let all my smoking friends know of the outcome. Makala is looking out for you ... hahaaaaaaa.

Chonde-chonde I wouldn't advise any Malawi male abroad to start having sex-change, *zinthu zikadali boo*, it's still manageable to survive as a male in Malawi. Of course the minute *Boma* starts talking about banning men from chewing *dzipalapatilo* then I will be the first one going abroad for a sex change operation, so that I can come back as *abiti Makala Amoto* or *AnyaAmoto.*

PRISONS ARE OVERCROWDED

There are certain songs you tend to forget the tune the minute the song finishes playing on the radio. But then there are those songs that stay glued to the walls of your brain from puberty all the way to adulthood. For me one such song is *Waba wekha! Usalile...Waba wekha!!! Usalile.*

Back in the day this was the instrument-less song we used to sing as the crowd of us children, grown-ups and skinny dogs (with flies all over their bleeding ears) followed a thief who had just been captured by the Youth Leaguers (Red Shirts.) It was a tantalising and lovely tune for us and not the thief, simply because while we were dancing and chanting, he was being whipped with bamboo canes and paraded along kuma plot. The thief's arms would be tied behind his back in what was the famous "*nyakula*" (chest-out) on his way ku *Eriyo kwa a* Chairman. Right behind him would be an overzealous mean looking Youth Leaguer carrying the items (supposedly stolen by the now bleeding, battered guy) which usually tended to be a few maize cobs or *Maluwa* soap and at times a skinny looking one-legged chicken.

Those were the days before armed robbery became a sophisticated art it has now become. This was before AK-47's flooded the scene, curtsey of the Mozambican war just across the border. This was an era when thieves simply specialised in stealing petty items; *nzimbe*, fresh maize, shirts and bras from the clothes line etc. Once in a while you might get a thief brave enough to dip his hand into someone else's pocket not realising that the dude was an off-duty MYP commando (*malodza mai.*)

It all used to culminate into some weekend fun for us kids once the poor thief had been caught ... the screams of *Wakuba!! Wakuba!! Wakubayo!!* Would resonate and we would stop whatever it was we were doing; be it eating, playing or bathing, sometimes even if I was in the middle of being spanked by Father he would pause and say,

"*Pita ukaonele wakuba kunsewuko* but make sure you rush back so that I should finish punishing you." Father would say while setting the whooping stick against the wall as I dashed over to see the captured thief and join in the chorus of that melodic tune,

"*Waba Wekha Usalile,*" all of us would be singing and running while one of my hands was massaging (*kusisita*) the throbbing tender *thako* from the recent spanking (*Masiku amenewo.*)

Nowadays things have now changed and the balance of power has drastically shifted in favour of thieves, who we now call robbers. These robbers have become hardened, callous and brazen, they no longer steal things – rather they take things.

When a small army of armed *dzimbalangondo* break into your house and demand that you help them pack and load your property into a waiting pick-up, that's no longer stealing – in my language that is simply classified as "*kutenga*" no matter from what angle you look at it.

That's exactly what happened at Simioni's house last week. They even came with a hydraulic jack (*Jeke wa* Lorry) and brazenly lifted up the burglar bars. They entered and went straight to Simioni's bedroom to wake him up. For some unexplained reason the thieves of today don't even have the decency of *kuba mwakachete-chete.* They are so arrogant and *a ulesi* that they expect you to help them pack your own property into their waiting pick-up. *Malodzatu bwana.*

So I was somehow shocked when I read in the newspaper of some idiotic suggestions that the President needs to pardon some thieves who are in jail to alleviate over-crowding.

"*Akuti mundende muli kathithi, ma* in-mates *akupondana mapazi.*" I told Agogo who harbours more draconian methods.

"Shouldn't they be left in an overcrowded jail so that it teaches them a lesson?" Agogo responded. He reckons that it would send a good message to other would-be-thieves that if you specialise in the art of stealing you will end up in jail which is so overcrowded, you will have to sleep while standing up, *njoooo*...as if you are listening to the nation anthem on 6 July.

Agogo tells us that you never used to hear of prison over-crowding back in the day. I asked him if this had to do with the fact that justice was usually handed out the old-fashion way, which made thieves to think twice before *kupisa nthumba la mwini?* Maybe we should revert back to those days of lashing and serving mob justice. Agogo agrees with me, he even suggests that we can take it one step further and feed thieves to starving lions or hyenas.

"Hahahaha, Agogo that's taking it too far I am sure if we take that path, yes it might alleviate the over-crowding but the Human Rights brigade will come knocking on our door. I think we should stick to *chikwapu* and *nyakula*." I said to my 102 year old Agogo.

I know *chikwapu* and *nyakula* still sounds a bit barbaric and primitive to most of you, but according to Simioni who was very upset, shaken and angry the following morning after they robbed his house, has an opinion that might differ from those of you who have never experienced armed robbery.

"When you have just been cleaned out by eighteen men brandishing *dzikwanje* you wish *nyakula* was back in fashion." Simioni told me and I agreed with him not just because *Nyakula inkabeba* for those of us watching, but because it also used to free up space in prisons. Any would-be thief used to think twice or thrice before stealing.

The problem according to Amalume is that modern day-thieves have also realised that they are entitled to human rights. They are aware of the privileges enjoyed by their fellow thieves and prisoners in UK or America; TV's in jail, eating three meals a day, taking a bath in the morning and now they want to be housed in 'one in-mate one cell.'

Amalume says that in UK and America prisoners have access to Facebook and internet as part of society respecting their human rights.

"Eeeiishhhh! Next thing we will hear that our Malawian prisoners are demanding Spaghetti with Sausages for their lunch, *inenso ndiye mungo-ndimangatu bwanji.*" I told Amalume.

Stop this nonsense about over-crowding in jail and remember that over-crowding is part of our Malawian characteristic, something we should be proud of. We have over-crowding in our jails, our minibuses, our bars, our tarvens, our churches, our parties, our cabinet, our parliament, our funerals, our weddings, our dzinkhoswe and especially our homes.

Yes over-crowding is our way of life so much that *enafe* in our houses, this is normal daily life. The majority of Malawian homes are overcrowded with relatives; *ana a masiye, ana azichimwene, ana a masistazi, atsibweni, azilamu,* alendo, (who have stayed for so long at your house that the alendo status doesn't make sense anymore), *ma khanda* who have been dropped off because your son impregnated your neighbours daughter and the girl's mother comes *molalata,*

"*Mulela nokha khandali, ine mwana wanga ndikufuna apite ku Amereka kumaphunziro.*" she screams before storming off leaving you wondering how you are going to feed another extra mouth.

Yes most of our houses are so overcrowded, but we don't go crying to the government seeking for presidential pardons. *Akuti* the President is not pardoning enough prisoners that's why *muli kathithi.* Aaaaaah! Comeon, there are certain things the President can be criticised on but not about pardoning thieves. Next thing we will hear that our President is being criticised for the torrential rains or the earthquakes we have been having. *Kathithi ameneyu* is not only *mundende zathuzi*.

Why then should the prisons be seeking pardons just to alleviate the over-crowding? Who is going to pardon these family members we are looking after? *Boma litithandiza*? Especially when you consider that all these *azilamu, ana a atsibweni* and *tiadzidzukulu* who am looking after didn't commit any crime to end in my overcrowded house? *Koma tikuwalela basi*, some sleep on the sitting room others in the kitchen, the grown up ones sleep in the Morris Marina. If you come to my house at midnight you would think my Morris Marina *ili paulendo*, it's always full of people sleeping *chokhala* leaning against the steering wheel with skill so as not to set off the *hutala*.

According to Simioni, they should all be left in the overcrowded jails. He even thinks the government should throw in a few crazy horny monkeys (with *utitili*) in the jail cells to spice things up. If word goes out that if you go to jail you end up sharing a jail cell with *anyani achiwewe* who fancy humans, crime will surely go down.

If packing these jails with mentally disturbed monkeys infested with blood thirsting *utitili* sounds drastic, then maybe *nyakula* technique needs to be revived. I know I am older now, but I wouldn't mind once in a while running by the road side and joining with a crowd of excited vigilantes dishing out mob-justice and singing.

"*Waba-wekha, Usalile*," while we throw rocks and bricks at the thief, especially if he was caught trying to divorce me from my Flat-Screen TV. Aaaaaa! *Fotseki* the only option I would give him is,

"Bwana kodi timange nyakula or ndege?"

Waba-wekha!! Usalile... Waba-wekha Usalile! ...
Kanyimbo kali boo aka am even beginning to dance and getting nostalgic all over.

IMPORTERS PAY 20% DUTY

Amalume has got this skill of coming up with statistics on everything and anything. It's quite amazing, even though I have a feeling he just makes them all up – but since he is older than me, I try not to dispute the validity of his data. This was the case today after lunch when Amalume started on his statistics infested conversation.

"99% of Malawian males think that the barber shop (*kometetsa*) is the most important institution and only 1% thinks that Parliament is the most important." Amalume said.

I raised an eye brow and was about to mumble, 'Oh! Lord here we go again' but succeeded in keeping my mouth shut. Amalume concluded by saying that the average Malawian male makes sixty visits to the barber shop per annum whereas most men never pay attention to what is discussed at parliament. I tried to make sense of what he had just said, found it a bit disjointed and figured for the sake of world peace – I will not labour over it.

While Manyuchi Darling and her friends were getting ready for a bridal shower – us men; Simioni, Amalume, me and Shasha jumped in the Morris Marina to go and visit that most important male institution, Meta-Meta Barber Shop which is only fifteen minutes away.

Amalume wanted to get his shiny *mbonga* retouched, Simioni wanted his beard and moustache trimmed and I had noticed that my Tyson was fading and needed an overhaul. Shasha whose hair is braided was just coming along for the ride (he gets his hair done at the female beauty-salon).

It's a short drive from my house to Meta-Meta Barber's and we really didn't talk that much apart from asking Shasha what happened the day the two big guys chased him through the neighbourhood. Shasha vows that he is not going to pay them *nta* one *tambala*, they would have to catch him first, he boasts. After seeing Shasha's sprinting skills, I had to agree with him. There is no way any *wangongole* was going to catch Shasha, not the way the boy was running. They would have to surprise him while he is fast asleep or else forget about getting paid.

It took us seventeen minutes to get to Meta-Meta Barber's and I parked my Morris Marina next to this massive American Ford Excursion 4x4 with a personalised plate 'L.A Lakers.' Amalume just mumbled,

"Mmmmmh, *koma pa* Malawi *abale,*" is all Amalume said and he didn't have to say much because I knew what he meant, it was a loaded statement that had all sorts of extrapolations resonating from it. You have to be a Malawian to comprehend the full meaning of a sentence like that.

Being a Friday, the Barber Shop was packed with men and boys getting ready for the weekend and those who simply came in to feed on gossip about the latest political goings-on. Meta-Meta Barbers is a good place to get the latest breaking news if you are one of those people who is not into the whole newspaper gig; either because of *kuchuluka ma* advert *m'manyuzi(zopweteketsa mutu,)* the exorbitant newspaper price or if you simply hate the way newspapers smell.

I had a feeling that today's topic at the barber's was going to be about the two gay men who have just been pardoned, it seems like the whole country is buzzing with this presidential pardon. Others are claiming that the UN (which has strong contacts with the IMF) had applied pressure on the government but then some were claiming that the pardon was simply out of the president's Christian forgiving heart. I couldn't wait to hear what the majority opinion at the Barber's was going to be like but I was surprised that the topic had nothing to do with the Presidential pardon of Auntie Tio.

Half the clientele in the barber's were young entrepreneurs who go abroad *kumakagula katundu* for resale and they like to call themselves 'importers' (*abweletsi*) or dealers. Your typical Malawian business men, in khaki shorts and t-shirt pockets stuffed full of thousands of Kwacha…*akuti zomwaza pa Kamba* or *Chez Ntemba*. You see them taking out a massive fat roll of K500's when they only want to buy bubble-gum. *Dzinkhwaya dzachinyamata dzachi-Malawi*, who wouldn't be able to tell you the difference between a Balance Sheet from an Income Statement nor can they differentiate Assets from Liabilities but can show you how to make K5000 out of K100 in a single day. That's Malawian entrepreneurial acumen right there which would leave most Oxford, Harvard or Yale University business graduates drooling with envy.

Since today Meta-Meta barber's was fully of these *abweletsi* or dealers, it came as no surprise that the hot topic was the recent Parliament bombshell of 20% Duty on trucks being imported into Malawi. One of the dealers who was in the barber's chair getting a Mohican hair-cut spoke in a deep booming voice,

"*Koma a* Minister of Finance *akufuna kutipha eti?*" He said annoyingly while wincing after the barber nicked his ear accidentally.

"Doesn't he know that bringing in trucks from abroad is bread and butter (*nchele*) for us importers?" another dealer who had just gotten a *mbonga* cut concurred.

For those who are not up to date with Malawi's current affairs, word on the street is that the Minister of Finance has just introduced a 20% Duty on all imported trucks. This basically spells an end to the duty free status heavy-goods trucks have enjoyed. The buzz inside Meta-Meta Barber's is that the government has sniffed a rat after *Boma* has realised that other devious importers have been taking advantage of the system.

Sitting in the corner was heavily built boyish looking man in a massive afro-hairdo and dressed in a basketball outfit with the words 'Lakers' emblazoned on his bright yellow over-sized shorts, matching jersey and baseball cap cocked to one side. I could see Shasha looking at Afro-man with envy and I whispered to my friend Simioni who was sitting next to me,

"*Zakumana mphongo zapa* States." I said while gesturing to where Afro-man was sitting.

I later discovered that this Afro-haired importer (owner of the flashy 4x4 outside) has got seven Freightliner trucks coming in from USA. He has already sold them to a famous transporter although they haven't arrived in Malawi yet. But because these trucks have already been paid for, Afro-man will now have to come up with a 20% Duty to clear them. He laments that this is a cost which wasn't factored into his selling price as a result he will be taking a 20% hit on profit. Afro-man was so incensed he spoke *mwachibwibwi.*

"*Ko-ko-ko-komadi* Parliament *i-i-i-i-itipha nayo* Duty *ime-me-me-meneyi.*" He stuttered in anger.

I had a feeling that there was an unspoken animosity from Shasha towards Afro-man. Either because of Afro-man's fancy Lakers outfit or maybe the Ford Excursion parked outside or simply the fact that here was someone who looked as if *zinthu zikumuyendera.*

My feelings were confirmed with Shasha's comment which was like a poisonous spit from a black mamba,

"*Hahahaha,* tough luck to those of you in the importing business, *munvetsa afana,* I wish the Honourable Minister had slapped 200% Duty on trucks." Shasha mouthed off much to the annoyance of the whole barber shop.

Afro-man who had been holding a pair of sharp-pointed scissors clipping his Billy Dee Williams moustache stopped, slowly standing up revealing a height of what must have been close to Shaquille O'Neal 7 foot 1 inch. He dismissively looked at Shasha from head to toe, the same way Tyrannosaurus-rex aka T-Rex would look at a tiny fragile delicious *gwape* gritting his teeth in a way that reminded me of the rapper 50 Cent.

This didn't look good, there were too many sharp objects in here and I could smell blood already. I looked at Amalume for help because two of Afro-man's associates were also slowly standing up, cracking their knuckles and purposefully blocking the only door, our only exit to freedom. I thought to myself '*pafa m'Malawi pano.*'

Amalume had to intellectually jump into the 20% debate, because it appeared like Afro-man didn't quite like Shasha's tone of voice and even with Simioni's karate background, I don't think we could take this bunch one-to-one if a scuffle was to break out.

"Shasha that comment exposes your ignorance towards a legitimate point this nice gentleman was trying to make," said Amalume with a '*we-come-in-peace*' smile while looking at Afro-man before continuing,

"You know that Malawi is a landlocked country and this means that all our imports come in by road. This means that this nice gentleman will have to put a 20% mark-up on his selling price in order to cover for the Duty the government is introducing." Amalume said, stressing on the word 'nice gentleman' which appeared to be working because 7 ft 1 Afro-man sat back down and his two equally large associates moved away from the door. Amalume breathed a sigh of relief and continued,

"Transporters in turn will pass on this 20% to the end-users. The end result is that the cost of goods and services will definitely go up accordingly. Everything from Kaunjika to China goods is going to go up since they all come via road and all of us in here will be impacted by this 20% Duty directly or indirectly."

Amalume had articulated his case so well that the whole barber shop fell silent. Even the Che Meta-Meta the Barber paused and I noticed that Afro-man had even lowered his scissors to his side in a gesture of truce. I wasn't sure whether Amalume's little lecture was factual or whether he was just trying to save Shasha's skin from Afro-man who was about to do something unmentionable with those pointed pair of scissors.

Simioni who is always on top of current affairs looked at Afro-man and asked him politely so as not provoke unnecessary beef or *zitopotopo*.

"Boss, why don't you just start importing buses?" He paused just to make sure that Afro-man wasn't going to get aggressive.

"I understand that buses are still exempt from Duty?" Simioni said with a fake smile on his face. Afro-man looked at Simioni and for the first time he smiled in the familiar 50cent teeth-gritting smile that revealed gold plated teeth.

"Naah, there is no profit in buses. They are difficult to source abroad and they are prohibitively expensive to ship." Afro-man responded.

"And even if you manage to get a bus over here, there aren't that many people buying buses compared to trucks." He said with some air of someone who knew what he was talking about.

As a minibus owner myself, although both my minibuses *ali pamitondo* awaiting spares from Okinawa Japan, I hated the idea of buses flooding Malawi and I was somehow relieved with what Afro-man had just said. As a member of the Minibus Association of Malawi

(MAM,) we have lobbied the government viciously to ensure that buses don't flood the cities. But what does our esteemed distinguished Honourable Minister do? He increases the Duty on minibuses up to 50% squeezing minibus owners like a vice.

I really felt sorry for Afro-man (even though he had a fancier car than mine and was spotting gold teeth), I also had my deepest condolences to all those in the trucking business because this industry is already suffering from huge running costs. From expensive spares to high fuel costs, and that is not to mention massive insurance costs.

But who I really felt sorry for was the ordinary Malawian who in the end is the one subsidising the transporter, because all these expenses are passed on to the end-user.

The barber gestured for me to take a seat while he vigorously flipped the white cloth to get rid of the hair from the previous customer.

"*Kodi a* Biggie *timete* style *yanji?*" Che Meta-Meta asked while oiling the clippers and I told him to give me the usual Tyson-cut. He took a short pause before surprising me that the price had just gone up 20% from K100 to K120.

BE THERE FOR YOUR WOMEN

Usually whenever Simioni visit my house, he tends to go back to his around 8pm, but last Sunday he was here until 10pm. I don't mind him staying up until late but the thing is it inconveniences the sleeping logistics of my household which after a certain time have to be executed with military precision.

Some of you already know that I look after a battalion of relatives, which means that after 9pm the sitting room is magically transformed into a bedroom; blankets start appearing out of nowhere, sofa-cushions are turned into pillows, as mattresses are ferried in and trousers are removed revealing *akabudula ogonela*. This is that time of the night when the sitting room becomes a no-go zone area for females until 6am. There are usually so many half naked male bodies in there stacked side by side and if the government was to walk in, everyone would be getting fourteen years.

You now begin to see how Simioni's extended visit derailed all these bedtime preparations. I could see some of my nephews standing impatiently in the kitchen waiting and annoyingly looking at the clock on the wall which was saying 10:15pm.

Agogo couldn't take it anymore and being short on the skills of diplomacy, he called it as he saw it.

"*Che Simioni, kwada dzipitani.*" Agogo said this while gesturing towards the door with his walking stick.

Agogo is not the one to mince words. There are people who often speak and then think after this but Agogo usually speaks and hardly thinks of the consequences of his words.

"*Tiyeni Mbuya nyamukani ife tidzigonano.*" He insisted to Simioni who was still rooted to his chair.

I could tell my friend wasn't planning on starting the exodus across the street to his house any time soon.

"Is everything ok?" I asked Simioni who looked as if his mind was far away and wasn't hearing what was being said.

Apparently things were not ok at his house. I later learnt that his Madam had told him not to come back home, telling him;

"*Ukagone kwa Makala wakoyo.*"

This was a revelation which seems to have tickled Agogo and he cracked out laughing sarcastically.

"*Bwanji dyomba, akunvelani kuti mwapeza mbeta penapake?*" Agogo sarcastically teased Simioni.

I thought this was uncalled for because Simioni is a very good and close friend of mine and I know that he only has eyes for his madam. Infidelity is one thing you couldn't accuse him of and this made me wonder for what reason would she bar him from going back home. I gave Simioni the 'tell-me-what's-up look' (*takamba brazi.*)

It turns out that Simioni's madam has been complaining that he never spends enough time with her. She complains that he is always at my house or hanging out with Shasha, Amalume and the boys. He usually eats at my house and only goes home to take a bath and sleep.

She had a point there because Simioni indeed does spend a considerable amount of time at my house. What makes it worse, according to his own words, is that she is getting tired and frustrated that he always falls asleep while she is talking to him. She claims he has changed from the Simioni she first met while at Secondary School.

I remember back in the day, amongst our group of friends, Simioni was the romantic type. He used to go over on the outskirts of the graveyard to pluck fresh flowers for his Madam. This is something we all thought was a bit devilish but he saw it as romantic. Every Valentine's Day Simioni would spoil her with all sorts of confectionaries from Gluco Power, Marie Biscuits, scones with powder on top (*miliki skonz*) and her favourite Cocopina drink.

I had forgotten about those days and I started smiling as memories came flooding back. Most boys used to call him Graveyard Casanova, but it was just out of jealousy because he had more class and no sass and knew how to treat a lady.

Apparently all this Casanovarism had faded with the passing of time. I almost laughed when he lamented,

"Do you expect me at my age to be going *kumanda kukazula maluwa*?"

The more Simioni talked of the calamity at his house the more I started thinking about myself and Manyuchi Darling. I sat there wondering if I have I also changed like my friend Simioni? Do I take everything for granted?

It was as if Agogo had read my mind because of his next remark which jolted like I had just been zapped with electrical shock.

"That's the problem with you men, you do all these nice sweet little things for your woman at the beginning of a relationship, promising to always be there for her, to protect and care for her." Agogo said while shifting his gaze back and forth between me and Simioni.

"But like an African politician who promises his electorate manna and golden bridges, once elected this politician starts spending more time with his homeboys forgetting that courtship and tight relationship he had with the electorate during campaign." Agogo articulated himself and had a point.

I looked where Manyuchi was sitting, my heart beating faster like someone who is just about to be pardoned from a fourteen year sentence. I tried to force my mind back to the first days I had met Manyuchi Darling. It felt like just yesterday even though ours started back in primary school. Was I the same man or had I slipped too just like Simioni? Was I like an African politician who tears up the manifesto just after being elected?

I know a couple weeks ago Manyuchi had remarked after coming back from shopping, cooked, taken a bath and watched TV, while all along I had been on the computer totally oblivious to my surroundings and her presence, I was engrossed in Facebook world with my Facebook friends.

"Koma ndiye computer *ikukupatsanitu* busy." She said it with a hint of loneliness which I failed to pick-up on.

Ever since Amalume came with his Acer laptop I have been spending some considerable time on it. There have been occasions when I type with one hand just because I am holding a piece of *chipalapatilo* in the other, which can be quiet annoying when I am trying to press two keys simultaneously.

A day or two after Manyuchi's made that remark, Agogo also commented that my eyes have gotten so big because of concentrating on the screen. I told him that it's because of these painfully tiny little letters used on Facebook which are so small you need eyes the size of tennis balls if not bigger.

"And you are stupid enough to be spending all that time forcing yourself to read words the size of a baby bacteria?" Agogo said his voice revealing his hatred for anything technological. Agogo hates technological gadgets to the point he would rather eat cold food than have it warmed up in the microwave.

I started thinking that Agogo had a valid point. Maybe we were really neglecting our women? Between *ma* gain, *timaganyu*, our weekly *bawo* tournaments and training sessions during the week, Facebook in the evening, long stints at the barber shop, a visit to the local watering hole (coming back *dzandi-dzandi*), maybe us men were spending too much time together and neglecting that which was priority.

The ironic part was that Simioni was the only one amongst us who was always standing up for women's rights. To think that someone like him could neglect servicing his own relationship at home was a bit scary and gave me goose bumps when I thought of my own. I had to make a promise that I will start putting in the time, life is too short.

Agogo told Simioni that spending a night here might not be a good idea. He suggested for him to pluck some flowers alongside the house and go home on his knees like Romeo, his exact words were;

"*Tapitani kuseliku mudimba lamaluwa muzule ofila ndi obiliwilawo, mukawapatse* madam, *zikhala bwino dyomba.*"

We know Simioni's madam is not the type that goes about throwing frying pans or hot irons, and I concurred with Agogo that plucking a few Rose buds and promising to cut-down on his visits to my house might just guarantee him a bed tonight. I told him I will not lock the front door just in case all fails, he could come back and lay on the small sofa with one of my nephews.

As I curled up in bed next to Manyuchi Darling, she curled up next to me and started talking. I forced open my tired eyes and prayed;

"Please God don't let me fall asleep while she is talking."

Manyuchi Darling must have read my mind because she softly asked;

"You look tired, do you want to sleep?"

"No am good, I want you to tell me everything about your day Manyuchi Darling." I lied through my teeth.

I was surprised I really enjoyed our long conversation, we laughed, giggled and I even made a promise that I will cut down on my computer time so that I can spend more time with her like the way it used to be before.

Mukaona zii just know that Makala has just realised that Manyuchi Darling is priority and I don't want to see what Simioni saw. Like what Agogo once told me, "your spouse is the last person you see at night and the first person you see when you wake up, the rest are just visitors who will come and go."

ECONOMY SAVED BY GONDOLOSI

Since Simioni's Madam imposed a curfew (lockdown) two weeks ago on my friend, I have really missed his company. There is a void-like feeling, the same feeling you get when the Obamas visit your house and after one week they say goodbye. In short Simioni's absence had left an Obama void in my house.

But as much as I miss Simioni's company, I will admit there are positives that have come out of his marital lockdown. On their side of the road, my friend and his madam seem to be getting along like two young rabbits, whereas on this side of the road things between Manyuchi Darling and I have been romantically sweet and satisfyingly hot. We have been having some quality time, retreating to bed earlier than we used to.

For some unknown reason we are always smiling before going to bed (at night) and laughing when we wake up in the morning, all the while looking at each other as if it's the first time to see each other. I have even been bringing Manyuchi her favourite breakfast in bed.

This morning when Manyuchi Darling told me that she was going to the beauty Salon to get her hair washed and retouched, I lovingly tossed the keys of my Morris.

"Drive mine and I will drive yours if I have to go out." She caught the keys, giggling and blew me a kiss.

"I hope there is petrol in it dear, because there is half tank in mine." Manyuchi said while giving me a cheeky warning look.

Mmmmmh! *chikondi chidzitelo abale*, I thought to myself while sitting down and calling *nyamata wantchito*, even though I had nothing to tell him. I was sure that by the time he got here, I would have found a task for him, typical Malawian *bwana, kukonda zotuma-zotuma*.

As soon as my butt settled in the comfortable sofa there was a knock on the door. Didn't I just tell you that calling *nyamata wantchito* would bear fruits? Like a typical Malawian bwana I sent him to see who it was and I was surprised more so glad to see my friend Simioni walk in followed by Shasha. It felt like the Obamas had decided to come back to fill that void.

"Are you alone?" Simioni asked almost in a whisper while peeping inside as if he was trying to hide something.

"Agogo is in the bedroom and Mother is at the back of the house, gossiping with the neighbour about the rumour that those two gay guys might be seeking asylum in the UK," I answered while gesturing for him to sit on the opposite sofa facing me.

"Why are you asking?" I quizzed my friend whose eyes kept darting all over the place like a mouse in a cheese house.

"You have to see this," Simioni said while pulling out a rolled up local Newspaper from his jacket, gesturing to a story on the front page about *Gondolosi*.

I immediately jumped up defensively waving my arms all over the place like a lollipop man who guides a taxiing plane at the airport.

"No! no! no! I don't need any aphrodisiac or artificial assistance for my relationship with Manyuchi Darling." I told Simioni who appeared not to be listening to my protests but exchanged funny looks with Shasha.

I have heard stories about *Gondolosi* that is a highly potent Malawian aphrodisiac that, supposedly, gives men some much needed stamina. Its aim is to give the man a boost or jump-start as far as pleasing the woman in the bedroom department was concerned, so the saying goes. This is one path I have never contemplated venturing on for the simple reason that I always considered myself to be on top of my game, although the frequency has lately been reduced from 7 to 5 per week. Or as Manyuchi liked to joking express it in ratio terms as 5:7, meaning 5 times a week.

This reduction has got nothing to do with biological slackness but rather the fact that feeding a house full of relatives on top of taking care of my business interests is so energy draining. That's why the frequency has slowed down to 5 a week as opposed to 7:7 or 14:7 back in the day when Manyuchi and I were still carefree teenagers. But this does not mean that I need to resort to *Gondolosi* to spice things up. Maybe in the near future I might have to walk down that road.

Simioni was quietly looking at me as if I was talking Hebrew mixed with Chinese and a little bit of Ibo. The same way your dog looks at you when you give him a plateful of *thelele*.

"Brazi, I don't know why you are all up in arms defending your manhood as if am insinuating or casting doubts about your bedroom capabilities, take it easy," he said with a smirk look on his face which only lasted a few seconds and was immediately replaced by a serious look.

"Have you ever heard of Viagra?" he asked with a stern face.

I have never heard of Viagra, but for the sake of not wanting to look ignorant in front of my two best friends, I mumbled an inaudible response.

"A little bit." I said while reaching for a glass of *thobwa*.

Shasha knew I was lying through my teeth, so he jumped in and started lecturing me about Viagra. By the time he finished I realised that I had been looking at this whole *Gondolosi* aphrodisiac issue from a totally different perspective. That's why I had gone in a defensive mode.

I had taken a romantic view on the matter but my friend Simioni was presenting it from a business perspective. I sat back in the sofa, scratching my unshaved chin while looking at the ceiling momentarily, losing interest in the *thobwa*.

I was digesting the sermon Shasha had just eloquently delivered, which, coming from someone who didn't have a female companion was a bit weird but educational nonetheless.

According to Shasha, if he is to be believed on his facts and figures, the sales of Viagra topped $1 billion in the first year it was launched; no drug has ever generated that much revenue in its initial year. Shasha claims that Viagra raised the profits of Pfizer, the company that makes it, 38% in the first 4 months of its launch.

"*Bwana Shasha kodi mwayamba* night school?" I asked impressed by my friend's business acumen. His synopsis in a way prompted my business wired brain to shift gears from 1st to 3rd, skipping 2nd without stepping on the clutch. I could see where Shasha was going with the story and I clearly understood why Simioni had dashed to my house upon seeing this *Gondolosi* article.

In our three-way friendship, Simioni and Shasha always come to me with anything that's business related, just as me and Shasha always dash to Simioni's casa if faced with an academic issue or dilemma. Simioni and I would always seek Shasha's council if faced with issues pertaining to America issues, hip-hop or anything auto related vis-à-vis which car has got more horsepower or cylinders. Our friendship complimented each other with such reciprocating dynamism, it was like a match made in heaven. And since *Gondolosi* was a business related issue, that's why we were having this impromptu *indaba* that needed my urgent council and input.

Unless a miracle of some sort happens and someone discovers that Malawi has been sitting on vast reserves of Diamonds, Gold or Oil, (which seems highly unlikely) farming appears to be our only destiny. As of now Tobacco, Tea and Sugar are the only sources of revenue we can point at, unfortunately these are not enough. We need more and we need something highly lucrative to give our economy a boost.

Our friends in Columbia and Afghanistan are blessed with some high revenue generating crops, albeit

391

illegal, in the name of Cocaine and Opium respectively. The problem with these kinds of cash-crops is that on top of investing in *makasu* you also need a few 12 gauge shotguns and AK-47 assault rifles as part of your farm tools, *dzipangizo*. I am glad that my country chose not to take up this deadly and murky form of farming despite the high lucrative returns that can be generated. One just has to look at the horror and massacre happening in Juarez, Mexico caused by *ulimi wa chamba*.

Fortunately Malawi has *Gondolosi*, a drug which we have had for as long as I can remember. As matter of fact we have been having *Gondolosi* long before Pfizer discovered Viagra. Am sure by now you are starting to see the high correlation between these two drugs both of which work by causing vasodilatation in the male, which eventually culminates in pleasure for the female. Since this is not a biology/sex lesson I will leave the rest to your imagination and if you are still lost then reach me on *www.makalasexclinic.com...* hahahaha. Let's stick to the economical side of the issue at hand.

This means that Malawi, just like Pfizer, could also be sitting on $1 billion a year aphrodisiac industry, which is well over K150billion a year. This is a lot of money, no matter in what denomination it's viewed and it's so big it almost provoked *kanfuno,* as you well know I tend to get nose bleeds whenever I hear obscene monetary amounts.

According to the Newspaper Simioni had just brought, there is a small-time entrepreneur who is selling *Gondolosi* in Blantyre. But because of our Malawian inability to see the bigger picture, Simioni says this businessman like many who are in the *Gondolosi* trade are basically selling Gold Bullion bars at a price of a brick. There is no way this entrepreneur is going to generate sales revenues of $1 billion, definitely not in this life time or the next.

In Malawi we have a lot of doctors who have never walked past a medical school let alone been inside a medical school lecture theatre, and this local entrepreneur of Gondolosi falls in this category. He claims to be a doctor and has been telling the media that he has customers coming from abroad demanding his product. If there are indeed potential foreign customers, Simioni thinks that there might be great potential in this *Gondolosi* venture. I agreed with him as my entrepreneurial brain shifted into 4th gear but immediately ground to a shuddering halt as if I had quickly let go of the clutch inside my cerebral oblongata.

I envisioned a couple of problems already looming on the horizon if this *Gondolosi* venture was to be taken at Platinum or Gold level.

Problem number one: Malawian herbal medicines or any concoctions you can think of don't look attractive unless you are really sick and woozy. Try visiting one of our African Doctors, not the ones graduating from the posh School of Medicine along Mahatma-Ghandi Road in Blantyre. I am talking about the doctors whose skills are passed on from generation to generation at a secret ceremony held deep inside the cemetery forest in the middle of the night. The kind of doctors who have on display; a glass bottle containing a whole brick inside as proof of what kind of miracles they can articulate [a gimmick that makes you wonder, surely if this old *juju* man can insert a whole brick in a Gin bottle he should be able to cure me of my influenza].

The presentation of our medicine is not like the kind you would find in your everyday chemist or pharmacy somewhere in Birmingham or Indianapolis. At Dr *Juju-man*, you often see on display roots resembling cassava lumped together with human finger-nails and hyenas genitalia. Next to these fingernails or goats eye balls, you might see some alien looking mounds of different coloured powder neatly stacked up like little Egyptian pyramids. Dr *Juju-man's* products tend to be in their raw state (hence the term *dzitsamba*), a state that might not be appealing if you are trying to attract rich white people to switch from Viagra and go *Gondolosi*.

I have always wondered how come we are so good at coming up with these medicinal remedies but fail to successfully market them to the world. It doesn't take a rocket scientist to realise that you would have to be an exemplary salesperson from Harvard or Yale University in order to convince a white customer to chew human hair and toenails that have been mixed together with hyena's urine. No wonder our medicines are confined within the borders of our lunacy, never going beyond Mwanza, Milanje or Chipata.

To convince a white or westernised customer to switch from Viagra to *dzitsamba* then these ghoulish looking ingredients of ours need to be hidden inside a nice sterile looking capsule that will explode once inside the stomach away from sight.

Problem number two: to transform our *dzitsamba* into a pill or capsule requires mind boggling financial investment enjoyed by the likes of Pfizer and other Pharmaceutical companies who have bottomless pockets. Can we really find Malawian millionaires willing to invest in Project *Gondolosi*? Very doubtful albeit having Malawian Financiers out there who are willing to sponsor a political party with their millions for returns that they will probably never see.

Do we have the technical know-how to address problem *number one*, that of creating a drug that meets the world standards required by the likes of WHO (World Health Organisation) or the ICH (International Conference of Harmonisation?)

Are there any solutions to these stumbling blocks? We brainstormed and debated amongst the three of us.

It's obvious with a gazillion PhD holders we are blessed with highly educated Malawians out there, who eat, dream, think and breathe chemistry, biology or whatever subjects or disciplines people need to create pills like Viagra. Can't they help us come up with our own $1 billion *Viandolosi*? In so doing cementing their names globally as Malawi's geniuses whilst at the same time propelling Malawi to the status of one of the leading countries on the cutting edge of medicine.

Surely there are Malawian political heavyweights whose cough or sneeze is powerful enough to cause the Governor of Reserve Bank to have talks with his counterpart at the World Bank or IMF (International Monetary Fund.) Am sure if we took the initiative, these giant financial institutions would be willing to cut us a cheque that would finance a research on how we can *Gondolise* our economy out of poverty. I can see the adverts already;

"Viagra might take you to *Sapitwa* but *Gondolosi* will take you to *Kilimanjalo* – because once you go *Gondolosi* you can't go Viagra."

It's somewhat sad this so called Doctor/Entrepreneur in Blantyre is vending his lucrative "bedroom dynamite" out of a cardboard shack – instead of jetting all over the world in his own personal Dassault Falcon Private jet; to board meetings with global business leaders, finalising multi-billion dollar deals for his patented *Viandolosi* which, let's face it, would also be beneficial for Malawi.

In the short-run *Dr Juju-man* would overtake Bill Gates as the richest *njonda* in the whole world and Malawi would definitely be propelled into the G-8, transforming this sacred group into G-9... hahahaha (*koma abale anzanga eti*). And in the long-run this Dr *Juju-man* wins, MRA wins, Malawi economy wins and not to mention satisfied marriages/relationships all over the globe all thanks to *Viandolosi* made in Malawi.

I thought of all the money I had wasted into sponsoring aspiring politicians who in the end never delivered at all. If I had only sponsored someone like this Dr *Juju-man* whose aphrodisiac is already in a working stage and just needs refining and a little tweaking to give it that much needed presentation appearance. Imagine what $1 billion a year would do to the economy of my country. Imagine how a billion dollars would transform my country's balance of payments. Imagine, just imagine.

"*Amwene* how much capital can you come up with?" Simioni asked with a business frown on his face, jolting me back into reality. The last time Simioni

Makala Amoto

had a look like that was when we had a meeting about launching our own minibus venture, but I had a feeling that this *Gondolosi* angle was going to be bigger than the minibus stint.

"Are you really serious about this?" I asked while looking at my friend. He didn't have to answer, I could tell by his look in his eyes, so I sat up, grabbed the keys of Manyuchi's car and headed for the door and my two friends, who were still sat, looked at me smiling and glad that I was on board.

"Let's go guys and see this *Gondolosi* Doctor and talk business." I said as we rushed out of my house like three Venture Capitalists on the verge of investing in the next Microsoft or Google.

Mother was still standing by the fence gossiping with her neighbour friend about the famous Malawian gay couple when I told her on top of my voice before jumping in the car,
"I will be right back Mother, am just going to town for some *Gondolosi*."

397

MASAPOTA AGANYU

Those who are wondering why Makala has been missing either don't have a TV or someone forgot to tell them that there is something of great importance happening in South Africa. The World Cup is upon us and for the first time there is a slim chance that an African team might be lifting this golden trophy, a possibility that has brought about hysteria and anticipation the whole of Malawi. There are celebrations the whole of Africa, Malawi included as if an African team has already won the World Cup.

At my house we have taken the festivities to a whole new level. We have stocked up on a supply of Vuvuzelas and the Amoto women have made sure that all food was pre-cooked by Thursday evening; buckets of rice, pots of red kidney beans, goat-meat in *nsunzi wa* curry, roasted pieces of mild and hot spicy *dzipalapatilo, anyani owamba-wamba* waiting to be salted and sliced into edible pieces.

As far as the Amoto household is concerned, we are ready for the World Cup. To show you how serious we are taking this whole South African shenanigan, a few of my village elders on their way to my house stopped by Nkula Falls and some at Tedzani Hydroelectric power plants to sprinkle some *juju* powder around the parameters of these massive Escom complexes. We are not leaving anything to chance and we aren't going to let any unexpected Escom blackouts spoil our football. Although I don't believe in the dark *juju* arts of exorcism, I figured if *juju* is going to guarantee a flawless supply of electricity then so be it. We will let these elders of ours do their thing with their pouches full of magical powder ground from a hyena's genitals, human bones and some arm-pit hair, *ife bolani tiwonere mpila basi.*

Agogo is the only one who seems to be annoyed about the World Cup fever that has gripped our household. He is not a football fan and finds no fun in the sport and he says that it really annoys him like an itchy throat.

He once commented about a local match between *Chakuti-kuti* Football Club and *Ijayi* Football Club.

"Look at those stupid grown up men chasing after an inflated round contraption instead of being constructive like herding cows or planting maize."

His dislike for the sport has reached a record high since the World Cup kicked off on Friday. He has constantly been chiding and ridiculing us that we are nothing but a bunch of *masapota aganyu,* likening us to those promiscuous women who ply their trade along Hanover Street at night advertising their merchandise to potential customers who drive by in fancy cars.

Agogo had a point albeit unsavoury one that *Amalawi tonsefe ndife aganyu.* Like *kamunthu ka chimaso-maso* earning a living along Hanover red light district; on Friday we were supporting South Africa and of course when Serbia plays Ghana; it shouldn't come as a surprise that my household will be flying the Ghanaian flag. Our promiscuity or ganyurism will continue likewise when Cameroon plays Japan on the 14th. *Kuchemerela yachi-*

Firikai is the Malawian mantra during this World Cup and the so many World Cups to follow.

But are we really that promiscuous that we will sell our services to any African country that enters the football pitch? Is this what life is like for those who don't have a steady madam or steady *njonda*? As a Malawian, I wondered to myself whilst for the first time experiencing what it must feel like to be a Hanover street candidate. I had a feeling my Nigerian and Cameroonian brothers and sisters had differents compared to mine – they had a steady partener in the form of their national team and I didn't.

Amalume thinks that Malawi National team has continuously let us down embarrassingly, but doesn't think that the whole blame lay with the Flames alone.

"It's the poor state of sports in Malawi as a whole which is to blame" Amalume reckons.

"There is basically no future in sports, that's why our footballers also work as carpenters or vendors to supplement their earnings," Agogo lamented and he strongly feels football in Malawi cannot put salt on the table. And by salt, Agogo was referring to the fine grade 'A' salt not *wamibulu uja*.

As much I tend to disagree with Agogo on most issues, on this occasion we were on the same wavelength, I totally agreed with him. To financially survive as a football player in Malawi you probably have to be an MP during the week, debating government Bills from Monday to Friday and then chase a round inflatable ball over the weekend for your *Khwakhwakhwa* Football Club. It's as simple as that really.

Simioni concurs that we can't ignore the high correlation between a poor economy and a declining sports sector. Agogo dipped a piece of *chipalapatilo* in his *nkebe* of abnormally hot *piri-piri* cutting Simioni in mid-sentence.

"There is no pool of footballers from where to draw and build a successful team, there is no talent here. Gone are the glory days when our National Team used to win things"

Here of course Agogo is alluding to the days of great Malawian football legends like Jack Chamangwana, Kinnah Phiri (our current coach), Lawrence Waya just to mention a few.

I sat back thinking and comparing my country with other African countries wondering how come they have managed to produce players of a unique calibre. Players that are considered to be crème-de-la-crème even by European standards; names like Essien, Drogba, Kanu, Eto, Adebayor all Africans playing in the top most leagues of lucrative football and yet neither of them is Malawian. Should it then come as a surprise that the Flames didn't make it to South Africa?

If we can't churn out celebrity footballers that make it to these big sporting events is it no wonder that our team is still languishing at the bottom of the basket of mediocre teams? Should we even wonder then that for this whole month we will be *masapota a ganyu*? We will be busy *kuchemerela zachifirika*..

Simioni, as if reading my mind, claims that "Malawi will never make it to the World Cup" he says it with finality and conviction the same way a wise man would reaffirm how nsima will never go out of fashion.

But Amalume cautions that in life 'never say never', maybe our time is coming when the Flames will play side by side with the likes of Argentina, Brazil or Portugal.

I agree with Simioni but disagree with Amalume's fluffy dream. I have watched the likes of Kaka, Robinho, Viera and others show their natural talent. They give the game of football some finesse, something that lacks in our local football. I don't see Malawi producing that kind of football wizardry, at least not in the next gazillion years.

But it would really be nice and astonishing if I was to be proven wrong. If the Flames made it to the big stage I would be the first to swallow my pride and blow my *vuvuzela* with all the air in my lungs in support of our boys. Unfortunately as things stand now, to delude ourselves that somewhere beyond the horizon we will kick it with the Argentinas or the Brazils of this world is a fallacy. It's like believing that a time will come when America will come to us asking for financial assistance. Only those who strongly believe that 'once upon a time elephants used to fly' would stake their reputation on the line that Malawi will one day hit the football jackpot.

Simioni who is an avid sports freak and seems to be in agreement with Amalume went on to say that,

"Instead of progress and moving forward, our football has been in sharp decline. Do you remember the time Malawi National team used to be feared?" Simioni asked to no one in particular before adding,

"But now we are expected to lose?"

It's perhaps why when we won against Algeria in the African Cup of Nations the whole sporting world couldn't believe it and even Malawian supporters couldn't believe it. I was definitely one of the many sceptics astounded that my country had notched a win against Algeria. I celebrated all the same albeit holding on to my strong belief that in the grand scheme of things, the Flames still stood no chance of upsetting the odds.

I was right because we fizzled out quickly like a flaming candle deep on the ocean bed. Our boys came back home and went about their daily jobs as carpenters or MPs and we the fans went about doing what we know how to do best, supporting more successful African teams vis-à-vis *ganyurism*.

Whether this is a reflection of our (not so good) economy or lack of footballing skills is a matter open to debate. This being a tête-à-tête about the World Cup (sports) it's best not to bring the economy into it, but concentrate more on sports although the two overlap considerably.

What cannot be argued against is that if (and that's a big IF) the Flames had made it to South Africa life would have excitingly jubilant for the Malawian nation, especially for my family. We probably would not have been watching the World Cup on TV as we were doing right now. With Malawi in the World Cup the Amoto clan would have crammed ourselves in my brother's 7 ton Penda-Penda Bedford truck and started a long trek to Jubeki to support the Flames. We could have been blowing our own Malawian made *vuvuzela* (*dzitolilo*) while flying the black, red, green flags and singing patriotic sports

themes ... *amalawi national team...limbikani mitima...
amalawi national team ... kuti mupambane...*

Even Shasha had an opinion, an opinion that comes back
to the theory on economy. He claims that in America
football (which they call soccer) ranks 4th or 5th and yet
they still managed to make it to the *Jubeki* whereas in
Malawi football is supposed to be our number one sport
and yet here we are cheering for our African neighbours
and very ecstatic when Ghana won.

Shasha, intelligently and surprisingly, articulated
himself that our sporting woes hinge on the lack of
resources. We simply are too poor and have bigger fish
to fry than to be worried about sports. We cannot pour
money into sports when we have hungry stomachs to
feed and empty medicine drawers (in hospitals) to fill.

Shasha went on to say that in Europe sports is an
industry, but here in Malawi it's just sports or like we say
in our vernacular it's *masewela basi* nothing more. You
play football in your childhood and then you grow up
to find a proper job so that you can sustain your family
because football is not a career.

Shasha, who was on a roll, went on to say that, "in
dreams a person can never be arrested for dreaming the
impossible. This is why the majority of American soccer
fans are right now dreaming that the World Cup might
be heading to Obama-land, but common sense tells us
that it's just a dream and they are entitled to have dreams
of that nature.

But a Malawian can't even dare dream that one
day the Flames will lift the World Cup...hahaaaaaaa...
awo ndiye masewela eni-eni and such a Malawian would

make it into the Guinness World Book of Records as the first person to be arrested for having *maloto otelowo*. Such is the appalling level of our football that we are not even accorded the privilege of lifting this golden trophy in the privacy of our dreams. The World Cup is not for *anthu amasewela,* it's only for those who have embraced sport as an industry", Shasha concluded.

Mother was at pains listening to our back-and-forth and she couldn't take it anymore. She cut in interrupting our analytical tête-à-tête.

"There is no point in debating what-ifs, why-not's or how-comes" she said in her usual calm and soothing voice

"The fact and reality of the matter is that Flames didn't make it to South Africa but some of our African neighbours did" Mother went on just pausing slightly to look at our attentive eyes before continuing.

"So let's enjoy these delicious *dzipalapatilo*, rice and drinks while throwing all our weight behind *abale anzathu achifirikawa*. After all most of these African players look like our relatives, they need our support... just look at Ghana winning 1-0, doesn't that make all of us Africans proud?" she finished, shifting in her sitting position to readjust her *chitenje*.

Most of the Amoto females seem to agree with Mother. Even my younger sister added that sometimes it is better to be admiring Drogba's tight stomach or Samuel Eto's bright smile than looking at our local heroes. All of the younger Amoto females broke into loud cheerful *nthungululu* the minute little *Chemwa* mentioned Drogba the Captain Ivory Coast.

I always wonder whether the female football supporters of my clan have sinister or clandestine motives for watching and supporting these African athletes.

Personally I wish they could ban players taking off their shirts whenever they score, it gives us un-athletic Amoto men too much competition and unnecessary pressure. Most of us the only cardio vascular exercise we get is our daily lifting of the barbequed meat and heavy mugs of *thobwa*. This explains the disappearing muscular six-packs that have been replaced by the expanding flabby bullet proof bellies that would make Homer Simpson look like an amateur. Even Manyuchi Darling's eyes always light up whenever these celebrity footballers expose their fake annoying six packs. It was no surprise to me that she was one of the females giggling when little *Chemwa* mentioned Didier Drogba.

The only female not smiling was probably Auntie after her country was let down by a goalkeeping error in their opening match against USA. It was a horrendous blunder which brought about an amusing remark from Agogo

"If that was someone who grew up chasing and catching *mbewa* there is no way he could have fumbled that slow moving ball", Agogo sarcastically chided, chewed and swallowed his spicy piece of chicken leg, looking at Auntie and then piled more on her

"Anyway you are married to a Malawian now so you are also a supporter *wa ganyu* by default, forget England my daughter and join the African bandwagon"

MAGALIMOTO AMAWAYA

There is something about the male species and cars that go beyond the norms of a two way love affair. It doesn't take a medical degree to diagnose that men tend to get this car virus or disease at an early age in life. I might have gotten the car virus while inside my mother's womb but the signs and symptoms started showing by the time I turned six-years old.

I have come to accept it that as a man, my chances of ever being cured of the car virus are probably zero. As a grownup high on testosterone, I have now graduated to real cars that are propelled by complex combustion engines. In its early stages this car virus was clearly evidenced by toy cars, fabricated from copper wire and propelled by our own legs.

I remember so vividly as a young boy, me and my friends had our own company of *galimoto za mawaya*. It was me, Simioni, Shasha, young Tchale, Nyenga and other friend's full time job to craft and fabricate these automobiles out of stiff copper wire which was then held together by flexible wire known on the assembly line of our factory simply as *mangilisho*. The raw materials were sourced from unsuspecting residential fences and refrigerator motors for the stiff copper wire and *mangilisho* respectively.

We used to visit each other's houses while pushing these hand crafted toy wire cars, we would go to football matches, the market and pretty much everywhere pushing these contraptions covering long distances each day. Appropriate sounds would come out of our mouths depending on what you were driving; bus, truck or small car. No matter what vehicle you had the distance covered on a daily basis was extensively long and the weekly mileage was phenomenal.

As a grownup I now shudder and shiver when I look back at how far I and my friends used to trek. I remember my parents sitting me down to give me an ultimatum that my shoes should better last three months or I will be walking barefoot to school. I was wearing out my shoes so fast, worse than a Formula One car wears out its tyres and am positive that over the years we covered a distance equivalent from Earth to the Moon and back. Such was the high mileage we used to clock on our *magalimoto amawaya*, the good old days. To think that nowadays I am so lazy to get up from my chair to go and get the TV remote control perched at the stool near my feet.

Of course not all boys were into this auto (*zamawaya*) industry. Some were more into toy guns (*migani*) playing cowboys or soldiers – and funny enough most of these boys ended up in the army as grownups whereas some are in the police.

Then there were one or two boys who were neither into *magalimoto amawaya* nor into guns. They were more interested with their sister's baby dolls (*tidzidole)* and stealing their mother's make up, applying lip stick and *kudziphoda-phoda* like females while their mother was at work. Most of these ended up as Auntie Tiwo and co, but this is a story for another day.

Today's topic is about testosterone and the lessons I learnt from manufacturing/fabricating and being a proud owner of a fleet of *magalimoto amawaya*. Lesson number one (and the only lesson I can really think of) is that when it comes to cars men never really grow up.

Men still live in an auto la-la-land unlike our female counterparts who tend to mature and become realists when it comes to automobiles. Women often think logically and strategically, constantly asking questions; do we really need a car? Can we afford such a car? Why should we buy a 4x4 when a Mini will get us to the same destination economically?

Men, on the other hand, don't think like this but are more obsessed with status or image and the statement they will make upon arrival at their destination. Men thrive on remarks made by other people in reference to what they are driving.

"*Wawa Amakala, mukubwela dunyu.*" My friends will cheer as I pull up in my Morris Marina at Baby Shower (yes you heard me right... Baby Shower.)

"*A* Biggie *njale ili shapu.*" Friends will often pump up another man's ego as he pulls up at a barbeque in a Range Rover Vogue or BMW 850.

"Boss, *katundu akudza hard.*" Men will whisper to another man as he gets out of his ridiculously expensive car at a funeral (*zoona*, even *kuzovuta*).

All these compliments, support, morale boosters, *dzichemelelo* or whatever you want to call them achieve one thing and one thing only. They pump up testosterone to astronomical levels that clouds a man's judgement inducing a false feeling that he is the only *njonda* in town. That's why it's very vital to make sure, for any amount of money, to find a female who will think logically for you and bring your testosterone levels to a legal limit. This is not to say that women are not car fanatics.

There are females out there who are also petrol heads – there is nothing wrong with this – just as there is nothing wrong with a stick of dynamite. The problem surfaces when you try to marry that stick of dynamite with a flaming stick of matches. A couple who are both petrol heads will probably result in two or more expensive cars parked outside the house but no salt or toilet paper inside the house. I am not sure where female petrol heads pick up this virus, but I know for men it can be traced way back to the era of *magalimoto amawaya*.

I am sure some of you are wondering and scratching your heads as to why Makala Amoto is trying to have this tête-à-tête about *magalimoto amawaya* and males. Shasha whose wallet-o-meter has always been on zero, (*khwakhwakhwa*) as far as his department of finances go, is the reason I am talking about this. Ever since he came from the States he has been moving from point A to B to Z via minibuses, borrowing bus fare or pleading with the conductors.

Funny enough every time he is inside a minibus you see him looking at the cars outside, making absurd little comments,

"There is no way I can drive that kind of a car and not be ashamed," he would say while standing awkwardly in a crammed minibus, *aShasha mwakwela minibus yaulele koma mukunyonza galimoto ya anzanu…* Eeiishhhh!

Apparently Shasha's parents moved back to their home village about a month ago, their reason being that they have had enough of town life and needed some fresh village air, and the open spaces to pursue their passion of raising *dzifuyo*; goats, chickens and *nkhuku ndembo*.

Shasha being the first born, his parents transferred and left the title deeds of the house in his name. What followed next was a chronology of events on comedic proportions. It was an all familiar Malawian story of children inheriting their parent's real estate property and the madness that usually ensues.

Shasha sold the house and bought himself a Sports car from someone who just came from America. He has been ecstatic about this car that looks like the Enterprise Spaceship from Star Trek. He has been telling the whole town that it's a six-speed Supercharged V8 with a 6.0Litre engine, riding on 20inch chrome low profile tyres, donning a custom made steering wheel like that of Kitt from Knight Rider. I even hear that there will be a car-warming party… Hahahaaaa… such is Shasha's level of bonkerism. All of this doesn't make sense to me nor do I have the time or inclination to understand it all.

I drive a Morris Marina; which has a regular round-shaped steering wheel and gears that go from 1 to 4. The boot is big enough to carry a bag of maize, *dzipalapatilo* and *feteleza*. That's all I need to know.

I will admit that when I first bought the Morris, Manyuchi was against the idea, querying me if we could afford it, insisting that we needed to wait. But back then

David Whitehead and Sons Ltd was closing down and they were getting rid of their fleet of cars at fire-sale prices. I knew it was now or never, the opportunity had risen for us to own our own four-wheels or remain at the bottom end of the minibus masses. I remember the Transport Manager of DWS responsible for the vehicle auction telling me that this Morris was the perfect entry vehicle into the auto ownership class. He even put an icing on the cake by informing me that I would be the proud second owner, the first being a white British engineer. If that was bait and I was Chambo then it worked, because I bit into it and presented the case to Manyuchi. She initially protested but in the end she fell for my boyish excitement and two days later a Morris Marina was parked outside our house. But I never had to sell my house so that I could afford a car, no way sir.

We had all gathered at my house, tossing *dzipalapatilo* on the barbeque grill, (the Torpedo 2000) waiting for the World Cup to kick off when Shasha pulled up my driveway revving his monster of a sports car, smiling from ear to ear like one of those famous crocodiles from the lower Shire valley during the *Tambala Wakuda* era.

The question that was nagging us all, the question that was eating our conscious had to be was the one that Simioni ended up asking.

"Which of the 12 banks did you rob to afford such luxury on wheels?" He asked with no sense of diplomacy whatsoever.

Shasha laughed reassuring us that there had been no bank heist to acquire this beast of a car, (that could go faster than Air Malawi's 737) instead he had to sacrifice his house for the Ford. We all went dead quiet you could hear a pin... no ... you could hear a feather drop.

That's when it hit me that boys will be boys; Shasha still lived in the era of *magalimoto amawaya*. Although the toy had gotten a bit expensive, his IQ had staunchly stayed stagnant as that of a twelve year old.

Agogo went ballistic and almost had a heart attack when he heard that Shasha sold his parents' house and invested all the money in a car. Rumour has it that he gathered his younger siblings and gave them a short brief parting sermon.

"*Mwakula aphwanga, pano mpatauni muone m'mene mungachitile.*"

Agogo could not believe what he was hearing, he knew what Shasha's parents went through to build that house, how they struggled to pay the builders and forgo eating meat, saving up for *malata*.

"*Matembelerotu awa,*" he lamented.

"What is with you boys of today and cars? Do you really think life revolves around these things? And where are your younger siblings staying?" Agogo asked resignedly.

Shasha thought that we would be applauding when he pulled up and wasn't expecting the tide of disapproval he got from us. He shook his head in annoyance and told us he didn't really like the negativity he was receiving especially from Agogo.

"Look here Gramps, I don't really know why you are hating? As a matter of fact I don't even need to be here listening to all this bad Karma? Yo! Makala, am gonna bounce dawg, peace."

And with that statement Shasha jumped back in his flashy car, did the whole roof thing to reveal that it's a *mpanda-denga*. My friend is a showman, (that would make Krusty the Clown glee with envy) and he did not get disappointed. He stretched over the passenger's side to get a remote control for his *Bang & Olufsen* in-car stereo. Why he had to stretch that far when he could have used the controls on the steering wheel, was as strange as it was obvious and amusing to watch. But when he pressed 'Play' on that chrome plated remote, the heavens opened up and a sound louder than a million Vuvuzelas blasted out of the gazillion speakers. The music was so loud, it sounded as if Busta Rhymes was holding a live concert right on top of your ear-drums.

He sped off, Lord knows to where… but definitely not home because that's one asset he doesn't have.

Manyuchi Darling always tells me that girls tend to mature early and this was proof of that. She even reminded us of a few similar cases that have befallen some families whenever sons have inherited assets from their father.

It really takes someone so mentally empty and psychologically disturbed to substitute a house for a car. Most people laugh at this stupid and nonsensical swap, but spare us males a thought and remember that while growing up, in the world of *magalimoto amawaya*, we (boys) didn't have *nyumba zamawaya* to prepare us for the significance of real estate when we reach adulthood. While growing up real estate wasn't factored into the whole equation, it tends to develop later on in life for some. Unfortunately for the likes of Shasha, the brain stays locked in car mode. Shasha articulates his argument that you can't drive a house around town while posing, can you?

We couldn't see the Ford Mustang, it had disappeared from our view like a NASA rocket but we could still hear the blasting music from the *Bang & Olufsen* stereo. Even Che Supanala, my mechanic shook his head in disapproval, commenting,

"The amount of fuel that car consumes while idling at the traffic lights is enough to get your Morris to Zomba and back, you really need to talk to your friend Boss."

Right now Shasha was in no mood to be listening to any boring advice about priorities and prudence from people who drive Morris Marinas. What makes it even worse is that he doesn't have a woman in his life, someone who could dilute the testosterone that makes us males behave like little excited boys.

Shasha is a strong advocate of the motto: "live fast, die young." I could see Shasha ending up the same way some of these Malawian boys ended up. Those who managed to "live fast" but unfortunately never "died young" but lived even longer after all their inheritance and the flashy cars had evaporated.

SHASHA BURNS DOUGHNUTS

For those of you who follow Shasha's antics you are well aware that he sold his parent's house, used the money to buy himself an American Sports car, *akuti* Ford Monstering or is it Mustang, I can't quite remember the surname but I am positive the first name is Ford.

And am sure you also know that Shasha's stay in South Bend was cut short because he was deported after the American legal system got tired of his traffic violations. Yes, yes, yes... you guessed it; Shasha is the first person ever to be deported from America because of traffic offenses.

If you recall, there was a long list of traffic violations that ranged from driving while suspended, driving under the influence, driving with no insurance, driving on the wrong side of the road, driving up a one way street, driving at 50mph through a school zone in reverse, driving with his leg hanging out of the window (*kusongola* Shasha style), driving while talking on his cell phone while holding a glass of gin and juice, driving while blind-folded trying to impress a girl, just to mention a few.

The thing is, *anatopa naye mwanja* Obama *ndi achina* Hillary, they had reached a point where *anangoti,*
"*Uyu adzibwelela asanatiphele ma* citizen *athu,*"
Hillary was overhead telling Obama which culminated

into Shasha being unceremoniously bundled out the US of A.

Anyway, Che Shasha was at it again in his Ford Ma... Ma... Ma... Mustang (Amalume advised me.) He was zooming all over downtown Blantyre at terrifying speeds overtaking and skidding like a lunatic. He then ended up *pa dziboli-boli* where he started doing doughnuts. When I heard that he was doing doughnuts my first thought was ... "Shasha *wayamba kukazinga mandasi pa dziboli-boli?*"

Amalume had to school me that doughnuts is a term that refers to a car stunt where the driver steps hard on the brakes while simultaneously pressing the accelerator all the way down pushing the rev-counter to its maximum. This results in the car rotating 360 degrees on the same spot without moving forward while blowing a lot of smoke from the spinning tyres as they viciously rub against asphalt... *akuti* tyre burning...*kuotcha Mateyala.*

Why anyone would want to do this is beyond me, especially *m'mene limadulila thayala pa* Malawi. There are three kinds of people who can afford to waste their tyres through such a meaningless stunt: [1] you would have to be *mwana wa Uje,* [2] you would have to be related to *a Onalabo (Anduna)* [3] you would have to have been smoking something abnormally strong. It should be noted that it's possible to be all of the above.

But *kuno nkumbali* and we all know Shasha does not tick the first two boxes, which means he must have been delirious from something he had either inhaled or injected (instinct tells me to go with inhaled, I can't see Shasha affording a syringe.)

Anyway, Shasha's doughnut escapade *padziboliboli* didn't go according to plan due to some unforeseen setbacks pertaining to the status of our asphalt roads [I will come back to this later.]

Shasha's history of doughnut making goes way back to his heydays back in Michiana USA. Apparently he used to burn doughnuts when he was still living at Irish Hills Apartments in South Bend, a stunt that led to his eviction after fellow neighbours complained to the landlord about the noise and safety concerns sorrounding Shasha's stunts.

He continued with his tyre burning antics when he moved to Indian Springs Apartments where he got evicted again only two months into his tenancy. He ended up staying with a friend in Elkhart where his serial doughnut rampage took him to the parking lots of Meijer's, Wal-Mart until one fateful day at the parking lot of Scottsdale Mall (before they demolished the place, he smashed into other vehicles and ended up at St Joseph County Jail.

The good thing with the road surfaces in the USA is the absence of potholes, that's why Shasha was able to execute his doughnuts to perfection, even better than Lewis Hamilton did in Australia (before he too ended up tangling with the law.)

Anyway, (I remember I promised that I will get back to you,) there are two variables Shasha forgot to factor in his doughnut burning equations. The first is that back here in the Warm Heart of Africa, we have potholes and the second is that in America passerby's will often watch from a safe distance in disgust, here in Malawi we tend to get closer to the action. *Kujijilika ndi za ziiiiiii* so that we can give our vocal support and cheer at something which will probably not even benefit us *nta pan'gono*.

So as usual, in keeping with our Malawian curious nature, people started congregating to watch Shasha circus-circus brouhaha; vendors, forex-dealers, shoppers, others jumping out of minibuses, respectable men in respectable suits, little boys knocking off from school, even some receptionists from nearby banks came out to see what the hullaballoo was all about. Strange enough not a single white person stopped to watch – *anzathuwa samajijilika ndiza ziiiiiii*. Maybe our Malawian lives are so full of *mavuto*, we need things that can amuse us and make us forget about *ngongole* or marital issues. And Shasha was surely providing that release valve.

Shasha was in the zone – *amadzinva* – as people cheered him on. With the top of his *mpanda-denga* removed, his dreadlocks flying in the wind, he stepped on the accelerator of his V8 Sports car hard, (with the same ferocity used when trying to crush a cockroach so as to squish its yoghurty insides) spinning the rear wheels faster than *Bwana Nodie* used to spin *20tambala* while playing *juga* at Apollo.

There was smoke everywhere and loud screeching sound as the Michelins vehemently protested against asphalt with the Ford turning in successive 360's. That's when the car hit this massive pot hole which has been there since the UDF era, the sudden jerk causing Shasha's foot to come off the brake. The car shot forward towards *nfanzi yo chemelela ija*.

Anyway I will spare you the gruesome and bloody details, but let's just say thank God that no one died. But six vendors are on drips *ku Gulupu*, two receptionists (lucky enough had MASM through their work) were rushed to Mwayiwathu Private Hospital with broken arms and lacerated bums, all sorts of *dziboli-boli* valued at an eye watering K0.5m were destroyed, the Ford Mustang is a total right-off. It had literally bounced all over the place like a ping-pong ball and ended up smashing one of the ATM cash machines of the bank opposite the chemist/pharmacy.

There was cash all over *padziboli-boli* and as usual Malawians started fighting for the K500 and K200 notes flying as far down as the immigration and FBM in the other direction. Not surprisingly everyone ignored the injured people as people jumped over bleeding bodies making unemotional comments.

"*Iiiii kaya zawo izo, abadikira ambulansi ife tikonze kaye ya nchele.*" they were overhead saying while chasing bank notes like people chase *ngumbi* at night.

This was like payday in the middle of the month as paper money fluttered out of the busted up ATM machine and unbelieving Malawians joyously sang; "*ambuye ayankha madandaulo athu.*"

Women dropped their children rushing to scoop as much dosh as possible, decent looking Malawians jumped out their decent looking cars to stuff their pockets with as much decent looking money as they could, vendors emptied their basins of *mandasi* so as to fill them with crisp bank notes, a few fights broke out as people bumped heads while chasing the same K500 note, one man who had jumped out of a flash Mercedes Benz was ruthlessly chased by screaming vendors,

"*Inu anamadya bwino, tisiyireni, lero ndi tsiku lathu.*" they yelled throwing stones and half bricks at him.

It was snowing money and everyone couldn't believe Christmas had arrived in so early in June. Shasha lay there slumped on the steering wheel moaning and groaning in what sounded as agonising pain, his head buried in the now deflated airbag.

Right now as we speak Shasha is in hospital under police guard with a broken rib or two, a black eye. *Kuno nkumbali abale ndi alongo* but you all know that for a black guy to have a black eye *ndiye kuti nkhani inali* serious. *Diso linachita kuthimbilila* as if someone was trying to decorate him with kiwi black shoe polish.

But a black eye and broken ribs are the least of Shasha's problems. As it turns out the relatives of the injured people, the owners of the damaged *dziboli-boli*, the proprietor Bank to the ATM and even the person who had sold Shasha the car, (apparently he had only paid half) are all after my friend.

Although there was an insurance disc on the windscreen it turns out that *nsonkho unali wa feki* which means that as far as insurance compensation is concerned, *ma* claimants *aiwale*. I am beginning to see why my friend was kicked out of America. He only had his Ford Mustang for less than 2 days but has managed to cause damages in the millions of Kwachas. At this rate he would probably end up being the first person to be deported out of his own country. They say there is always first time for everything, right?

Chonde Chonde Chonde abale, don't come here *kumudzi kuno* with ma show-off *akunja* like my friend Shasha. If you have a nice car, which these days most people do, just *drive bwino-bwino*. Just because you are driving a flashy car doesn't turn you into a James Bond. You might feel like Bond inside but outside you are still you.

Shasha is now in the hospital handcuffed to a bed like a fugitive and there is a drip of what appears to be water. I wouldn't be surprised it's just tap water with a bit of salt and sugar added, although the nurse keeps checking it as if there is really any anaesthetic medicine in there because I heard that Shasha was really screaming his lungs out in pain.

But then all the blame shouldn't just be apportioned to the Shasha's of this world. *Ifenso a Malawi kutengeka* so much that whenever we see someone doing something that we only see in the movies *basi makosi thyolele* supporting and cheering as if we will get paid. *Za ziiiiiii zeni-zeni*.

Amalume says that when he was living in Gorton in Manchester, just behind the Police Station, the place where they now built Tesco, someone tried to do a similar thing. No one was impressed and no one was cheering or congregating, instead an annoyed Nigerian shop owner from across Hyde Road just picked up the phone and rang the police... 999.

And as you know their police over there takes less than five-seconds, (*Hahahaaaa bambo Makala five-seconds yachepetsa ikani nthawi ina yachilungamo*)... ok less than six-seconds to get there. This *mzungu*-yob was arrested right there, no questions asked as that is deemed endangering the lives of others.

The same cannot be said of our beloved police. Although someone rang the police and ambulance after Shasha's Mustang had climbed over a few bystanders, they took so long by the time they arrived at *padziboliboli, ovulala* were still there *kubuula-mwa ukali* but the money from the cash machine was all gone. Someone even stole the smashed up ATM, *koma abale inu*...who steals an empty cash machine and for what? I surely can't see it ending up at the market where potential customers would show any interest in it, or would they?

"*Kodi cash machine yanuyo ikupita pa bwanji?*" asks the potential buyer.

"*Inu muli ndi zingati Boss?*" replies the vendor... hahahaha I can't see this kind of transaction taking place, *koma paja* this is Malawi *akuti* never say never.

Our Malawian roads are not big enough for people to be showing off in their flashy cars. I wish government could pass a law that all these powerful imports; Chrysler 300s, Range Rovers, Ford Mustangs or Hummers should be modified to run on Lawn-Mower engines. Instantly this could guarantee a lot of work for our local mechanics who would be tasked with the job of modifying all these imported cars. The rise in employment would surely be a boost to our economy.

It would also, simultaneously and importantly, make our roads safe due to the reduction in speed of these very powerful vehicles since they would be propelled by a one cylinder Lawn-mower engine.

Like a positive knock-on effect, this decrease in speed would equate to decrease in road traffic injuries which then would create bed-space in our hospitals so that our limited resources are concentrated on serious ailments i.e. *kamwazi or malungo.*

This would also ensure that hospitals start filling the drip pouches with proper anaesthetic fluids instead on tap water mixed with half a teaspoon of sugar, if at all.

Because of Shasha's moment of mad fun, eight people (including Shasha himself) are now in hospital with broken limbs, bones and severe broken dreams. This is very true for one of the receptionist who was supposed to be getting married this weekend but is instead on a hospital bed with tyre marks across her thigh.

Simioni, Manyuchi Darling and Simioni's madam have gone over to visit Shasha, I think *ali ku* 5B. They have taken a container of *nsima* and yesterday's left over beans which I thought was very generous although Manyuchi wanted to take some *dzipalapatilo*, but I gave her my don't-provoke-me-look. I could have gone with them, but I hear he is under police guard and seeing that I already have some issues with the police (*nkhani yaitali,*) I think I will just wait until he is discharged otherwise *tingakatsale nkonko.*

My worry is *kaya afikila kuti* since the car is gone and his house is long gone. *Uyu bolani angobwerela ku* States *basi.* Please *chonde* to all those *abale* ndi *alongo* in South Bend can you sort him out with bank statements and any other documentation needed *kuti timukonzele visa*? He shouldn't be a problem once he gets there since he already has his Social Security Card.

MALAWI 3 – ENGLAND 0

It's been over a week since Shasha had that bad accident in his Ford Mustang right by *dziboli-boli*. He has now been discharged from hospital and is now staying with Simioni for the time being. We went over, carrying containers of rice, beans and some Sobo, *kukazonda* since I didn't get a chance to do so while he was in hospital for reasons already stipulated in our earlier dialogue vis-à-vis the presence of Police by Shasha's bedside. This meant that I couldn't really see myself entering the Ward with the hope of coming out a free man, seeing that I had some unresolved issues with the long arm of the law as regards to a small matter of unpaid taxes and an accusation I once levelled at our police as being inefficient. You would have thought that after all this time the police would have forgotten about it, but they hadn't.

Whether it's due to the injuries sustained to his head during the accident or the effects of strong anaesthetic medication he was under, Shasha has been talking a lot of nonsense that actually makes sense. The problem for me is that he is talking about numbers and some maths.

It's not a secret that I hate numbers with a passion and I hate maths with a vengeance. I am not talking about complex maths here and I am not even talking about calculus or hard-to-solve quadratic equations. What I am talking about is your simple everyday 2+2 arithmetic, your basic every day numbers. You can laugh at me all you want but I just happen to be allergic to numbers .

I hate numbers so much that if you take a look inside my Morris Marina you will see that my Speed-o-meter is covered up by a photograph of Manyuchi Darling. I would rather be looking at her picture than to be watching the Speedo-needle pointing at numbers that really don't make sense to me. I have always struggled to comprehend what 30kmph really means and I long gave up trying to make sense of it all, hence the picture over the speedo.

So when Shasha started yapping about 3+1 is the same as 1+3 because they both give you the answer 4, I will be honest with you, I was a bit lost and so confused. I have no idea how he was getting the same result, but when I tried to work this out on my (Nokia 3510) cell phone calculator it was coming out right.

"(3+1=4) and (1+3=4), Aaaaahhh, *zikutheka bwanji*, was this *matsenga* or what?" I whispered to Amalume.

"Because the values of the variables in both equations are the same the result should also be the same." Amalume explained to me although I comprehended nada! As a matter of fact I was even more confused than before. Amalume had just spoken Greek to me.

I was about to ask him to clarify more, but Shasha switched gears and surprised everybody. He claims that on this basis it means that Malawi beat England 3-0. That assertion got me laughing like a hungry hyena.

"Shasha is your head ok? *Munamenyetsadi mutu wanu pangozi ija eti?*" I asked while clutching my stomach as my lungs couldn't take Shasha ridiculous assertions.

I was actually chocking with laughter but Shasha just ignored me. He went on with his theorising using numbers as if he was a calculus specialist.'

"We know that Malawi beat Algeria 3–0 but England drew with Algeria 0–0 then we can effectively say that Malawi beat England 3–0," my bandaged up friend said with some conviction that made me wonder if he had mixed his strong morphine with some strong alcohol.

There were just too many numbers in what Shasha was saying, no matter how hard I tried to wrap my head around Shasha's mathematical jinx I still couldn't get it.

I looked around the room and it looked as if everyone (apart from me) was on the same page with Shasha, I ignorantly scratched my head so hard that there were bits of hair and skin stuck to my finger nails. I looked at Amalume for some feedback, clarification or *chithandizo*. Amalume just stared back at me, shrugged his shoulders in agreement with what Shasha was saying. *Zodabwitsatu izi*, did the accident suddenly turn my friend into a genius, some sort of an Albert Einstein?

I hit a rewind button in my brain to replay what Shasha had just said;

"(Malawi 3: Algeria 0) + (England 0: Algeria 0) = (Malawi 3: England 0)." I replayed it in my head and was surprised that it actually started making sense. Shasha's mathematical nonsense was really making sense.

I couldn't believe it and I suddenly stood up speaking on top of my voice.

"We could actually win this World Cup then, Malawi could actually lift the World Cup." I rushed out of the bedroom screaming.

"AYOBAAA!!! AYOBAAA!!!" everyone looked at me as if I was the one high on morphine and what not.

I was screaming so loud that I failed to hear Amalume's reminder that the Malawi-Algeria game was during the 'African Cup of Nations,' not the 'World Cup.'

It didn't really matter and it's not like I would have cared anyway. I grabbed my car keys and dashed outside shoving six or seven of my little nephews into the Morris Marina giving them a Vuvuzela each. We managed to find a two [Black, Red & Green] Malawian flags, so we attached them to the aerial of the Morris and went cruising around town.

I looked at the photograph of Manyuchi Darling pasted over the speed-o-meter, I had no idea how fast I was going and I didn't really care. The Malawian flags were fluttering in the wind, my nephews were blowing hard on those Vuvuzelas and I was screaming jubilantly at the bewildered pedestrians.

"Malawi 3 – England 0" "Malawi 3 – England Zero" "Malawi 3 – England Nada!!" came out like a song out of my smiling mouth while my hand pressed on the horn of the Morris that was blaring in unison with the Vuvuzelas. Hahahahaha what a good feeling knowing that Kinnah Phiri (our Coach) is far better than che

Fabio Capello (the England Coach) who earns £6million a year.

"Ayobaaaaaaaaaaaaaaa!!! Ayobaaaaaaaaaa!!!!!"

ROMANCE COLLIDES WITH CULTURE

My British Auntie likes to say that 'something good always comes out of every bad situation', but to be honest with you when Shasha smashed his car into the ATM machine near *dziboliboli*, I didn't see anything good that came or could come out of it. Maybe because I wasn't one of the many people who walked away with a free K500 notes.

Somehow as days go by I am beginning to agree with this saying, Auntie might be right after all because it looks as if Shasha's bad accident is beginning to bear some good fruits.

Since I didn't go to visit my friend at the hospital for reasons that pertain to my previous friction with the law, it seems like I missed out on some new and exciting developments that took place whilst he was admitted *ku Gulupu.*

For those of you who have been Makala's friends for long time, you will remember that there was this nurse who came from America. The very same *Namwino* whose house burnt down because relatives had constructed it using shoddy *azimisili* and later on the house-boy had accidentally switched on the kitchen lights which resulted in a fireball inferno [*see story: Malawians on Accidents and Zomanga-manga.*]

Apparently it is the same nurse who was looking after Shasha during his tenure at *Gulupu* Hospital. And it so happens that this Patient-Nurse relationship blossomed into something romantically serious and exciting.

Simioni recently told me that things are so serious that Shasha is moving out of his house where he has been staying since being discharged. He will be moving in with *Namwinoyu* who will double as a nurse and *chibwenzi*, in what some would call killing two birds with *mwala umodzi*.

Even Manyuchi Darling and Simioni's madam are so excited and happy for Shasha, they can't stop talking how Shasha looks so happy whenever this beautiful *Namwino* comes over to visit. To them this is something out of a Mills and Boon novel and it looks like all the neighbourhood women have taken a liking to this *Namwino*. Apparently she was at Simioni's yesterday evening feeding Shasha some Cerelac because my friend still can't chew solids since his car crash in the doughnut stunt. The whole feeding process was done with her right hand while the left was gently and lovingly stroking Shasha's breaded hair, *achimwene che* Shasha *nkumangomwetulila. Chikondi abale anzanga... akuti* Puppy Love, *zachizungutu abale.*

But this happy romantic story apparently has just been involved in a serious head-on collision with Malawian cultural norms. This collision resembles that of a Car and a Train whereby the seriousness of it depends on which of the two you had been passenger at moment of impact, the train or the car? As things stand at the moment I would probably say that Shasha and *Namwino* were passengers in the car and Agogo and Shasha's elders were probably riding the train. I will leave it up to you to judge who came out with the worst bruises or broken limbs.

Agogo has been hearing of this Shasha-*Namwino* saga since my friend was discharged from hospital and has had enough. Listening to Manyuchi and her friends giggle and the constant chit-chats about these two love birds is too much for Agogo, he couldn't hold his reservations inside him any longer. Very few things push Agogo beyond boiling point and this was one of those few.

Agogo is a staunch old school disciple who strongly and wholeheartedly believes that no woman can stroke a man's head in public. Those are affections best conducted behind the closed and locked doors of the bedroom. Worse still, Agogo fiercely disapproves two members of the opposite sex sharing the same house unless if they are husband and wife or related. Keep in mind in Agogo's books, relation only goes as far as first cousins - he doesn't even condone to second cousins sharing the same roof, unless there is an elder to referee. This is why the stories going round that Shasha is cuddling with a female who he is not married to and the looming prospect that he might be moving in with this *Namwino* have affected Agogo a lot as if Shasha is one of his grandchildren.

We didn't know that Agogo had sent uthenga via *nyamata wa ntchito* to Shasha's parents at the village that their son was planning to elope with a Nurse he met at the hospital. Shasha parents came over instantly. This shows you how serious my 102 year old Agogo and Shasha's parents view this whole Shasha-Namwino issue in relation to what happened in Shasha's life recently. He sold the house his parents left for him (making his siblings homeless.) And on top of that, he was involved in a serious accident.

As far as his parents and Agogo were concerned, these two incidents are minor compared to him moving in with a nurse. This is evidenced by the fact that his parents didn't even bother to visit him after the accident, especially when they heard that the accident was his own fault due to recklessness, they figured "that will teach him a lesson."

The notion of Shasha moving in with a woman before wedding bells was enough to send his parents packing and hastily head towards town. As far as they were concerned this was a situation which had to be diffused and extinguished into oblivion.

All along I have known that our culture norms are strict but I didn't realise that they are this strict. The elders from Shasha side have descended heavily on him. They have explicitly told him that he needs to marry this Namwino woman first before he can even start dreaming of sharing the same roof with her or else *awona malodza*. When your own parent(s) threatens *kukulodza* you know that this is serious.

But Shasha confided in me that, it's too early to start thinking of marriage. He says he deeply loves this woman, he has been with so many women while in the States but he has never felt what he feels with this nurse. Whenever he is with her, he feels like he is walking on a fluffy cloud.

"These feelings are real Makala, I can feel it from deep down the pits of my stomach," he told me with a twinkle and a unique smile he has never displayed before.

I asked him why then don't they just marry so that they can move in together without breaking any culture laws? Shasha claims that now is not the right time, he wants to get his act together and most importantly get a job and start being responsible.

The last time Shasha had held a job was way back in the States at a clothes shop inside University Park Mall. This accident was proving to be beneficial after all. This makes sense to me that he should find a job first before tying the knot, and I asked Amalume if he could put in a good word for Shasha to the elders.

Amalume did, telling Agogo and Shasha's parents that even in the UK and USA people do this.

"*Kunjakutu* Malawians live together responsibly even though they are not married, it's normal, it's acceptable and it makes sense," my well travelled uncle commented. I had wanted Amalume to really help Shasha out, but the minute those words came out of Amalume's mouth, I knew that he had gone about it the wrong way. Even Amalume himself realised *kuti anyula* and had to clasp his mouth with the palm of his hand as if that would un-say what he had just said.

Too late, it was as if Amalume had just poked a hornet's nest, *kutosa chisa cha mavu*. Agogo's response was so scary I found myself shutting my eyes as if someone was just about to slap me with both hands on both cheeks.

"*Amataaaaani?*" the words shot out of his 102 year old mouth like some sort of a black mamba spitting lethal venom. He was actually foaming by the mouth like *galu wachiwewe*, telling us off and berating our immoral ways, only pausing to handover the assault to one of Shasha's elders. It was like watching *nkhalamba* playing tennis or ping-pong, and Shasha was the ball even though the assault was levelled at all of us who were the same age as Shasha's.

We all sat there quietly, knowing that Amalume had just opened up a can of worms that a lot of elders in Malawi weren't aware of.

"*Kani ndi zimene mumapanga kunjako eti? Mumativutitsa za ma* visa *kuti mudzikapanga zauchitsiru kunjako?*" so they said, as the tirades and condemnations rained on us all. They were coming thick and fast, which ended up reducing my British Auntie to tears because she couldn't see anything wrong with what Shasha and the Nurse were planning on doing. "It's not like we are talking about kids here, these are two consenting adults," Auntie tried to rescue Shasha from the onslaught, an attempt that rendered futile, as it was useless because in my clan culture had its boundaries that transcends notions of two consenting adults. You could actually see streams of tears cascading down Auntie's cheeks which had no effect whatsoever on the hardened up elders led by Agogo.

The old generation view this whole issue from a moral perspective, while the young generation look at it from a practical perspective, that of realism. I have heard that two unmarried people can live together as a couple and that this is a common thing, but I wondered and seriously doubted if it could ever be accepted as normal within the borders of my country.

I honestly wanted to offer my opinion, but there are times when you have to learn to shut up, especially in the mood

Agogo and Shasha's parents were in. And if there was a 'shut up time' this was definitely that time. I honestly didn't feel like playing James Bond the hero, otherwise it will be the first time Bond dies in his own movie. The concept of "*mwini filimu saafa*" didn't apply here, after all this wasn't the TV series 24 or Prison Break, this was real, this is my Agogo we are talking about here.

Manyuchi gave me a look as if she was pleading with me to defend my friend and his *Namwino* girlfriend. I couldn't believe Manyuchi Darling actually wanted me to jump in and say something; she always told me that of all Agogo's grandchildren he always had a soft ear for me... "He listens to you Makala," she would always say. But today I gave Manyuchi that look that clearly said;

"I love you Darling and I also like my friend Shasha but no way am I putting my neck on the line, especially when it's Agogo holding the knife." Even Jack Bauer knows when to call it a day.

Now I know that there are other families whose elder's *ndionvetsetsa* or *amakono*... but in my family there are certain issues that are best left alone, as we say in Amoto clan;

"Never poke dry *ndowe* or you will expose the fresh inside and find out how much it stinks."

I know Amalume did the same when he was in UK, moving in with Auntie before they got married, but that was UK and this is Malawi where culture rides a freight train and always comes out the winner in a head on collision.

To be honest with you, I really don't know *kuti zitha bwanji.*

MAKING IT BIG BY ANY MEANS NECESSARY

It's been almost five months since that fateful day at dziboliboli when Shasha crashed his sports car. A lot has happened since then; the vendor who stole the ATM was caught trying to sell it to an undercover police, the two receptionists who were admitted to Mwayiwathu were discharged although one of them has got a permanent limp sustained from the injuries. Shasha and Namwino are now living together and listen to this... Shasha is thinking of buying a six bed-roomed house with a swimming pool (somewhere near Sanjika). On top of this, he just bought himself a 4x4 Hummer H2 about 3 weeks ago.

I know most of you are scratching your heads, wondering; 'how can this be possible when dzulo-dzuloli Che Shasha *amanvencha* ma minibus.'

Shasha is now the Senior Partner and proud owner of Shasha Attorneys at Law, (SAL) a legal firm which everyone is now talking about in Malawi. His client list comprises of the crème de la crème of Malawi's wealthiest. I am sure some of you have already heard about this amazing legal firm but those of you who haven't... trust me you will be hearing about it soon.

When Shasha told me that he was going to launch a legal firm, I thought the accident had loosened some screws in his head... I have never laughed so painfully in my life and I only stopped laughing when I realised that my friend wasn't joking.

He came to me soon after the *indaba* that was held about him and his new Namwino girl-friend. I could tell that Shasha was not going to let the words of the elders drive a wedge between him and Namwino. My friend was in love, it had to be love just by listening to him talk.

"I am serious about this lady and I will do whatever it takes to prove to her that I can put food on the table." He vowed and I could tell that he was serious, there was something about my friend that was somehow different, it's as if both the accident and his romantic encounter with the nurse had made him mature. He had suddenly grown mentally and perhaps emotionally too.

But when Shasha told me that he will do whatever it takes, I honestly didn't realise that he was going to literally do 'whatever it takes.' It was no holds barred whereby he was going for broke evidenced by the fact he was vowing that the sky was the limit.

"*Achimwene chichitike-chichitike, ndatsala pati*, I am going to open a Legal Firm." He said it with such calmness, I was 101% certain that he was joking, but was he? I wondered.

"You are going to whaaat? Shasha you don't just wake up one morning and decide you want to be a Lawyer, people spend years studying and writing gruelling bar exams before they can start practicing." I tried to reason with him.

But my friend was unfazed; he looked at me, waiting for me to finish spilling out my concerns and bewilderment. When I paused to take a sip from my glass of cold *thobwa*, he slowly opened this folder he had been holding, revealing a Degree from one of the most prestigious Universities in America. The authentic looking document stated that Shasha was a Lawyer, who had passed his Law Degree with Honours.

I couldn't believe this, surely this document couldn't be real? It had to be a fake, but how could a fake look so real? I was having trouble dismissing it as a fake because I had a feeling I had seen a similar looking Degree somewhere but maybe I was just imagining things. Perhaps I was having one of those déjà vu moments.

"Shasha you are my friend and you know that I know that all those years you spent in America you have never walked past any school let alone graced the halls of this well known University where this Degree supposedly originated from." I said to him while running my fingers over the authentic looking document. It felt so real and genuine.

Shasha didn't bother lying to me and he came straight out revealing how he had acquired such a lucrative Degree (especially in this day and age of legalised lawsuits.) There was a time when lawsuits where unheard of in Malawi, they were as scarce as gay people but now everyone wants to sue everyone. Even bosses are now suing the *khukhi* for gross misconduct vis-à-vis *kupseleza ndiwo*. Shasha wanted to corner this niche market with a demographic that happens to be the whole of Malawi.

"I was online, chatting on Facebook with fellow Malawians who are still in the States when I stumbled across this website." Shasha camly revealed going on to say that for $19.99 only, this online company can manufacture a Degree that can be delivered to you in five business days and if you pay by Visa Credit card they throw in a free gold plated frame for your Degree.

"Since I don't have a Credit card, I had to Western Union my $19.99 that's why I didn't get the frame but the Degree just arrived this morning." Shasha said with a faint smile as if what he was doing was legal and above board.

"So you bought your Degree?" I asked in disbelief and Shasha calmly answered me as if I had just asked him to tell me the time.

"Yes, and this website claims that for $50 they can send you three Degrees: Law, Medicine and Accounting, unfortunately I could only raise $19.99 – that's why I could only graduate with a Law Degree." My friend informed me with the smile and excitement of a fresh graduate.

"Shasha, you didn't graduate," I yelled at him, but he gave me a look that simply said; 'how come am holding a Degree?' This was unbelievable; I looked at my friend hoping to see signs that he would start laughing telling me that this was all one big joke. But he didn't so I pressed on.

"You mean you were actually contemplating on becoming a Lawyer, a Doctor and an Accountant for only $50?" Shasha just nodded saying.

"Good deal innit? It could have been like one of those joint Degree Programs people do at these Universities."

"Do you even think people will believe this scam of yours? And even if they do, can you even stand in court and argue a case in front of a Judge or against another lawyer who has actually been to school and studied law?"

I asked while slowly sitting down, because I was actually getting dizzy from this entire unbelievable shenanigan. There are so many stunts my friend has pulled in the past, but this was the mother of all stunts. I was sure this was worse than Bernard Madoff's $50billion Ponzi scheme but Shasha only saw it as his one way ticket to making it big.

Shasha came closer to me stooping so low his mouth was closer to my ears and whispered his second shock of the day,

"Who is your favourite Dentist?" he asked, with a devious smile on his face. I thought this was a silly question, because there are so many Dentists in Malawi but there is only one who is the best, people even bribe his receptionist just to get on his patient list, he can only be seen by appointment and the good thing with him is that you can even pay by instalments (although he keeps some of your good teeth as collateral until you have finished paying, then he inserts them back in.)

"Of course you know who my favourite Dentist is." I answered, wondering why the change of subject. "Did you know that this so called celebrity Dentist got his Dental Degree from the same website I got mine?"

No it can't be... but the minute Shasha said that, that's when it hit me. My Dentist did have a Degree that looked exactly like Shasha's. How could I have missed that? It's the first thing that you see when you enter his posh looking Dental Practice and it stares at you as you wait in the lounge while reading Ebony Magazines. He is the only Dentist the whole of Malawi who speaks fluent English with a hint of American accent and has got this infectious smile that makes you forget about your toothache.

"Are you trying to tell me that this well known and respected Dentist who has been taking care of all the teeth of the Amoto clan bought his Degree online just like you have?" It was a question directed at myself than at Shasha. And my friend patted me on the shoulder before leaving and landed one below the belt.

"Bwana, how hard can it be to pull out a bad tooth?"

The following morning I asked him if he thought it was ethical to go ahead with his deceit. Apparently he didn't view it that way, only saying that there are those with time on their hands who can afford to spend years studying and buying expensive textbooks.

"Bwana I don't have the time or the inclination to sit in a classroom or lecture theatre, all I have is $19.99 and street smart, that is the hand that fate dealt me." Shasha calmly told me as he got up to leave, pausing right by the door to look at my disapproving face.

"You can judge me all you want Makala, but for me this Degree is a Game Changer, it's now or never Bro... it's now or never," with those words he calmly closed the door behind him and was gone.

That was five months ago and today we are in Shasha's massive Hummer H2 going over to inspect this mansion he is planning on buying. I have never seen Shasha so happy and so chatty; "did I ever tell you that I once worked at a factory in Elkhart USA where they make these Hummers?" Shasha mused while drumming his hands on the steering wheel as Fat Joe the rap artist wafted out of the enormous speakers singing 'Lean Back' and Shasha was literally leaning back in his driving position as if he was in bed.

Recently he has taken to talking about his life like a rags-to-riches story. As much as Shasha's newly found wealth makes me uneasy and all queasy inside, you certainly have to admire what he has done for himself. He might not be academically programmed but Shasha has got some tactical street wisdom that makes you pause in awe and admire.

In five months, Shasha has managed to win some high profile cases, demolishing the other Lawyers with his flawless Americanised English. Wealthy Asian-Malawians (*amwenye*) and some prominent Malawian business tycoons have been spreading the word around town about a new whizz kid of a lawyer who is mesmerising the jury and wowing judges.

I am not a man of law but whatever Shasha was doing, was working and was generating enormous amounts of wealth to the point I was itching to ask him about this website. But Manyuchi warned me not to even think about it, saying that even if I did, what Degree would I be buying? I told her; "Anthropologist" she cracked up laughing hysterically.

"Do you even know what Anthropology is?" Manyuchi asked while clutching her stomach. I had no clue but to me Anthropology sounded like something that could upgrade me from a Morris Marina owner to a proud owner of a Hummer H2. I have never seen Manyuchi Darling so tickled out of her senses,

"*Amunanga amenewo, inunso mukufuna mutsegule* an Anthropology Firm since *anzanu ayambitsa* Legal Firm?" She asked not really expecting an answer from me.

"And what are you going to be doing in there?
Helping Malawians with their Anthropological needs?
Hahahahahahahaaaaaaaaaa!"

POLYGAMY GETS YOU TO DZELEKA PRISON

Amalume was still not talking to me since the American Tax-Return issue, I wanted to tell him to behave *ngati munthu wankulu* and move on, but I did not. The only reason why I held back was because his brand-new TV (*yanyu-nyu*) from UK will be baptised today and I didn't want to miss out.

Everyone was mesmerised by the sheer size and thinness of the screen (*kopya-pyala*). We had moved all the sofas and dining table to make room for all the relatives and friends who came to feast their eyes on this technologically advanced 42inch Sony Vista. It was more of an initialisation ceremony and an experience of how it feels like to have *kanema* in your own house. Most of you have already got TV's in your homes, but for the Amoto family this was the first time to experience the thrill of no longer gathering around a radio but staring at a TV... *kunvetsela nyuzi ndi maso.*

Unfortunately there was no football match, so we had to settle for TVM News whereby the face of our Minister of Gender came up on the screen saying ... Malawi government will soon table a bill proposing criminalizing men who marry more than one wife.

It was as if Malawi had just scored against Algeria because all the women in the room broke out into a cheer, *nthungululu* ringing out as if we were in the middle of *chinkhoswe* while most of the men sat there in silence as

445

if there were *pazovuta*...worse still as if they were Algerian supporters.

According to the Minister, if passed into law, violation would attract a maximum of five years imprisonment. Five years might not seem long, but someone once said one hour in a Malawian prison can feel like one hundred years.

But the more I analysed the proposed Bill the more I told myself that '*ma* Lawyer *adyapo zawo apa*' because it sounded as if there was going to be a clause in this soon-to-be law, that those who already have more than one wife will not face any prosecution.

All in all, this was still devastating news for the Amoto clan (especially the male department) and I am sure other Malawian men as well. I could see the frowns and discomfort at some of the men in the room. I have a few *azimalume* who already have two or more wives ... it is well known that my family is affected by the *Zuma*-factor. In my culture, the number of wives symbolises a man's status and this has been the case for generations just like Zuma the South Africa president or King Nswati (a hero of my 102 year old Agogo.)

Agogo actually thinks that King Nswati has more clout and commands more respect than the British royalty, because in his eyes a man's status can only be quantified by the number of wives he has. He argues vehemently whilst pounding the floor with his walking stick.

"Prince Charles *sangakhale Mfumu kumudzi kuno.*" Agogo barked and *tonse tinangoti pheeeee*. We know better than to correct Agogo, and none of us was brave enough to tell Agogo that the reason Prince Charles cannot be *Mfumu* back here is because he is white and British not because he only has one wife. But no-one wants to provoke Agogo's *ukali* so we keep our eyes glued to the flat-screen TV.

This has always been a source of controversy in the Amoto Kraal. There are those who still cling on to our ancestral ways of life and then there are those who have moved on and hold on to the belief of one woman for one man (or one man for one woman.)

So you can imagine when the Honourable Minister's voice boomed on the Sony surround sound system that; "Polygamy (*mitala*) was going to be made illegal." There was one camp that was smiling but there were some of *azibambo* in the sitting-room already contemplating, calculating and thinking if it was possible to marry as many wives as they could before this bill became law.

My friend, Simioni, whispered to me that the news had already reached Malawians abroad. Travel agents have reported an increase in the number of air-tickets sold to Malawian men from Manchester, Nottingham, Birmingham, London, all heading for the Warm Heart of Africa to beat the deadline. He couldn't give me any feedback about the situation in America because *nkhani ya misonkho siinazizire* and no one is not trusting anyone to start answering survey questions. *Ku* Obama-land *kudakali* tense, so as of now we are only getting reports from UK.

For those who were planning on becoming transporters, forget investing your money in trucks or trailers. Now is the time to start thinking of buying stretch limos because all market indicators and forecasts are suggesting that wedding business will boom before this bill becomes law as men rush to marry multiple wives just to beat the deadline.

Shasha's legal firm, 'Shasha Attorneys at Law' has already started assisting Malawians who are abroad, who won't be able to travel this year or anytime soon due to all sorts of reasons; *mwina sangathe kupempha* holiday *kuntchito, kapena* school *idakali nkati-kati* or simply *mapepala sanalongosoke bwino-bwino...akangotuluka ndiye kuti atulukilatu (wayenda wapenga)*.

I know he is charging premium rates but when you consider that his legal firm is the only one the whole of Malawi willing to tackle these cases, you begin to understand why his charges seems to be on the higher side.

I hear that 'Shasha's Attorneys at Law' is able to backdate marriages so they comply with the law of the land. Even if you are planning on coming back home in ten years time, for a small fee Shasha's legal firm can backdate pa *chiphaso chanu cha banja* as far back as April 1990 or any date of your choice. If you want to beat the system then 'Shasha Attorneys at Law' is your firm.

I know it sounds like am condoning to this whole concept of polygamy, let me state that I am a one-man-one-woman believer. I have never really understood the reasons why a man in his right mind would go and marry more than one wife. But if a man feels that his overflowing libido warrants him to marry an army of wives, who am I to judge otherwise. If the woman feels like sharing a husband with ten other women, again, who am I to say otherwise?

There are of course, religious and (as already stipulated above) traditional pressures expected of certain tribes or clans like the ones prevalent in my family. My reasoning has always been, how would the male species react if the tables were reversed, vis-à-vis women marrying more than one man? I imagine myself waking up and sharing the sitting room with husband number two, while husband number three was outside sorting out firewood and Manyuchi Darling was somewhere in the house with husband number four. It's thoughts like these that made me concur and smile at what the Honourable Minister was preaching that soon polygamy will carry five years or more ku Dzeleka Prison.

INTIMATE ROMANCE OR PORNOGRAPHY

For some unexplained reason strawberries have always been synonymous with romance and I have never questioned; 'how come strawberries, why not *bwemba*.' Maybe it's one of those natural phenomena we just have to accept. Maybe that's why I vividly remember the first time I ate strawberries and yet I cannot recall the first time I ate Bwemba.

What makes this strawberry moment so memorable for me is because I was with Manyuchi Darling when I first chewed these small red exotic *dzipatso*. I don't remember the exact date or time, but I remember it was the time when we were ascending Zomba Mountain on our way to Chawe Inn. This was when we were young, adventurous, flirty and floating on teenage love. This was long before the Morris Marina, which explains why we had gone to Zomba by bus.

We had dropped off by the Kwiksave and started our ascent on foot meandering our way through the lush cool forest like two tourists in our own country. It was the longest walk we have ever embarked on together but it felt short because it was a romantic exploration and a sweet exodus. We were giggling as we chased each other and held hands, much to the fascination of the vendors of *dziboliboli* and strawberries who we met as we walked up the narrow road. These vendors were so intrigued by us and our unusual display of affection that they gave us five strawberries, even vendors appreciated the high correlation of this fruit with romance, I gave four to Manyuchi even though my stomach was making noises of hunger.

We arrived at Chawe Inn; exhausted, excited, elated and broke, so broke I could only afford one bottle of Fanta. We shared this sweet orange tasting drink between us, laughing and accusing each other that one was taking bigger sips than the other. After an hour of laughing, talking and exploring this lovely Inn we started our descent back to Zomba to catch the bus home.

Meeting the same vendors on the way down Zomba Mountain I really wanted to buy Manyuchi some more of these sweet delicious tasting strawberries, but simple arithmetic told me if I executed such a move we probably wouldn't have enough money left for bus fare. So I made her a promise that next time we come Ku Chawe I will buy her a basket full of strawberries.

We never went back as life kept throwing us all sorts of reasons or excuses (*mabize.*) Days turned into weeks, weeks into months, and months into years, to the point that Ku Chawe had become all but a faded memory.

It was just last week that Manyuchi Darling remarked that we are not investing enough time in our relationship like we used to. She wasn't accusing me but she was merely stating the obvious. Business coupled with family issues and friendships were robbing us of the time we used to spend together. Manyuchi Darling lovingly reminded me that I owe her a basket of strawberries. I had completely forgotten about this promise I made years ago and thinking about it carved out a smile on my face.

So on Friday we packed our clothes; my Gucci underwear (even though it says made in Afghanistan and is spelt as Gucchi) and Manyuchi packed the Victoria Secrets lingerie I bought for her last Valentines. I was already getting excited before we even set off, at the prospect of going up Zomba Mountain, just the two of us. I wondered if those strawberry vendors would still be there and if they were, would they recognise us. It felt like back in the day, only that now we had the Morris and we could afford to spend two nights at Chawe Inn. The feeling was so surreal, I was so giddily all over and I could feel the juices racing inside me at the prospect of a romantic getaway.

Time flies when you are in love and sure enough the weekend went by so quickly like a blur. It was a weekend to remember and we had captured it on a zillion pictures with the Sony Digital Camera Amalume had so kindly lent us. We asked various people to take our pictures while; we posed next to the Morris or while feeding each other strawberries.

I couldn't wait to get home and upload these pictures on the laptop for the whole family to admire our Romeo and Juliet Kodak moments, especially the ones (taken by a waiter) of me carrying Manyuchi on my back while attempting to run like a horse. The overzealous waiter even managed to capture the moment when I dropped Manyuchi as we both fell clumsily in a heap of fun, rolling and laughing non-stop before limping off to our room.

I couldn't believe that it was already Sunday and we were arriving home. I had to park outside the gate because the driveway was full of cars.

"Home sweet Home," Manyuchi said with a hint of sarcasm because, just like me, she was looking forward to some quiet time of just the two of us.

I could see Shasha's flashy Hummer H2 and a few other cars of relatives parked all over the yard, with a few *njinga za kapalasa* (*Hamba*) propped up against the wall. Even Manyuchi Darling had to ask while looking at the number of cars and bicycles outside our yard.

"*Kwagwanji?*"

Being my house I didn't see the need of knocking to announce our arrival and I was curious to find out what this *indaba* was all about. After a marathon weekend of romance I had hoped we would get back to a quite house, so Manyuchi and I could unwind and maybe feed each other the strawberries we had bought. We had agreed that today was just going to be us time and then tomorrow we would invite everyone to come see our pictures on the laptop. But it appeared as if this wasn't going to be the case.

The house was packed like beans in a can (*nyemba za nchitini*) and as soon as I walked in, Amalume gestured for me to sit down while whispering in my ear,

"*Khazeni wanu wanyula zedi,*" he said it with the same tone of voice you hear when someone is telling you that *auje* was talking *zotsutsana ndi boma*.

Apparently, while we were romanticizing under the stars at Chawe Inn, unbeknown to us, one of my distant Cousins had just dropped one of the biggest Malawian bombshells which others are billing it to be larger than the Monica Lewinsky saga. The story has been on the news and people are talking about it from the Northern region of the country to the very South.

My culprit of a cousin was so embarrassed he went AWOL and abstained from attending the *indaba*. He was so scared to come face to face with the *Amadoda* of the family. Unfortunately his bedroom antics landed the whole young generation of the Amoto clan in hot soup; we are basically being whip-lashed by *azikulu-akulu* on his behalf.

For reasons know to himself, my cousin had recorded an explicit sex video featuring him and his Madam. Unfortunately or fortunately (depending on which side of the equation you are standing) this juicy video had found its way out of their bedroom into the public domain, which by Malawian standards means DVD vendors.

Mind you, this is not the first time in Malawi that lurid bedroom shenanigans have come out in the public. But what makes this the grandmother of all sex scandals is the length of the video. It runs for a quarter of an hour which (many would agree) is quite long when it comes to bedroom antics especially in this day and age of "*khamani-khamani* time is money."

The news/scandal first broke on one of the internet forums and spread like a wild fire from there and comments were flying all over the social networks, drinking holes and offices.

"*Kodi mwanva.... hehedeeeeee.... zamalodzatu.... koma iwowa amaganiza chani... matembelerotu awa... masiku omalizadi ano eti?... imeneyi Hollywood, Bollywood,*

Nollywood kapena Nyasawood?" This was the buzz at Chez Ntemba and so too at Kamba's Bar.

When Agogo heard of this he blew a gasket, swallowing four of his high-blood pressure prescription pills instead of the usual two. He was literally forming by the mouth *ngati galu wachiwewe*, calling for an impromptu *indaba* so that he could grill each and every member of the clan.

Instead of chillaxing with Manyuchi and reminiscing about our from '*Zomba Mountain with Love*' experience we had landed right in the middle of a family drama where Agogo was venting his wrath.

"What do you young ones think, Mmmmmh?" Agogo fumed at us dangerously waving his walking stick, it felt like being near rotating propellers of Second World War Luftwaffe plane. We all kept quiet, this wasn't a time to be clever in sticking up your hand to answer, it was a time to look down at your toes as if you have never seen them before, especially with Agogo walking stick rotating over our heads.

"Am I talking to monkeys or am I preaching to the wall? What do you stupid kids think?" Agogo repeated the question, louder than before but simply sat there quieter than the wall.

"Don't just sit there *ngati Abubu*, answer me. Why are you letting cameras in your bedrooms?" He fumed his eyes looking at us in fury.

The minute he mentioned the word 'camera' we all instinctively fumbled in pathetic attempts to conceal our mobile phones. Agogo attentive 20-20 vision was too quick for us, catching some who had bigger phones, clumsily fumbling to stick them into tiny pockets. I simply dropped my flip phone catching it with my foot to cushion its landing.

"Go on, hide your camera phones. It's because of this stupid technology of yours, now you have cameras everywhere. You have cameras on your stupid cell phones and on your stupid laptops, I bet you have cameras on your stupid microwaves or stupid irons as well." Agogo gestured in the direction of the kitchen with his walking stick.

"Back in the day, only photographers used to take pictures, this is not the case these days. You people want to be taking stupid pictures of yourselves in compromising situations. Don't you know that what happens in the bedroom stays in the bedroom? Nowadays you want to record everything for posterity. How stupidly naive can you be?" Agogo paused to let his words sink into our young generation-x skulls.

Simioni slightly leaned over to where I was sitting, tapped me on the shoulder and whispered,

"If Agogo asks where you have been the whole weekend make sure you tell him that you were at a friend's funeral." Simioni advised me, because when the scandal broke Agogo had been asking about my whereabouts and Simioni had covered for me. Simioni was right, this wasn't the time to be telling Agogo that we had been on a romantic rendezvous and had taken a gazillion pictures of ourselves (although none of them were taken while naked, I must set the record straight.)

Agogo's alert eyes saw Simioni whispering to me.

"*Mukunong'onezana chani*? Do you have a stupid comment you want all of us to hear?" He said this while slowly advancing to where we were sitting, his walking stick still flaring about like a Jedi's sabre from Star Wars Movie. Simioni simply shook his head, clamping his mouth shut with immediate effect.

In a way I understood Agogo's anger and that of other family members or the Malawian society at large. I also wondered what had possessed my Cousin to play the roles of the actor and director of his own sex video.

Was Agogo right that technology had warped the rules of bedroom antics? He is right that if it was back in the day, you would have to have hired a photographer to come and record or take pictures since personal cameras weren't readily available. Would my cousin have been able to go through with the shooting of this XXX-rated home movie if a third party had been recording it? I doubted this. Technology, so it seems is really taking us into horizons we never envisioned we could end up in.

On the other hand though, isn't my Cousin and his madam two adults, it's not as if we are talking about two thirteen year olds here. What they do in the privacy of their bedroom is surely nobody's business. Whether they decide to bring in cameras, knives, handcuffs, bananas or pliers in their bedroom should be a matter between the two of them, shouldn't it? But should then this be made available to the public, and when does a romantic Kodak moment turn into pornography?

I was jolted back into reality when Agogo regained his composure and was seething his hands trembling in anger.

"This is a disgrace to our culture and to the family. Why don't you people think of the consequences of your actions?" With that he stormed out of the living room slamming the corridor door so hard I felt the foundation shake as a couple of lizards fell from the ceiling landing on top of my flip phone.

At that moment I realised that the pictures we had just taken at Chawe Inn would not be shown to the family on the laptop anytime soon, this would otherwise be deemed as *kunyula ntembo*.

WOMEN AND THE ARK OF NOAH

I have always believed that the Ten Commandments are a prerequisite for getting into Heaven, that is; if you happen break one of them, then you are guaranteed a seat on the next plane to Hell where you shall suffer in eternal fire while the Devil constantly pokes you with his scorching hot sharp-pitch fork.

While I was growing up these Ten Commandments were the first and last law in our household, which meant that you had to know them by heart just like you know your own name. It was no surprise that once in a while Mother would surprise anyone of us while taking a bath or in the middle of lunch to recite the Seventh Commandment.

Whereas most of my friend's homes had a portrait of the Head of State, in my house we had this massive placard of the Ten Commandments hanging in the living room staring down at us and at visitors (or thieves.) There were also smaller placards in each of the rooms including the toilet. The one in the toilet was so low so that you could read it while sitting down while executing your toilet transactions.

With so many reminders all over the house and the constant chiding from my parents every time one of us strayed off the path of righteousness, it was no surprise that I turned into a straight individual who did everything by the book. By the time I was a teenager I knew, deep down, that I had booked myself on the next train or plane to Heaven. There is no way the Devil was going to be poking my behind with that red-hot pitchfork of his. I had earned my heaven credit or pass through the strict adherence to each and every Commandment, I knew there was a chair with my name on it in heaven.

Put simply, I knew each and every commandment like I know my first, middle and last name;

Thou shall not kill; I have never murdered or killed a living soul; that is if chickens or mosquitoes are not part of the deal. If for some reason they are then game *yavuta*. I have lost count of how many mosquitoes have met their demise after coming in contact with my palm. But surely there is no mention of slaughtering mosquitoes in the Holy Book is there?

Honour thy father and mother; I have always done this to the fullest... I respect my parents like a true Malawian, except that one time I called my father by his first name, I was young and I happened to be reading out loud what was written on his Certificate, his name just came out before I realised what was happening. Surely that wouldn't work against me, it was an honest child's mistake.

Thou shall not steal; on this one I know I am good to go. I have never taken that which is not mine. Maybe once, during my teenage years, when father was sleeping I took his keys and quietly left the house. Making sure that the keys did not jingle, I careful inserted the Union key unlocking the chain that secured father's cherished *Hamba* bicycle and quietly pushed it all the way to the road. Once safely out of sight I pedalled the black gleaming bike to a night disco party, picking up friends on the way; two on the carrier and one across *pa-ntanda*.

Of course when I got back, the *Hamba* had sustained a few scratches and the front mudguard was out of alignment. I arrived back home a little bit after 5am only to find Father waiting for me *pakhonde* in his vest, wearing a serious face and the familiar leather belt dangling from his fist. There was no need for questions or answers, no point in talking or narrations, accusations or refutations we both knew what was about to transpire. What followed next was bigger than the 1974 Ali vs. Foreman's Rumble in the jungle title fight held in Zaire. Father whooped me so bad I had problems sitting down for two days so much I had to stand during lessons at school. This punishment surely must have exonerated me from having to go to Hell for a second punishment.

It was like this for all the Ten Commandments (I adhered to them) so you can imagine my shock when I found out that everything that I had so far believed wasn't going to be so. It was Manyuchi Darling who broke the strange and shocking news. She simply started by saying,

"Darling MA, I have something here but before I show it to you, I want you to think outside the box." Manyuchi said in her soft calm melodic voice abbreviating my name in a way that always sounded as if she was sprinkling sugar from Nchalo all over my heart.

She was holding an official looking letter (resembling a scroll) that had an ancient looking seal on it. It wasn't written in English or Chichewa but strangely enough I could read these Hebraic scripture-like-writings without a problem. As a matter of fact it was the best and easiest language I have ever read. It was addressed to Manyuchi Darling and it simply said;

The world is coming to an end in two weeks' time. There will be a Ship similar to the Ark of Noah but there is only one special requirement to get onboard this Ship. Only women have got a Pass to get onboard, but they can choose one other person they want to take with them; any ONE person. You are a woman, please choose wisely but do not reveal your choice until the day the Ark gets here.

I read this over and over and over and came to the conclusion that Manyuchi Darling was trying to play a sick joke on me. If not Manyuchi, then perhaps one of her friends; she had one or two friends who liked playing silly jokes and I wouldn't be surprised if it was one if not both of them.

It could also be that my own friends had sent this letter, especially Shasha. He had this devilish sense of humour and enjoyed winding me up whenever he got a chance.

These were all viable possibilities but what I couldn't figure out was the strange language the ancient scroll like paper the letter was written on and that strange red official seal which looked real and so authentic.

I was still scratching my head when Simioni busted through my living room door panting heavily as if he had been in a marathon with lions (behind him.) Guess what he was holding? In his right hand he was carrying an identical scroll like letter that his madam had also received with a worried look on his face too. He was about to say something when we heard Shasha's Hummer H2 pull up the drive way at a high speed and loud revs.

We heard the dog yelp as the massive front wheel of the 4x4 Hummer run over its fluffy tail. Shasha jumped out, ignoring the yelping dog, dashing straight in holding a similar scroll like letter. His mouth was open about to say something but nothing came out as his eyes saw the similar looking letters from Manyuchi and Simioni's madam resting on top of the stool.

All along I had been raised up to believe that if you adhere to the Ten Commandments you are on your way to that place without eternal fire; the place of angels, laughter and joy, a place where everyone wears white robes and guavas grow on mango trees. But it now turns out that only females had a guaranteed Green Card to this place and it all depends on females who they wanted to accompany them.

How I wish I was a female, I thought to myself. Life is not fair when you look at how I had abided by the rules whereas Shasha had pretty much broken each and every rule that could be broken. Enjoying ill-gotten wealth from a fake degree and yet he could enter the Ark if his Madam Namwino choose him?

Whereas there was a possibility that I could end up in eternal fire if for some reason Manyuchi Darling decides to choose Che Supanala over me? The thought alone gave me goose bumps in places where I have never had goose bumps before.

I looked at my friends and wondered how we were going to debate this issue, we only had two weeks and by the look of things this would probably be our last debate.

There was nothing to discuss or debate here, this was the real deal because by 10am it was obvious that each and every female world-over had gotten this letter. Shasha hastily got up bidding us farewell.

"Ma Bro, *tichezabe*... I gat to bounce," is all he said while hurriedly walking out as quickly as he had come in. I tried to walk him to his car, like I always do, *kuperekeza*, but I could tell he didn't want me to get close to it. He appeared to be blocking me but I managed to peek inside the plush interior of his Hummer H2.

On the driver's side there was a box of chocolate, a beautiful card, female Jimmy Choo shoes and a nice looking alligator skin hand bag. That's when it hit me. Shasha had already figured out how to make his Namwino Lover choose him when the Ship gets here in two weeks' time.

"He was trying to Jimmy Choo his way into the Ark." I thought to myself while at the same time admiring his ingenuity.

"Clever bastard!" I cursed him as the Hummer pulled out in reverse missing my gate with inches.

"This is serious eti?" I thought to myself as I walked back to the house to tell Simioni what I had just seen.

But the house was empty, Simioni was gone, only *nyamata wantchito* was standing there clearing the empty glasses and bottles from the stools, he looked at me with that face of someone who has got something to tell.

"*Anzanu aja* went out the back door and plucked a few flowers *m'mbali mwa nyumba* and he told me to

tell you; '*Auze abwana ako ndiawonabe Ambuye akalola...*
masiku omaliza ano."

So Simioni too was playing Mr Loverman just to
make sure he gets a seat on the Ark. My friends were sure
desperate to dodge Hell.

By 2pm the whole country was buzzing with romance
and strange behaving men; men taking their women for
a stroll in the park, men telling their women to relax
for the next two weeks the dishes and the mopping was
going to be done by them. Men taking their women to
the beauty salon and waiting for them while their hair
got washed, dried, permed, chemicaled, straightened,
braided, woven... without even complaining that it was
taking so long. Arriving back home to cook and bathe
the children, hand over the TV remote control to the
madam etc

For years men had adhered to the Ten Commandments
and now for two weeks they had to do something totally
different so as not to be left behind when boarding begins.
Would I make it on that Ark? I wondered.

I remember the time I had refused to give
Manyuchi money for petrol when her car had run out
fuel. Would she use that against me? What about that
time I had finished the whole relish of garlic beans while
she was out shopping without saving any for her? Surely
she couldn't hold that against me to the point of choosing
someone or would she?

I couldn't hold it anymore, this was killing me,
I was just going to ask Manyuchi who she was going to

take onboard; me or her little brother or our pet cat or even Agogo...or... or... I just had to know.

Where was she? I couldn't see her? I started calling out her name loud... louder... very loud...

"Manyuchi D! Manyuchi D! Manyuchiiiii!!!" I only stopped when I felt a light gentle familiar tap on my shoulder.

"Makala Dear, wake up you are having one of your nightmares again?" Manyuchi's voice sounded as if it was coming from a deep well which made me sit upright from the bed, kicking the blanket off my feet.

"Manyuchi, where is the letter?" I asked a bewildered looking Manyuchi while my hands tried to wipe sweat off my forehead.

Manyuchi Darling raised her eyebrows as she dabbed my sweaty forehead with a nice cool cloth before asking,

"What letter Dear?"

DUAL NATIONALITY

It has been three weeks since I last drove to Lunzu, on the outskirts of Blantyre, a bustling town a few kilometres from Kameza Roundabout. As you all know Lunzu is my favourite meat abattoir, where the meat is fresh... I repeat fresh, not frozen, but fresh...*yochucha magazi*. Friends have tried to convince me otherwise, *akuti* I should be buying meat from Shoprite because it's hygienically sound and professionally butchered. My argument to them is; in all my years of feasting on meat from Lunzu never have I once suffered from *kamwazi* or *phanzi ndi pakamwa* (foot and mouth).

What worries me about meat from these fancy places vis-à-vis PTC or Shoprite is the 'Expiry Date' they stamp on it. Meat from Lunzu has got no 'sell-by-date or eat-by-date.' Being rebellious in nature, I don't like people to be telling me when I can eat my meat and when I can't eat it.

That is why today I drove into Lunzu, a buzzling place of sorts; bottle stores, brothels, outdoor clothes-mall aka *kaunjika* and anything you can think of. Mother asked me to buy *dziboda* and hoofs for her home-made soup, two items you rarely find at Shoprite or PTC. That's the good thing about Lunzu Abattoir because it provides you with an array of all parts of a cow; from tail to nostril including all the underside organs that are deemed too graphic for repetition here. But those of you who salivate at eating these unmentionables are smiling right now and your stomachs are rumbling at the prospect of a plateful of '*zimenezi.*'

Anyway, am not here for a tête-à-tête on meat-ology but rather what transpired the minute I got out of my Morris Marina. My meat vendor, who always comes to greet me and open then shut the door of my car as if I am some sort of cabinet minister, today did no such thing. This made me feel as if I have just been dropped from the cabinet and no longer had any clout. It felt rather strange shutting my own door, so this is how dropped ministers must feel... after endorsing the flag-change, *lero awadomola mu* Cabinet... mmhhh.

Anyway, like a recently dropped minister, I approached my vendor who greeted me in a rather unusual cold way I had to ask him;

"Che Vendala, *koma zabwino-bwino lero?*" I asked, extending my arm in the usual Malawian *mulibwanji* greeting.

He ignored my five fingers offer of *moni* and looked at me from head to toe as if he was Bruce Lee about to Taekwondo or kung-fu my butt. Che Vendala's follow-up words were like a jab which felt like Mike Tyson had just punched me below the belt, yes that area where no man wants to be punched.

"There is a strong rumour going around that you are not a Malawian, people are saying that you are from Zambia," Che Vendala said while turning away to serve another customer who was there to buy 2 metres of *matumbo.* Any other day, the prospect of someone ordering intestines as if they were buying *nsalu* would have made me laugh, but not today. Me? Zambian? This is a serious allegation that could actually get me deported or jailed.

For those of you familiar with Malawi's *malamulo*, you know that it's illegal to hold dual nationality or citizenship. You cannot be a Malawian and Zambian at the same time, *kuno zimenezi amakaniza.*

Even Che Vendala knows this and I could understand his distaste on such allegations about me. All these years he has been charging me Malawian prices on the meat when he could have been charging me a Foreigner's fee.

I felt rather perplexed and somewhat baffled by the Zambian rumours but I just didn't have the energy or inclination to stand here at Lunzu market trying to convince a meat vendor about my true Malawian identity. I muttered more to myself than Che Vendala;

"Fotseki, am going to Shoprite for my meat, Mother will have to do without *dziboda* or hoofs"

It's when I got home, angry that I had spent four-times what I could have spent at Lunzu for half the amount of meat I could have gotten from my vendor. I was also seething in anger for being doubted about my Malawian identity. I am not Zambian and even if I was, so what? I said to Amalume.

Amalume told me to be careful about this because this dual nationality issue is a bit sensitive in Malawi. If you are not 101% Malawian by birth or otherwise, there are so many things you are not entitled to. If this Zambian rumour gathers momentum I could find myself losing my farm which has been passed on from father to son, generation after generation.

"Can they really do that?" I asked Amalume and he nodded his head;

"Yes they can."

Agogo who had been listening quietly sat up from his low sofa, clearing his throat making sounds you often hear coming from a clogged sink or bathtub before speaking softly;

"Do you remember that famous Malawian footballer way back in 2004 whose football career ended after the government refused to renew his Malawian passport?" Agogo paused to give my brain time to engage reverse and go back in time to the era he was alluding to.

I had forgotten about this player whose father was Malawian but the mother was South African. He had wanted to play in the World Cup qualifier against Morocco but could not after his immigration status revealed he was not a 101% Malawian.

"Sanali wathu-wathu amene uja," Agogo said with an evil like smile as if glad that the government had extinguished all hopes of this once Malawian footballer ever kicking the round ball in a Flames uniform.

Mother, who was disappointed I came back without *dziboda* for her soup, joined the debate and reminded us of the recent on-going case about this lady from Mulanje who happens to hold a British nationality via marriage.

This woman plays a vital role in taking care of Malawian orphans (*ana amasiye*) but now her real estate holdings, especially the land she recently bought, are under scrutiny by the government authorities.

By law, she shouldn't have been given first priority in purchasing land in Malawi. This, despite the fact, she is a woman who can cook nsima in reverse with her eyes closed. Her blunder, so it appears, is to have married a British national.

Shasha who came over to my house, after he had heard that I had gone to Lunzu for *maofozi*, joined in the debate.

"I am going to play the devil's advocate here," he started his mumbo-jumbo lawyer talk telling us why government is a bit strict on this whole dual nationality and ownership of assets in Malawi.

Akuti boma is just trying to protect the indigenous Malawians otherwise if they let foreigners start acquiring land it will be to the disadvantage of Malawians who don't have as much disposable income compared to foreigners. If you force your otherwise critical mind to commit to this line of thinking, then everything the government articulates actually makes sense.

It is true that some scrupulous foreigners go as far as marrying a Malawian just to have access to land, but it is also true that there are other Malawians who have found themselves on the wrong side of the equation for reasons that are beyond their control vis-à-vis marriage.

Should people chose love over country? I wondered to myself, thinking of many Malawian sisters who have found genuine love and married non-Malawian men.

Will the children borne out of such marriages ever be entitled to a piece of Malawi soil?

Surely if Obama, a 50% Kenyan national, could become the 44th President of the most powerful country on earth... surely if Arnold Schwarzenegger aka Terminator aka Commando aka Conan the Barbarian could become the Governor of California, shouldn't it be logical to let people of Malawian descent, albeit married to non-Malawians, enjoy the benefits of their Malawianism? My somewhat liberal and logical brain wondered.

Agogo, as usual doesn't think so, and he did the whole throat clearing procedure before coming out with his, rather, venomous remark.

"Mapanga awiri avumbwitsa," he vehemently argued. You can't be *wakunja* and then be a Malawian at the same time he claims.

"You want to have properties kumudzi kuno and properties kunjakonso? That is simply *kuphanga*." He barked, waving his walking stick violently as if he was trying to lash out at all Malawians who had dual nationality.

I didn't have the energy to argue with Agogo's narrow outlook on life and his ignorance on how globalisation is transforming the way we look at things and the way we perceive and respond to the ever disappearing borders as we know them.

The sad truth is that there are more people, in powerful legislative positions, who think like Agogo. Which means that simple ordinary Malawians who have no clout to warp Malawi's laws, but find themselves on the wrong side of the nationality issue, have no chance in hell of overcoming this debacle. To borrow an American terminology, which Shasha like to use quiet too often, 'such Malawians are basically screwed.'

The more I thought about this Malawian-Mulanje-British woman... the more I thought about thousands of children being born from Malawian couples abroad, assuming foreign nationalities... the more I thought about thousands of Malawians who left home and have now become Americans, British, Chinese or *matalibani*, is the more I started realising that my confrontation at Lunzu abattoir with Che Vendala was a minor altercation.

There are Malawians out there who have bigger headaches than mine, *mutu weni-weni wachi ng'alang'ala.* As much as I would have loved to have come home with a *dengu-ful* of *dzipalapatilo, maofozi* and cow genitals, I realised being told you cannot own land in the country of your birth is the worst nightmare of all.

And just in case you are wondering, I think I am Malawian.

PAUL THE OCTOPUS PICKS
THE NEXT PRESIDENT

Call it witchcraft, psychic *matsenga, ulosi,* sorcery or simply *zaufiti,* but one thing for sure Paul the Octopus has amazed the world with his 100% correct prediction. Let me pause for a second here for those of you who just came back from Planet *Ujeni* or just woke up from a long coma and have no idea who Paul the Octopus is.

For the past four weeks here on Planet Earth there has been an on-going football tournament aka World Cup taking place in South Africa. No, it was neither Brazil nor England who won the golden trophy; it was Spain just like Paul the Octopus had predicted.

If you are wondering what Paul the Octopus has to do with football, just ask anyone who has been present here on planet Earth for the past month or so. They will tell you that Paul the Octopus is a fish-like squid which has eight tentacle arms and also happens to hold German nationality. During the World Cup this amazing fish has so far predicted which team is going to win with such accuracy leaving many scientists baffled and in awe. Don't ask me how this eight tentacle squid has been achieving this 100% prediction rate because Makala, just like the rest of the footballing world, is clueless and mesmerised at the same time.

With the World Cup over, we at the Amoto clan were a bit sad that Paul the Octopus will be retiring from his psychic duties. The Amoto family loves placing bets on anything; like the time I lost a lot of money betting that there is no way someone with a name like Obama can become the President of America or the time Agogo lost a few Kwachas betting that One Party System will never come to an end.

During the World Cup we were no longer betting on which team was going to win – we started betting against Paul the Octopus. We wanted to see if this sea creature with eight tentacles would be right or wrong and this was more fun than betting on the actual matches. That's why, today, we were sitting outside quiet as if *tili pazovuta* now that the World Cup is now over. The only sound you could hear was that of dzipalapatilo sizzling on the Torpedo 2000 barbeque grill as oil dripped onto the hot charcoal below; *tchuweeeeeee.*

There was a distinct rumbling sound of V-8 engine and we all looked up as Shasha pulled up in his massive 4x4 Hummer H2. He had a wide smile that could probably be seen all the way from the Hubble Space Station. His smile reminded me of Agogo's stories about the human eating crocodiles from the lower Shire during the *Tambala Wakuda* era.

Ever since Shasha opened up his legal firm, his constant smiling has been getting on my nerves. If he wasn't my friend, I swear I would have gone to the authorities to spill the beans that the academic Degree he was using to practice his Law was a fake, bought on the internet. Since our friendship runs deeper than deep, I just had to control the urge to run and tell.

Agogo was the first person to break the silence as soon as Shasha got out of his over washed 4x4 with its gleaming over polished massive Goodyear tires.

"*Bwana* Solicitor Che Shasha, *mwetu-mwetu ameneyu kwagwanji?*" Agogo asked not really interested in the answer Shasha was going to give as much as he was interested in the piece of *Chipalapatilo* that I had just removed from grill to the plate. I don't really think that anyone was interested to hear the cause of Shasha permanent annoying smile. My guess is; either he had won another important case or had just ordered something from the States; maybe a roof-rack for his obscenely expensive 4x4, who cares?

"I am thinking of running for Presidency." Shasha's responded cheerful while grabbing the long wire we use as *chobayila-nyama* to poking at one of the chicken piece with precision of a hungry man.

"Whaaaaaaaat?" rang out like a chorus from a choir from all us. I even turned around so quickly knocking the basin of dzipalapatilo to the ground (something I have never done in my barbequing career).

"Pre… Pre… President of what?" Amalume asked getting up as if remaining seated was somehow making it difficult for him to hear Shasha properly.

Shasha told us of how the voice of God had said to him in a dream that he had to run for the Presidency in 2014. He said it so frivously whilst taking aim at another chicken piece on the grill although he hadn't even taken a bite on the first one.

Mother, who is fiercely religious and despises the Lord's name being used in connection with politics, was the first to cut my friend down.

"You are telling us that God spoke to you in your dream?" she said with a faint hint of sarcasm.

"Was there a burning bush too?" said Agogo referring to the story of Moses from the bible.

Shasha was about to respond when one of my uncles who has never liked Shasha when he was struggling and vehemently dislikes him now (a hundred times over) that *zinthu zikukhala ngati zikumuyendela*, got up standing between Shasha and the Torpedo 2000 blocking him from assaulting anymore meat.

"Shasha, you have no academic qualifications and the only Degree you have is a fake one", he said annoyingly with much emphasis on the word 'fake'.

Hate him or love him, one thing for sure, Shasha had the knack to spark up debate(s) or conversation more than any friend I have ever had. This *indaba* was turning into a 'Shasha bashing' as he was bombarded by criticisms and told to be realistic.

"Being President of a country is not a small task. How are you going to communicate with the likes of Obama or Cameron on the world stage?" My uncle argued before sitting down breathing heavily and a bit frustrated that Shasha didn't seem the least bothered, just glad that he was no longer blocking him from the Torpedo 2000 grill.

Stabbing at another chicken leg you could tell Shasha was not fazed by the pouring condemnations. Instead he cited the likes of Jacob Zuma who, Shasha claims; doesn't have a gleaming academic career and yet his country was able to host one of the most memorable footballing tournaments the world has ever seen. Whether he was insinuating that once he became our president he was going to bring the World Cup to Malawi is something Shasha didn't elaborate on.

He also remarked that there have been leaders with meagre academic qualifications, citing the likes of Tony Blair and Ronald Regan. Amalume immediately cut Shasha down on his assertion and told him not to compare himself with these esteemed and accomplished Heads of State.

"Shasha my friend, do you really think Malawians can vote for someone like you?" Simioni asked slowly. I had a feeling why Simioni was bringing this up in that demeaning tone of voice of his.

Malawians have now learnt that to be a Head of State, one has to have credible academic qualifications and no criminal record.

Shasha has always vehemently denied his criminal conviction in the USA that led to his deportation, even though it remained as a dark stain on his CV. He claims that his conviction was a result of racial profiling. He once told us that; if his skin colour looked like milk he would still be in the States. Anyway, that's Shasha's version which can't be substantiated because of the logistics and/ or proximity pertaining to the Geographical relationship of Malawi and America.

Shasha looked at all of us, unabashed and still smiling sucking on that chicken bone as if it was ice cream.

"The short period of time I have practiced law, I have met so many people, I have helped so many especially the poor. I have fought for *khukhi*-boys and garden-boys without charging them a Tambala and I have donated maize and fertilizer to villagers. I have bought a pickup that is used at funerals of people who can't afford to hire a car and I have built a few *dzigayo* and *dzitsime*" he paused briefly pacing up and down looking at us the same way the late Johnny Cochran looked at the Jury in court during the O.J Simpson trial. I was actually impressed the way he articulated his case.

"These are the things that I have done and once I am in office I am hoping to reduce taxes for Malawians especially for religious institutions and I will kill the whole debate about the Flag Issue just to mention a few" Shasha the fake Lawyer said with such conviction I started thinking to myself; 'this bastard might pull this thing off'.

"Do you really think that I can be worried about the so-called educated electorate with access to Facebook or the internet? These are those who prophesize to be academically inclined and criticise me behind computer keyboards, hand-held Blackberry's and all sorts of web based forums? After all these people only make up less than 1% of the voting population in Malawi and the majority of them are in Diaspora anyway that is why I don't give a rat's ass what they think of me. As long as I remain a champion of the poor, as long as the man or woman in the village knows that Shasha is willing to fight for their cause, as long as I can garner enough support from the forgotten masses, who make up the majority chunk of the electorate, I know I will be alright, because these represent the largest voting segment of this country and I am their soldier." Shasha closed his somewhat long political speech.

"We might have a Malawian Obama in the making here," I thought to myself.

I have never heard my friend Shasha articulate himself in such fashion, like a graduate from the Havard Law School. Shasha might have a fake Degree but I think all these months going in and out of courts, using his wits to argue and win cases was like a correspondence school for him.

I still didn't think that Shasha was eligible to own keys to Sanjika and I told him so without mincing words.

"Shasha, I don't know how you are succeeding at this whole Lawyer façade because we all know you never went to any Law School or any school for that matter. But I will give you credit because you seem to know what you are doing and maybe it's better if you just concentrate on Law than trying to do Politics." I told my dear friend while looking at the pieces of *dzipalapatilo* scattered all over the grass due to my clumsiness earlier on.

Shasha calmly bent over where the plate of *dzipalapatilo* had dropped picking up one and wiping it with an expensive looking handkerchief he had just taken out of his expensive looking double breasted Armani suit.

"I am sure you have heard of Paul the Octopus." Shasha calmly said while taking a bite before continuing.

"I have been in communication with Paul the Octopus' people in Germany and I told them about my dream.

"Paul the Octopus predicts that I will win if I run." Shasha paused to take another bite before continuing. He was speaking slowly and deliberate.

"I am not trying to be rude or anything, but it seems like God is on my side and so is Paul the Octopus."

With that statement Shasha tossed the bony *Chipalapatilo* together with the handkerchief into the rubbish bin and walked back to his 4x4. Such was the level of Shasha's *kuchita bwino* he could now afford to throw away handkerchiefs as if they were disposable tissues.

He must have pushed a master-switch because all windows except the windscreen slowly came down and we all heard the music from his Bang and Olufsen car-stereo blasting a Lucious Banda's song. He was still smiling as he slowly reversed out of my yard, the massive V8 engine rumbling as if it was mocking all of us.

"Was Paul the Octopus right? Could we really be looking at Malawi's next president?" were questions that kept dancing in my confused mind and I bet, in the minds of all my relatives and friends.

RESEARCH BEFORE MARRIAGE

Recently there have been malicious rumours flying around that Makala is Schizophrenic, whatever this word means. These poisonous rumours started after the recent tête-à-tête at my house about the authenticity pertaining to the nationality of some African presidents. Some people who visited me on this particular day went away and later, Shasha told me, were overhead *pa*-bottle store preaching that I have started politics.

"*Mwamuona Makala ujatu, wajailano wayamba kutchaya ndale...ine sim'mene akundibowelamoyi... mmmmxxiiii.*"

These persons are busy, from one bottle to the next, one market to the other, articulating their presuppositions that the politically shy Makala is changing colours (*ngati mbendela yafuko lathu) akuti 'ndikufuna ndidunphile nawo mu* Cabinet.

What these rumour-spreaders are not aware of is that there are underlying reasons why politics is not my cup of *thobwa*.

In public I like to boast that I don't have the time or inclination to tango in this 'dog-eat-dog' dance, but in private I prophesise the real reason why I don't politic. It's simply because of 'fear' aka *mantha...ndimaopa*. It is the raw naked fear of Malawian politics that has been passed on from generation to generation in the Amoto family like some sort of a family heirloom. And it is this subject of fear which brings me to today's dilemma surrounding weddings.

I know some of my reader-friends are scratching their heads how I can jump from fear of politics to a subject about weddings;

"*Koma iwe Makala mutu wako umagwira ntchito bwino-bwino,*" I can hear you, my reader-friend asking. Yes reader-friend, my head functions properly most of the times anyway, except Mondays to Wednesdays and Sunday after 5 *Koloko.*

The fear I have for African politics is identical to the kind of fear that permeates *dzikwati*, something Simioni agrees with and something most honest Malawians will agree with.

I know the majority of *abale ndi alongo* believe that weddings are moments of joy where laughter is interspaced with the jovialities of people tossing K500 notes in the air gripped in a trance of cultural *perekani-perekani* chaos. Touché, but am not talking about the goings-on during the actual day, the fear I am alluding to exists prior to the days before the big day…before the *perekani-perekani* or *bevu* madness. Yes, there is something about wedding preparations that instils fear in those involved *mutima*-committee *tadzikwati.*

There are a lot of shenanigans that take place prior to the reception and/or church ceremony. It's these that make a lot of families apprehensive, dreading and loathing the whole wedding circus… *mantha adzaoneni.*

No one has ever explained to me why we, homo-sapiens proud descendants of Zinjanthropus, put ourselves through such agony when even our closest cousins vis-à-vis chimpanzees or baboons, are clever enough to opt out of such excruciating pre-marriage hullabaloos. ... *anyani sakambirana zaukwati.*

The element of *mantha* and *dzinjenje* is borne from the fact that a wedding brings together two families that don't know each other but are expected to work together *ntima*-committee *ta*-transport, *ta-dzakudya* and the like. Since families are different, there are bound to be sparks flying during these meetings because the boy's side wants a white helicopter on the convoy while the girl's side wants a stretch-yacht *akuti ngati ya* Abramovich. *Koma abale inu.*

So when I heard that *mwana wa-Asisi*, who is currently abroad *kumaphunziro*, is planning on getting married, my first reaction was; "I wonder whose daughter she is he wants to marry?" I was already envisioning the distasteful meetings prior to the big day. Will her family 'needs or wants' be compatible with the Amoto's 'needs or wants?'

Being the Uncle of *mwana wa-Asisi* I knew I would be parachuted into the Fallujah-like frontline, meeting with Azimalume of the girl to debate about intricacies and nuances of this and that... *kodi adzakwela chani?* Benz or BMW?... Hummer or Knight Rider?... *za ziiiiiii.*

Today we were all sitting in my living room, nibbling on leftover *dzipalapatilo* whilst waiting for an important phone call from abroad. *Mwana wa-Asisi* did not disappoint, he called at exactly 5pm to tell us the big news, *akuti* he wanted to get the ball rolling on his road to matrimony since he had met and fallen in love with a certain *kachiphadzuwa*. Like a loving Uncle I asked him about the particulars of his wife-to-be;

"*Kodi ndi mwana wandani?*" I posed the question warmly after he had spent a good twenty-minutes telling me how much in love he was with this girl who he met at college *kunjako*.

The instant he mentioned her name... her surname... I almost dropped the phone as if it was a hot brick. Mother, who had been standing next to me with a wide smile on her face due to the fact that *amatengeka ndi dzikwati*, looked at me;

"Is everything Ok?" She asked in her calm diplomatic voice while adjusting the knot of her *chitenje* with the deftness and skill of a Malawian woman.

I didn't answer her because my mind had gone numb and my clammy fingers were limply clasping the phone it's a miracle I hadn't dropped it. I could still hear *mwana wa-Asisi* at the other end of the phone;

"Hello! Hello! Uncle Makala, are you still there? Hellooooo!"

I slowly regained my composure, knowing that the packed living room was staring at me wondering why I had all of a sudden started sweating in the July breeze. I slowly spoke into the mouth piece of the Motorola Razr;

"*Iwe*, can you repeat her surname?" It was more of a whisper like that of a thief communicating with another thief in the dark while trying to steal silverware in a church.

Mwana wa-Asisi's response made me dizzy and a bit nauseated. How could this be happening? I thought to myself while struggling to regain my composure. I was finding it extremely hard to formulate my follow-up question;

"Have you two already... I mean... are you two sharing the same bedroom?" The minute the badly mumbled question slithered past my lips I was already dreading and fearing his obvious response.

"Yes Uncle, we have already consummated the forbidden fruit, as a matter of fact she is three-months pregnant and that's why we want to speed up these wedding preparations." Was his instant response which knocked the wind out of me, I reached for the nearest chair, slowly easing myself into it like a boxer who has just suffered twelve gruelling rounds.

Globalisation has seen a gazillion Malawians exodusing abroad in droves for greener pastures or *mamphunziro*. Most find love *kunjako* and some end up getting married over there while others, whose immigration papers are still valid, come back home *kudzakwatitsa choyela* amongst family. This is exactly what *mwana wa-Asisi* and his pregnant girlfriend were planning on doing; to come over *kumudzi kuno*, get married and then go back *kumaphunziro* as husband and wife.

After hanging up the phone I could feel all eyes were on me, especially Agogo's who has the propensity to smell disaster a gazillion miles away like a hyena smells a dead carcass.

"*Kwagwanji?*" Agogo asked with a frown and a hint of annoyance. I didn't know how to diplomatically interpret the telephone conversation I just had with *mwana wa-Asisi*, so I said it as it was...*mwachindunji*.

"The wedding preparations will not have *akuchikazi.*" I started, while reaching for a glass of water and gulping all of it in one swing because my throat felt dry and parched like the Sahara.

"What do you mean the female side doesn't exist? Doesn't she have relations over here?" Agogo interrogated me as if I was the one getting married.

"*Ndiwamasiyenamwaliyo?*" Mother diplomatically asked in her usual calm voice, her earlier smile replaced by a look of concern and worry.

"No Agogo, it's because we are both the boy's side and the girl's side," my voice sounded coarse like someone was scrapping together two pieces of sandpaper. Time stood still as my words slowly embede themselves into the minds of those present, there was an eerie silence like the calm before a storm hits and in this case the said storm came in the form of Hurricane Agogo. At approximately 5:26pm Hurrican Agogo struck the shores of the Amoto compound and at approximately 5:27pm all hell broke loose.

"Whaaaaat! We are both *chani*?" Agogo grilled me as if I had just dropped my trousers in public revealing the un-revealable.

"The girl is *mwana wa-Achimwene aku Nancholi,*" the minute I said that the whole room which had already been silent apart from Hurricane Agogo, fell even more silent. It was so silent I could hear the breathing of chickens outside and Agogo beating heart.

The tension was so unbearable to the point Simioni and his madam slowly departed in reverse (*chanfutambuyo*) without saying a word. Even though Simioni and his madam were the god-parents of *mwana wa-Asisi*, I am sure they were thinking; '*izi zapachiweni-weni zanu...ife tazidomoka.*'

The silence didn't last for long. If Agogo wrath was category 5 previosly he cracked it up a notch and he came back as category 6 if not 7 worse than Hurricane Katrina. He violently swung his walking-stick onto a DFS-stool Amalume had brought from UK, smashing the glass-top into a gazillion pieces while screaming like a possessed being.

"Nooooooo!!! *Malodza! Malodza! Malodza eni-eni*! They can't get married, it's a travesty, and I won't let it happen for as long as I live!!!" Agogo raved and ranted and we could all see the meandering *mitsempha* protruding along his neck, his eyes were blood-shot red with rage. The women who had been sitting close to him started heading for sanctuary in the kitchen. No one wanted to get poked in the eye or whacked on the head with that walking stick.

"Agogo, she is already three-months pregnant," I said, glad that I wasn't anywhere near his lethal walking-stick. The minute I said this, the remaining women in the room let out a chorus of gasps and Agogo slumped back into the chair like a boneless mass of meat. Mother shook her head from side to side like someone trying to wake up from a ghoulish nightmare;

"Koma you kids, what do you do *kunjako*? You mean you don't research or *kufufuzana kuti kumudzi nkuti musanafunsilane?*" She lamented.

Most of you know that there are well documented long-term ramifications that arise when two closely related individuals bite the forbidden fruit. There have been cases of distant cousins playing '*za-abambo ndi amayi*', and in some cultures it is even encouraged to marry between cousins, *akuti* keeping it in the family.

But *zatigwela ifezi* is a whole different ball game because *mwana wa-Asisi* and *Mwana wa-Achimwene aku Nancholi* are as close as it gets. *Pa mwambo wathu wachi* Malawi they are brother and sister. In western culture they would be first cousins. This is a mega-dilemma and Amalume suggested that we call for an emergency impromptu meeting.

I had a feeling that this story was not going to stay under wraps for long, I had observed Simioni's madam before their *nfutambuyo*-departure, the way her ears had fluttered like those of an excited elephant. I know how she loves to flap her bright-red lipstick-lips, she might be highly educated but she is a serial gossiper with the expertise and talent of spicing up a story by sprinkling her own *adyo* and sugar. Simioni's madam could take a boring story of two chickens mating, re-tell it with much sensationalism and stir up so much excitement you would think she was talking about two aliens not chickens. I gave me goose bumps just to think how much controversy she was going to whip up with *zationekela ifezi*.

As a result you don't have to be a psychic to know that by tomorrow the whole neighbourhood would be talking and laughing.

"*Kodi mwanva malaulo akwa Amoto? Apatsanatu mimba pachibale*"

"He-he-deeeee Uluuuuuu"

I had a feeling the impromptu indaba, suggested by Amalume was going to be unique, since *akuchimuna ndi akuchikazi* were the same family, us, the Amotos. I was really afraid and not looking forward to this meeting. I also had my doubts if it would achieve anything at all; the three-month pregnancy was like a white elephant in the room.

Nkhani yochitika kunja was having devastating consequences *kumudzi kuno*. This was a bit tumultuous for us as a family and I tried to remember if there was something similar in my clan's past but nothing came to mind. Not even cousin's video taping his bedroom shenanigans came close to this 'inbreeding' that was beyond abomination.

Agogo who had gone abnormally quiet suddenly looked up and I thought to myself; 'here comes Hurricane Agogo'

"*Akangobwera anawa tiwalande ma* passport *awo,*" he said maliciously before adding;

"I want those passports burnt, *mwanva? Zidzaotchedwe akangofika.*" We all nodded in agreement, the same way Ugandan army Generals used to nod in agreement at anything Idi Amin Dada said. The scary bit is that Agogo meant what he had just said at which point I realised that this was more serious than African politics.

NAME CHANGER OR GAME CHANGER?

Amalume once told us that there are only 4 ways of getting rich [1] you are born in riches (by default) [2] you marry into riches [3] you work hard to get riches [4] you lie your way into riches.

[1] Blessed are those who this option is accorded to them by birth-right. We all know that *ana a Uje* will never have to worry about how to pay for that holiday abroad. Their biggest problem might be that there are only seven days in a week and yet they have twelve cars.

[2] It is becoming a bit harder to get rich via this route because nowadays people with money sign Prenuptial Agreement which means you cannot inherit their wealth after divorce. But if the opportunity presents itself go for it madam, even if he is ugly as long as he is willing to leave the prenuptial out of the marriage.

[3] The chances of getting rich via this route go beyond nil (into negative territory.) Many people have tried to get rich through working 7:30-5 or *ma shifiti*, hoping to be the next Bill Gates but so far only one person has succeeded – Bill Gates. *Ambirife* we just work so that we can pay taxes and maybe if we have any change left over we go out and buy air-time for our phone. 100% of all those who are working will never get rich, if your boss is not even a Thousandaire how do you expect to become a Millionaire? Hahahahaha, *osatheka bwana*.

[4] Is the most common, it sounds easy but this option is perhaps the toughest of the four. It is an option which requires an IQ ten times that of Albert Einstein, because *kulikunga bodza loti udye nalo ma* million is not everyone's cup of tea, otherwise we would all have been zillionaires. You are most likely going to meander on the wrong side of the law in order to execute this option. Go ask Bernard Madoff who managed to tell a $50billion lie. It is on this fourth option that today's drama hinges on.

We were all outside by the barbeque grill and it was the first time in the Amoto barbequing history that *dzipalapatilo* did not feature. Our friend Tchale who just arrived from Mozambique brought this massive tentacle squid like fish.

"Is that Paulo the Okutopasi?" Agogo asked referring to *chinsomba chimalosela* World Cup *chija*. It was so massive it sprawled across the whole grill, its natural oils dripping onto the fire underneath emitting the most amazing smell my nostrils have ever been bombarded with. It was one of those smell you cannot quiet describe or believe that you are really experiencing it. The signals were sent from my nostrils via my brain then down to my stomach which responded by making these loud grumbling noises like thunder.

Tchale claims that the fish-monger who sold him this squid assured him that it was indeed Paulo the Celebrity Octopus and that its meat is so soft it feels like biting into a cloud. *Izi ziribe umboni* but I was looking forward to sinking my teeth into this boneless *lebede-lebede*-fish. The smell was tantalisingly nice no wonder the whole neighbourhood dogs converged in my yard wagging their tails as if it was mating season. I felt sorry for the dogs since it was obvious there would be no leftovers and for the first time in my life I was thankful that I wasn't a dog.

I was just about to flip the Octopus over when Shasha pulled up in his Hummer H2 with a passenger who neither of us recognised. Shasha's mysterious friend just arrived from abroad *akuti ku* Sweden over two weeks ago. Shasha wasn't even blasting loud music as he usually does when he is driving, a strange phenomenon indeed.

The passenger in Shasha's 4x4 claims to be the son of Malawi's Great man who passed away back in 1997. And we later learnt that Shasha has used his legal firm 'Shasha's Attorneys at Law' to help his friend to change his name to take that of the late-Great man. We all paused the minute Shasha said told us of the name changing that had just taken place, apparently yesterday.

"He Whaaaaaaaat?" Was Agogo's reaction who all along had been eyeing the sizzling-cooking Octopus ignoring looking at the Hummer or its occupants but now looked up in shock with a hint of disgust.

You have to remember that Agogo is one of the few people present at Chileka Airport in welcoming back the late-Great man back in the 1960's and he is one of the few still living who knows the history of the late-Great man more than anyone else.

I remember Agogo telling us how the late-Great man had led a rather strange celibate life; not marrying nor fathering any children. No woman ever came forward to claim that she had been impregnated by the late-Great man. Not even weeks or months after his sad passing at the age of 101 did any one come forward with claims that she mothered him a child, something which confirms Agogo's stories that this Great man had borne no children.

So you can understand our shock when Shasha turned up with a mysterious friend who was claiming to be the son of the late-Great man. For us, it was shocking to hear such a claim, but for Agogo it was simply catastrophic on a Titanic level to the point that he was started shaking with rage and twitching of his left eye. This was a sign that the shit was about to hit the fan and someone was bound to get sprayed in some stinky gooey.

"How old are you again?" Agogo asked menacingly pointing at Shasha's friend with his walking stick.

"Oh boy, here comes the walking stick," I whispered to Manyuchi who was standing next to me. I didn't like where this was heading, I had a feeling Agogo was about to poke Shasha's prestigious Swedish friend in the eye. My fear was; what if this Malawian was really the late-Great man's offspring, *sitiwonapo ma* lawsuit apa?

"He is 34 years old." Shasha answered on behalf of his un-usually quiet friend and Agogo didn't like Shasha playing Lawyer with him.

"Why are you answering for him, *iwowa samanva chichewa?*" Agogo angrily vented while his walking-stick kept rising higher and higher getting closer to eye level.

"Calm down Agogo, my client has proposed to pay K75000 out of his own pocket for a DNA test to prove that he is the son of the late-Great man." Shasha said while protectively stepping in between Agogo and his

Swedish friend. The minute Shasha mentioned money, we immediately smelled a rat, because this K75000 felt like a down-payment to something else. Mind you, we are Malawians and viruses of suspicion runs in our blood. Yes he might be the late-Great man's son, but the 'suspicion virus' was denying my brain to accept that possibility.

Simioni who had been sitting quietly all this time stepped forward standing side by side with Agogo. This was the first time Simioni and Agogo had taken a stance like this, it was like the Jews and Palestinians being on the same side as allies.

"Shasha why is your friend coming out now I mean, where was he all this time?" Simioni asked a question we all were dying to ask since we all knew that the late-Great man had left a lot of wealth but no off springs; something which had been drilled in all Malawians to the point it became factual, or was it?

Everyone knows that the late-Great man was the richest man in Malawi with properties spanning as far wide as South Africa and United Kingdom. There was no one else in Malawi who owned as much land as he did. And Agogo, who is roughly the same age as the late-Great man, told us of how there are some active Swiss bank accounts with millions of American Dollars still intact.

"Has Shasha friend sniffed chinyezi?" I heard one of the men, I think it was Amalume's younger brother, whisper into the ear of another man, who was a relative but I couldn't recognise. It was a pathetic whisper because it carried over and we all could hear it, including Shasha and his friend.

"My client-friend is not motivated by money, he just wants Malawians to know who he is." Was Shasha's weak argument, which he tried to substantiate by saying that his client was not motivated by greed but by the right of everyone in knowing their biological father. But Agogo wasn't buying this.

"Why go through with the DNA testing? Why not get together with the relatives of the late-Great man instead of *kutsogoza ma* lawyer?" Agogo asked poking Shasha on the cheek with his walking stick, with amazing lightning speed, Shasha never saw it coming. He must have struck a bone because Shasha staggered backwards, holding his cheek in pain and telling his client-friend from Sweden.

"Let's go brother, these people are just hating." Shasha murmured to his friend while walking towards his car pressing the remote ignition which started the engine before he had even gotten in.

After Shasha's Hummer had disappeared, we all started debating and discussing about this strange development, arguing amongst ourselves.

"Is he or isn't he?" Was the question that was being debated on with passion and some heated emotions one would think we were related to this Swedish young man. I stood there thinking of the many facets to this peculiar story: the DNA, the K75000, the Name Changing, the Swiss Bank Accounts, the Real Estate Portfolio, the various companies. I concluded that this character is not a fool and he must have done his Swedish-homework down to the last digit. Combine that with Shasha's American cleverness, I had a feeling we haven't heard the last of this saga. So many Malawian conspiracy theorists will be analysing this latest saga with the majority of fingers pointing to the 4th option (of getting rich) that was mentioned above.

I wondered; "is he or isn't he," it was 50/50 chance according to me, that is until one of my little nephews let out a terrifying scream.

"*Ankolo Makala, chi Paulo the Okutopasi chikuphyelela!*" The boy yelled as if he had just seen the Angel of Death. We all dashed back to the grill, which we had neglected because of the debate, but unfortunately the Octopus had been reduced into 'ashes to ashes' all because of this Malawian from Sweden. It was at that moment that I made my mind up.

"No, he is not his son."

LIES

When you are four years-old it is reinforced in you over and over again that telling lies is wrong. A lie will guarantee you a one-way ticket to Hell where you will burn in eternal fire – the kind of fire that inflicts excruciating pain but does not kill you. By the time you reach ten years or thereabouts you are totally brainwashed that any form of lying is punishable by a firing squad if not worse.

I remember how I narrowly survived the death sentence aged only eight when I had been faced with a 'should-I-lie-scenario.' Father was standing over me; angry and interrogating me to death.

"Did you urinate all over the edge of the toilet?" he asked in his Barry White bass. It was a 'lose-lose' situation for me; telling the truth was going to invite belt whooping, but telling a lie would also invite a belt whooping. I figured I might as well lie and earn my whooping.

"No it wasn't me, it was my little sister." I pathetically lied... *mayo ine*...big mistake.

It's only when you come out of puberty and start crossing over into adulthood that you start discovering that not all lies warrant the death sentence.

I started realising that the very same people who used to bark at me not to tell lies weren't as honest as they purported to be. This happened at Primary school when I had boasted to friends that my Father used to be 'Number One' in school. Guess how surprised I was to learn that every child was told the same story by their father. This was a bit puzzling for me and raised all sorts of question; 'surely if every child's father the whole of Malawi was Number-One at school, who was 'Number-Two then?' That's when it dawned on me that everyone from Mzuzu to Nsanje tells lies with amazing precision.

By everyone, I mean everyone; you, me, him, her, *ajawo, iwowa, inde inuyonso.* I can see some of you looking behind as if I am talking about the person behind you even though you know you are there alone. We are all liars.

The question is why do we lie when we were told that it is wrong to lie? Even those who are religious know that; 'Thou Shall not Lie' is one of the most sacred Commandments (the 9th if my memory serves me right) and yet they don't minding spinning what they consider an innocent lie.

We lie because while growing up we have innately convinced ourselves that there are harmless lies and there are harmful lies. How lies are placed in these two categories depends on personal preferences, judgement and perhaps level of desperation or what is the outcome or rewards of *kulikunga.*

For example; if you are an economic migrant from Malawi and the Immigration Officer at Heathrow or O'Hare Airport looks at your passport suspiciously as if it's a fake one and then fires a question at you,

"While you are here in the UK/USA, are you planning on taking up employment?" then looks at you straight in the eye as if you luggage is full of cocaine or some contraband. Although you know you signed on your visa application that you will not work, you look at that Immigration Officer with cold fake-innocent dry eyes replying with a slightly trembling voice with that hint of Malawian accent,

"I swear on my great-great Grandmother's grave I am just here for holiday/school, I have no interest in stealing jobs from indigenous British/Americans Sir, I will not work 1000 hours a week Sir, I promise... *mbambadi,*" the Chichewa word stumbles out of your mouth accidentally as you stutter because you are talking faster than normal, your dry lips sticking to each other as if someone smeared super-glue and your tongue struggles to swallow saliva that isn't there.

The Immigration Officer looks at your stuttering dry mouth and abnormally dilated eyes, stamps you passport 'Enter-Lowani' – but tells you politely with a hint of sarcasm;

"All you had to say was No, I will not work."

One week later, after Social Security or National Insurance Card *yapelekedwa*, you are already pounding the streets of London or Indiana, filling up employment application forms – *zantchito*.

And a month later you are at Western Union, *kuzitumiza mwakathithi* and a year later, they send you pictures of the house or church your money has built back *kumudzi*. *Chimanshoni* comprising of seven or eight bedrooms even though you only have one child, guest wing that has two bedroom and boy's quarters to house an army of workers even though *muli kunjako* you were doing your own dishes and mopping your own floors.

This might sound wrong but this is the approximation of the chronology of events. Between the Visa application and building of the *Manshoni* (or buying *mutu wa thraki*) there is a whole lot of multi-complex lies that cement this process.

Usually the seeds of *mabodza* start with the adding of extra zeroes on the bank statement to facilitate the visa. Then comes the lie(s) told at the port of entry, which culminates into the lie(s) on the job application that you have been in the UK or USA for more than five years when you know that you haven't even been in that country for five weeks. Then they are those lie(s) told with crocodile tears, when caught by immigration, that if they send you back you face, forced circumcision or incarceration because you once overtook the Presidential Motorcade along the highway.

All these are categorised as harmless lies, after all we have some pastors who had to spin one or two harmless lies that enabled them to go to the States or UK. If a Pastor will knowingly twist (not forge but twist, forging is for criminals) a 7 and turn it into a 9, why shouldn't Makala twist a 1 into a 1000000? Touché.

If you were honest upon arrival at Heathrow or O'Hare and responded 'Yes' to the Immigration Officer, he would have sent you back on the next plane home. But common sense tells you that... 'namani' because the reality of the situation is that; a whole village back in Malawi is counting on you in alleviating its poverty. Yes it was a lie, but subconsciously you place that lie in the harmless category.

Then there are some lies that are just plain wrong, lies that don't benefit anyone in particular, lies that will not feed a family or a village. Lies that go beyond the realm of normalcy like the lie that shook up our neighbourhood and rocked the very core foundation of our friendship just two days ago.

If lies were earthquakes then this would have been bigger and devastating than the one that crippled Haiti. As far as lies go, this was the mother-load, a heat-seeking bunker-buster missile of a lie dropped from an unmanned drone like the ones hovering all over Pakistan but piloted somewhere in America.

We were watching BBC news about Britain as one of the richest countries in the world and that its leader, David Cameron has travelled to America. He did not travel by Private Jet, but bought a ticket on British Airways, he did not sit in First Class but sat in Business Class (between First and Economy) by doing this, it is claimed he saved the British Government £200,000. Why would the leader of such a rich superpower nation want to save his country £200,000? I wondered and noticed that Agogo was about to make a comparison with Malawi when we heard a loud smash outside as if a glass had imploded. It was followed by a loud piercing car-alarm.... *tuli-tuli-tuli-tuli-tuli*...

We all dashed outside and saw the whole front-windscreen of Shasha's Hummer-H2 broken to bits and Simioni standing right next to it with a big axe. I have never seen Simioni like this and I was about to ask what this was all about when he took another hard swing, this time smashing the passenger's side window. It was all happening in slow motion and yet so fast. You could hear the axe going whoosh! Followed by a loud Phwaaaaaaaa! Whoosh! Phwaaaaaaaa! Whoosh! Phwaaaa! Window after window after window.

It was amazing and a bit peculiar because as the expensive Hummer-H2 was being pounded to bits in what was perhaps worse that Demolition-Derby, Shasha did not run to confront Simioni but stood right behind me in fear.

If someone had been scratching my Morris with a toothpick or even thinking of scratching it with *nthenga ya nkhuku* it would have resulted in World War 4 and yet here was Simioni about to smash the last window on the Hummer and Shasha was cowering behind me in fear.

Simioni went around the whole car methodically and ruthlessly smashing any glass or window that could be smashed. He then slashed all the tires Whoosh! Boom! Whoosh! Boom! Before standing right in front of the Hummer H2 and taking a mighty swing axing the bonnet right through, chopping the Turbo in half.

Breathing heavily he menacingly started walking toward us, his abnormally big arms sweating and gleaming in the afternoon sun, that big axe looking deadlier than a loaded bazooka, his eyes red like fire, gritting his teeth like the rapper 50cent. He looked past me at Shasha who was still behind me trembling. And the million dollar question came out of Simioni's mouth like a volcano seconds before eruption.

"Have you been having an affair with my madam?" Simioni coldly asked, pointing the axe that was still dripping motor oil squarely at Shasha. I had a queasy feeling that soon that axe was going to be dripping blood.

Now you all know I love my friend Shasha to bits. I once told him that I wouldn't mind taking a bullet for him as a token of our friendship. But the minute Simioni asked that question while holding an axe; I did what anyone of you could have done.

I immediately and unceremoniously detached myself from Shasha as if he had the highly contagious deadly Ibola virus. Even Agogo who had been standing in line of fire jumped back indoors slamming and locking the door just incase Simioni decide to throw that axe like a tomahawk.

Simioni got to a touching distance and I could see Shasha's brain making all sorts of calculations whether to stay or to leg it like Usain Bolt. Common sense told him that if he took off, that would leave Simioni with two options; chase after him or throw the axe at him. He opted to stand his ground and take it like a man.

"I am only going to ask you this one more time, have you been having an affair with my madam?" Simioni said while tap-poking Shasha on the chest with the blunt end of the axe forcing him to take two steps back in pain.

In life, once in a while we all arrive at a difficult juncture where we are only served with two options; tell the truth or spin a lie. At this very moment my dear friend Shasha was at that juncture and his life, literally, depended on what answer was going to come out of his dry mouth.

It reminded me of the toilet situation I had faced when I was eight-years old. I could tell that Shasha's mind was trying to categorise the lie he was about to tell; harmful or harmless? Whilst factoring in Simioni's past and capabilities to inflict pain that would make torture by water-boarding sound trivial.

Everyone knew Simioni's past; the weightlifting, Karate, Judo, Boxing and something called Taekwondo. Put simply, Simioni is one of those people you don't want to have for an enemy. I remember while growing up, Simioni used to take pleasure in slaughtering chickens without the aid of a knife. He could literally give one lethal *nkhonya* to the chicken's head and that was it, no blood spilled ready for the hot water before *kusosola nthenga*.

We all knew that axe or no axe, either way Shasha was basically a dead-man-walking and I couldn't see how he would come out of this one alive.

What Shasha said next amazed and surprised all of us and it reinforced my belief that we all lie when faced with a life threatening situation. Everyone would spin a lie if it guaranteed them life. In most instances a lie tends to be a Game-Changer especially if you are standing at the wrong end of an axe.

If presentation of false information is going to save a life or lives would you go ahead and fabricate one? Would you? Well Shasha did and lived to talk about it.

LONG DISTANCE RELATIONSHIPS

While growing up I used to think that cheese was another way of saying; 'show us all your teeth,' because every time a photographer would say; 'cheese' we would respond with a smile. It was later on in life that I realised that cheese was a dairy product.

One thing for sure though, saying cheese used to do the trick because all the photos we took back then show us with smiling faces; whether we were leaning on walls, standing next to a rose flower, posing with hands on hips or balancing on top of *chulu*. What stood out most were the happy smiles, the cheerful faces, the joy captured in these Kodak moments. Unfortunately this is not the case anymore.

These day's people take pictures with serious faces, *akuti* looking cool... *dolo samwetulila*, practising Niggarism. I used to wonder, 'why take a picture if you are going to come out angry? A face so devoid of cheerfulness, contorted in agony as if you are in pain from constipation. If that's a way of portraying and protracting coolism then leave me out of it, am Ok being uncool.

Last Sunday I became one of those people who take pictures with an unsmiling face, I wasn't trying to exhibit the Niggarism philosophy nor was I harbouring any thoughts of becoming Malawi's next Ice-T. I just wasn't in the smiling mood. Everyone tried to make me smile but it didn't work, I just couldn't bring myself to display my canines or dental structure, even Agogo commented,

"*Koma ndiye mwalundatu* as if she won't be coming back." Agogo said while sifting through the sizzling *dzipalapatilo*.

On this particular Sunday we had gathered not to welcome anyone else (like we often do in my family) but to bid Manyuchi Darling farewell. She was going away for a month; but to me it felt like a century.

I was so depressed to the point that I asked Simioni to be the pilot of the Torpedo 2000 (our barbeque grill.) I just didn't have the desire *yowotcha nyama* and for the first time I didn't have any appetite for *dzipalapatilo* that were deliciously sizzling on top of the Torpedo 2000. It didn't even bother me at all when I saw some people hiding meat in their pockets and plastic bags so that they can take it home with them. I just didn't care and did have the tiniest inclination to be bothered by these unauthorised take-aways.

Amalume once said; as far as relationships go, there are three kinds of states any individual will be at any given moment in time. [1] Living together happy with your significant other [2] Living single, not in any relationship and [3] Living in a long distance relationship.

It is the third one that I could never really comprehend although I have heard so many people being in that state.

"*Amunanga ali ku* States *kumaphunziro* for nine-years or *Akazanga ananka ku* UK two-years ago *timangotchayilana foni pena Fesibuku basi.*"

I have heard of people talk like this but I never gave it that much serious thought. I always assumed, 'surely it can't be that hard;' as long as you love someone, distance and time are nothing but intangibles which can be quantified numerically and romantically compressed into their true nothingness. So at the end of the day, it didn't really matter whether the person you love is a gazillion miles away or whether they were in the next room or standing right next to you bumping heads. It was all the same, no difference whatsoever. I was wrong so very wrong – if anything, then the opposite is true.

Before Manyuchi left, I thought the young gentleman running around Malawi looking and chasing for his DNA was going through the most excruciating pain known to man. But his pain wouldn't compare to what I was going through right now. In his case he is not sure what he lost, in my case I am 200% certain of what I don't have. I don't need DNA to alleviate my pain or curb my suffering, what I need is, Manyuchi to be here with me. His DNA might suffice this afternoon or tomorrow, cutting short his suffering once he ascertains the identity of his biological father, but for me I know exactly how long I will have to suffer alone before Manyuchi comes back home.

In real time it has only been a week since Manyuchi Darling was last here with me, but it has been the longest week I have ever endured. In romantic time this one week morphs itself into one year, those in a long distance relationship will concur with me here. There is some sort of a time warp when the one you love is not around with you. It could be 4pm now but for some unexplained reason after one hour the time will be 3pm.

I sat in my living room, sniffing Manyuchi Darling's blouse and bra she left behind for my sake because I have always remarked how they remind me of our last valentine day. Everything smells like her and I keep thinking she will reappear like magic right next to me. But no such thing happens, so I agonisingly stare at the anti-clockwise ticking Seiko on the wall, watching the seconds hand move in a slow tick-tock-tick-tock motion like a knife right through my soul.

All my friends have stopped coming over; they say I don't pay attention when they are talking, am always oblivious, my eyes constantly far away and my mind not in the here and now. But wouldn't you be if the person who completes you was not there with you? Wouldn't you be if the love of your life was so far away? Wouldn't you? Wouldn't you?

I went in the shed outside to rummage through my old stuff, looking for old cassettes that Manyuchi and I used to listen to; they were dusty but they still worked, TDKs in their original plastic O.G Issa covers; Tony Braxton, En Vogue, Boyz-2-Men, Luther Vandross and Mr. Kenny G. I figured, listening to these gentlemen and ladies doing their roma-roma thing would somehow make me feel better, it would bring a smile, it would give me a cheese moment. Wrong, it just made things worse.

Romantic music is a dish best eaten with your lover, is what I concluded. Listening to romantic music all alone is like having a barbeque all alone; flipping sausages and then chewing them alone, no one to share the deliciousness with – Yuk! They would probably taste like the leg of a dining chair.

That's exactly how Tony Braxton and Boyz-2-Men were sounding right now; it was like listening to *Mangolongondo* Acapella that is off-tune played by a drunken person. No disrespect to *Mangolongondo* music or to all my drunken friends.

To all those who are in a long distance relationship; I feel your pain, I feel your loneliness and I now understand the absence of smiles on your faces. I never thought that being in a long distance relationship requires courage and bravery beyond that needed by *Sojazi* in the battle fields of Kandahar or Fallujah Afghanistan.

I have only endured one agonising week and there is only three more to come, I know there are brothers and sisters out there who live without their loved for months if not years on end. All I can say is; 'you are strong and you are brave,' so brave you deserve a Love Medal.

I sat there in the dark; Kenny-G had long stopped blowing his Saxophone and I didn't feel like getting up to go and rewind or turn the tape to side B. I hadn't enjoyed it anyway, because of my aching heart, Kenny-G's saxophone had sounded like a badly tuned Vuvuzela.

I figured I was better off listening to the tick-tock-tick of the Seiko clock resonating in the silent night. I couldn't tell what time it was but I could tell it wasn't moving fast enough.

Last Sunday when everyone was eating and laughing I sat there looking in Manyuchi's eyes telling her that no distance, river or lake is big or deep enough to keep us apart. What a lie that had been and all those in a long distance relationship will agree with me 'time' is the guillotine and 'distance' is the enemy, no phone or mail can ever shrink it.

I was alone in the living-room feeling like the jailed white owner of the vicious dog that attacked his security-guard. Agogo had spoken about this dog-owner currently locked up in prison for breaking the Malawian law of keeping dangerous animals. He was languishing after being denied bail, but what law had I broken to languish alone like this? I could hear laughter and music coming from Simioni's house.

He came this morning to borrow the Torpedo 2000 grill and had invited me for a barbeque that would later on morph into a full blown party. Apparently it was a make-up barbecue, something to do with him and Shasha reconciling their differences. I didn't feel like being there, so I diplomatically refused.

It was dark outside, the music across the street (at Simioni's) was loud and I could hear distinct laughter which signified to me that the barbeque part was over and the party phase had now began, just as my friend had advised. I tried to bury my head in the cushions to muffle the festivity sounds to no avail.

I heard the door connecting to the kitchen open slowly and the lights came on. I had to shut my eyes from the intense glare, I felt like an owl caught in the headlights. I knew it had to be Simioni or Shasha coming to drag me to the party. I was about to scream to be left alone, I didn't want to go to their barbecue/party but it wasn't who I thought it was. It was Mother, standing there looking worried at my sorry state and unkempt facial features.

"Why don't you go hang out with your friends," she said slowly and quietly shutting the door and walking over to where I was sitting.

"Do you know that once loneliness gets out of control you end up being chronically depressed?" she went on in her motherly voice about how there is sweetness in missing your loved one, it's like an emotional Gluco Power or Switi wa Mapanga.

"It's nice to imagine Manyuchi's smiles or kisses and it is also Ok to miss her but don't let it become too intense my son," she said while putting her hand on my shoulder.

"If you miss Manyuchi beyond the normalcy of missing, it's just going to become a constant ache inside you, a feeling of emptiness that can't be filled. Go out and have fun with your friends Makala." She said with a faint smile on her face and I looked up at Mother; she has never called me by my first name since I was a teenager, always referring to me as 'son' and she has never talked to me like this.

I walked over to Simioni's and was glad that I did because everyone was laughing and shouting happily. I even made new friends. Actually one of them hasn't seen her significant-other since January and will probably not see her until next year, she told me. I wanted to ask her, how come she looked so happy, talking and laughing as if she was complete. But I figured maybe doing such a thing will just bring about unnecessary pain. So we sat there talking about general things.

Talking to people like this gave me courage and in a way made me feel not so depressed anymore. Surely if this new friend of mine could survive a year before being reunited with her other half, who am I to cry and weep for not seeing Manyuchi for one month? I thought about the Love Medal again and realise that there are a lot of people out there enduring twenty-four long hours, month after month who deserve such a medal.

With that thought I reached for a piece of *Chipalapatilo* that Simioni had just deported from the Torpedo 2000 to the plate. I took a hungry bite and noticed it didn't taste the same like those seasoned by Manyuchi. Three more weeks Makala, just three more weeks... I said to myself whilst struggling to swallow the strange tasting piece of *Chipalapatilo*.

ZACHIKONDI-KONDI

The whole Amoto family, including some of my neighbours and friends, has gone to the Lake. My family is, perhaps, the only family the whole of Malawi that goes to the lake in a Bedford 7-ton truck...my brother's *Penda-Penda* Transport.

They took so much food I started thinking they were going they wouldn't be coming back. There was food in baskets and bags, pots and plastic containers. I wanted to ask them why they were busy loading meat when there is plenty of affordable fresh delicious *chambo* where they were heading. I also wondered why they were busy taking a gazillion plates, pots, a basketful of spoons instead of items that could be used at the beach. No one was worried about beach towels or bathing suits or sun-lotion (for those with lighter skin.)

Since I wasn't going along with them I figured it was best left alone. After all the sooner they left the better for me and Manyuchi. As soon as *Penda-Penda* loaded with laughing men, cheering women, screaming children and excited workers left the yard, the house was so quiet it felt abnormal and surreal. I couldn't believe it was just me and Manyuchi Darling.

"Hahahahahahaaaaaaaaa," I found myself laughing getting goose bumps in the process as I dashed back in the house.

"Manyuchi Darling! Today is the day! Today is the day!" I kept yelling as I entered our empty house. Manyuchi who had been taking a bath was now standing there in the middle of the living-room wearing one of my big T-shirts which was even bigger on her and was almost touching her knees. I could see the dampness on her lovely skin and hair. It excited me so much I started wishing the 'Lake People' would just stay there until eternity.

We locked both doors; front and back and made sure that all the curtains were drawn. We weren't taking any chances with any unannounced visitors. I had instructed the garden boy to tell any visitor that; '*anthu onse achokapo.*'

"*Boyi* if by tomorrow you still want to be employed by me, make sure that nobody knocks on the front door." I sternly warned him but gave him K500 note for motivation.

We didn't want anyone disturbing our romantic safe haven, this was our "*us*" time and it felt good just to be in such an environment. It reminded me of back in our younger days when I had brought Manyuchi over to my parent's house after they had gone to a funeral. It had been a wonderful experience but today's was ten-times better because this was our place and we didn't feel like two naughty thieves.

It was just the three of us in the house; me, Manyuchi and Kenny-G who was melodically wafting out of the speakers (*nyamata odziwa kukodola* saxophone.)

We sat on the big sofa and I was playing with Manyuchi's long beautiful silky hair. She always likes it when I massage her head, *akuti ndimamulefula* and she reciprocated by gently squeezing my inner thigh, her little soft fingers sending all sorts of sensations throughout my body.

It was as if we were teleported back in time; I remember the first time she gave me an inner thigh squeeze. I remember that day with the same urgency I remember my name, it was the day when I realised that what I felt for Manyuchi Darling was true love, it was not infatuation like other people had told me.

I could kill for moments like this, when neither of us says a word only communicating in silence. I love looking at those beautiful eyes of hers, eyes so pure and so honest. Manyuchi has always told me that she likes watching me smile. She says whenever I smile she feels sugary inside like sugarcane dipped in honey. This is exactly what we were doing right now, silent love... *chikondi chakachete-chete abale anzanga.*

Because Manyuchi had just taken a nice deep bubble bath, the lovely scent of her favourite lotion was making me dizzy and woozy... *kafungo kamandilefula mokoma moyo.* It's the same lotion that tantalised my senses years ago when I first caught her scent. After we started seeing each other, I had told her that as long as she puts that sensual tantalizing body lotion I will never leave her no matter what. And years later here we are, I was still sniffing her and liking every ounce of that scent oozing out of her, it felt like those yesteryears, it felt like today and it felt so real I just had to smile – her favourite smile.

As Kenny-G softly whispered to us with his saxophone through the speakers, we could hear the July wind blowing outside and the sound of leaves chasing each other. It sounded so chaotic, nasty and cold out there. But inside it was the opposite; life inside was calm, quiet and warm, especially Manyuchi's body which felt warmer through the big T-shirt of mine she was wearing. I wrapped both my long arms around her body, hugging her tight as if I was afraid she might escape. I sniffed her hair and sniffed her neck, inhaling hard and long as if I was a drug junkie snorting on cocaine.

"Do you remember the first time you told me you love me?" She asked me in her soft voice, knowing that I will get the answer wrong. We always argued, laughed and disagreed on the specificity of when this four letter word was first uttered or said.

"The day you tripped and landed on your bum." I answered fully knowing that this answer was going to invite a flurry of playful punches from her. She always punched me whenever I bring up this day, which was a bit comedic in a way.

The reason I like bringing up this particular day is because it was the day when I first touched Manyuchi Darling. It was the first time I looked into those cute big lazy eyes of hers. It was the first time I felt a tug like pull on my heart.

She had been with her friends messing about during break-time at school. Whatever it was they had been doing she lost her footing and fell awkwardly, landing with a mighty thud in a sitting position.

Everyone started laughing and jeering at her misfortune but I went over where she was still sitting, pain evident in her eyes. I didn't say a word but simply extended my arm so that I can help her up. She grabbed my hand and I pulled her back on her feet with so much force our faces almost touched, she had to stop coming any closer by placing her left hand against my chest in a reflex action.

It wasn't the first time meeting her, but it was the first time touching her, feeling that silk-like complexion, it was the first time our eyes locked albeit for a fraction of a second which felt like eternity, it was like peeping into the future. It was the first time I had really been so close to her I could smell the lovely lotion on her skin. She shyly looked down, retrieved her hands and started dusting her behind with her palms.

"Thank you." was the only thing she said to me. She said it so faint it was almost barely an audible whisper. But for me it was the smile that tickled me more than the fact that she had thanked me. My heart was beating so fast it reminded me of the time I had found a K10 note on the living room floor. I didn't know what to do; take it to Father or pocket it as "finders' keepers" I chose the second option; quickly tucking it in my pocket, just to hear Father's booming voice from behind

"What are you doing?" Father had asked in his usual Barry White bass, my heart stopped, literally, then started beating fast like a crazy frog. This is exactly how my heart was beating on the day I first touched Manyuchi Darling.

"For me it was during that brief eye contact when I realised that I love you." I said it gently looking in Manyuchi Darling's watery eyes while massaging her slender shoulders.

"I tried to tell how much I love you just staring at you." I stopped the massage knowing that what I had just said was going to illicit uncontrollable laughter from her. And it did, she doubled up pounding her fists on my thighs.

"Hahahahaha, why didn't you just tell me instead of just looking at me?" She asked fully knowing that that's one question I will never answer.

I waited for Manyuchi to calm down and I gently wiped a tear drop that had cascaded down her cheek from all the laughing.

"Ok, my turn now," I said to her while palming the sides of her head and tilting her head to face.

"When did you fall in love me?" I knew what Manyuchi Darling's response was going be and that it was going to reduce her to tears again. I like the way it always made her laugh.

"It was the day you first met my Father." Manyuchi said then immediately broke into a hysterical laughter.

I vividly remember the day in question as if it was today. I had gone over to her house just after 3pm, walked over and sidestepping the thorny rose bushes growing on the flower bed under her bedroom window. I started tapping lightly on her bedroom window fully knowing that it would open and I will be greeted with a beautiful smile.

I used to write these poems for her and would take them to her house, tap on her window and give them to her as soon as she opens and run back to my house. She used to call me crazy, but she used to say that with a smile on face. For me this meant that she didn't mind my poems.

At the time I thought my poems were romantic but looking back now, I cringe at what a bad poet I was. I have always wondered why she never told me off or reported me to her Father and I have never understood why she kept each and every poem in her diary up to this day. Now that am all grown up I dread looking at these poems from a bygone era which are marred with a gazillion grammatical mistakes, misspellings i.e. rove instead of love and things that didn't even make sense i.e. if you were a fruit you would be fruity.

This particular day in question, I went over to her place at 3pm knowing that her parents were still at work, and tapped on her window. Their vicious dogs were barking menacingly behind the house but I wasn't bothered because I knew that they stayed on a leash until 6pm. So I continued tapping.

Usually her window would open after the second tap, but today I must have administered a gazillion taps on it, and nothing happened. I was about to deliver my gazillion and one tap when from the corner of my eye I saw a figure that had to be her Father.

Just by the *tsinya* on his angry looking face, I knew there wasn't going to be words like '*uli bwanji*' coming from him so I started backing away slowly. But what he said next put raw fear in me. I felt my bladder contract as if someone had stepped on it squeezing out its contents and immediately there was this embarrassing wet patch around my *lisani*.

"Killer, Hunter, Poacher... get him!!!" Her father yelled a command that was followed by growling and then loud barking.

I don't need to spell it out that these were names of their three vicious dogs. Long fanged hellish looking K-9 hounds and rumour had it that they were only fed flesh meat doused in *tsabola* to induce *ukali*. As the hounds from hell sped towards me, I took off thankful that I was wearing my Adidas running shoes.

All along Manyuchi Darling had been watching from one of the windows as the drama unfolded. I zoomed off, yelling in fear, running as if my life depended on it, huffing and puffing, making sure that those three dogs will not close the distance between me and them.

I could hear my heart beating from the sides of my temples and this was the first time I had really yelled out a genuine prayer

"Lord if you let me get out of this one alive I promise I will be a good boy."

I don't remember jumping over the fence, I don't I remember crossing the road in front of an approaching bus and I don't have any recollection how I ended up with one Adidas on my left foot only.

Manyuchi later told me that the dogs did not even get outside their yard, but because I never looked back and the loud beating of my heart muffled out all exterior sounds, I thought I could still hear barking and approaching paws.

Manyuchi was laughing so hard, the picture of me running and almost being hit by a bus and one of my Adidas shoe flying off from my foot.

"It's the way you jumped over our fence that made me realise that you were the one. You had risked your life just to come and give me a poem." Manyuchi softly said while looking at me.

"The way you ran Darling, you should have been an athlete." she said jokingly.

We both sat there laughing together with Kenny-G, savouring the moment and enjoying each other's company, *chikondi cheni-cheni*.

As a couple life had been good to us. We were so blessed to be surrounded by family, friends and most importantly be in good health. To have each other was a bonus on everything that was good in our lives.

We have been through a lot but we always came out together, intact and solid. I looked at Manyuchi Darling, realising that I was more in love with her today than I was yesterday and yesterday than I was the day before which meant that tomorrow my love for her was going to be greater than today. Our love for each other was growing everyday and realising this was like winning a lottery. Having Manyuchi Darling was like winning a lottery. Holding and being held by Manyuchi was like winning a lottery. Imagine waking up each and every morning and realising that you have won a lottery. Imagine that, just imagine it.

The house was quiet, even Kenny –G had stopped doing his thing with the Saxophone. I wanted to get up to change the CD but Manyuchi stopped me, we lay there enjoying the silence, quietly just the two of us. I held her so close I could feel the faint beating of her her heart, a lovely and loving heart.

I love my family to bits, but at this moment in time I was glad that there was no one else around; no dzipalapatilo, no debates, no politics, no business just pure silence. We stayed on that soft sofa until darkness enveloped the whole living room. I could no longer see Manyuchi's face but I could hear her soft breathing and I could smell her lovely scent. I had been playing with her hair for so long it finally put her to sleep. Stroking her cheek I whispered so softly in her ear.

"Good night my love, good night my everything."

MEMORIES FROM MY COFFIN

The soft mellow funeral hymns were constantly punctuated by the wailings of mourners. These wailings were slightly muffled by the velvety white cushioned interior of the oblong-box which was my coffin.

Judging by the sorrowful sobs, there must have been over 3800 mourners out there. The distinct cries of Mother and the piercing shrieks of Manyuchi Darling's wailings were two of the loudest. It was strange hearing my British Auntie grieve like a Malawian woman, crying out and pronouncing my name in that proper English accent of hers;

"Meykalaar, Meykalaar my nephew, sob! sob! sob! Ooooohohoho my dear Meykalaaaaar!"

Laying here in my coffin felt rather chillingly calm and somewhat peaceful. Everything I had imagined and dreamt about the state of death was not to be. Most of my friends and relatives had come to pay their last respects. *Osalephela* there was a minority of mourners that came just to make sure that Makala *wankadi*, I could hear their faint hypocritical sobs and could picture them shedding crocodile tears whilst staring at my coffin *uku akutafuna dzipalapatilo* and *nsima*; typical funeral hypocrites.

I had a feeling my dear Agogo was somewhere amongst the men, holding on to his *nkebe* of *piri-piri* while silently crying for my sudden departure. For all Agogo's hard-core stance or poking people in the face with his walking stick, deep down he was highly emotional and prone to crying. It was no secret that Agogo considered me his favourite grandson and I knew his eyes must be gushing tears more than Nkula Falls.

I could hear Amalume angrily telling off a demented relative who had callously ventured inside the house grabbing a few of my suits, shirts and shoes; funeral scavengers...*akuti kulanda za-Achimwene.* Amalume, then, shouted advice to the grief stricken Manyuchi;

"Go lock the bedroom door and hide the key inside your blouse!"

I felt like sitting up, pushing the coffin lid open, telling them to stop this unnecessary grieving – I was ok, or was I? It felt strange, somewhat heavy not to be able to move my own limbs. I tried to lift my eyelids but they too felt like a ton of bricks were clamping them shut. I felt nothing; I was neither hot nor cold. Surely if I was dead, my body temperature should have been lower than an ice-block. I had to be alive and all this had to be one of those hellish-nightmares whereby you woke up drenched in sweat.

If I was dead how come I could distinctly hear the funeral noises of hungry men asking for nsima? I also heard Simioni's familiar voice giving, what sounded like, a eulogy.

"Was this some sort of a joke?" Maybe if I started yelling they could stop this funeral masquerade and get me out of this confined space. I had to be alive but something told me this was not the case. The cries and shrieks of;

"*Ndidumphire momo...*"

"Makala why you? Waaahahahahaaa!!!" All these were like a guarantee that I was no longer one of the breathing but the dead. There was also the vivid memory of that big truck heading straight at my Morris Marina.

As soon as I turned the bend, my hands tapping on the steering wheel to the tune of Julio Iglesias... I froze. I was staring straight at the menacing grill of a Freightliner truck hugging my side of the road, attempting to overtake a minibus and heading right at me at breakneck speed.

Everything happened so fast, I had no time to react or scream the only words that came out of my mouth were a whisper;

"I will always love you Manyuchi Darling, always."

There was no recollection of the impact, just this searing burning white pain after something metallic and sharp struck and punctured my neck. Wind and blood exploded in a cocktail of red mist through the gaping hole at the base of my neck, momentarily blinding everything in front of me. It felt like the biggest burp as my lungs painfully depressurised, perhaps exhaling for the last time.

Time stood still, somehow prolonged, as my body rattled like a 'snakes-and-ladders' dice inside a cup. I could feel and hear my ribs and limbs breaking as I was bashed about against all sorts of twisted metal and broken glass. I was flung sideways then violently lurching forward, out through the windscreen. The floating sensation was somehow calming as I was suspended in mid-air like an eagle.

The moment of hitting the tarmac-asphalt of Zalewa-Road did not arrive nor do I recall the exact time when I stopped living.

The crescendo of the grief-stricken shrieks outside the coffin's comfortable interior grew louder and agonisingly sorrowful. I had never heard cries of my name belched with such pain.

The wailings were getting louder and stronger to the point of annoying me to death – or rather back to life. That's when I heard a heavy thud as something landed on top of the coffin. It took four, five identical deafening thuds before I realised what was happening.

Someone was throwing shovelfuls of damp *katondo* dirt on top of the coffin. They were burying me, how could they? Didn't they realise that I was inside this stupid oblong-box? Why would they be trapping me six-feet under? I was overwhelmed by the urgency to get up and smash my way out of the coffin. I wanted to scream out to Mother, she could make them stop shovelling the earth on top of me. But I couldn't move and the ferocity of damp earth raining down the six foot hole increased as well-fed *anyamata* vigorously shovelled.

As more katondo-earth enveloped my coffin, the cries and shrieks of the women grew faint and were replaced by a frightening silence, an almost deafening quietness I have never experience in my life or death before. Thoughts of;

"What happens if I ran out oxygen," came and passed. I wanted to hear the reassuring voice of Mother and the loving touch of Manyuchi Darling. None of that happened.

It's the first time I felt how it really means to be alone. I started having regrets at not having prioritised my life. I wish I had said 'thank you' to *nyamata wantchito* a thousand times.

I wished I had said 'I love you' to Manyuchi last night before she went to sleep? I wish I had spent more time with her instead of mulling over Facebook?

Why didn't I say 'sorry' to Agogo after I broke his smoke-pipe deliberately?

Why didn't I stop to give a lift to my primary school teacher who I saw soaking in the rain by the stage?

Why had I procrastinated in buying Mother that *chitenje* I had promised her last year?

How come I never acknowledged the blind *masikini*-beggar I used to walk past daily, oblivious to his grinding poverty and at times annoyed by his extended hand; would it have hurt me to once in a while toss a few coins in his hat?

There was a sickening realisation that I would probably lay in this black darkness until eternity. There was nothing to look forward to, not even death for I had already used up that card.

What was that smell? There was a very unpleasant putrid smell of decay that interrupted my deathly thoughts. It took me some time to realise that the smell was my own flesh decaying, transforming itself into soil.

How long have I been laying here? I wondered. Has it been hours, days, months or years already? I honestly couldn't tell because there was no concept of time down here. It was a continuum eternal like blackness with zero interruptions.

There was a slithery movement as several big red earthworms exited my nostrils. I was no longer inside a comfortable coffin; the rotting pine box had long imploded under the pressure of the warm earth. The roots of the cemetery forest had penetrated around me enveloping my exposed bones. Their firm grip over me felt like the once warm embrace of Manyuchi Darling.

Down here in the damp darkness of the underworld there was no reference to my past material possessions; the-house, the-TV, the-fancy clothes, the-minibuses and Morris Marina did not matter here. All the things I had obsessed over while alive were nothing but frivolities down here.

My aggressive pursuit of wealth and material things was one long wasted opportunity to what could have been or what should have been. Even the expensive Armani suit they had buried me in had long decayed into soil. The shiny brass cuff-links lying uselessly besides my now exposed wrist bone.

If only I had experienced death before life, I could have done things differently and right. Now here I was, left alone in this coliseum of deceased relations, each one of us lying at six foot depth level and each one of us thinking what was and never became. Our past glories were all but compressed down to mounds of earth and few flowers or wreaths, most of which had long withered replaced by stubborn weeds obscuring the headstones.

"Here sleeps Makala Amoto, he came, he tried, he left… 19-*chakuti-chakuti* to 2010"

COMMENTS (FROM FACEBOOK FRIENDS)

I enjoyed reading all the comments that were posted by you, my friends, on my Facebook Wall. I wish I could reproduce all of them, but that would be a whole book in itself, instead I have randomly chosen a few of those comments.

I thank each and every one of you for taking the time to make these wonderful comments. My thanks, in equal measure, also go to those dear friends who took the time to read Makala Amoto but did not make comments for very understandable reasons. You became more than friends, you became family and I will forever look at everyone as family.

The fact that you took (your precious) time to read Makala Amoto on Facebook is something that I will always hold dear to my heart. It really meant a lot to me and motivated me to dig deeper.

Here are a few of those comments, in alphabetical order, which the owners gave me their permission to reproduce;

- Aileen Q. Mendoza- Ramirez: *My stomach aches form laughing... thanks Makala... I can imagine the faces of the couple watching their buffet table swept in an instant.*
- Alfred Mvula: *Packed like beans in a can, ndiyetu nyumbamo munadzadza zedi!!!.*
- Alinane Chimimba: *We want more!! We want more!! It seems we can't get enough of you, Makala.*
- Andrew Chipangula: *Hahahahahahaha, Makala umakhala kutiko? Ndinu aluso man.*
- Andrew Chipangula: *Makala you are a legend, papa I like you man.*
- Angelina Digolia Chinema: *That's what I keep telling these folks laughter is the most expensive thing that money cannot buy.*
- Annah Kondowe: *hahahahaha, Makala you are three much.*
- Arthur Chihana: *Makala, umanditha nzeru osati masewela.*
- Bertha Madi: *Makala Makala Makalaaaaa.*
- Bertha Madi: *Oh my, ndikungoseka am speechless. I can imagine a Malawi ndi buffet.*
- Brandon Mafuleka: *That's what it do....moto moto Makala Amoto.*
- Brigitte Dambuleni: *Lets Forgive Makala for hiding Himself because being mysterious is part of Makalaliness.*
- Chakongela Mtegha: *Way to go Makala, we need this.*
- Chancy Lodzani: *Makala Makala you amaze me.*
- Chipiliro Khonje: *I'm your number one fan. Inbox us these pieces so we don't miss them.*

- Chris Chipi Minofu: *Wawa Makala...dude thus the south bend that I know...I had to stop my car to read this one...keep 'em coming...ifenso timenya exodus...lol.*

- Clement Mwakikunga: *Thanks Makala, you are inspiring man. You keep it up.*

- Comfort Khembo: *My new found secret. This is where I come for my laughter dose after a day's hard work, thank you Makala.*

- Elias Dziko: *I was watching a movie as I scrolled (down) the script. I love the way you write.*

- Elsie Thandie Subili: *Hahahaha! It doesn't get any better than this.*

- Elsie Thandie Subili: *I sure can't get enough of your stories. Makala you rock. Keep it up!! You have just made my day.*

- Elsie Thandie Subili: *Makala keep on keeping on. Nice stuff, at least you make some of us smile. Please write again. Kikikiki.*

- Ernest Ernest Wadza Phoya: *am smiling though I haven't read it yet....shaaaaa!!!!*

- Ernest Ernest Wadza Phoya: *One day the writings will be classics...can't wait for the first edition.*

- Evelyn Solomon: *Iiiiii koma Makala ake ndiye ndi oyaka bwino...moti sangachedwenso malonda... ndi kuziziraku angakome kuothatu amenewo.*

- Gabriel Nkhoma: *Makala Amoto, wapalamulatu iwe tsopano tawona anthu amene ayankha status yako. Kikikikikikiki. Kodi unalemba dala eti? That's good observation Akulu!!!!*

- Jayne Vungs: *Koma Makala mutu wako sulibwino.*

533

- Jennipher Phiri Sagawa: *interesting I just like your stories, people ask him more so that I 've something to read.*
- Judith Didi Kamphero: *Yes Yes Yes. I love this Makala a FIRE.*
- Katie Zhoya: *Makala you are becoming kilevala.*
- Kb Kamanga: *Wow for a second I was home then abroad and then back home wow am speechless... you must revised our books Timve and Tsala so it will b interesting so much with your writing which brings me to the question, who are you Makala?*
- Linda Leanora Muthala: *The past is my root, the present my stem & the future is where I will bloom!!!no need for the reverse button...nice one Makala.*
- Linnie Vyachi Kaunda: *you have just cheered me up I can't stop laughing.*
- Lisa Barratt: *Ndikulira ndi kuseka ine!!*
- Lizie Pashane: *lol.... you are something.*
- Loyce Trizer Kambwinda: *He is really wonderful and amazing! Good job Makala, keep it up.*
- Lusu Wa Owen Zimba: *Makala woyeee.*
- Mada Lisa Matupa: *That's a good one always be there for your loved ones.*
- Mali Kaunda: *HAHAHAHAHA!!...Makala, this is funny but very very true!*
- MamaNgina Fachi: *very funny and very true.*
- MamaNgina Fachi: *lol.. Mpaka ice-cream mu mpunga...classic Makala, buffet yavuta*
- Maria Ndasowa: *Hahahaha I love this*
- Maria Ndasowa: *ooh thanks for this....ndaseka and ndaphunzirapo and I love it really.*

- Maria Ndasowa: *this is fantastic....thanks Makala.*
- Mark Uko: *I have been trying to remember that name for a long time, George Matewere...he writes just like him.*
- Mark Uko: *this Shasha guy is a character.*
- Molly Chosa Whayo: *You should really compile your writings so that you can make a book in future, I really enjoy every master piece of your writings.*
- Mona Kachitsa: *Anthropology yomweyo, hahahahaha, mukadzathana nayo bwana mudzandigulitse ine, on a second hand price.*
- Patricia Bonongwe: *I can't stop laughing.*
- Pauline Patience Kaude: *Koma Makala you're a genius.*
- Pauline Patience Kaude: *Makala and his long entries. Man inutu muli ndi luso lolemba.*
- Phunjex Bling Bling: *ha ha ha ha ha ha ha ha ha ha ha ha ha ha I love this.*
- Sheila Banda: *Hahahahaha, I can't stop laughing.*
- Shupie Kamwendo Puckett: *Happy Easter Makala Amoto, you never cease to amaze Fuko la a Malawi.*
- Sylvester Ngambi: *Auze Makala amanama tonse ndife a Malawi*
- Sylvester Ngambi: *Hahahahaha Shasha wayitha. Payelepayele Makala*
- Sylvester Ngambi: *The story teller Makala*
- Temwa Mapunda: *Walking to and fro Kuchawe!? Makala you do bring back old memories. What we do for love!*

- Temwa Mapunda: *your relation to current affairs reminds me of malemu George Matewere. Keep it up*
- Thandiwe Buttercup Mkandawire: *Ha ha ha ha ha, mwanditseketsa bwanji!!! My mom must read this*
- Twammie Candymama Chimungu: *Why not write a novel am sure you would sell*
- Upile Chitete: *there you go again! Big up Makala!*
- Vikhu Kubwalo: *Koma nkhondo imeneyi yovuta ndithu, that's why we do not prosper Makala. Good one man!!! Watzapu!!! kikikikiki*
- Vikhu Kubwalo: *You need to write a book Makala! koma ma gangster wo afika bwanji kumeneko?*
- Yassin Mwachande: *Makala- you are the Shakespeare of Malawi. I agree with these guys that we treasure your writing skills and some of us we are sharing the stories at home with our family who does not even know what internet is let alone how to use a computer. We call our Agogo a BBC (Born Before Computers),and they are enjoying your stories. Keep up the great work brother.*
- Yassin Mwachande: *Pen master par excellence- Makala. Thanks for the edutainment u bring us. Thumbs up*

Thank You, Thank You, Thank You All for the wonderful comments above.

I appreciate your enormous patience, the patience of putting up with the mystery of Makala Amoto, the patience of not knowing who was behind this character. I purposefully withheld my ID for two reasons. First I wanted you my friends to have your own perception of Makala that is why I neither revealed his age nor physical attributes. Secondly, the idea of working as Makala gave me the freedom to come up with material without any constraints or invisible chains. Thank you my friends for putting up with the mystery.

It was really fun and a rollercoaster experience for me. I will forever cherish the Makala moments we shared; the laughs, the lessons and most important the bonding.

Much appreciation for the ideas and the assistance I received in coming up with some of the material. A special Thank You to Vera Ulemu Shaba for your time and tireless help, you were always there, a dedicated Grammatician and a true friend.

To Sandra, my friend, my rock, my wife and my everything… a gazillion thanks for being there.

Stay Blessed.